Gay Romance Holiday Collection

Also by Keira Andrews

Contemporary

The Spy and the Mobster's Son
Honeymoon for One
Beyond the Sea
Ends of the Earth
Arctic Fire

Lifeguards of Barking Beach
Flash Rip
Free Wind

Holiday
The Christmas Deal
The Christmas Leap
The Christmas Veto
A Baby for Christmas
Only One Bed
Merry Cherry Christmas
Santa Daddy
In Case of Emergency
Eight Nights in December
If Only in My Dreams
Where the Lovelight Gleams
Gay Romance Holiday Collection

Sports
Kiss and Cry
Reading the Signs
Cold War
The Next Competitor
Love Match
Synchronicity (free read!)

Gay Amish Romance Series
A Forbidden Rumspringa
A Clean Break
A Way Home

Gay Romance Holiday Collection

by Keira Andrews

Gay Romance Holiday Collection
Written and published by Keira Andrews
Cover by Dar Albert
Formatting by BB eBooks

ISBN: 978-1-988260-46-4
Print Edition

Eight Nights in December

by Keira Andrews

Acknowledgements

Thank you to Anara Bella and Davina Jamison for their invaluable help with this reworked novella.

Chapter One

AS HE ROUNDED the staircase, Lucas McKenzie could already hear the pounding bass emanating from above. He cringed, knowing without a doubt it was coming from his room.

Well, Sam Kramer's room.

It was also technically Lucas's room, but Sam didn't let that stop him from doing exactly what he wanted to do, when he wanted to do it. As the star forward on Brookfield University's basketball team, Sam was used to getting his way, and Lucas didn't have the energy to argue most of the time.

Lucas trudged through the hallway, weaving around revelers celebrating the end of the December exam period. Everyone on the floor except Lucas was a senior, and although he knew some of them well enough to say hi to, it didn't go further than nods and smiles.

Heart already skipping at the thought of making small talk, he stepped over the drunken people sitting in his doorway and was greeted by a can of cold beer that bounced off his chest and rolled to a stop under the foot of his bed.

"Buddy!" *Everyone* was Sam's buddy. "School's out!" He whooped loudly, his muscled arms thrust over his head. Dark-haired Sam was tall and gorgeous; his chiseled features and sculpted muscles would be just as at home on a movie screen as they were on the basketball court.

Lucas ignored the acid flooding his belly and gave Sam a thumbs-up. "I'm totally stoked!" He'd learned early on in the semester that the best way to deal with Sam was to agree with everything he said. Besides, Lucas *should* be stoked. Exams were over, and what kind of college student didn't love partying and getting wasted?

From Lucas's estimation, he was apparently the only one.

"Grab a beer and party with us!"

Nodding and smiling, Lucas retrieved the beer from under his bed and popped the top after stashing his backpack in the closet—currently the only part of the small room that wasn't occupied by a fellow student. How were there so many people crammed in? Sweat prickled the back of his neck, and beer foamed out over his fingers. He gulped from the can.

A girl Lucas recognized as living down the hall was sprawled on his bed, sticking her tongue down the throat of a guy who looked old enough to be in his seventh or eighth year of college. Lucas thought wistfully of curling up under the covers and watching a movie on his laptop.

"Holidays are here!" Sam's proclamation was met with a loud cheer from the partygoers. Lucas kept the rictus smile on his face as he worked his way into the hallway, holding his can of beer aloft in a toast. He escaped back toward the stairwell, hoping that he wouldn't run into—

"Lucas!" Andrea Price materialized in front of him, grinning widely.

"Hey, Andrea. Um…" *Say something. This is the part where you say something.* "How's it going?"

"Great! I'm so glad exams are over. I can't wait to go home."

"Me either." Lucas found it easier to just lie. "Uh, well, enjoy the party."

Andrea touched his arm, her fingers light on his bicep. "I thought maybe we could hang out in my room downstairs." She looked up at him from under lashes thick with mascara.

Lucas groaned inwardly. Andrea was a fellow freshman and a beautiful girl—blonde and petite with a bright smile—but she just wasn't Lucas's type.

Not by a long shot.

He'd dated girls before, and he knew plenty of them found him attractive, but he wasn't sure why. He had no fashion sense to speak of, and although he was almost six feet, he didn't have bulging muscles like Sam and the other athletes. Yet the other day he'd overheard Andrea and her friend cooing about his "golden hair" and "sparkling green eyes—like emeralds!"

Vast exaggerations.

Unfortunately, he didn't find women attractive. At least, not in the way they found him. "Oh, I… Um, I've got a really bad headache. I'm just going to get some air." *Wait, would she think that was an invitation to go make out?* He blurted, "Alone."

Her face fell just a fraction before she smiled again. "Sure, I understand. Feel better. And merry Christmas if I don't see you again tonight."

"Right. You too. Um, thanks." He forced a bright, "Merry Christmas!" and winced inwardly at how awkward he sounded.

Leaving a disappointed Andrea in his wake, Lucas reached the stairwell and headed up one more flight to the roof. He would love to have her for a friend, but she seemed incapable of reading his signals, so he'd started avoiding her a few weeks earlier. He didn't want to lead her on or anything.

He'd briefly considered dating her so he could meet some other people, but he'd sworn when he left Michigan he'd stop pretending. Besides, it would be a dick move to date Andrea knowing he was using her. He had to come out and start being himself—whoever that was.

All signs point to being a total loser, he thought, cursing himself.

He was too chickenshit to join the campus gay association, so now he didn't date women *or* men. He told himself it would be his New Year's resolution to have the balls to join the club and at least *meet* some other LGBT people. Joining would make it official—still a bit of a scary prospect.

Frigid night air greeted him as he pushed the door open. A group of five or six people huddled together nearby, puffing away on cigarettes. Lucas nodded to them and walked to the other side of the roof, which was usually deserted. Leaning against the waist-high brick wall, he peered out, his breath clouding in front of his face.

He knew being antisocial wouldn't help him fit in at Brookfield, but parties made him stupidly anxious. What if he said the wrong thing? He was terrible at small talk. Plus, he looked like he was having a seizure when he danced, and he hated loud music and having so many people around.

Maybe he could just tell Andrea he was gay, and she would be cool with it and they could hang…

But what if she wasn't cool with it? His stomach clenched. What if she told everyone and Sam freaked out? Sam had been pissed enough to get stuck with a freshman roomie, and though he'd warmed to Lucas in his way, what if he was a homophobe? Lucas hadn't heard him using any slurs, but…

Thanks to his father's job in sales for Ford, Lucas had moved around a lot over the years and never made lasting friends. He'd hoped college would change that, but so far, not so much. He only had himself to blame, but the more he stressed about making friends the more he screwed it up and wanted to hide.

The bass from downstairs thudded through the soles of his sneakers, more bearable now at least. The campus spread out before him, lights twinkling merrily on the trees that lined the drives, winding their way around the stately old buildings.

It was December eighteenth, the last day of the fall semester. Lucas was fairly confident he'd done well on his last exam—

organic chemistry, ugh—and he had hoped Sam's parents would have already picked him up. Sam lived in New York City, a few hours away from the tiny town in upstate New York that was home to Brookfield. Lucas wanted nothing more than to relax in his room and have an early night after being up late studying for the past two weeks.

Clearly he'd have to wait until tomorrow when the campus emptied to get some peace and quiet. Yet as much as he wanted some time to himself, Lucas knew that the next couple of weeks would be a little *too* quiet.

Tomorrow, all the students who hadn't already gone home would be taking off, leaving the campus a ghost town. The dorm advisor had told him he was the only one on his floor not going home for the holidays, and although he would be glad for the respite from the constant partying, spending Christmas completely alone was a depressing prospect. He enjoyed being by himself for the most part, but he was afraid loneliness would creep in and make itself a home.

He thought of his father and quickly took a gulp of beer to ward off the tightness in his throat. Some more smokers arrived, laughing gaily as they piled out onto the roof. Taking another swig of beer, Lucas stayed in the shadows.

"UHHH."

Another sharp rap on the door echoed through the room, and Lucas forced himself to open his eyes, since it sounded like Sam wasn't yet able to form words. It didn't feel like Lucas had been sleeping long, but the light streaming through the window told a different story.

"Samuel, it's your mother." Her voice was soft yet firm on the other side of the door.

"Uhhh," Sam repeated, his head still buried under his duvet.

Lucas kicked empty beer cans under the bed and tried to cover up the evidence of the previous night's activities, shoving Sam's bong in a drawer. When he opened the door, he smiled brightly, not without some effort. "Mrs. Kramer? I'm Lucas."

"How nice to finally meet you." She extended her hand and shook his firmly, the jewels on her tasteful rings sparkling.

He stood aside as she swept into the room, surveying the piles of Sam's dirty clothes, books, and discarded pizza boxes. Mrs. Kramer looked to be in her early fifties, although Lucas couldn't be sure. Sam rarely mentioned his family; most of his conversations revolved around basketball, partying, and girls. Many, many girls.

Sam's mother was an average height, with dark brown, bobbed hair betraying no hint of gray. Her black skirt and camel-colored coat were crisply pressed.

"Samuel."

Sam groaned again unintelligibly.

Lucas smiled at Mrs. Kramer. "He's not really a morning person, but I guess you know that."

"Indeed I do." She marched the few steps over to Sam's bed, heels clicking on the tile floor. With a brisk motion, she yanked off the duvet. "Time to get up, young man."

Sam, clad only in his briefs, groaned again before rolling over onto his back and opening his eyes. "Mom, chill. I thought you were coming later."

"It is later. Almost noon."

Sam whined, "What's the rush?"

"Hanukkah starts tonight at sundown, which I've mentioned to you a number of times. So get up and get moving. It's a three-hour drive home, and I have things to do."

Grumbling under his breath, Sam stood and shuffled off to the bathroom down the hall, leaving Lucas and Mrs. Kramer alone. Lucas smiled. "I'd offer you a seat, but…"

Returning his smile, she perched on the side of Sam's bed. "This is fine." She glanced around the room one more time before focusing her attention on Lucas. "Are your parents coming today as well?"

Lucas hated this part. The creased faces and murmured apologies. The pity. "No, I don't have any family." He forced a smile. "But it's cool. I'll get the place to myself for a couple of weeks. It'll be great."

"No family? None at all?" Mrs. Kramer regarded him with a new interest that unnerved him a little.

"Well, I have some cousins in Texas, but I've never met them."

"What happened to your parents?"

Lucas blinked in surprise. Usually people beat around the bush for a while before getting to that question. "My mom died when I was little; my dad in September. Cancer."

"I'm so sorry to hear it." Her face pinched in concern. "That must have been very difficult for you."

Difficult didn't really begin to cover it, but Lucas nodded. "Yeah."

"That's why you didn't start school until October. I remember Sam wasn't too happy to find out he'd be sharing a room after all. I told him he should have moved off campus, but he insisted on the dorm. I can only imagine that's due to the large number of young ladies living here." Her smile was wry.

"Yeah, Sam was *thrilled* to have me move in. But my profs were all really good about me starting late, especially since I'm only a freshman."

His father had insisted Lucas finally enroll in university for the fall, since the doctors hadn't expected him to make it to summer. When September rolled around, Lucas and his dad fought for days, Lucas refusing to leave his bedside while his father was adamant that at twenty, Lucas had already put off his future for long enough. Lucas won the battle, and had held his father's hand as he slipped away.

The school had been very accommodating about his late start, but now he was alone on a campus where everyone in his classes already made friends at the start of the year and, thanks to a housing shortage, his roommate was a senior jock. Lucas could move out—aside from the life insurance, his dad had left him a fair amount of money—but then he'd be even more isolated.

He cleared his throat, eager to move on to another topic. "So, Hanukkah starts tonight. That must be fun."

"Yes, it's a nice time of year. What will you do for Christmas?"

"Oh, just hang out or whatever. I'm not religious, so it's no big deal."

"Hmm." She stood and surveyed the room again. "Do you have a suitcase, or one of those duffel bags my son likes so much?"

"I'm sorry?" Lucas's duffel was somewhere at the bottom of his closet, and unless—

"Pack your bag, Lucas. You're going to spend the holidays with us."

"Oh, that's so nice of you, but I couldn't impose." Despite how lonely he might be over Christmas by himself, he was definitely looking forward to time away from Sam.

"You can, and you will. There's simply no way I'm leaving you here all alone."

"I really appreciate your concern, but I'll be fine. Really."

Sam returned, looking marginally more awake than when he left. His mother turned to him. "Samuel, Lucas will be coming to spend the holidays with us. Do you know where he keeps his overnight bag?"

Getting to his feet, Lucas was very tempted to tug on Mrs. Kramer's arm to get her to pay attention to what he was saying. "Thank you, but I'm not even Jewish. I don't want to intrude on your Hanukkah."

She waved him off. "Don't be ridiculous. You're more than welcome, and I'm not leaving you to..." She gazed around, nose wrinkling. "*This.*"

Yawning widely, Sam clapped him on the shoulder. "Dude, there's no point in arguing. Trust me."

Lucas opened his mouth to protest, but he couldn't think of a single good reason he should stay on campus alone for the holidays. Even if he had to put up with Sam, maybe he could do some sightseeing or something.

Half an hour later, Lucas found himself in the back of the Kramer family SUV, heading toward New York City as the first snowflakes of the season drifted down.

Chapter Two

AS THEY CROSSED the bridge to Staten Island, Lucas peered out the window as the city passed by. Sam snored lightly in the front seat, and Mrs. Kramer listened to a talk radio station that Lucas had tuned out near Poughkeepsie.

"Have you ever been to the city before?" Mrs. Kramer asked. Her voice jolted Lucas from his reverie.

"No, this is my first time."

"We'll have to show you around."

"Oh, you don't have to do that." Lucas already felt awkward enough.

"I insist. I'm sure Sam would be more than happy to take you into Manhattan. There's a wonderful Degas exhibit at the Frick."

Lucas realized the best way to deal with Mrs. Kramer was the same way he dealt with Sam: He nodded and smiled. "Thanks, that sounds great." Of course, the idea of Sam voluntarily going anywhere that didn't serve beer seemed highly unlikely.

They were only on the island for ten minutes before they pulled into the driveway of a large, two-story brick home. The lawn and shrubs were as neatly manicured as Mrs. Kramer, and large picture windows glowed with soft lights in the overcast afternoon.

"What a beautiful home you have."

Sam roused from his slumber and grunted. Mrs. Kramer

smiled widely in the rearview mirror, her lipstick still somehow untouched despite the cup of coffee she'd had. "Thank you, dear."

Inside, a man Lucas assumed to be Sam's father shuffled into the foyer to greet them. He was tall, thin, and balding, with glasses propped on his head. He looked as if he'd just woken from a nap. "Hello, son. Good drive home?" He pulled Sam into a hug.

"Hey, Dad. Yeah, sure."

"He slept the whole way as usual, Benjamin. Just like you would have done."

Mr. Kramer shrugged sheepishly. "Like father, like son, I suppose." He suddenly noticed Lucas hovering just inside the door, holding his duffel bag. "And who's this?"

Mrs. Kramer ushered Lucas forward with a gentle hand on his arm. "If you'd check your phone for messages, you would know that this is Sam's roommate, Lucas. He's going to spend the holidays with us."

After blinking in surprise, Mr. Kramer smiled broadly, shaking Lucas's hand firmly. "Welcome! It's good to meet you."

"Thanks, nice to meet you too." Lucas peered around at what he could see of the tastefully decorated home. The living room featured dark redwood, accented with rich reds and yellows. He glimpsed the kitchen at the end of the front hall and saw more redwood cupboards and stainless steel appliances.

"Sam's room is still a disgusting mess from Thanksgiving." Mrs. Kramer glared at Sam as he opened his mouth. "I told you I'm not your maid anymore." Glancing at her delicate gold watch, she pressed her lips together. "I've got to get organized in the kitchen; everyone will be here before we know it. Nathaniel has the extra bed in his room, so Lucas can stay there."

Lucas followed Sam up a plush staircase off to the right. "Lucky you, you get to crash with my geeky little brother."

"Are you sure he won't mind?" Lucas certainly wouldn't be happy, and he had to admit the thought of rooming with a kid wasn't his idea of a good time. Sam was bad enough.

"Who cares? What Mom says goes." At the top of the stairs, Sam pounded on the first door on the left. "Yo, loser! Open up." With that, he continued down the hall, which was decorated in muted tones of green and brown.

"Wait, aren't you going to introduce us?"

"Dude, I've gotta piss." With that, Sam disappeared into another doorway, kicking the door shut behind him.

After waiting a good twenty seconds without a response, Lucas knocked tentatively. He didn't hear any movement inside, so after another half minute, he knocked a little louder. This time he heard what sounded like a curse, followed by a barked, "What?"

Lucas slowly poked his head in. The large bedroom had two twin beds jutting out from the left-hand wall, and Sam's brother sat at a desk straight ahead against the window side of the room. Lucas saw immediately that he wasn't a little kid at all. From the back, he looked at least Lucas's age, with short, wavy chestnut hair.

"I'm reading, Sam."

"Um, I'm sorry to bother you." Lucas stood in the doorway awkwardly, not sure how to proceed.

Nathaniel spun in his seat. "Who are you?" He stared with big eyes through a pair of black-framed glasses, his soft features making him more pretty than handsome.

"I'm Sam's roommate. From college. I guess I'm going to be your roommate for the holidays." He glanced around the neat room, covered in childish wallpaper depicting sailboats and anchors. In the center of each wall was a large, framed black-and-white photograph. The stark and beautiful pictures of mountains and trees seemed out of place.

Nathaniel took this in before he smiled ruefully. "Clearly this was my mother's doing."

"How'd you guess?" Lucas smiled back. "Look man, I'm sorry.

I wouldn't be too happy if I were you."

He shrugged. "It's cool."

"Thanks. I'm Lucas, by the way." He dropped his bag and walked to the desk, putting his hand out.

Nathaniel stood, and Lucas could see they were almost the same height, Nathaniel perhaps an inch or two shorter. He regarded Lucas for a long moment before taking his hand. "Call me Nate."

Butterflies flapped in Lucas's stomach, and he said too loudly, "Okay, Nate!" He cleared his throat, pulling his hand away. "Um. I mean, cool. Or whatever." He glanced around again. "You like boats?"

Nate smirked. "Not for about ten years. I need to update my room, I know." He watched Lucas for a few moments, his eyes flicking down and then back up to Lucas's face. Then he reached out and squeezed Lucas's shoulder, sending sparks down his arm. "Make yourself at home, okay?"

Lucas could only nod before turning to grab his bag. Sam's little brother was *hot*. He scolded himself sternly. *Do not crush on him. Don't be lame. Don't make sharing a room weird!*

When he turned back, Nate was bending over his desk, tapping at his laptop. His firm, denim-clad ass was on full display, and Lucas could barely tear his gaze away. Sam was such a doofus that Lucas wasn't attracted to him at all despite his good looks. He was a little too muscle-bound anyway. But Nate was long and lean, his skinny jeans hugging his thighs…

Nate glanced over his shoulder, pushing his glasses up his nose. "Do you need anything?"

Hell yes. Lucas managed to squeak out, "No!" and busied himself with rooting through his duffel bag.

The *need* had been simmering for years now, but he'd been too afraid to hook up with another guy. Lucas ordered himself to get a grip and make sure he didn't embarrass himself. Maybe he should have stayed alone in the dorm after all.

Yet he couldn't help sneaking peeks at Nate, who seemed oblivious as he pecked at his computer, still leaning over the desk.

There was no harm in looking, right?

LUCAS SMOOTHED DOWN his shirt with the palm of his hand and wished again that he'd thought to ask Mrs. Kramer for an iron. The black button-down was the only good shirt he owned, and after being squashed in his bag for a few hours, it was a little worse for wear.

He leaned against the doorframe between the living and dining rooms, watching as Sam's relatives chatted happily. There were grandparents, aunts, uncles, and cousins. Fourteen people in all. They'd been very friendly when he was introduced, but Lucas couldn't help but feel out of his element. He hadn't been to many family gatherings, and never any Jewish celebrations.

"All right, time to light the menorah!" Mrs. Kramer clapped her hands once for attention. "Samuel, why don't you do the honors and read the blessings?"

Sam didn't look too excited, but he dutifully stepped up to the ornate candleholder in the front window. From the elevated candle in the center, two wings of four candles curved down gracefully to the left and right. After a moment, Sam spoke in what Lucas assumed was Hebrew.

Almost all of the guests recited the blessing along with Sam. Two more blessings followed, and Lucas wondered if he should bow his head. He glanced around the room and found Nate watching him from the other side. Cheeks going hot, Lucas focused on Sam as he lit the center candle on the menorah, followed by the one farthest to the right.

"Nathaniel, come and say the *Hanerot Halalu*. Stop hiding in the back." Mrs. Kramer extended her hand, and Nate came forward.

Taking a small book from his mother, he straightened his glasses and began reading quietly. His voice was soft and melodious in contrast to Sam's, and Lucas could hardly believe they were related at all, let alone brothers.

When Nate was finished, Mr. Kramer burst into song, everyone else following suit. Lucas couldn't understand the lyrics, and as the verses went on, it seemed like only the older people knew all the words. After the song ended, Mrs. Kramer brought out trays filled with what looked like lightly powdered doughnuts without holes.

"Hands down, the best part of Hanukkah." A pretty young woman with long, reddish hair smiled eagerly at Lucas, a tray in her hand. "Try one."

Lucas returned her smile and picked up a doughnut. "Thanks. Um, uh…" He managed to ask, "What's your name?"

"I'm Rachel. Sam and Nate are my cousins. You're Lucas, right?" She beamed at him.

"I am." Lucas glanced at Nate, alone across the room, thumbing through the prayer book. "So what's Nate like?" He hoped his tone was casual.

"Nate? He's always been quiet. He's twenty-one now, but he's still never had a girlfriend. Always too busy studying and taking pictures. I don't know; he's weird." Shame flickered across her face. "I mean, I love him, of course! He's a really good guy."

He nodded. "Oh, of course." Mrs. Kramer walked by, apparently in the middle of an argument with an elderly man.

Rachel rolled her eyes. "Don't mind them. Papa still thinks we should observe the Sabbath every Friday. That would mean going to synagogue and not cooking anything or using cars to get home. No electricity at all. It's just not practical."

"Does he follow the rules every week?"

"Yes, but he and Bubbe—our grandmother—are the only observant ones in the family." Rachel leaned in and lowered her voice. "Except if there's a Mets game on a Friday. Then all bets are off."

Laughing, Lucas took a bite of his doughnut, and a divine sweetness filled his mouth. "Wow, you're right. That's delicious. I didn't know you guys had holiday doughnuts."

Laughing, she said, "*Sufganiyot*, but yeah, that's basically what they are."

"And you eat them before dinner?"

"In our family we eat them before and after. Sometimes during," Nate said, appearing beside Lucas and reaching out to the tray.

Lucas laughed. "Beats turkey, that's for sure." Not that he and his father ever had a traditional Christmas. They'd made their own tradition: pizza, junk food, and football on TV. His dad had loved football, and even though Lucas didn't, he never complained.

He remembered their last Christmas, when his dad couldn't keep anything down thanks to the never-ending chemo. All his thick, dark hair was gone, his face puffy and body frail. He'd fallen asleep in his armchair at halftime, but Lucas had kept the game on, just in case his dad woke up.

Nate frowned. "Are you okay?"

"Huh? Oh yeah." Lucas nodded vigorously and took a huge bite of doughnut.

"Rachel, I think my mom needs you in the kitchen," Nate said.

As she scurried off, Lucas swallowed, blinking rapidly as he looked at the floor. He was going to make a fool of himself if he didn't get it together. After a calming breath, he took another bite of his doughnut and tried to act normal. "So, you guys eat like this for eight nights in a row?"

Nate smiled softly. "No, we just have a big dinner on the first night and once again before it's over, depending on everyone's schedules. We light the menorah every night, but that's about it. Hanukkah's actually not that big a deal. It's not a high holiday like Yom Kippur or Rosh Hashanah."

Another tray went by, and they both grabbed another sweet treat. Lucas knew his dad would want him to move on and be happy, and he'd worried so much about leaving Lucas alone. Lucas had promised to make friends, and since he'd failed utterly so far at school, maybe he could start with Nate. He asked, "What other Jewish delicacies await me tonight?"

"You like potatoes?"

"Does anyone *not* like potatoes?"

Nate seemed to ponder the question seriously. "No one I can think of." He added, "Tonight the potatoes will be in pancake form. *Latkes.*"

"I really hope there isn't maple syrup involved."

As Nate grinned, a dimple appeared in his left cheek, and Lucas felt a flutter in the pit of his stomach. He'd made Nate laugh! This was going okay. He wasn't saying anything stupid. Not yet, anyway.

He reminded himself again that the last thing he needed was to crush on his roommate's brother. The brother he was sharing a room with for the next two weeks. He was going to make a friend, and that was all.

Mrs. Kramer dashed by, insisting that Lucas eat the last sufganiyot on her tray. He gratefully obeyed and stuffed it in his mouth.

"It's time to sit down." Nate's hand was warm on Lucas's shoulder, and there was that tingle again. He nodded and followed him into the dining room, hoping his cheeks weren't too bright.

LUCAS WOKE TO pressure on his bladder and the faint sound of running water that had permeated his consciousness. He opened his eyes reluctantly and took in the early morning gloom. According to his phone it was after eight, but evidently it would be another gray, cloudy day.

He sat up and surveyed the room. Nate's bed beside him, closest to the windows, was empty. Across the way, an extra wardrobe stood in the corner beside the bathroom, and light shone through the half-open bathroom door, the water running in the shower.

Lucas couldn't wait to pee. He got up to venture into the hall to find another toilet, but hesitated as he glanced back at the half-open door. Without really knowing what he was doing, he tiptoed toward it. A couple of feet away he stopped suddenly, breath frozen in his chest.

Through the doorway he could spy the large mirror over the white sink. Reflected in it was Nate, who Lucas could see quite clearly through a completely transparent shower curtain. Nate's head tipped back under the water as his hands soaped his body.

A body that was more toned and defined than Lucas would ever have guessed.

Lucas forced a breath into his lungs as his pulse thrummed. With a start, he realized he was hard—not unusual first thing in the morning—and he clenched his fist to avoid touching himself.

Nate began stroking himself lazily as if on cue. He leaned a shoulder against the white tiles, and his eyes closed as he worked his hand up and down his shaft. He tugged a few times, and Lucas whimpered with need.

The water sluiced down Nate's firm, long body, steam rising as he worked himself. Lucas moved a step closer, squinting at the image in the mirror to get a better look. With his other hand, Nate fondled his balls, and his strokes increased in tempo.

Lucas wasn't sure when it happened, but his own hand was

down his pajamas, fist tight around his cock and moving like a jackhammer. The mirror in the bathroom was fogging, and Lucas knew he couldn't risk getting any closer. He heard Nate's muffled moan, and the sound was enough to put Lucas over the edge as he emptied, the rush of pleasure practically knocking him over.

There was a soft thud as he caught himself on the wall, and in the fogged mirror he thought he saw Nate's head turn his way.

Shit! How much can he see without his glasses?

Lucas stumbled backward and dove onto his bed, pulling the covers up and flipping on his side toward the door.

With his eyes jammed shut, he tried to catch his breath and keep still. A minute later, he heard Nate pad into the room. Lucas feigned sleep as Nate dressed, ignoring the fact that now he really, *really* had to pee.

When Nate finally left the room, closing the door gently behind him, Lucas waited thirty seconds and then hurried into the bathroom to relieve himself. His pajamas were a sticky mess. He couldn't exactly hang them to dry, so he spread them out under his duvet after a quick rinse, knowing he might have to sleep in a damp bed that night.

He needed to get a grip, and fast. As he pulled on jeans and buttoned up a plaid shirt, he muttered to himself, "Just not a grip on my dick this time."

Downstairs, Nate and his father talked quietly at the kitchen table, sipping coffee. Wearing jeans and an unzipped purple hoodie, Nate got up and poured Lucas a steaming mug, their fingers brushing when he handed it over. Lucas stammered out his thanks. Nate seemed totally normal and went back to his conversation with his dad, taking off his glasses and polishing the lenses with his gray T-shirt.

Soon Lucas was embroiled in a discussion with Mr. Kramer about Sam's many achievements in basketball. As Mr. Kramer waxed poetic on a game-winning layup Sam had made, Lucas pondered what Rachel had said about Nate's lack of girlfriend.

It didn't mean anything. Probably Nate dated around like Sam and didn't tell his family about it. It didn't mean he was gay or bi or anything. Lucas was gay, and he'd never even had the courage to kiss a guy. Nate not having a girlfriend proved nothing.

Every time Lucas glanced at Nate across the kitchen table, his temperature rose with a rush of desire. God, he wanted him, and now they'd be in close quarters for days on end. Looking, but not touching.

It was going to be a very, very long holiday.

Chapter Three

LUCAS SPENT THE afternoon with Sam and his father in the den, watching football on a big-screen TV that made Lucas practically drool. Nate had disappeared into his room after lunch, and Lucas tried not to obsess about what he was doing.

It was just after five when Mrs. Kramer told them it was time to light the menorah. Sam groaned, and Lucas could have sworn Mr. Kramer did too, but they obediently headed to the front room.

Nate was already there, the matches in hand. As Lucas watched Nate, he couldn't help but remember how Nate had looked naked and wet and jerking himself, and he mentally slapped himself with the reminder that this was a religious ceremony.

Nate seemed to only recite two blessings before lighting the middle candle and two on the right, doing the outer candle last. Lucas thought there had been three blessings the night before, but couldn't be sure. As if he could read Lucas's mind, Nate said, "There are only three blessings on the first night, and we don't bother with the prayer and song when it's just us."

"Can we get back to the game now?" Sam looked at his mother.

Her hands found her hips and she good-naturedly said, "You know this is supposed to be a time for family, not for TV."

"Sweetheart, it's the fourth quarter." Mr. Kramer gave his wife a beseeching smile.

With a laugh, she shooed them out, her husband kissing her soundly on his way. "Go on, Lucas. I'll be in with dinner in a little while."

"Do you want any help? I don't really care that much about football." Nate was already at the foot of the stairs, and Lucas willed him to turn around and stay.

Nate smirked. "Don't care about sports? That's sacrilege in this house." Then he was gone, his steps fading as he went back upstairs.

Sam's voice bellowed from the den. "Dude, you've got to see this play! Come on, you're missing it!"

With a smile for Mrs. Kramer, Lucas reluctantly returned.

AFTER A DINNER of leftovers on TV trays, Lucas and the Kramers watched an action movie about an alien invasion on Netflix. Nate had come down for dinner, but disappeared back up to his room halfway through the movie. Lucas fidgeted in the stuffed armchair in the corner of the plush, dark den. What was Nate doing up there? Not that it was any of Lucas's business.

You already invaded the guy's space without warning. Give him his alone time.

The nanosecond the movie credits appeared onscreen, Lucas yawned widely and said goodnight. Mrs. Kramer gave him a plate of sufganiyot to take up to Nate, saying, "He's always hiding away up there. He doesn't eat enough."

Lucas knocked softly on Nate's closed bedroom door, waiting a few moments before opening it. To his surprise, Nate wasn't in the darkened room, and the bathroom appeared empty. The space around the closet door glowed with a strange reddish light, and

Lucas blinked at it, thinking of the 10-foot, red-eyed aliens from the movie. After a moment of debate, he approached and knocked.

"Hold on," Nate called.

"Um, okay." Lucas stood there with the plate of doughnuts, wondering what on earth could be going on inside.

Two long minutes later, Nate opened the door and Lucas flooded with embarrassment for not figuring out that the red light was indicative of a darkroom. *Duh. I'm such a loser.*

The walk-in closet had been fashioned into a working space with a counter running around the perimeter holding trays of developing liquid. A clothesline ran across the back of the closet, large photographs pinned to it.

"You're a photographer?"

Nate chuckled, but not in a dickish way. "You clearly have a future as a detective."

Face hot, Lucas shuffled his feet, laughing awkwardly. "Clearly." He suddenly remembered the plate in his hand. "Here. Your mom thinks you need to eat more. I can just leave them."

"You wanna come in? I've just got to develop a couple more shots."

Lucas nodded and pulled the door shut behind him. Enclosed in the small space with Nate, his pulse raced. In the soft red glow, Nate looked better than ever, and Lucas fought the urge to reach out and touch him.

He cleared his throat and attempted to clear his mind. "I guess this explains why you keep your clothes in that separate wardrobe thingy."

"Yeah, Mom was overjoyed when I made this a darkroom, as I'm sure you can imagine." He glanced over his shoulder as he splashed some fluid into one of the trays. "You ever develop a picture before?"

"Uh-uh." Lucas had been examining what looked to be a couple of little moles on the back of Nate's neck and didn't feel capable of complete sentences. Lucas had removed the hoodie, and his back flexed through the white tee.

"I'll show you."

As Nate went through the steps, Lucas tried to pay attention. At one point, Nate handed him a pair of rubber-tipped tongs, and Lucas dutifully plucked out a developed photo and hung it on the line. They worked in companionable silence, and Lucas found he enjoyed watching the photographs come to life. They were all black-and-white cityscapes, and a frisson of excitement zipped through him. He'd finally get a chance to see New York for himself in the days to come.

Maybe Nate could show me around.

"You took all of these?" Lucas admired the clean lines and unique angles of the photos.

Nate waved his hand dismissively. "Yeah, I'm just messing around."

"I'd like to see what you can do when you're taking it seriously because these are amazing."

"It's nice of you to say so." Nate wiped his hands on a towel and plucked a doughnut from the plate Lucas had left on the counter. "We just need to wait now before we open the door."

Nate didn't seem comfortable with praise, so Lucas stopped talking and took his own doughnut, relishing the sweet, fruity flavor. He couldn't understand why Nate trivialized his talent. Lucas was no expert, but he found the photographs beautiful, particularly one taken from a low angle of a cathedral, a balloon floating away in the corner. He wondered what color the balloon had been but didn't ask. It was probably a stupid question.

They ate in silence, and Lucas noticed a blob of jelly filling on the corner of Nate's mouth. Before he could think, he reached out, swiping at it with his finger. Their eyes locked, and Lucas froze, his hand still at Nate's mouth.

Oh God, what was he doing?

He stayed in place, not breathing as he and Nate stared at each other in the muted red light. Before Lucas could process what was happening, Nate's tongue curled out and licked the jelly from his finger. A jolt of desire shot right to Lucas's balls, and he swallowed thickly, his throat suddenly dry.

Then Nate turned his head just a bit and sucked Lucas's finger into his mouth, his gaze behind his glasses locked on Lucas's face.

As Lucas moaned low in his throat, heart pounding, Nate yanked him close, and they were kissing. Lucas's head swam from the explosion of sensations.

They. Were. *Kissing.*

He was actually kissing another man. He'd dreamed of it, and somehow it was happening. He opened his mouth, and Nate's tongue dived in, probing and stroking as his hands ran over Lucas's back, down to his ass.

Quiet, allegedly mild-mannered Nathaniel Kramer was grabbing his ass.

Head swimming, Lucas kissed Nate back, his body alive in a way it had never been while kissing a girl. The scratch of Nate's stubble, his musky scent, his strong body hauling Lucas close— everything about him was so *male.*

I really am gay! I'm kissing a guy!

Giddy and burning with lust at the same time, Lucas explored Nate's mouth, their kisses sweet from the doughnuts.

They both gasped for air, and Lucas realized his jeans were now undone as Nate sank to his knees. "What are you…?"

As Nate grinned wickedly and took Lucas in his mouth, all intelligent thought fled. Lucas leaned back against the counter, his hands searching for purchase as he moaned at the wet heat of Nate's mouth. His right hand slid into one of the developing trays, liquid splashing as Nate sucked him into his throat.

Lucas's whole body vibrated. Nate's tongue was doing things

he'd never imagined possible, and it certainly hadn't felt like this when Paige Gallner had awkwardly sucked him off on prom night.

It felt like his cock was pulsing in time with his heart, all his nerve endings on fire. Nate pushed up Lucas's plaid shirt with one hand, fingers skimming over Lucas's belly and up to his nipples.

"Oh!" Lucas cried out, then slapped his own hand over his mouth.

Nate pulled off and said, "Yeah, keep it down, okay?"

"I'm sorry."

"It's okay." Nate caressed Lucas's belly, making him squirm, watching him. "Have you done this before?"

"I… No. Not really. A girl did this to me once, but it wasn't anything like this."

Lazily stroking Lucas's shaft, Nate waggled his eyebrows above his glasses. "Well, you're in good hands now."

"Literally. I never thought—Sam said you're a geek, but you're not at all."

Nate dipped his fingers behind Lucas's balls, pressing the sensitive skin there. He grinned as Lucas trembled and bucked his hips. "Geeks can be good at fucking. I promise."

Lucas could only moan, his breath hitching.

After licking along the bottom of Lucas's cock, Nate asked, "You like guys? You like this?"

"Uh-huh." He nodded jerkily. "Doesn't it seem like I do?"

Nate grinned. "Yes, but I just wanted to make sure." His smile faded, and he teased the tip of Lucas's cut dick before asking, "Want to come in my mouth?"

He could only whimper and nod, and Nate sucked him almost to the root, his cheeks hollowing. Lucas quivered, his knees shaking as Nate cradled his balls with his other hand. He tipped over the edge, red-tinged stars exploding in his vision as he came and Nate swallowed.

Nate held Lucas up with strong hands on his hips, standing a few moments later. He swiped his mouth with the back of his hand and straightened his glasses. Then casually unzipped his jeans and shoved them down his hips before pulling out his cock. It was cut and thick, the tip gleaming in the red light.

"Uh…" Lucas still couldn't seem to form a sentence, which made Nate smile as he began jerking himself off. Lucas watched, wide-eyed. "Can I?"

Nate dropped his hand. "Be my guest."

So many times Lucas had imagined what it would be like to touch another guy's dick. He'd done it as a kid once with a schoolmate, but that had only been mutual curiosity. They'd been too young to really know what they were doing, and had only poked and goofed around.

This was a man's cock Lucas was wrapping his hand around. It throbbed hot against his palm, and he twisted his hand to get a good angle as he stroked. His fingers brushed wiry hair at the base, and Nate's puffs of breath tickled Lucas's face as he leaned closer, his hand slipping around Lucas's shoulder, holding on.

"That's it. Just do it like you'd do to yourself."

Lucas lifted his hand to spit into his palm a couple of times, and Nate took his wrist, bending his head to lick Lucas's hand, spitting into it himself. Lucas's balls tingled, his dick twitching already at the rough sensation of Nate's tongue.

When Lucas stroked Nate again, Nate groaned, his hand sliding farther around Lucas's shoulder, fingers reaching up to tug at the short hair at the back of Lucas's neck.

I'm really doing this. I'm touching his dick. I'm jerking him off!

Of course his stupid brain felt the need to blurt, "So, you're gay too?"

Nate raised his eyebrows, smiling as he breathed hard, arching his hips into Lucas's hand. "Detective material for sure."

"Did you know I was gay as well?"

"I hoped you were when you walked into my room. You're so

fucking hot. But I *knew* when you watched me jerk off in the shower."

Blood rushing to his cheeks, glad the red light of the darkroom would conceal it, Lucas squeaked. His rhythm on Nate's cock stuttered. "You saw me? I'm sorry. I shouldn't have—I didn't—"

"Shh." Nate caught Lucas's mouth in a kiss, and Lucas moaned as he realized the musky salt he was tasting amid the lingering hint of sugar was his own cum. Nate leaned back, eyes twinkling. "I left the door open on purpose. I figured if you fell into my trap, this Hanukkah could be a lot more fun than the usual games of dreidel."

"I…" Lucas's mind spun. Nate's other words registered belatedly. "You think I'm hot?"

Nate's brow furrowed. "Uh, *yeah*. Have you looked in a mirror?" He thrust his hips against Lucas's hand. "You get me really hard."

"Uh, thank you?" Blood rushed in Lucas's ears. This had to be a dream.

Laughing softly, Nate kissed him again, just a gentle press of lips. "You're welcome. What do you say we have some fun this holiday?"

"Okay." Breathless, Lucas nodded. "Yes."

Nate arched an eyebrow over the black rim of his glasses. "Now how about you make me come?"

Lucas had never been happier to oblige a request in his life.

Chapter Four

"**L**OOK AT THIS fog—sticking around all day! There's a gorgeous view from this bridge, but I'm afraid the weather's not cooperating."

Lucas spoke up from the backseat. "Don't worry, Mrs. Kramer. I'm sure I'll see the view another day."

"You simply must. Perhaps you can come back into the city on the ferry. You'll get a good look at the Statue of Liberty too. I'm afraid I don't like heights, or I'd take you up the Empire State Building myself when there's better visibility." She glanced in the rearview mirror. "Sam, you'll take Lucas back tomorrow?"

"I've got stuff to do with my friends. I already spent a whole day at a stupid museum with you guys. Why did I have to come?"

"*Samuel.*"

The truth was, Lucas couldn't have cared less about seeing the city anymore. What he cared about was that Nate had been an arm's length away from him all day and he couldn't touch him. Nate had taken the front seat after a heated debate with Sam, and he was tantalizingly close, yet out of reach. Lucas's leg jiggled, and he noted the traffic with impatience. He just wanted to be back in Nate's room.

Back in his bed.

Well, he hadn't slept there or anything. After they'd made out again and Nate had given Lucas another mind-bending blow job, they'd slept in their separate beds. Lucas knew it was stupid to sleep together in a tiny twin bed when Nate's parents could walk in at any time, but he still wanted to. When he'd woken that morning, Nate was already downstairs, and they'd been on the go all day.

"Mom, I've got plans!" Sam whined.

Lucas cleared this throat. "You know, I can just come back by myself."

"I can take him." Nate's voice was so quiet, Lucas barely heard him.

"Will you, darling? I thought you'd be busy with your little hobby. So many hours you spend locked up in that closet."

It occurred to Lucas that he didn't know if the Kramers knew Nate was gay. Was he in the closet in that regard as well? Lucas could hardly blame him. He'd only come out to his dad near the end. He hadn't wanted to upset him, but the thought of never telling him the truth was unbearable.

Thinking of how his father had kissed his forehead and told him he loved him just as he was, Lucas's eyes burned. He pushed away the memories before he burst into tears and freaked everyone out.

"It's not a problem." Lucas thought he could detect an edge to Nate's voice now.

"Yeah, because King Geek doesn't have any friends." Sam cackled.

"*Samuel.* Your brother has lots of friends at NYU. He's in the law society, after all."

"Just no friends I'd introduce to you, asswipe," Nate added.

Lucas turned his head to the window as Nate and Sam continued bickering. There was something oddly reassuring about it, and the way Mrs. Kramer interjected every so often. The sense of familiarity with each other left him yearning.

After what seemed like an eternity, they were home. Lucas

wanted nothing more than to escape to Nate's room and spend the whole night there, but he had to make more small talk and sit through another dinner.

First they gathered in the living room and lit the candles on the menorah, adding another to the right-hand side, but lighting them in order from the middle. Mr. Kramer recited the blessings beforehand, and Lucas tried to listen and not think about how he wanted to lick Nate's Adam's apple. Trying to be sociable, he asked, "What's the story behind Hanukkah? Something about oil, right?"

Mr. Kramer grinned. "Well, there's an old joke that every Jewish holiday boils down to: They tried to kill us; they didn't—let's eat."

Mrs. Kramer jumped in. "After the Maccabees reclaimed the Temple in Jerusalem from their enemies, there was only enough oil to light the eternal flame for one day. However, the oil lasted for eight nights."

"A miracle." Mr. Kramer clapped his hands together. "Okay, let's eat."

At the dinner table, Lucas pushed Thai takeout around on his plate, and afterwards he tried to concentrate on the game of Rummikub Mr. Kramer suggested, but ended up with the most tiles every time. Although Nate had retreated to his room, Lucas couldn't think of a good reason to go to bed at eight o'clock.

When he finally escaped an hour later, he thought he might explode with pent-up desire and frustration. He practically ran up the stairs and burst into Nate's room without knocking. Nate, lying on his bed, looked up from the book he was reading, the lamplight glinting off his glasses.

"Good game?"

"Not really; I kept getting stuck with high numbers I couldn't get rid of."

"Too bad." Nate yawned widely. "I was just about to go to

sleep. So if you want to read or anything, can you use that little lamp on your side?"

Lucas was speechless for a moment. "Yeah. Sure." That was it? Nate was going to *sleep*? Shame and embarrassment flooded Lucas like a hot, prickly tide. He wished he could be anywhere else. Apparently Nate wasn't interested in him at all anymore.

Standing, Nate pulled his sweater over his head, stretching his arms up high and yawning again. He unzipped his khakis and stepped out of them before carefully folding his clothes and placing them on his desk chair, clad only in his boxers. Lucas, still standing dumbly, watched.

Nate strolled back to his bed and stretched out. He glanced over at Lucas and burst out laughing. "Oh man, I should take a picture of your face right now."

Son of a... "This is your idea of a joke?"

As Nate patted the mattress beside him, Lucas didn't know whether to kiss him or kill him, but when he had Nate's warm skin under his palms, he knew it would be the former. He covered Nate's body with his own as their mouths met.

They kissed for minutes or maybe hours, until Nate propped himself up on his elbows and took a breather. "You took forever to get up here. It was torture today not being able to touch you. That's why I insisted I sit in the front. Man, I thought you were going to jump me at the dinner table. Good thing my family's so clueless."

"So they don't know you're gay?"

"Nope. Like I said—clueless."

Lucas wondered why Nate didn't tell them, but as he rubbed against Nate, his dick hard in his jeans, he figured he'd ask another time. "So you were playing hard to get just now?"

"Of course." Nate grinned, displaying his dimple and sending another rush of blood right to Lucas's cock.

"I thought maybe... I thought you weren't interested anymore." Lucas glanced away. Why did he say that out loud?

"Shit, I'm sorry. I shouldn't play games with a virgin."

He cringed. *I'm so lame.* "A girl blew me after prom. Does that count?"

"If you want it to." Nate ran his hands over Lucas's back down to his ass.

"Not really. It was super awkward. It just felt…wrong, you know? Not like with you." Clearly Nate was experienced, considering the things he could do with his tongue. "How many people have you been with?"

"No *people.* Just guys." He looked thoughtful for a moment. "I don't know. My fair share. I went to a gay bar during frosh week, and the rest, as they say, is history."

Wow. Nate had been with men. *Multiple* men.

"Don't worry. I get tested regularly, and I'm careful."

Lucas had been wondering how to bring that up. "So you've dated a lot of guys?"

Nate laughed. "Dated? Not really. I guess I've kind of dated a few. Well, I had sex with them more than once." He peered closely at Lucas, his brown eyes intense behind his square-ish glasses. "Just so you know, I'm not looking for a boyfriend."

"Oh. Why not?" Lucas hoped he didn't sound as needy as he felt. He was lying on top of the guy and it seemed so *intimate.*

It's just fooling around. Go with it. Don't be a loser for once.

"I can't exactly bring home a nice boy to Mom and Dad. It's easier this way. Besides, I'm not good at that stuff." He smiled. "I like sex. I'm *good* at sex. Why complicate it?"

"But—"

Nate leaned up and caught Lucas's bottom lip between his teeth. "Let's stop talking," he whispered.

They kissed again, and Lucas explored Nate's body. He'd never been able to handle another man so freely, and he reveled in touching and tasting. He sucked one of Nate's nipples into his mouth, delighting in the soft moan that escaped Nate's lips. As he moved lower, his heart pounded in excitement.

He was really going to do it.

He'd thought about it a million times and wondered what it would be like to suck a dick: how it would taste, how it would feel, what it would smell like. He nuzzled the trail of hair that led down from Nate's belly button, and Nate lifted his hips as Luke pulled off his boxers.

Lucas was still in his jeans and green Henley, and Nate's nudity fired his blood. Especially when he spread his legs wide, unashamed, his cock flushed, standing up from the trimmed patch of hair. He watched Lucas patiently, keeping his hands at his sides.

Taking Nate's cock tentatively, Lucas rubbed it on his cheek, his chin, his lips. He wrapped his hand around Nate's shaft, exploring and working up his nerve. His pulse raced, stomach clenching. It must have shown on his face, because Nate stroked his hair gently and said, "You don't have to."

Screw that. He wanted to. More than that—he'd explode if he didn't. With a deep breath, he swallowed the head of Nate's cock, wrapping his lips around him as far as he could. The shaft was heavy and hot in his mouth, and saliva dripped down his chin. Lucas moved his head up and down, sucking and licking like he was enjoying a popsicle on a hot summer's day.

A dick popsicle. A dicksicle, even.

Slurping, loving the musky, slightly bitter tang, he remembered what Nate had done, and fisted the base of Nate's shaft as he sucked what he could into his mouth. He traced his tongue up the ridge on the back, and Nate moaned, making Lucas even harder in his jeans. He humped the mattress between Nate's spread legs to get some friction on his straining dick.

Nate's fingers tangled in Lucas's hair, and he muttered under his breath. "That's it. Like that. You're doing so good."

Lucas experienced a rush of power and pride unlike any he'd

ever felt and sucked even harder. Ducking lower, he explored Nate's balls, boldly licking them as he continued stroking Nate's cock with quick, firm movements. Remembering a porno he'd watched a dozen or possibly a hundred times, he sucked one of Nate's balls totally into his mouth.

Nate exhaled sharply and shuddered as he came, spurting up onto his chest. Lucas raised his head to watch, and he drank in the sight of Nate with his head thrown back, his smooth chest and hard stomach splattered with semen.

Going up on his hands and knees, Lucas dipped his head and impulsively licked Nate's stomach, savoring the salty taste. Nate chuckled softly and pulled Lucas up for a kiss as he reached down and rubbed Lucas through his jeans.

"You're wearing too many clothes."

There was a knock on the door, and they froze, eyes wide. After a beat, Lucas scrambled off Nate and dived onto the other bed and under the covers as Nate pulled up his duvet. Nate cleared his throat. "Yeah?"

"I'm going out shopping tomorrow with Aunt Linda, so I've left you and Lucas some money on the counter. Have fun in the city. Be home in time to light the menorah, please."

"Okay, Mom."

They listened to her footsteps recede down the hall, both breathing heavily. Then they looked at each other and burst out laughing.

"You need a hand over there?" Nate whispered.

"That would be nice."

Nate flicked off the light and crept over, and they giggled quietly as he jerked Lucas off, which didn't take long at all.

Chapter Five

"THERE YOU GO. Statue of Liberty approaches to starboard, or possibly port. I can never keep them straight."

Lucas nodded. "That's her all right. Looks pretty much like she does on TV."

"You mean you're not filled with a burst of American patriotism at the sight of Lady Liberty?"

"Oh, wait... There it is." Lucas thrust his arms in the air. "USA! USA!"

Laughing, they ignored the stares of people nearby and found an empty bench. The wind was icy out on the water, and most passengers sat inside. Lucas pulled his scarf closer around his throat and wished he'd remembered his hat.

"Wait, stand by the railing," Nate directed Lucas as he pulled a large camera from his messenger bag.

Lucas did as he was told and posed. It felt good to be the focus of Nate's attention, and despite the cold air, a warm glow filled him. He asked, "Your glasses don't bug you when you shoot?"

"Nah. I'm used to it. My eyes hate contacts, and I'm too blind to go without anything. Some people adjust the diopter to compensate for bad vision, but my Nikon has a high eye-point and it works great with my glasses." He huffed out a nervous laugh. "I know I'd probably look better without them, but..."

"What? No way." Lucas glanced around to find they were still alone. "Your glasses are super hot." Nate had seemed so confident about sex that Lucas was surprised to hear any insecurity from him. It was strangely reassuring.

"Yeah?" Nate smiled, clearly pleased.

"Hell yeah."

When Lucas rejoined Nate on the bench after a few more pictures, he leaned back and watched the city skyline get closer. The sun peeked out through the clouds, and Lucas couldn't remember the last time he'd felt so content.

The only thing that could make the moment better would be holding Nate's hand, but he was too afraid to try.

"What's your major?" Nate was watching him with the intent gaze that seemed to be his default expression.

"Chemistry. Premed."

"You want to be a doctor?"

The $64,000 question, as his dad used to say, although Lucas was never sure why. Something about a game show. "Well, I'm really good at science."

"Not exactly a resounding 'yes.'"

"My dad always wanted me to go to med school. I don't want to disappoint him."

Nate was quiet for a moment. "Mom said he died a few months ago. I'm sorry."

"Yeah. Thanks." Lucas tugged off one of his gloves, suddenly preoccupied with an itch on his palm. "You're prelaw, right?"

"Yep." Nate didn't sound thrilled about it.

"Following in your father's footsteps. Well, it's not like Sam's going to."

Nate barked out a laugh that sounded too loud coming from him. "The golden child? Not likely. He'll be too busy basking in the warm memories of his b-ball glory days and probably making a fortune as a salesman at my uncle's company."

"It occurs to me that I don't even know what his major is."

"Technically it's business, but mainly hoops and chicks."

"Okay, I don't understand why he's so special. I mean, he's not a bad guy, but Sam's just such a…"

"Stereotypical jock asshole?"

Laughing, Lucas nodded. "That about sums it up. You're smart and studying to be a lawyer. And you're such an amazing photographer."

Nate shifted on the bench, a little smile tugging at his lips. He took off his glasses and ran his finger over a scratch on the top right of the frame that Lucas assumed was from his camera. "You think so?"

"Of course. Your folks should be putting you on the front cover of their yearly newsletter. They seem like the type to do one."

Gaze still on his glasses in his hands, Nate said, "My parents think Sam walks on water. The thing is, he's always been this…miracle. Mom had a bunch of miscarriages, and they never thought they'd have a baby. When they had Sam, it was the best thing that ever happened to them. Then he turned out to be this amazing athlete, unlike anyone else in my family, and he's been the star of the show ever since."

"But you—"

"Have never been anything to write home about. It's not like my parents don't love me. Sam just became the center of their universe when he was born, and that didn't change when I came along. And if they knew I was queer…" He grimaced and slipped his glasses back on.

"Have you tried talking to them about it? I was terrified of what my dad would say, but he was awesome. Maybe if—"

"No. Everything is fine the way it is. I don't need to tell them."

He wanted to argue, but if Nate wasn't ready to come out, that was his choice. It wasn't as though Lucas had been brave and honest himself at school. "I'm sorry." He couldn't think of anything else to say.

"Don't be." Nate stood and slung his bag over his chest. "Come on, we're almost there."

Lucas knew the conversation was over, and he didn't push it. He felt the urge to grasp Nate's hand again, but instead simply followed him into the surge of passengers downstairs.

An hour later, they stood at the top of the Empire State Building in crisp sunlight, and Lucas marveled at the view of the city. Central Park was an enormous green rectangle holding the surrounding skyscrapers and buildings at bay.

With his camera, Nate seemed to have tunnel vision as he snapped shots of the city below. Lucas divided his time between watching him and peering out at the view, and eventually Nate garnered the majority of his attention.

Nate noticed Lucas's stare after taking about twenty shots of the Flatiron Building. "What?" Lucas swore he saw a blush tint Nate's cheeks.

"You look so happy."

"Yeah. I love photography. I wish..." He shook his head and nodded over his shoulder. "We should check out the other side."

Lucas reached for Nate's arm. "You wish what?"

Nate looked out over the city. After a moment's hesitation, he said, "I wish I could do this all the time."

"Why can't you?"

"Oh, sure. Drop out of prelaw and transfer to Tisch for photography? The 'rents would love that."

"Tisch. Is that in New York?"

"Yeah, it's part of NYU."

Suddenly it made sense to Lucas why Nate hadn't gone away to college. "That's exactly what you want to do isn't it? That's why you went to NYU in the first place."

Nate looked at him sharply and yanked his arm away. "You

don't know anything about it."

"You're in third year, right? What are you waiting for?"

"Look, I just can't." Nate jammed the cap back on his camera and zipped it into its case. "It's freezing up here. Let's get some lunch."

"Nate, I don't understand—"

"What was that you were saying about medicine? I think your exact words were that your *father* wanted you to be a doctor."

"That's different." Was it though? Crossing his arms, Lucas shivered. "You're right, let's go inside. It's too cold."

They descended in the elevator, Nate's glasses fogging in the sudden heat, the chatter of a group of German tourists filling the silence. The black cloud hanging over them didn't dissipate as they headed up West Thirty-Fourth Street. Lucas wanted to say the right thing, but with every minute that ticked by, it became more and more awkward.

Despite what they'd shared, it hit home that he and Nate didn't really know each other. Lucas had been feeling so comfortable with him, and now there was only weird, strained silence he didn't have the right words to break.

Nate had told him he wasn't looking for a boyfriend, and perhaps all he wanted was sex and not even friendship. Which was totally fine! Or should have been, but it left Lucas feeling hollow.

Instead of suffering through an awkward lunch, Lucas faked a headache. They spoke to each other in clipped sentences when necessary, and Nate felt like a stranger on the ferry back to Staten Island.

Lucas impulsively accepted an invitation from Sam for pizza and poker with him and his friends that night, even though Sam had clearly only asked because Mrs. Kramer made him. Hopefully poker would involve less small talk than hanging with Mr. and Mrs. Kramer.

Before Lucas and Sam left, they dutifully participated in lighting the menorah. It was the fourth night, and after lighting the middle candle, Mrs. Kramer lit the four candles to the right. Nate disappeared as soon as they were done, and Lucas tried to brush it aside. Much to his surprise, he actually had a good time with Sam's friends, and almost forgot about the tension with Nate.

Almost.

He and Sam came home late, smelling of pot and the can of beer that had been shaken and sprayed on everyone in attendance in celebration after a guy named Mutt won a particularly big prize. They were only playing with dollar bills, but apparently twenty bucks was a lot to Mutt.

Lucas pushed open the door to Nate's darkened room as quietly as he could, tiptoeing inside. Nate slept, curled toward the windows. After weighing his options—go to bed reeking or risk waking Nate by having a shower—Lucas crept into the bathroom and closed the door behind him. Stripping his clothes off, he stepped into the tub, enjoying the hot water flowing down.

He was on his second shampoo when he realized he wasn't alone. Through the transparent curtain, he saw Nate closing the bathroom door behind him. Leaning against it, Nate watched him.

"Sorry. Did I wake you?" Lucas shifted uneasily. He felt like he was on display in the bright light of the bathroom and resisted the urge to cover himself.

Nate took off his glasses, then his boxers. He slid back the shower curtain. The shampoo trickled down Lucas's forehead, and Nate washed it away with his palm. Stepping back, Lucas silently invited him into the shower.

Since it was far easier than talking, they silently moved into each other's arms and kissed, tongues winding together as their hands explored. Lucas wasn't sure when Nate had picked up the soap, but he leaned into his touch as Nate lathered him.

His cock was at full attention, and Lucas could feel Nate's

hardness against his ass as Nate turned him around to face away from the spray of water. His hands still roamed over Lucas, and then one of his fingers pushed just inside Lucas's hole. Lucas tensed, his eyes popping open.

"Relax." Nate whispered in his ear before sucking the lobe gently.

Lucas tried to do as he was told, and Nate's finger probed a little deeper, stretching him. Filling him with a low burn, the pressure of his finger feeling... God, it felt good. *Really* good. He must have said it aloud, because Nate chuckled. "Just wait. It gets better."

"What are you going to do?" Lucas's heart hammered wildly. He knew he was entering uncharted territory.

"I'm going to eat your ass."

The words sounded so wonderfully dirty on Nate's tongue. Lucas had read about rimming, but reading and experiencing were two very different things. He took a deep shuddering breath, excitement thrumming through his veins. He could only say, "Uh..."

Nate smoothed his hands down Lucas's flanks to his hips. "As long as you want me to?"

"Yes, yes. Uh-huh."

Chuckling, Nate kneeled behind him, spreading open his cheeks. At the first touch of Nate's tongue against his hole, Lucas thought he might come right then and there. He leaned forward, bracing his hands wide on the slick tiles as Nate licked and nibbled at his ass, thrusting his tongue inside. If Nate hadn't held him up by his hips, Lucas was sure his legs would collapse as flashes of pleasure shot through his whole body, all the way to the tips of his fingers.

He moaned, breathing heavily as Nate worked magic with his mouth and tongue. When Nate's hand snuck around to stroke Lucas's cock, sparks ignited and his balls tightened. Nate was fucking him with his tongue now, stroking Lucas in time, and Lucas had to press his lips together to keep from shouting.

He shook with his orgasm, whimpering in little gasps as the pleasure overtook him, centered on his cock and his hole, where Nate had his head buried. Propped up by the wall, Lucas tried to catch his breath. Nate's tongue traveled all the way up his spine until Nate nuzzled at the back of his neck.

"Like that?" Nate whispered, nipping at Lucas's skin.

Lucas could only nod. Nate's erection was hot against his ass, and he thought about what it would be like to bend over and let Nate fuck him, to have that hot cock pressing inside. Before he could do anything, Nate turned him around and put Lucas's hand on his rigid cock, urging Lucas to stroke him. He did, and Nate leaned into his touch, his eyes drifting shut.

Nate didn't take long to come, and when he was done, they cleaned up under the hot spray of water. Lucas was just finishing rinsing the leftover shampoo out of his hair when Nate said, "Sorry about today. I was a jerk. I can get like that sometimes."

"It's okay. I didn't mean to push or whatever. I was a jerk too."

Nate turned off the water and stepped out onto the bathmat, wrapping a towel around his lean hips before putting on his steamy glasses. "It wasn't your fault. It's just..." He stopped, his hand on the doorknob.

"What?"

"No one's ever read me that easily before." Then he was gone, leaving Lucas alone in the steam.

Chapter Six

WHEN THE PHONE rang in the kitchen, Nate snapped it up off the cradle. "Hello?" He was silent for a moment. "Mom, you know we've got tickets for *Wicked*. In fact, it was you who bought them and insisted I take Lucas to this stupid musical in the first place."

Lucas shifted uncomfortably in his chair at the kitchen table. He hated witnessing fights, even if they were one-sided. They'd been waiting for over half an hour for Mrs. Kramer to return home, since she'd requested they light the menorah with her before going into the city.

"Okay, Mom. I know." After a beat he added, "I love you too." He hung up and turned to Lucas. "Come on, we've got to light this thing and hit the road."

Lucas followed as Nate went to the living room, pausing to stick his head down the hall toward the den. "Dad! Mom says we should just light it without her tonight."

"Oh." There was a pause, and then Mr. Kramer called, "You boys go ahead without me. And take my car into the city if you want."

Nate's eyebrows raised. "Yeah? Okay, Dad." At the front window, he whispered to Lucas. "He usually doesn't let us within a hundred yards of his Audi."

He struck a match, and Lucas blinked in surprise. "Don't you have to say those things first? The blessings?"

Nate sighed, smiling. "You're worse than my mom." He closed his eyes and spoke the two blessings quickly, and Lucas told himself he shouldn't find it hot. He failed miserably. Nate opened his eyes. "Okay, now you can light the candles."

"Me? I'm really not qualified."

Laughing, Nate struck another match, lighting the middle candle. "This is the *shamash*, which means guard or servant. So we take this"—Nate picked up Lucas's hand and put it on the candle, his palm warm as he covered Lucas's hand with his own—"and then light the other candles with it."

Lucas let Nate's hand guide his as they lit five other candles, three still unlit. Standing so close to Nate, Lucas felt the warmth of his body and yearned to touch him. They placed the shamash back in its place, but still held it as their eyes met. In the soft, flickering light, Nate had never looked so gorgeous, and Lucas leaned in to kiss him.

"You should get going. Traffic's always bad getting to the theatre district." Mr. Kramer's voice boomed out from the hallway, and Lucas and Nate sprang apart.

Mr. Kramer rounded the corner. "Ah, candles lit. Very good." He pulled out his wallet. "Here's some money for gas, and to have a bite after the show if you want." He handed Nate a wad of bills. "It's very nice of you to entertain Sam's friend." He turned to Lucas before going back to the den. "Merry Christmas."

Lucas blinked, realizing he'd forgotten it was Christmas Eve. "Oh, right. Um, thanks." His first Christmas without his dad was upon him, and he hadn't even noticed it. Guilt soured his stomach, and he had to swallow hard to get rid of the lump in his throat.

In the car, they were quiet as Nate headed to the Verrazano Bridge. "Are you okay? I know it must be hard, with your dad gone and everything. Mom said you don't have any other family?"

"No, not really. And yeah. Thanks." Lucas blew out a long breath. "It sucks. You'd think…" He shook his head.

"What?" Nate reached over and rubbed Lucas's thigh with his palm.

"I knew for months that he was going to die. So did he. He fought hard, but he knew it. So you'd think I'd be more used to it by now or something. Sometimes I'll see something and think, Oh, I need to tell Dad about that. Or, Dad will like that movie. Or whatever. Like I actually forget."

"I think that's normal." Nate rubbed gently, his hand warm on Lucas's thigh. "It's hard too with the holidays. Those old traditions."

The way Nate was touching him—not in a sexy way, just comfort—filled Lucas with longing. He knew he shouldn't get too attached. Nate had made it clear this was only a holiday fling. But maybe…

Forcing a laugh, Lucas said, "Football and junk food isn't really a hallowed family tradition that should be passed on. I don't even like football."

"Well, my dad and Sam will be more than happy to keep the tradition alive tomorrow, I have no doubt."

Lucas laughed. "No doubt." Watching the passing lights of the city as they entered Manhattan, he was quiet for a minute, relishing Nate's caress. Then he said, "Thank you for letting me light the candles. It was…nice." He cringed inwardly at how lame he sounded.

"Yeah." Nate put his hand back on the wheel. "No big deal."

Exactly. No big deal. So don't make one of it, moron, Lucas scolded himself.

When the play let out a few hours later, Lucas and Nate walked into the crisp, clear night, squeezing past the horde of teenage girls waiting at the stage door for the boy bander who was currently playing Boq. Cabs honked incessantly, and the city was alive with light and sound as Nate led him to Rockefeller Center to see the Christmas tree.

Light snow started to fall almost on cue as they approached and shimmied their way into the crowd jostling for a look. Lucas took in the massive tree, which dwarfed the skating rink below, where at least a hundred people circled. A vendor sold hot chestnuts nearby, the smell wafting on the December air. It was like being in a movie.

After a minute, he realized Nate was chuckling. Lucas asked, "What's so funny?"

"You look like Dorothy arriving in Oz."

"Don't make me start singing." Lucas put on a mock serious expression.

"Start? You've been humming and skipping since we left the theater!"

Lucas shoved Nate's arm playfully. "So I like musicals, okay? Besides, don't tell me you didn't enjoy it. You know you got *verklempt* at the end."

"Ohhhh, busting out the Yiddish! Impressive. Very impressive."

"Your bubbe taught me a thing or two the other night."

Nate's cell rang, and while he pushed his way out of the crowd, Lucas followed, gazing around in wonder. Manhattan at night was as vibrant and intoxicating as he always imagined. He thought fleetingly of the sleepy little college town to which he'd soon be returning, where he had felt so alone, and lost a bit of the spring in his step. New York City just seemed so full of *possibility*.

Pocketing his phone, Nate turned to Lucas and eyed him critically, unzipping Lucas's navy jacket. "You've gotta lose the plaid."

"What?" Lucas glanced down at his outfit of jeans, black tee, and plaid shirt over top. "You said this was fine."

"I believe my exact words were that you'd fit in with the other tourists," Nate teased.

"Okay, so where are we going now?"

"To a flannel-free zone." Nate grinned slyly. "Don't worry, you'll like it."

LUCAS SHIVERED, RUBBING his arms as he tried to restore circulation. The line for the club was long, but Nate had insisted Lucas take off his shirt and jacket and hold them, even though the night was only growing colder. Nate had peeled off his sweater and jacket and was clearly trying not to shiver in his white tank-top style undershirt.

The neon sign on the building screamed *Gomorrah* in scarlet. Lucas was amazed how many people were clubbing on Christmas Eve. He'd really rather just go home and curl up with Nate in one of the twin beds, but he didn't want to be a killjoy.

Sure, the club would be crowded, and the music was so loud the sidewalk practically vibrated with the bass, but when in Rome and all that. Besides, he was with Nate, and it was about time Lucas went to a gay club. He'd seen them in movies and on TV, and his heart skipped excitedly at the thought of actually going into one. It was all very Officially Gay.

Leaning in close, Lucas whispered to Nate, "Have I mentioned I'm not twenty-one?"

"Shhh. Just look cute, which will be easy. I'll handle the rest."

Their turn came at the front of the line, and Nate handed two pieces of ID to the bouncer, who looked them over carefully before giving them back and miraculously waving them inside. In line for coat check, Lucas tried to play it cool, but couldn't.

"What did you give him?"

The thumping bass was muted in the vestibule, but still loud. Glasses fogged, Nate put his lips right up to Lucas's ear, sending a shiver down Lucas's spine. "My driver's license and my library card, plus fifty bucks from my dad."

Lucas didn't stop laughing until they pushed open the doors to the interior of the club. He gazed around, speechless. The cavernous, multilevel circular space was full of men. Young, hot men. Strobe lights pulsed in time to the deafening beat, and Lucas could barely hear himself think.

A few women were here and there, but by and large it was the most male place Lucas had ever been. The most *gay*. It was like heaven. Granted, a very loud, crowded, and sexed-up heaven. But thrilling nonetheless.

Nate must have spotted his friends, because the next thing Lucas knew, Nate took his hand and was pulling him along as they weaved through the crowd surrounding the dance floor. Lucas didn't mind; as long as Nate was holding his hand, he'd go anywhere.

"Hey!" A very good-looking guy with light brown skin and the clearest eyes Lucas had ever seen waved to them. Those eyes raked over Lucas, taking him in from head to toe. He winked at Nate before dropping a quick kiss on his lips. He then turned to Lucas, extending his hand and speaking loudly over the din. "I'm Yaman."

Four cute young men sidled up, all also kissing Nate on the mouth in greeting, which had Lucas staring and trying to hide his surprise. Also the bolt of raging jealousy. Nate had dropped his hand when they'd found their little space in the crowd, and Lucas fought the urge to sling his arm over Nate's shoulders possessively.

After Lucas was introduced to Jamie, Ryan, Gord, and Dave, he tried to pay attention as they all chattered about people he didn't know. It was strange to see Nate with his friends, talking and laughing and being so much more outgoing and confident than he was with his family. Lucas had glimpsed this side of him when they were alone, but it was startling to see him so relaxed.

He tried valiantly not to obsess about whether Nate had slept with any of his friends. He knew it was none of his business, but his mind kept returning to thoughts of Nate with other men. He wanted him all to himself.

When Gord—Lucas was pretty sure it was Gord and not Dave—slung an arm around Lucas's shoulders and asked, "And what's this cutie's story?" Lucas eloquently replied, "Uh…"

Nate swooped in and removed Gord's arm. "Hands off."

Nate's friends all shared a glance with eyebrows raised and chorused, "Ohhh!"

Yaman grinned at Lucas. "You must be something special all right."

Jamie added, "Don't tell me Mr. No Boyfriend—No Way, No How is smitten?"

"Shut up!" Nate jammed his hands in his pockets. "He's just new. I don't want you to scare him off. I don't care what Lucas does."

The hurt struck more deeply than it had any right to. Lucas knew he should laugh it off, but he could only stare at his feet, wishing he was anywhere else. A hand patted his shoulder, and he raised his head to find Ryan smiling kindly. "Don't listen to him. Come on, let's dance."

Lucas shook his head. "I'm a terrible dancer."

"So am I! Come on, baby. We'll be terrible together." Ryan extended his hand, and well, why not? It was better than hanging with Nate, who apparently couldn't care less.

After a couple songs of a jerky approximation of dancing, Lucas relaxed into the music, for once not minding how deafening it was. It make it almost impossible to think, and that was just what he needed.

Yaman and Dave joined them too, and Lucas forced himself not to look for Nate. If Nate didn't care, why should Lucas?

Maybe I shouldn't, but I do anyway.

He told the voice to shut the hell up and jumped around getting sweaty when the new Lady Gaga came on. After a few more songs, he waved to the guys and squeezed off the dance floor, in desperate need of—

There was Nate, holding out a bottle of water. Lucas took it gratefully and chugged half before wiping his mouth. "Um, thanks!" he shouted.

"Do you want a real drink?" Nate yelled back. "I'm driving, but I can buy you one."

"Nah. But thanks." Lucas tried to think of something else to say and failed miserably.

Then Nate blurted, "I'm sorry. I was an asshole. It's not up to me to say who can touch you, and…" He shrugged up his shoulders with a deep breath and let them drop, his words rushing out, barely audible above the blaring techno. "I do care. I care about you. And it's freaking me out."

"I care about you too."

"I just don't know if…" Nate shook his head. "But I was a total asshole, and you don't deserve that."

"I forgive you."

His eyebrows shot up. "Just like that?"

Lucas shrugged. "Yeah. I don't want to be mad at you." He reached out his hand, and Nate took it, drawing him near for a long, slow kiss.

When they parted, Nate asked, "Do you want to dance again?"

"Nah. I just want to watch."

With a nod, Nate led Lucas upstairs to the second floor. A glass-fronted balcony with a railing ran all the way around, and they looked out over the dance floor. Nate stood behind Lucas, his arms snug around Lucas's stomach. It was incredible to be in a place where they were allowed to touch. Where no one would judge or hate them or want to beat them up. The thrill was a heady rush that went right to Lucas's head like champagne.

A mass of male bodies writhed as one below them, bare skin glistening with sweat and glitter that rained down at regular intervals. Some men simply danced, but others rubbed against each other, limbs tangled, kissing desperately. Lucas realized he was half hard, and he wiped sweat from his brow. "It's hot in here," he shouted.

"How's that song go? I think you're supposed to take your clothes off now." Nate nipped Lucas's earlobe.

Gripped by an insane impulse, Lucas peeled off his T-shirt, hooking it through one of his belt loops. Glancing over his shoulder, he saw Nate's expression suddenly grow serious, his eyes dark with desire as he descended on Lucas's mouth, kissing him thoroughly.

Catching his breath, Lucas turned back to the dance floor as Nate moved in even closer, his hands drifting upward, caressing Lucas's chest. Nate raked his short nails through the sprinkling of chest hair before teasing Lucas's nipples, one and then the other. As he sucked at the juncture of Lucas's neck and shoulder, adrenaline sang in Lucas's veins.

When Nate's hand deftly unzipped Lucas's jeans and slipped inside, Lucas glanced around furtively. Bold eyes were on them from all sides, and he found to his shock that being watched sent a bolt of excitement straight to his cock.

As Nate stroked him, he whispered in his ear, "You like that? Like being the center of attention?"

Lucas nodded, licking his lips. He watched the dancers below, arms and legs and torsos slithering through a sea of smoke and glitter. He was a *real* gay man. He'd always felt like an imposter somehow, but now look at him. He was at a gay club being wilder than he'd ever imagined. He didn't need a drink to feel intoxicated.

Nate tightened his fist around Lucas's cock. Then his free

hand squeezed down the back of Lucas's briefs, finger touching his hole. Lucas shivered and gasped, his eyes closing. Nate stroked him faster, the tip of his finger dancing around Lucas's pucker.

With the deafening music, Lucas didn't try to bite back his moans of pleasure, and as Nate pushed his finger inside him and crooked it just so, Lucas came with a cry that sounded like it echoed on every side of the club.

Nate supported him, wrapping his arms around Lucas as he kissed his cheek. "I knew you'd be a screamer if you got the chance."

Clinging to the railing, Lucas blinked down at where his semen splattered the glass. He could still feel the heat of anonymous gazes on him, and knew he was blushing furiously. "Holy shit. I can't believe I just did that."

He should have been horrified, but it was exciting to be so *free.* To be surrounded by hundreds of people like him, where he could kiss Nate and not be afraid. More than kiss! He repeated, "Holy shit."

Glasses bumping Lucas's head, Nate kissed his neck as he tucked Lucas back in and zipped him up. "Maybe this'll be a new Christmas tradition?" he shouted as a new song that sounded just like the last one came on, and everyone cheered.

Lucas laughed. "I don't think so." He glanced around, the high of his orgasm wearing off. Fortunately the spectators had moved on. "I wouldn't want to come here too often. Sorry, I'm super lame."

Nate turned him around and brushed back Lucas's sweaty hair. He leaned in close, looping his arms around Lucas's waist. "You want to know a secret? I'm not a huge clubber either. My friends love it, so I end up going with them sometimes. I figured you should have the experience and judge for yourself. It's all right, but I'd really rather be home playing the new *Dead of Winter* expansion pack."

Lucas brightened. "The zombie game? I've always wanted to try it, but my dad couldn't concentrate enough, and I haven't had any friends, so…"

"So what do you say we blow this joint and head home?" He waggled his eyebrows. "Where we can blow each other too."

"I'd say merry Christmas to me."

With a grin, Nate took his hand and led the way, Lucas practically floating behind.

Chapter Seven

LATE THE NEXT afternoon after countless hours spent trying to survive the zombie apocalypse—punctuated by blow jobs and make-out sessions—Lucas and Nate squeezed into the back of the Kramer SUV for a trip to visit Mrs. Kramer's sister. Lucas sat in the middle, and Sam took up so much room to his right that Lucas had no choice but to lean against Nate, their knees pressing particularly firmly.

Nate's cousin Rachel opened the door at the ranch-style house, greeting them—especially Lucas—enthusiastically. The house was smaller than the Kramers', but just as stylishly decorated. Most of the family from the first night of Hanukkah was there, and after lighting the shamash and the menorah's six candles just before sunset, the children began a game of *dreidel* on the carpet.

Lucas sat on the couch, watching the kids spin the four-sided top, making bets with chocolate coins wrapped in gold. Depending on how the dreidel fell, the players sometimes gained more coins or added another to the pot, and on some spins nothing happened at all.

Nate's grandfather joined Lucas and began clapping his hands, singing in a low baritone. "Oh dreidel, dreidel, dreidel, I made you out of clay. Oh dreidel, dreidel, dreidel, with dreidel I shall play."

The children joined in, and Lucas noted with amusement that

Nate, watching the game by the window, sang along too. Nate caught his stare and abruptly stopped singing, his flush visible across the room.

When the game was over, Linda, a shorter, plumper version of her sister, and Mrs. Kramer produced a pile of gifts from the other room. The kids squealed in delight as they tore the paper off video games and what Lucas could only guess were the latest trends in Barbie doll fashion. Nate perched on the arm of the couch beside Lucas to unwrap his gift, and Lucas resisted the urge to lean in close.

"So you get presents on Hanukkah? It has nothing to do with it being Christmas today?"

"No presents traditionally, but I guess the little Jewish kiddies feel left out from the Christmas consumer madness. Adults don't usually get anything. Since most everyone has Christmas Day off work, it's convenient for the family to get together again today."

Nate carefully peeled the paper off a box his parents had given him, revealing a state of the art camera flash that made his eyes widen and a smile split his face.

"Maybe your parents are cooler about the whole photography thing than you think," Lucas whispered.

Nate snorted. "I wouldn't go that far. It's still just my 'little hobby' to them." He got up and hugged his mother and father as Sam let out a surprised gasp.

"Whoa. This is awesome!" He turned around a framed eight by ten black-and-white photograph of himself leaping up to make a basket. Sam grinned and yanked Nate into a bear hug. "Thanks, man. Sorry, I didn't get you anything."

"It's nothing; don't worry. I just thought you'd like it." Nate extracted himself from Sam's embrace as everyone admired the photo. It really was beautiful, capturing Sam in perfect flight.

At dinner—Chinese takeout, which Lucas was told was tradition now—Linda took advantage of the silence while everyone was chewing, telling Nate, "I saw Stephanie Stein's mother last week at synagogue, and she told me Stephanie's back on the market. Such a lovely girl!"

Beside Lucas, Nate stared down at his plate, pushing his chow mein around with his fork, and Lucas could feel the tension coming off him in waves. "I'm sure she's great, but I'm too busy with school right now. Thanks anyway."

"Too busy!" Linda clucked her tongue. "Your brother's never been too busy for girls. She's so pretty! Just take her out to dinner. You'll like her, you'll see," Linda added.

Lucas glanced at Mr. and Mrs. Kramer, who were looking at each other and seemed to be having a telepathic conversation.

Before Nate could reply, Sam spoke up. "Why don't you guys just leave him alone? He likes doing his own thing."

That put an immediate end to the discussion, and after a few moments of awkward silence, Mr. Kramer complimented Linda enthusiastically on the sweet and sour chicken balls, everyone echoing his sentiments.

Under the table, Lucas covered Nate's sock-clad foot with his own. Nate shot him a smile and speared his last chicken ball, putting it onto Lucas's plate. Lucas smiled back, and as he ate it, he realized Mr. and Mrs. Kramer were watching them, their expressions seemingly neutral.

Still, Lucas's face went hot, and he moved his foot away, dropping his gaze to his plate, suddenly very interested in his Peking duck.

As soon as they were inside Nate's room again, Nate shoved Lucas up against the door and kissed him hard. He pushed Lucas's legs apart with his knee and rubbed their crotches together as his tongue plundered Lucas's mouth.

Lucas gasped for a breath, a grin tugging on his lips. "Does 'The Dreidel Song' always make you this horny, Nathaniel?"

Nate practically growled, spinning Lucas around and steering him toward the far bed before taking his desk chair and jamming it under the door handle. Lucas waited, growing more and more excited by the lust in Nate's eyes.

Nate rustled around in one of the desk drawers, not bothering to turn on a light. The curtains were open, and the streetlight cast pale white light and long shadows across the room. When Nate peeled his clothes off, Lucas followed suit, and soon they were both naked and kissing on the tiny bed.

Nate pressed something into his hand, and Lucas realized he was holding a condom. His eyes jerked up to meet Nate's. "You want…"

Nate's gaze was steady and direct. "I want you to fuck me."

Lucas gulped. *Merry Christmas indeed.*

After putting his glasses on the side table, Nate kneeled and popped the lid off a tube of lubricant. He reached his hand behind himself. Lucas realized he was lubing himself up, and his cock twitched in anticipation. They were really going to do it.

He was going to fuck another man.

Nate fingered himself, his pale chest gleaming in the streetlight. A small smile graced his lips, and Lucas took a deep, calming breath, his pulse racing. He tore open the foil package, rolling the condom down over his cock. With a slick hand, Nate stroked Lucas's shaft, and Lucas tried to keep his cool.

When Nate got on his hands and knees, Lucas almost lost it, but he clambered up behind him, reaching out and holding Nate by the hips. He positioned the head of his cock at Nate's hole, taking another breath. This was it. He'd seen enough porn to know what he was doing, right?

"*Fuck me,*" Nate gritted out.

Heart thumping, Lucas squeezed inside him, moving into the

tight, incredible heat inch by inch. Nate pushed back, squeezing his muscles and establishing a rhythm. Lucas began thrusting in and pulling almost all the way out, pleasure shooting through his cock. After a tentative start, he felt like he got the hang of it, grabbing one of Nate's shoulders for better leverage as he worked his ass.

Nate grunted and breathed heavily, and their skin grew slippery with sweat as Lucas pumped into him. "Harder," Nate demanded.

Lucas pistoned his hips forcefully into Nate's tight heat, panting for air and biting his lip to stop from crying out. He was inside another man. He was inside *Nate*; he was fucking *Nate*. He never wanted it to end. He wanted to stay inside him forever, locked together in abandon and bliss.

Of course, he was about to shoot his load. Shaking, he stopped moving for a moment, willing his body to obey him as he sucked in air. Sweat dampened his brow. When he felt back in control, he rocked his hips forward again, plunging in and out of Nate's ass.

Reaching back, Nate took Lucas's hand and placed it on his cock as they writhed together. Lucas stroked him rapidly, jerking Nate's cock in tandem with the almost manic thrusting of his hips. Nate squeezed down with his ass, and then he was shaking as he came.

The pressure and heat on his cock was intense, and with a cry, Lucas shot into the condom, closing his eyes as the orgasm rocked his body. He collapsed on top of Nate, both of them breathing hard, skin slick. After a minute, he reluctantly pulled out and stood on quivering legs.

After he disposed of the condom, wrapping it in almost an arm's length of toilet paper just in case Mrs. Kramer was the nosy type, Lucas returned to the bedroom. He hovered at the foot of Nate's bed, not sure what to do. Nate was sprawled on his stomach even though it had to be wet, taking up the whole space.

Lucas suddenly felt very exposed, and he quickly put on his T-shirt and pajama bottoms. Turning to Nate, he sat on the side of his mattress and waited. Nate's eyes were closed, so apparently he was just going to sleep now? Was Lucas being creepy sitting there watching him? He'd just been *inside* Nate's body. Surely that meant something?

Eyes still closed, Nate crooked his finger. "C'mere."

Lucas knelt beside Nate's bed. He cleared his throat. "I guess we should get some sleep."

Opening his eyes, Nate reached his hand behind Lucas's head and pulled him close for a long, slow kiss. "That was amazing." A rush of pride made Lucas smile, and Nate tapped him on the nose affectionately. "You're a natural."

Saying thanks would sound kind of stupid, so Lucas just kissed Nate again before climbing into the other bed. They were only a couple of feet apart, but Lucas yearned to press against Nate's warm body and fall asleep holding him.

Stop it. This doesn't mean anything. It's just sex. A holiday fling. That's all.

Still, as his eyes grew heavy, Lucas couldn't help but *wish*.

THE NEXT DAY dawned bright and sunny, so Mrs. Kramer declared it a perfect time to visit the Bronx Zoo. Lucas hadn't expected the zoo to be so sprawling or state of the art, and the only thing that could have made wandering the exhibits better would have been holding Nate's hand.

He longed to touch him all the time and considered dragging him into a bathroom stall after lunch for a quick grope. Mr. Kramer put a kibosh on that by coming to the bathroom too. Nate had winked teasingly at Lucas just briefly at the urinals, so apparently Lucas needed to do a better job of hiding his sexual frustration.

After a volunteer gave them a lesson on lemurs near the end of the afternoon, Lucas and the Kramers wandered through the gift shop. Lucas was drawn to the magnets, and as he plucked a gorilla from the metal holder, he said to Nate, "My dad would—"

The next words lodged in his throat, and Lucas realized he hadn't thought of his father once all day. His dad had loved collecting silly magnets everywhere they went, covering their fridge from top to bottom.

Like a finger removed from a dam, guilt and grief flooded him, and he blinked back tears, the magnet clattering to the floor. He was only vaguely aware of Nate's hand on the small of his back, leading him out into the brisk air. He tried to breathe, leaning against the wall of the building.

From the corner of his eye, he saw the Kramers exit the store. Nate drew them away, murmuring, and Lucas willed himself to get a grip. After a few deep breaths, he walked over to them and said, "Sorry. Just had a moment. I'm fine."

Mrs. Kramer clucked her tongue. "Dear, you don't need to put on a brave face. We know how hard it must be for you. If you want to talk about it, we're all here to listen."

"Why?" Lucas blurted. He shook his head. "I'm sorry. I— thank you. What I mean is, I don't know why you're being so nice to me. You don't even know me."

Nate said, "Anyone who has the patience to room with Sam and not murder him—"

"Is always welcome in our home," Mr. Kramer finished, giving Nate a good-natured glare. To Lucas, he added, "It's been a pleasure getting to know you this week. I hope we'll be seeing much more of you in the future."

Lucas felt so stupid for causing a scene, and they were being so nice about it. He smiled weakly. "Thank you again. But Sam will be graduating and…"

Mrs. Kramer smiled. "Well, you and Nathaniel seem to be getting along like gangbusters. Aren't you?"

Lucas said, "Uh…" *Don't blush. Don't blush.* "Yeah."

She looked to Nate, who shrugged and nodded at the same time. There was something about her smile and a strange tension in the air that had Lucas's head whirling.

Does she know?

Before the moment could get any weirder, Mr. Kramer thankfully announced he was getting hungry and it was time to head home. He and Mrs. Kramer kept up a steady stream of chatter in the front seat on the drive, their forced cheer evident.

Lucas stared out the window, more aware than ever that no matter how kind the Kramers were to him, his father—his only real family—was gone. Nate was right beside him but out of reach. He didn't want a relationship; he'd said so, no matter how close Lucas felt to him. After the holidays, Lucas would be on his own again.

The evening passed in a haze—lighting the menorah and then watching another movie, this one about creatures from the deep attacking Earth. Lucas picked at a slice of pizza and told Mrs. Kramer he was fine. When the credits rolled, he excused himself for the night. Nate followed a few minutes later, shutting his bedroom door quietly behind him. Lucas climbed into bed, Nate watching him silently.

"I just want to sleep tonight, okay?" Lucas said. What he actually wanted was to simply be held, but could he ask that of Nate? It was only supposed to be a fling, and as kind as Nate was being, surely cuddling crossed some line.

Nate nodded, and soon he was in his own bed, the lights out. Curling on his side toward the door, Lucas tried to clear his mind, but it was useless. He couldn't stop thinking of the stupid gorilla magnet. His dad's magnet collection was piled in a box in some storage unit in Michigan with the rest of the stuff they'd had in their last apartment. Lucas had barely been able to bring anything to school, and when would he have an actual *home* again?

A sob gripped him, cutting off his breath, and he buried his face in his pillow to stifle the ones that followed. When his father had finally slipped away, Lucas hadn't cried. The nurses had hugged him and told him to let it out, but he'd insisted he was fine. Now the tears wouldn't stop.

After a few moments, the mattress dipped, and Nate's long frame spooned up behind him, his arms snaking out to hold Lucas close. As Lucas wept, Nate caressed his hair, whispering calming words in Hebrew that sounded like a lullaby.

Lucas wasn't sure how long he cried before his breathing became easier. Nate still soothed him, and soon Lucas wanted more. *Needed* more. He shifted, and in a tangle of limbs, Nate rolled on top of him on the narrow bed. Lucas pulled Nate's head down for a kiss, and their tongues wound together as Lucas's hands roamed over Nate, sliding up beneath his T-shirt.

Nate's body on top of his was heady, but not enough. "Please," Lucas breathed.

Nate pulled back and watched him for a moment, squinting in the darkness, asking without saying a word if Lucas was sure. "Please," Lucas repeated. He pulled Nate's shirt over his head, and soon their pajamas were tossed aside.

Nate was up and back before Lucas knew it. He bent Lucas's knees, placing his feet flat on the mattress, kneeling in front of him. Squeezing the lube into his palm, Nate warmed it up before his fingers found Lucas's hole, gently working the slick gel inside. He started with one finger, lightly stroking Lucas's cock with his other hand. Then two fingers.

When he had the condom on and lubed, he moved closer and placed Lucas's legs up onto his shoulders, opening him. Lucas had never felt more vulnerable, but he only shivered with anticipation.

He trusted Nate completely.

Nate slowly pushed his way inside, and Lucas felt like he was tearing open. His eyes watering, he gasped as the pain blossomed. Nate leaned down, kissing him tenderly all over his face: cheeks, forehead, and eyes. "Just breathe," he whispered, and Lucas felt a calm come over him, his body relaxing despite the pain.

Bit by bit, Nate moved farther inside him, the stretch both almost unbearable and something he never wanted to stop. They were both breathing heavily, and sweat glistened on Nate's forehead in the streetlight.

When Nate was almost all the way in, he hit a spot that made Lucas see stars, a moan of pleasure slipping from his lips. With another kiss and a little smile, Nate began shallow little thrusts, hitting that spot every time.

Lucas began moving with him, the pain ebbing away to become pure pleasure. Nate pressed Lucas's knees to his chest and drove into him, grasping one of his hands. Lucas felt like he was in a dream, drifting in a world where nothing else existed but him and Nate. Their eyes locked together as their bodies flexed and rocked. Nate was *inside* him, and Lucas could feel it in his soul.

His cock was hard and leaking, squeezed between their bodies as Nate increased his rhythm. He found the spot again, grunting softly as he hit it over and over. Lucas couldn't stifle his cry as he came, his orgasm ripping through him. As he shook, Nate thrust sharply two more times before shuddering in release.

Lucas winced when Nate pulled out of him. Nate dropped a kiss to his shoulder, murmuring something Lucas couldn't make out. Sitting up, Nate tossed the tied-off condom into the garbage pail by his desk. Before Lucas could even ask him to stay, he pulled the covers up over them, wrapping Lucas tightly in his arms.

Nate kissed Lucas's ear and whispered, "Sleep."

The fracturing grief for his father had receded for the moment, and he felt whole in a way he couldn't explain as he closed his eyes in Nate's arms. Lucas hadn't meant to fall in love, but he realized with a sense of wonder that was exactly what he'd done.

Chapter Eight

RUNNING, NATE AND Lucas barely made it on board the ferry before it left the dock, and they laughed, their icy exhalations puffing out in front of them. Most passengers crowded inside, but Lucas liked to watch the city glide by. On the upper deck, he and Nate leaned against the railing and caught their breath.

It had been a perfect day.

The Met was crowded with holiday visitors, but Lucas barely noticed. He and Nate were in their own little world, and Lucas vowed to himself to just enjoy it and worry about the future when it came.

Of course, as he stood shoulder to shoulder with Nate, watching the Statue of Liberty in the distance, his mind wandered to his inevitable return to school. He sighed audibly, and Nate nudged him gently, an eyebrow raised.

"I'm just thinking about the new year. Going back to school." Lucas's dour tone pretty much said it all.

Nate was quiet for a few moments. "So why are you going back?"

"Because I have to." Where else would he go?

"What are you doing at Brookfield? Even Sam notices you're miserable."

"What? You and Sam were talking about me?"

"Not in a bad way, but my usually clueless brother knows

you're not happy there." He took a breath, as if steeling himself. "You could move here in the summer. Transfer schools; there are about a million to choose from. Figure out what you really want to do with your life."

The thought of returning to Brookfield and the noisy dorm, going back to his chemistry books and the degree he didn't truly want, filled Lucas with dread. Maybe Nate was right. What was stopping him from coming to New York and living his own life?

His father had wanted him to be happy, and Lucas had pretended for long enough that his father's dreams for him were his own. "Well, it would be pretty awesome to live in New York if I could afford it. I mean, I have money from my dad, so I guess I could." A thrill zipped through him. "I guess… I guess there really is nothing stopping me. Whoa."

"Blowing your mind, huh?" Nate grinned.

"A little bit. Brookfield was where my dad wanted to go, but he didn't have the grades. So when I got in, he was over the moon." Lucas shivered as frigid wind gusted, his ears stinging. He stupidly had forgotten his hat. "But he'd want me to be happy."

"Of course he would."

Lucas couldn't stop smiling. "What about you? Are you going to quit law? Switch to photography?"

"What? No. I'm not good enough," Nate said dismissively.

"Yes, *you are*."

"You're being nice, but I don't have the talent." He smiled ruefully and muttered under this breath, "*My little hobby*."

"Your mother has no idea what you're capable of. You do *so* have the talent. You're afraid to take the risk, but you expect *me* to."

Nate was silent for a long moment, peering out to the horizon and the city slipping away. Finally he sighed. "You're right. I'm a hypocrite." He wrapped his arms around himself, shivering as the wind whipped off the water.

"You don't have to be. Neither of us is happy. We need to make a change. We could do it together."

Nate looked at him. "Together?"

"Oh, I mean...not... I don't..." Lucas took a deep breath. Time to stop being afraid. "Screw it. Yes. Together. You and me. I really like you. And I know you don't want that, a boyfriend, so I'm probably wasting my breath, and this is just a holiday fling."

Nate straightened his glasses, and Lucas realized he did it when he was nervous. After a deep breath, Nate said, "I've been thinking about that. You're only a few hours away. Sam goes on the road a lot for basketball in the new year, and he's going to Daytona for spring break. I could visit."

Lucas tried to tamp down his rush of excitement and failed completely. Then a thought hit him, and his smile vanished. "What about when we're not together? Will you still be seeing other guys?"

Nate leaned closer. "I don't want to see anyone but you, Lucas."

Warm happiness exploded in Lucas's chest like the creature in *Alien*. "I thought you weren't looking for a boyfriend."

"I wasn't." Nate smiled crookedly. "I guess one found me. If you want me."

Not caring if anyone was watching, Lucas threw his arms around him. "I want."

Nate held him close, their cheeks pressed together. Lucas watched the sun sink over the distant skyscraper in a blaze of red and orange. He had a boyfriend. He might move to New York City. He had a *boyfriend*. Maybe holiday miracles really did happen.

When Nate laughed and said, "Maybe," Lucas realized he'd said it aloud. He only hugged Nate tighter.

IN THE UBER, Nate checked his phone. "We missed lighting the menorah on the last night of Hanukkah. If we miss synagogue, I'm dead meat." When they'd gotten home to a darkened house, they'd quickly changed, Lucas borrowing a tie and jacket.

"But I thought you weren't that observant," Lucas said.

"We're not, but we always have to go to synagogue at least once every holiday, or we'll never hear the end from Papa. I kind of like it, actually."

Hopping out in front of the temple, Nate took the empty steps two at a time before he jolted to a halt and pulled a rounded, dark gray suede piece of material from his pocket. He placed it on the back of his head.

Lucas said, "Okay, this is going to sound like a stupid question, but—"

"How does it stay on?" Nate laughed. "Years of experience." He pulled another piece of material out of his pocket, this one black. "You, however, get a bobby pin for your *yarmulke*."

Lucas stood still while Nate gently pinned it in place. Their heads were close together, and Nate's warm breath ghosted over Lucas's cheek. Nate stood back. "There you go. Looks good. What about me?" He laughed suddenly, rolling his eyes. "I know, I look like a complete dork."

Fat snowflakes had begun to fall, nestling in Nate's hair and spotting his glasses, and Lucas told him the truth. "You look beautiful."

Nate leaned closer, their lips inches apart. Just then, a van pulled up, unloading a chattering family who rushed by them up the steps. Lucas and Nate followed, finding a seat near the back.

Lucas gazed in wonder at the blue and gold ceiling soaring high above. A center aisle separated rows of pews, and ornate chandeliers hung in pillared archways along each side of the room, with a gallery of extra seating on the left and right through the arches on the second level. It was a full house.

The rabbi spoke of freedom, and conquering fear and despair. As the service went on, Lucas was filled with a sense of peace he couldn't remember ever experiencing. He thought of his father and smiled. The pain was still there, but Lucas knew he would get through it.

Glancing down to his left, he saw Nate's hand on the bench beside him. Sliding his palm over the polished wood, he touched Nate's pinky finger with his own. He would have been satisfied with just that small contact, but a few moments later, Nate flipped his hand over. As the congregation began singing, Lucas covered Nate's palm with his own, threading their fingers together.

Lucas didn't understand the words, but he tried to sing along anyway.

After the service and socializing, Lucas and the Kramers pushed open the doors of the synagogue to discover the world had been covered in white. Large flakes of snow floated down, blanketing everything and giving the night an unnatural, serene brightness, the wind gentle now. They all paused to admire the beauty of the winter's first real snowfall.

Mrs. Kramer's fingers brushed over Lucas's yarmulke playfully. "It suits you, Lucas. You'll have to come and stay for Passover." She planted a kiss on his cheek. "And I won't take no for an answer!" Hooking her arm through her husband's, she led the way down the snowy steps. "Let's go home and eat."

Nate and Lucas followed side by side, neither of them able to hide their smile.

In the Kramers' living room, the menorah candles had burned out, and Lucas was sorry he hadn't had a chance to see all eight of them burning. Maybe next year...

Mrs. Kramer tutted as she examined her black high-heeled shoes. "I wouldn't have worn these if I'd known it would snow. At least the salt wasn't out yet."

Mr. Kramer took the shoes from her. "I'll give them a good

polish. Don't worry." He kissed her cheek, and she beamed at him.

Lucas found himself smiling as he watched. He caught Nate's eye, wishing he could show him affection like that. *My boyfriend. I have a boyfriend!* Nate gave him a little smile. Maybe they could go upstairs quickly and just kiss for a minute or two.

Then Sam said, "What are you two grinning about?"

"Huh?" Lucas jerked his head around. "Nothing. Just… Um, hungry. Looking forward to dinner."

Mrs. Kramer said, "Well, we have a lovely meal waiting. Everyone to the table."

"And where was tonight's delicacy ordered from?" Mr. Kramer asked.

"Baggio's," she answered. "Veal tortellini, our favorite burrata and tomato salad, that mushroom risotto Nathaniel loves, and garlic bread of course. And panna cotta for dessert." To Lucas, she added, "I'm sure you've noticed I'm not much for cooking."

"I'm not either, so."

They all laughed, and Lucas ran a hand through his hair, his yarmulke coming loose. "Oh! Sorry."

Chuckling, Nate came close and reached up to unpin it completely. "It's okay. We only wear them at temple." He straightened Lucas's hair, sending tingles down Lucas's spine. He couldn't wait until they were alone again and—

"So are you guys boning, or what?"

Lucas's heart seized violently, his stomach lurching and threatening to bring up the burger he'd had for lunch. Nate whipped his hands back to his sides, looking like he was choking on his tongue, his face beet red.

The Kramers turned in the wide doorway to the kitchen, mouths open. Mrs. Kramer snapped, "*Samuel!*"

"What?" He rolled his eyes. "Sorry. Are you two *making love?*" As Nate sputtered, Sam added, "Come on, dude. We know you're gay."

Chest rising and falling rapidly, Nate looked between Sam and their parents. He crossed his arms, and Lucas wanted to step closer so Nate knew he wasn't alone, but didn't think it would help. He jammed his hands in his pockets, waiting.

Mr. Kramer sighed. "Son, we've been waiting for you to tell us. Was that the wrong thing to do?"

"Unless we're mistaken after all?" Mrs. Kramer asked.

Nate laughed harshly. "You'd be relieved if you were."

She jerked her head back an inch, blinking. "No. That's not true at all."

"Oh, come on, Mom." Nate's tense jaw worked, his nostrils flaring. "I know you think gay people are *vulgar*."

"I do not!" She stood up straighter, her husband placing a comforting hand on her shoulder, frowning at Nate.

"Dude, what the hell are you talking about?" Sam lifted his meaty hands in the air. "Mom and Dad are totally cool with it."

Mr. Kramer said, "Nate, we love you. We haven't wanted to push. Rabbi Lowenstein said to let you come out when you were ready."

"You told the rabbi?" Nate shouted. "Great, now everyone probably knows. What about the rest of the family?"

"No," Mr. Kramer answered. "First off, Rabbi Lowenstein would never betray our trust. We asked for his counsel in confidence. And we haven't told anyone else in the family, although I'm sure some of them suspect. It's absolutely your choice as to when you want to tell them."

"Why did you say that? That I find gay people 'vulgar'?" Mrs. Kramer asked, her lips quivering along with her voice.

When Nate spoke, at least he wasn't shouting. In fact, it was barely more than a whisper. "There was a pride parade on the news. Ten years ago now, I guess. There were guys in Speedos on a float, and you said it was vulgar. With such disdain."

She exhaled sharply. "Well, men thrusting their pelvises while clad only in tiny bathing suits *is* vulgar. I've never been one for such displays. Bathing suits belong on the beach. It has nothing to do with being gay."

Mr. Kramer said, "She's never liked beauty pageants for the same reason. And there isn't even any pelvis thrusting in those."

Tears glistened in her eyes. "Nate, have you thought all this time that I wouldn't approve?"

Adam's apple bobbing, Nate nodded, staring at the beige carpet. His mother crossed the space between them in a heartbeat, wrapping him in her arms. Tears slipped down her cheeks, and he bent to rest his head on her shoulder, hunching since she was shorter.

"You couldn't be more wrong," she said. "I love you. I want you to be happy. That's what we all want."

Lucas's eyes burned, and he blinked rapidly, jumping when Mr. Kramer squeezed his shoulder. "Lucas, I know we've only just met you, but I hope you know you're very welcome here. Gay, straight, whatever. It doesn't matter to us."

"I… Thank you." Lucas swallowed hard, his voice trembling. "I am. Gay, I mean. We…" He glanced at Nate, who raised his head and stepped back from his mom, swiping at his eyes.

Nate nodded. "We really like each other. We're going to visit each other whenever we can in the new year and see what happens."

"I knew it!" Sam crowed.

Nate muttered, "Shut up," but there was no heat to it. He looked between his parents. "I'm sorry I didn't tell you before. That I'm gay. I really didn't think you'd be okay with it."

Now tears formed in Mr. Kramer's eyes. "I'm sorry we gave you that impression." He pulled Nate into a hug, and Lucas blinked rapidly, warmth spreading through his chest, his breathing steady now.

Sam punched Lucas in the shoulder playfully. "Man, it must be torture for you rooming with me and seeing me naked and stuff. But thanks for not hitting on me or anything."

A giggle bubbled up and Lucas tried to keep a straight face. He failed miserably, and Nate even smiled as he separated from his dad.

Sam shrugged. "What? I'm just saying! Hello, I'm hot."

Lucas nodded, trying to stifle his laughter. "It's a challenge, Sam. I appreciate your understanding."

"Gay people are just like everyone else, and I was thinking it would be hard to live with some hot chick I couldn't bang."

Nate eyed him skeptically. "You're really okay with me being gay? Dating Lucas?"

"Totally, bro."

Nate smiled, shaking his head. "I thought you'd hate me."

Sam was taken aback. "Dude, I could never *hate* you." He reached out and jerked Nate into a hug, slapping his back forcefully. "You're my brother. So what if you fuck guys?" He winced. "Sorry, Mom and Dad. I mean *make love* with guys."

Lucas said, "We really appreciate your support. It means a lot."

"Hey, we're friends, right? Of course I support you." Sam turned to Lucas and hugged him too.

As Sam slapped his back, Lucas grinned. "Definitely friends." He was happy to discover that he really meant it.

"Well. Now that we have that settled." Mrs. Kramer blew her nose delicately, folding the tissue after. "Our dinner's keeping warm in the oven, and we don't want it to dry out. Let's sit around the table instead of in front of the TV."

Nate and Lucas shared a smile as they followed toward the dining room. Lucas reached out and squeezed Nate's hand.

"Oh, one more thing," Mrs. Kramer said, turning back. "Now, I'm sure you know all about safety. In regards to..." She waved her hand.

Nate groaned. "Dad, make her stop!"

Mr. Kramer slipped his arm around his wife's shoulders. "Come along now, dear. Let's celebrate the last night of Hanukkah and leave the safe sex lecture for another day."

"Don't you mean safe *making love*?" Sam asked as he followed, apparently endlessly amused by his own joke. "Hey, since we're having Italian, we get to drink real wine with dinner, right? Not that sweet crap. I mean *stuff*."

As his family disappeared around the corner, Nate stopped. He appeared slightly dazed, his glasses askew. Lucas reached out to straighten them as Nate asked, "Did that really just happen?"

"It did."

"I can't believe it. Seems like I've been a real idiot."

"Seems like."

Nate burst out laughing. "Hey!" He frowned in mock offense. "I thought boyfriends were supposed to be supportive."

"My bad." With a glance around, Lucas gave Nate a quick kiss. "I'll make it up to you later."

"Deal." Nate grinned. Then he shook his head. "I can't believe my family is being so cool about this. I guess miracles really do happen at Hanukkah."

Lucas gave him another kiss. "I guess they do."

Epilogue

FROM JUST INSIDE the doorway, Mrs. Kramer surveyed the studio apartment, which now appeared even smaller thanks to the arrival of Nate's belongings. "Well, it's…cozy." She held her fur-trimmed leather gloves, her long black jacket still buttoned.

Lucas shimmied between some boxes and the left-hand wall and made it into the narrow kitchen, which was separated from the living room by an island counter. "Can I get you a bottle of water?" He'd worked up a sweat and had stripped off his plaid shirt, wearing just a white tee and jeans.

"No, dear, we really can't stay," Mrs. Kramer replied. She looked to the immediate right at the so-called bedroom, which was really more of a nook behind a half-wall, barely big enough for the double bed Lucas had brought from Michigan after sorting through the storage unit.

He'd gotten rid of a lot of stuff, but having his dad's brown leather couch and armchair against the right-hand wall in the living room made the bare-walled apartment feel like home already. The TV was still in its box, along with most of Lucas's possessions.

Nate and his father nudged Mrs. Kramer out of the doorway and inside, carrying the last of Nate's boxes. Mr. Kramer stretched his back with a soft groan and said, "All right, you're all set."

Mrs. Kramer scoffed. "Hardly. Look at how much needs to be unpacked. I thought Rabbi Lowenstein said this was a 'spacious' studio? And your view is a brick wall. Good thing you're on the tenth floor so you can glimpse the sky." She tutted.

Nate squeezed between stacks of boxes and grabbed water from the otherwise-empty fridge. "It is, Mom. We've looked at a thousand crappy apartments since the beginning of summer. This one is amazing for the price. Rabbi Lowenstein's cousin's sister's aunt cut us a great deal."

"After six months of sharing Nate's room at the house, I'm sure this will feel like luxury," Mr. Kramer said.

"Totally," Lucas agreed, then hastily added, "Not that your home isn't lovely! I appreciate you letting me stay so much." He'd transferred to NYU after finishing his year at Brookfield, and the Kramers had been incredibly generous by letting him move in with them while he and Nate hunted for an apartment, which was a blood sport in New York City.

The Kramers smiled, and Mr. Kramer clapped Lucas's shoulder. "We know, son. We also know how exciting it is to have a place of your own."

"And Hell's Kitchen has come a long way," Mrs. Kramer said. "So many restaurants right around the corner. Although it's really quite noisy." A siren wailed distantly on cue.

"Come on, Deanna. Boys, we'll see you soon. Hanukkah starts tomorrow, so we'll expect you for dinner. Call if you need anything." Mr. Kramer ushered his wife to the door.

She gave Nate a long hug and kissed him tenderly on the forehead before stepping back. "Be good, *bubala*."

As soon as the door closed behind them after more goodbyes, Lucas met Nate's eyes across the stacks of boxes, and they grinned. Nate gazed around, taking in the bathroom squeezed right across from the foot of the bed in its nook. "What are we going to do with all this *space*?"

Lucas laughed. "Just wait until you see the east wing. It's impressive."

"But it's *ours*." Nate took his phone from his pocket and snapped a few shots. "I'll take some real pics when we're unpacked, but I want to document the process."

"Should I model, Mr. Photographer?"

"Always." Nate winked and took a few more pictures as Lucas made faces and posed with boxes.

Nate had applied to Tisch for photography without mentioning it to his parents, figuring he'd see if he got in first. Naturally he did—Lucas had been confident it was a slam dunk—and he'd broken the news to his parents. They hadn't taken it very well at first, but had either come around or resigned themselves. Either way, they were supportive.

Nate eyed the bed beyond the half-wall. "We finally have a real bed that'll fit both of us. I can't wait to sleep with you every night."

While of course they'd still had sex in Nate's room, actual sleep had usually occurred in their twin beds. "Just sleep, hmm?"

"Fucking goes without saying. Duh." He bit his lip. "Speaking of which, maybe we should christen our new bed. You can scream as loud as you want."

Lucas didn't have to be asked twice. They sidestepped the boxes, falling back on the bare mattress. Nate's weight on top of him felt so good—so right. He carefully took off Nate's glasses and put them on the shelf built into the half-wall separating the bed from the entry and living room. Then he yanked Nate's sweater over his head and kissed his smooth chest, teeth on Nate's pink nipples, making him squirm and moan.

The taste of Nate's salty skin was heady. Lucas rolled over, his mouth moving over Nate's body, peeling away clothing as he continued until Nate was naked beneath him, both of them kicking off their sneakers and peeling away socks.

"I need to fuck you. Or you fuck me. Whatever. I need to feel you." Nate gritted the words out, and his already-hard dick was proof of them.

Lucas sat up on his knees and quickly stripped off his clothes. "Shit. Where did we pack the lube?" They'd stopped using condoms now that they were completely committed to each other and had clean bills of health.

"In the bathroom box? Oh, wait, wait. In my wallet. They were giving out those little packets on campus for some sex-ed drive or something."

Lucas dug through Nate's pockets and came up with the lube, tossing the packet to Nate. "Put it on yourself." Nate opened it and rubbed the lube between his palms before slicking himself as Lucas straddled his hips.

Nate stroked himself with one greased hand and the other found Lucas's hole. He pushed his fingers inside roughly. "Fuck, you're tight. You look so hot. I can't believe we're actually here. In our own place."

"Me either." Heart pounding, desperation ignited in Lucas's veins. Even though they'd given each other hand jobs in the shower that morning, he felt like it had been forever ago. He moved over Nate's dick, maneuvering himself into position.

With a loud moan, he slid down and the head of Nate's cock stretched him painfully. He bit his lip as he forced himself down the shaft.

"Whoa. I don't want to hurt you." Nate held Lucas's hips firmly, stopping his downward movement.

Lucas shuddered, the burn in his ass almost too much as he lowered himself. *Almost.* "I want to feel you tomorrow. I want your cock. I need it."

Eyes dark with lust, Nate reached for his glasses. "You're so beautiful. I could watch you all day. I want to take your picture like this. With my cock inside you." He bent his legs and thrust his hips up. Lucas cried out as he impaled himself fully, the pleasure and pain combining as he rode Nate. "Oh God, oh God."

"That's it. Be as loud as you want."

Lucas squeezed his ass on Nate's dick as he bucked up and down. His own cock was hard as rock, and Nate reached out for it, stroking roughly. Lucas cried out over and over. "Oh, oh, God."

Sweat dampened his brow and the back of his neck, their skin slick where their bodies met. A sense of abandon came over Lucas, a complete lack of inhibition as he slammed down on Nate's cock over and over again, making two bodies one.

"I love your ass. You're so tight, oh God," Nate muttered, and he squeezed Lucas's dick, his thumb flicking over the head. "Love coming inside you. Want you to come all over me."

Suddenly Lucas came in a rush, spraying Nate as he clamped down on Nate's cock. Lucas's cries would probably wake the dead, but he let them rip. Nate fucked up into him almost frantically, head tilted back and eyes closed. Voice hoarse, Lucas urged him on. "Fill me up."

After another few thrusts, Nate shuddered, his semen spilling deep in Lucas's ass. Lucas squeezed, trying to milk out every drop before flopping down on Nate's chest, kissing his throat. They panted, bodies a wet and sticky mess, and Nate lightly ran his fingers up Lucas's spine.

Lucas murmured, "I guess we should unpack."

"Five more minutes. Or ten."

After they cleaned up, Lucas yawned on the mattress, still naked. It had been a hella long drive from Michigan the day before. Maybe he could just close his eyes for a few minutes…

He wasn't sure what time it was when he woke with a fluffy duvet tucked around him. Stretching, he reluctantly sat up. The overhead light was on in the kitchen, illuminating the whole apartment, and Lucas was surprised to see through the windows it was already dark outside.

Peering over the half-wall, he focused on Nate in front of the fridge. "How long was I out?"

Nate jumped about a mile, spinning around. "Jesus. A couple hours. You were zonked. I unpacked a bunch, and I was just…" He glanced behind him at the fridge. "I don't know if I'm doing it right, but I thought you'd like it. Make it feel more like home."

Lucas realized the fridge was now covered in magnets. He'd brought a big plastic container filled with his dad's collection, and now they decorated the fridge. Wrapping the duvet around him, he shuffled over, taking in the familiar images.

There was a hot-pink magnet shaped like Florida; a cheesy plastic replica of a San Francisco trolley; a Hawaiian surfer with the words "Hang ten!"; a block of cheese from Wisconsin; an old-time Coke bottle; one from the National Air and Space Museum that proclaimed, "Failure is not an option."

Lucas swallowed thickly. They were all here, out of the box and displayed where they belonged. His dad would love it. "It's…"

"Obviously you can change the order. I'm sorry. I should have let you do it."

"No. Thank you for doing this." He met Nate's worried gaze. "It's perfect." He didn't have any other words, so he kissed Nate instead and brought him back to bed.

After finishing their unpacking the next morning and getting rid of the stuff that wouldn't fit, Lucas suggested a trip down to Union Square. The square was ablaze with Christmas lights and chock full of covered wooden artisan booths, and they wandered the rows of stalls as the light drizzle turned to fat flurries. Lucas was struck with the holiday spirit. "I have an idea."

Nate lowered his camera and cocked a brow. "Does it have something to do with sex?"

"Is that *all* you think about?" Lucas huffed in mock exasperation.

Nate leaned in, his breath warm on Lucas's neck. "When you're around? Pretty much, yeah."

Despite himself, Lucas blushed and a shiver of desire coiled around his spine. "Believe me, we'll get to that later. For now, my idea involves twenty dollars and this marketplace."

"I'm listening."

"I propose we split up for half an hour and buy each other a Hanukkah present. Twenty-dollar limit."

"Shouldn't you get a Christmas present?"

"Call it a 'Chrismukkah' gift, then."

Laughing, Nate said, "Okay. Twenty dollars. Half an hour." He returned his camera to its case and glanced at the time on his phone. "Meet back here." Then he was gone, disappearing into the throng of shoppers. Nate always enjoyed a challenge.

Lucas hurried off in the other direction, examining each stall's wares. He considered a pair of supple leather gloves and wondered if he could talk the seller down. In the end he didn't even try; the thought of haggling made him faintly nauseated.

Row after row, Lucas struggled against the crowd, considering and then discarding gift ideas. Everything was either too expensive or just not right. Perhaps this game hadn't been a good suggestion after all.

A large Star of David hanging from the top of one stall caught his eye, and Lucas angled through the crowd. Just as he reached the stall, he heard Nate's chuckle from his left. Nate joined him, smiling. "Fancy meeting you here."

Lucas laughed. "Well, I asked myself, what do you get the Jew who has everything?"

"Tell me the answer isn't a Star of David wall hanging to decorate our new place."

"Not on your life." Lucas glanced at the woman operating the stall. "Um, no offense."

The young woman waved her hand. "None taken. But I'll have you know those are very popular with Staten Island ladies of a certain age." She indicated the rest of her wares. "Maybe there's something else more to your liking."

Lucas and Nate looked over the collection of novelty yarmulkes and kosher dog treats. There was also a velvet case of jewelry containing silver necklaces and bracelets with dangling stars. Another case held rings, and Nate picked up a silver ring inscribed with Hebrew, spinning it around between his fingers.

"Ah, that's a beauty," the woman said. "It says '*ani ledodi vedodi li.*' It means 'I am my beloved's, and my beloved is mine.'"

Nate held it in his palm. "How much?"

"Wait, what?" Lucas blinked in surprise.

The woman sized them up. "I'll give you two for sixty dollars. Normally eighty." She took a quick look at Lucas's hand and pulled out another ring. "Try this one."

Lucas took it from her. The silver was decent quality and the ring felt solid in his hand. He smiled uncertainly at Nate. "Um…"

"Don't worry, I'm not proposing." Nate took the ring from Lucas's hand. He slid it onto Lucas's left ring finger, where it fit perfectly.

"Could've fooled me." The butterflies unleashed in his belly flapped like crazy.

Nate grinned. "Just want to make sure it fits." He tried on his own ring, sliding it on his ring finger. It was a bit too big, so the woman gave him another size.

She smiled. "They look good on you, boys."

Lucas didn't know what to say. "Uh… Thanks." His head swam as he looked down at the ring. He knew he loved Nate with all his heart, but they'd only been together a year. "I guess we're going over the twenty-dollar limit."

"Will you throw in two chains?" Nate asked.

The woman pondered it for a moment. "You drive a hard

bargain. What the heck? It's Hanukkah. Almost."

Nate took Lucas's hand and slipped the ring from his finger. "We can wear them around our necks until we're ready."

Lucas swallowed hard over the sudden lump in his throat.

Nate's smile vanished. "Shit, I totally freaked you out, didn't I? I know it's spur of the moment, and I was the one who used to be all, I don't want a boyfriend. But you changed everything, and I thought… Look, we don't have to—"

"Would you shut up? I love you, and you love me. So why not?" Lucas pressed their lips together. Turning to the beaming woman, he smiled in return. "We'll take them."

Riding the creaky elevator in their building an hour later, Lucas couldn't stop smiling. He loved the feel of the ring against his chest and knowing that Nate felt the same brush of silver. Lucas leaned in close to him. "Think I'll get lucky tonight?"

Nate caught his mouth in a kiss. "You just might. Good thing I told Mom and Dad we had too much unpacking left to make it tonight."

Guilt tugged at Lucas. "Maybe we should still go. Even if we miss the blessings and the menorah lighting, we could still see everyone. Rachel texted me a bunch of sad faces."

"The great thing about Hanukkah is that it's eight nights. We'll make sure we go to Aunt Linda's for her big dinner and gift exchange. I'm beat. I just want to curl up in our bed."

"I can't really argue with that." Lucas nuzzled Nate's cheek. "I love quiet nights."

At their apartment door, Lucas fished his keys out of his pocket, but when he twisted the knob, the door sprung open. Lucas knew his mouth was gaping, but he didn't know how else to react to the sight of what had to be Nate's entire family crammed into their tiny studio apartment.

Fifteen or so people stared back at him, some standing in the kitchen shoulder to shoulder, kids on Nate and Lucas's bed poking their heads out through the open space above the half-wall.

Lucas's first response was a flare of panic at all the people in such a small area, but at least there was no pounding bass or beer bongs being passed around. He took a long breath and blew it out slowly. It was okay. These weren't strangers. They were family.

Among the crowd, Lucas spotted Mr. and Mrs. Kramer, Nate's grandparents, Sam, Linda, and Rachel—who grinned. Lucas glanced at Nate beside him, appearing equally stunned. Nate shook his head and said, "I knew we shouldn't have given my parents the spare key."

Laughter rang out, and a few people shouted, "Surprise!" as Lucas and Nate took off their jackets and threw them on top of the overloaded coat stand behind the door.

Mrs. Kramer gave them a stern look. "Well, we had no choice when you said you weren't coming tonight. Besides, we have to give your apartment a proper housewarming and blessing."

Mr. Kramer held a blue rectangular case several inches long. Golden symbols were carved on it. He said to Lucas, "In this case is a *mezuzah*. It's a scroll of parchment with two chapters from the Torah handwritten on it and rolled very small. We hang the case on the doorpost to ask God's protection." He squeezed through the throng with a hammer and opened the door, nailing the case to the frame.

Nate's Aunt Linda recited a blessing in Hebrew, and Lucas bowed his head. When he lifted it again, through the maze of people jammed into the apartment he spotted the gleam of something in the window. Craning his head, he realized a golden menorah stood on the windowsill.

Following his gaze, Linda exclaimed, "Look at the time! The sun is almost down, and we have to light the menorah."

Nate noticed it for the first time. "You brought yours?" he

asked his mother.

She smiled. "No. This is for *your* home."

Nate hugged her and pressed a kiss to her cheek. His grandfather inched his way to the menorah as people shuffled out of the way. The old man, who always wore his yarmulke whenever Lucas saw him, smoothed it with a gnarled finger before reciting the blessings from memory.

Some of Nate's family spoke along with him, and Nate slipped his arm over Lucas's shoulder. Lucas wrapped his arm around Nate's waist, unable to wipe the smile from his face.

When Papa was finished, he pointed toward Lucas. Lucas glanced over his shoulder. "Me?"

"Yes, you. Come here and light the candles."

Nate nodded and gave him a gentle push. Lucas shimmied past the coffee table and a few of Nate's cousins, and took the long match from the old man.

"Do you know which candles to light?" Nate's grandfather peered at him with watery eyes.

Lucas felt as if he was answering the most important pop quiz of his life. "The middle one, then the candle on the far right."

The old man nodded, and Lucas exhaled and struck the match. When the candles were lit, everyone burst into applause, and after another blessing, they sang a joyous song. Nate stood next to Lucas, singing along. The new ring sat against Lucas's chest, the metal warm and solid.

Every surface in their narrow little kitchen was covered with food—latkes and sufganiyot and a dozen delicious dishes Lucas couldn't name yet. Nate's bubbe bustled around with Linda, heating everything in the oven and Lucas's old microwave.

Nate pulled out his camera and asked Rachel to take a picture of him and Lucas by the window, the menorah silhouetted by the falling snow. They stood close, and Lucas thought of how in a few hours when they were alone again, they'd sleep in each other's arms naked except for the matching rings.

In their tiny apartment in Hell's Kitchen, crammed full of family, Lucas knew he was home.

THE END

In Case of Emergency

by Keira Andrews

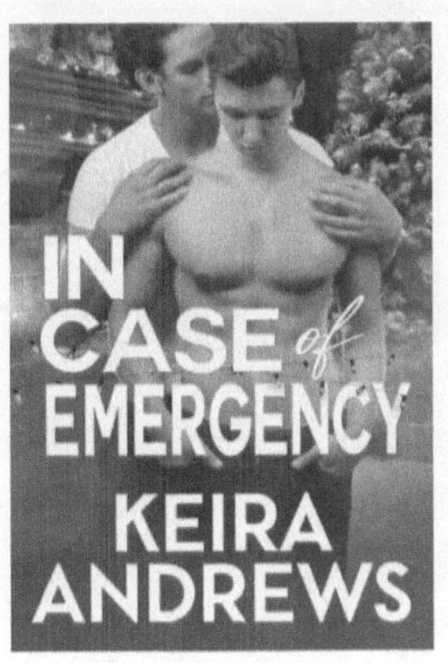

Acknowledgements

Thank you to Leta Blake and Davina Jamison for their invaluable help with this novella.

Dedication

To everyone who loves the Christmas season as much as I do. May your bells jingle and your winters be wonderlands.

Chapter One

Daniel wasn't sure how many ways he could say it, but he tried again. "I don't know a Nicholas Smith."

The woman on the other end of the line somehow persisted. "But this is Daniel Diaz?" She rattled off his number.

Daniel took the cell phone from his ear for a moment to glance at the screen. It definitely said Carleton University. Was this some student prank? Did people even make crank calls anymore? He said, "Yes, that's the correct number, but there's been some mistake."

"But you *are* Daniel Diaz, aren't you?"

He sighed. "Yes, but as I said, I don't know a Nicholas Smith." Ugh, he just wanted to get home so he could pack and get back on the road. He was actually taking an honest-to-God *vacation*. With his new, maybe-could-be boyfriend. *Which might be a complete disaster.* Stomach tightening, he pushed away the unease as the woman spoke again.

"I'm so sorry to bother you, but he's one of our students. He's had an accident. Your name and number are listed as his emergency contact."

"I don't know what to tell you. I have no clue who this guy is." He switched his wipers to the next setting, the rubber squeaking a little faster as it cleared the wet snow on the windshield.

Traffic crawled along the slushy 417 toward Kanata, a sea of red lights in the December darkness. Normally Daniel came home after eight and missed rush hour. He usually would've ignored the call while driving, but at five kilometers an hour, he figured he was safe. He really needed to get Bluetooth set up, but most of his communication was by text anyway, even for work. These days the only person who called him was his mother—

"Shit," he muttered with a sinking sensation, gripping the steering wheel, the heated leather warm under his fingers.

"Uh, excuse me?"

"Sorry. It just hit me. Is this *Cole* Smith? Our parents were married for, like, five minutes. It was a million years ago, but a few months back my mom mentioned he was moving to Ottawa. Grad school, or something."

"Yes, Nicholas Smith is enrolled in our master's degree in environmental engineering."

"Why the hell would he put *me* down for his in-case-of-emergency person? We haven't talked in years." He did the math. "*Ten* years."

"Well, I'm not sure. But he's been taken to the hospital, and it's policy that we inform his emergency contact. That would apparently be you, Mr. Diaz."

The woman didn't sound that worried, so it couldn't be a big deal, but... "He's okay, right? It's not anything *serious*?" He barely remembered nerdy, knobby-kneed little Cole, but he didn't want anything bad to happen to the guy.

"All I know is that there was an accident, Nicholas was injured, and an ambulance was called. But, no, I don't believe it's a life or death situation. However, the campus is closing now for the next three weeks, and I imagine Nicholas's classmates are already gone. Yours is the only contact number we have."

Shit, fuck, fuck. As the traffic came to a complete standstill, he closed his eyes for a moment and rubbed the bridge of his nose.

"I guess it's up to you whether you go to the ER or not."

Daniel groaned internally. He still had to pack and finish up a couple of hiring reports, even though the office had just closed for the holidays. "God, I hate hospitals."

"Doesn't everyone, Mr. Diaz?"

She had a point, and guilt attacked like a punch to the gut. "Which hospital?"

Of course it was back the way he'd come, and the next exit would take a good ten minutes to reach in the bumper-to-bumper procession. After hanging up, Daniel quickly dialed his mom. She answered on the third ring, and he said, "Hey, Mom. Look, I got a weird call to go to the hospital."

"What? Are you sick?" Her voice squeaked out at a pitch close to something only dogs could hear.

"No, no. I'm fine. Mom? Listen to me. I'm a hundred percent fine. It's about Nicholas Smith. Is that your ex's son?" Not that "ex" narrowed it down. He added, "Cole?"

She sucked in a breath. "Is he hurt? What happened?"

"I don't know yet. I'm on my way. Carleton called me because he had an accident on campus. Do you know why he would have put me down to contact?"

"Because I told him to, darling. He doesn't know anyone else in Ottawa."

"Uh, he doesn't know me either! I haven't seen him in forever." Not since the rebound marriage between Daniel's mother and Cole's father predictably imploded after only six months.

"Of course you know him. He's family. Oh my goodness, what do you suppose happened? Please let him be all right."

"I'm sure he's fine. Don't get worked up." He pushed the heat button on the Audi's dash, turning it down. "And Mom, he is not *family*."

"You don't divorce children, Daniel."

"You got that from *Clueless,* didn't you?"

She huffed. "Regardless, it's accurate."

Daniel wasn't going to argue with her about it. "How's Puerto Vallarta treating you?"

"Divinely! I've already had four mango margaritas and it's not even dinnertime. I wish you could come down, sweetheart. It doesn't seem right spending Christmas without you."

"Mom, you know I'll see you in the new year. Besides, it's a girls' trip with your friends. No men allowed, remember?"

"Yes, true. And at least you're actually taking time off work—although I know you wouldn't if you had your way. Thank goodness Martin believes in work-life balance. You need to learn from your boss, sweetie."

Martin Bukowski, the CEO of AppAny, insisted on being called by his first name, wore flip-flops in Ottawa in January, and had installed a massive tube slide between the floors of his headquarters. The work itself—creating apps for small business-es—was actually rather staid. Lots of back-end web development and whatnot. But Martin was determined his company would be edgy and cool, with playgrounds for offices, flexible work schedules, and a staff with a median age of twenty-five.

"Speaking of work-life balance, Cole is a lovely young man. Assuming he's all right, and pray that he is, maybe you could spend some time with him in the next few months? I'm sure he's been lonely, on his own in a different city."

"I barely have time to see my own friends, let alone some dude I don't even know." He finally reached the off-ramp and circled around to get back on the highway heading into Ottawa. At least there was less traffic going that way.

"As I always point out, you work far too much."

He rolled his eyes. "Yeah, yeah. Mom, I have to hang up now. I can't talk and drive. I'll let you know what's going on with Cole as soon as I can. Love you."

"Love you too, my darling."

He'd heard it a million times that he worked too much, but she didn't understand how important his job was to him. Not many twenty-eight-year-olds made HR director. Granted, he was one of three HR directors working under a VP at AppAny, but it was still an accomplishment.

So what if he worked damn hard? How was that a bad thing? And he was taking a vacation, wasn't he? At the last minute, even!

Daniel thought wistfully of the hot tub waiting. It was outdoor and boasted a view of the mountains and the frozen lake. Mont-Tremblant in Quebec already had a couple feet of snow, and it would be perfect to cuddle up in the steamy water with a glass or three of merlot. Oh, and Justin. Right.

With a mix of excitement and trepidation, he thought of free and spontaneous Justin. He was so handsome, with his strawberry-blond hair, blue eyes, and mouth that didn't quit—in more ways than one. Daniel usually preferred to make plans well in advance, but Justin loved the thrill of doing things on the fly. So Daniel had rented a whole chalet for them last-minute thanks to a cancellation. He could be fun too, damn it.

"It's going to be great," he muttered. "CYC."

It'd been his friend Pam who'd pleaded with him to accompany her to a self-help workshop called CYC: Change Your Cadence. Of course he'd flatly refused at first. He tried to keep Sundays completely free to cook and watch all the mindless TV he'd recorded. Crowding into the Kanata Best Western ballroom with a bunch of unhappy people and paying a hundred bucks to some con artist who promised to change their lives was not appealing in any way, shape, or form.

But tears had glimmered in Pam's eyes as she'd whispered that no one else would go. She and her wife, Christine—make that ex-wife now—had lived in the condo next to Daniel's rental, where he'd lived for a few years before moving into his new house.

Pam had always been so stoic and practical, the yin to Christine's flighty, over-emotional yang. When it fell apart, Christine took custody of most of their friends in the divorce, and at thirty-three, Pam had found herself starting over.

Daniel had never seen her cry before, so of course he'd gone with her. The guru was an ex-Marine sergeant from the States who'd made a new career for herself after being shot in Afghanistan and then abandoned by her loser husband in the same month. Her philosophy wasn't exactly groundbreaking—if what you've been doing isn't working, try something different—but her delivery captured people's imaginations.

As the other attendees, mostly women but some men, had hopped and twirled and even crawled over the burgundy-and-gray-checked carpet during one of the exercises, literally changing their cadence, Daniel had sat straight-backed in his chair.

Yet Sergeant Becky's message had permeated his consciousness—he still hadn't ruled out brainwashing—and later, after the workshop was over, he found himself often attempting to CYC.

Like with this trip.

He wasn't sure how much he and Justin had in common, but cuddling up together in the hot tub in Mont-Tremblant would be his chance to find out. Before CYC, Daniel would never have agreed to go on a date with someone as…exuberant as Justin, let alone go away with him for a week. And he'd definitely never date anyone in the staff group he managed. Luckily, Justin was under one of the other directors.

Besides, Justin had been so enthusiastic about Daniel, obviously into him and not ashamed to show it. How long had it been since anyone had been interested in that way? It'd been way too long since Daniel have even been willing to attempt a relationship.

Wonder what Trevor's doing for Christmas.

Grimacing, Daniel tried to banish the memories, acid flooding his gut. He'd simply been too busy to date the last few years. Okay, *six* years. But he was changing that, wasn't he? CYC. He'd committed himself to doing things differently, so that was that.

He jabbed a button on the steering wheel with his thumb and turned on the radio, an obnoxiously cheery Mariah Carey Christmas song filling the car. He lifted his thumb to change the station, then left it to prove to himself how open-minded he was being.

Justin had pursued him relentlessly at the office over the past month. He worked for AppAny's marketing department as a graphic designer and was fresh out of art school. Justin's attention was flattering, and although Daniel had put him off time and time again, he couldn't deny it was fun to have someone flirting with him. Of course Daniel insisted they keep it strictly professional at the office.

Except for when Justin had blown him in the Audi in the parking lot the previous week.

Usually Daniel could manage his own sexual needs quite handily—so to speak. But it had been an extra-long day and the lot was almost empty. Justin had smiled so prettily and practically begged to go down on him. Daniel hadn't been able to resist. CYC and all that.

They hadn't even actually kissed, but now they'd have a whole week at the chalet to get to know each other. After Daniel dealt with this Cole situation. He took the exit for the hospital, the blue and white neon H on the main building beckoning. What if Cole was really hurt?

"Fuck," he muttered. It was the last thing he wanted to deal with right then, but obviously he had to at least make sure his former stepbrother was okay.

He took a ticket from the machine, the mechanical arm lifting to admit him to the visitor parking lot. The concrete hospital was brightly lit against the dark sky, and Daniel shoved his hands in the pockets of his knee-length Burberry coat. The temperature hovered around the freezing mark, which was balmy for Ottawa in

December. He hadn't had to bust out his Canada Goose jacket yet, but he'd bring it to the mountains.

As he walked up to the ER, sirens approached, and by the time he neared the door, he was blinded by red lights and had to jump out of the way as paramedics shouted about a GCS of twelve and a head lac and wheeled in a bloody man on a stretcher.

Daniel followed in the stretcher's wake, stopping in the fluorescent-lit enclosure of the gray waiting room, where a chorus of coughs greeted him. One woman, who was hacking up a lung by the sounds of it, jiggled a wailing baby on her knee. A drunk-sounding man spoke too loudly, evidently to himself, the chairs next to him empty despite the mass of people in the small space, some leaning against walls.

Disinfectant seared Daniel's nostrils, but not enough to cover the stench of—yep, horribly pink vomit being mopped up in the corner. Sad little red and green Christmas decorations hung from the reception desk; one end of the garland trailed onto the floor. A brown-edged poinsettia sat in front of the clerk's computer.

Daniel didn't want to touch *anything*.

A middle-aged woman with a brunette dye job that showed an inch of gray at the roots glanced up as he reluctantly approached the desk. "Can I help you?"

"Yes. I'm here to see Cole Smith? Nicholas, I mean. He was apparently brought in by ambulance this afternoon."

She tapped her keyboard. "You're family?"

To avoid red tape, he nodded and told a big, fat lie. "He's my brother." Working in HR, he knew just how long it could take to deal with privacy regulations.

"He's in curtain seven."

Daniel exhaled. "Does that mean he's okay? Since he's not in the operating room or whatever?"

"Uh-huh. He's just fine." She read from the screen. "Broken hand. Mild concussion. He'll be ready for discharge."

Thank Christ. "Thank you so much."

"You're welcome. Go through the double doors to the right."

Another child's wail joined the baby's. Daniel shuddered. "Is it always like this?"

The woman smirked. "Only on a full moon. Fa-la-la-la-la."

Daniel gave her a smile and followed her instructions, pushing through the doors and into the ER itself, where another reception desk sat. The doors shut behind him with a *whoosh*, mercifully dulling the cacophony. A young woman looked up, and Daniel asked, "Curtain seven?"

"Take your first left and look up for the numbers."

In the long, narrow room, machines beeped and someone moaned behind their curtain, but it was mostly still. He felt like he suddenly had to tiptoe, his leather loafers silent on the linoleum anyway. Some curtains were drawn, while others were open, revealing patients on stretchers.

Electrodes dotted the sunken chest of one older man. A silver-haired woman who was likely his wife sat in a plastic chair beside him, gripping his hand. She glanced up as Daniel passed, and he gave her what he hoped was a sympathetic smile. She returned it, then looked back to the man, who snored lightly.

Curtain seven was drawn, and Daniel stood there for a few moments. There was nothing to knock on, so finally he cleared his throat and said, "Uh…Cole? Are you in there?"

Chapter Two

*H*OLY. *SHIT. DANIEL?!?*

Cole would know that baritone anywhere. It had fueled his teenage fantasies, and even now fire sparked in his veins, his tummy fluttering. Daniel Diaz was a few feet away, only a pale blue curtain separating them. What the hell was he doing at the hospital? How did he know—

Of course. Claudia had messaged Cole on Facebook in the summer when he was registering at school.

Congrats on the master's program! How exciting! Did you know Daniel's been in Ottawa for some years now? Do you have his number? I'll give it to you. You'll need someone local just in case, but you should call him regardless! I'm sure he'd love to hear from you!

Cole had been positive it was the last thing Daniel would want considering Daniel had never had time for him when they'd lived in the same house and shared a bathroom. Still, he'd put down Daniel's name and number on the school form as emergency contact—a silly little thing that had made him smile. He'd never expected for a moment said emergency would actually happen.

"Hello? Cole?"

Shit. "Uh, yeah?" His voice squeaked on the question, and he cringed, trying to straighten his hair with his right hand, which wasn't enclosed in a cast like his left. He was certain his hair was sticking up at the back of his head, but at least he'd had a trim last week. He sat up a little straighter, the top of the stretcher raised at an angle. "Come in."

The curtain drew back on its rounded track, and *holy shit* there was Daniel. Cole's throat went dry, and he blinked at the vision of hotness before him. He'd seen pics on Claudia's Facebook, but live in person was a whole new level.

Six-one. Dark, shiny curls kept short at the sides and back, a little longer on top. Full lips the color of a blush, and his skin a warm brown—almost golden. He was dressed impeccably, a gray scarf around his throat and a long, black coat that hugged his lean hips.

Does he have more chest hair now than he did when he was eighteen?

Daniel frowned. "Cole? It's Daniel Diaz. Do you remember me?"

"Yes!" He winced and lowered his voice. "Sorry. I'm a little out of it. They gave me something for pain. Um, hi. It's great to see you again."

"Yeah. It's been a long time. Look, the school called me. Something about me being your emergency contact."

Cole's gut clenched, and he tasted bile. Shit. Why had he put down Daniel's name? *So stupid!*

Yet Daniel only said, "I was worried, but clearly you're okay. Right?"

"Totally. They insisted on calling the ambulance. Shit, I'm sorry they bothered you." Daniel must have been *pissed*.

His closed-mouth smile was tight. "No, it's fine. As long as you're okay. That's what matters."

Cole blinked. Daniel had pretty much hated him when their parents had been married, but he was being kind of nice now. Granted, it'd been almost a decade. Cole still braced himself, waiting for a sneer. Or worse, to be dismissed altogether.

Nurses passed by with another stretcher, this one holding a

drowsy-looking older woman. Daniel stepped closer to let them by, coming in beside Cole now. His eyes were still a hazely-chocolate brown that made Cole think of Ferrero Rocher.

Daniel's dark brows drew together. "Dude, are you sure you're okay? You seem really out of it."

"Oh no, I'm fine!" His head throbbed, but he nodded. "It was stupid. I fell up the stairs. I mean, who falls *up* the stairs? Not even down."

A smile tugged at Daniel's full lips, hinting at the gleam of straight, white teeth. "You always were a klutz, if I recall correctly."

That he remembered *anything* about Cole made him giddy. Cole laughed too loudly. "Yeah. That's me."

Daniel nodded to the cast. "You broke your hand? At least it's not the right one, huh?"

"Yeah! Well, actually, I'm left-handed."

"Oh. Shit." Daniel shifted from foot to foot. "So you don't have any friends here?"

"I made a few at school, but they've gone home for the holidays. And doing a master's isn't like undergrad. A lot of people work part-time. We're all busy, not getting together for keggers every weekend. Everyone already has their own lives." *Except for me.* "You know what I mean?"

"Right. Fair enough."

"Yeah." Cole cringed internally. *Think of something smart to say!*

"No girlfriend, I assume?"

"Why would you assume that?" It was stupid to be offended, but the defensiveness reared up anyway.

Daniel frowned, which seemed to be his default expression, his thick, sculpted brows drawn together. "Because if you had a girlfriend she'd be here?"

"Oh. That makes sense." Now Cole just felt like an idiot. "I haven't had a girlfriend since senior year of high school." He took a deep breath, butterflies flapping in his stomach even though there was nothing to be nervous about. "I came out in university. I'm gay too."

Daniel's eyebrows shot up. "Oh! I didn't realize. Cool. Guess there's no boyfriend either."

"Uh-uh." Cole's cheeks went hot. Daniel must have thought he was so lame. "I was sorry to hear when you and Trevor broke up. Guess that was a while ago now."

Jaw tight, Daniel pulled out his phone, and said in a clipped voice, "Six years. Forever ago."

"Still, I'm—"

"Where's your dad these days, anyway?"

Okay, Trevor was off-limits. Good to know, although he desperately wanted to know what had gone wrong. They'd seemed so perfect together. Cole answered, "He still lives in Toronto in that same house, but right now he's on an African safari with my stepmom."

"Ah." Daniel smirked. "Which number wife is this?"

"Four." Cole shrugged. "It is what it is."

"Yeah, I hear you. My mom's still a serial monogamist too. At least she didn't marry the last few losers. How about your mom? If they were just going to call you Cole, why did they name you Nicholas, anyway?"

"I'm not sure. I'd ask her, but she's dead."

Daniel froze, his eyes going wide. "Shit. I guess I forgot."

"It was six years ago. Car accident."

"Oh. I'm sorry. That really sucks."

"Yeah. Thanks." Cole could think of her now and not cry, which was a vast improvement from the earlier years. Still, he didn't want to dwell, so he asked, "Is your dad still in Spain?"

"Yep. No plans to come back to Canada. He's got a whole new family there, so. You know." Daniel shrugged tightly. "Let me text my mom and tell her you're okay. She was super worried when I told her you were in the hospital."

A rush of warm affection filled Cole. "I'm so sorry to bother her. Claudia's always been wonderful to me. She's stayed in touch. Facebook and stuff." His belly swooped. "Actually, I sent you a friend request when I moved to Ottawa."

"Oh, did you?" Not looking up, Daniel tapped his phone. "I haven't been on Facebook in months. No time."

"Right. I hear you. It's a good way to stay in touch with people from high school and stuff, though."

Daniel glanced up. "Since I have zero desire to talk to anyone from high school, I'm good."

Right. Likely Trevor-related as well. Daniel and Trevor had been co-captains of the hockey team and out as a couple in senior year, which had blown Cole's little mind at the time. They'd been so *fearless* and had gone off to Western together for university as a total power couple. Cole was dying to know what had gone wrong.

Obviously he didn't ask, instead saying, "I'm sorry to bother you with all this. I'm sure you have much better things to be doing on the Friday before the holidays."

Daniel frowned at his phone as his thumbs flew. "Yeah, I'm driving up to Tremblant to meet my…kind-of boyfriend or whatever. We're staying in a chalet for the week."

"Oh. Sounds amazing." Whoever this "kind-of boyfriend or whatever" was, Cole immediately loathed him simply for existing. Which of course was entirely unfair and immature, but he could accept his shortcomings. "It was really cool of you to come check on me. It's good to see you."

Slipping his phone in his coat pocket, Daniel said, "What? Oh, yeah. Definitely. It's been a long time." His hazelnut gaze ran over Cole. "You're all grown up."

"Still short, but what can you do?" He forced a laugh. *Oh God, shoot me now.*

Before Daniel could reply and prolong their awkward reunion, the young doctor bustled by and skidded to a halt. "Oh good, someone came after all." She eyed Daniel and said, "I'm Dr. Hanratty. Are you taking Mr. Smith home? Did the nurse go over the concussion protocols with you?"

Cole said, "I'm sure I'll be okay. My head barely hurts. I'll be fine on my own." He sat all the way up, and as if to prove him a liar, the throbbing intensified and a wave of nausea had him salivating.

Dr. Hanratty shook her head, her red ponytail flying. "No, Mr. Smith. You cannot go home alone. I think it's a very mild concussion, but you did bang your head on concrete. Brain bleeds can be sneaky things and can quickly become a life or death matter. You must be observed for twenty-four hours to make sure your symptoms don't worsen. I won't discharge you without someone to care for you."

The idea of being cared for—by Daniel Diaz, no less—sent a pang of yearning echoing through him, but Cole said, "I've already been too much of a pain in the ass. Daniel, don't worry about it. Go to Tremblant. Have an amazing time." Cole had already resigned himself to spending Christmas alone poking at his thesis and marathoning a few Netflix shows. He'd be just fine.

Daniel looked between Cole and Dr. Hanratty, clearly torn. "You don't have anyone else here in Ottawa who can help?" At Cole's shake of his head, Daniel's shoulders sagged. "It's cool. I'll look after you."

Cole's heart leapt even as he insisted, "Seriously, I'll be—"

"Taken good care of," Dr. Hanratty said in a tone not allowing for argument. "You have a broken hand and a concussion. It's going to be a struggle just to feed yourself. We don't realize how much we use our hands until one is essentially tied behind our backs. Let your friend help."

To Daniel, she added, "You'll need to wake him every two to three hours tonight. Ask him simple questions: his name, the date, who's prime minister. Look for any changes, such as slurring, confusion, increased dizziness. He can take acetaminophen, but no ibuprofen, aspirin, or any NSAIDs. Lots of fluids to stay hydrated, and nothing too heavy to eat for a day or two. He'll likely experience some nausea tonight. He should be just fine, but you need to keep an eye on him. Got it?"

Daniel nodded. "Got it."

"But…he has other things to do!" Over the years, Cole had daydreamed about becoming friends with Daniel. Or maybe more—which was beyond ludicrous, a fantasy he should have outgrown. Still, being a massive burden was not going to make a great first impression. Well, second. Whatever.

Dr. Hanratty gave Cole's leg a pat, ignoring his protestation. "You don't need to stay in bed, but no heavy exercise. Relax and take it easy. No alcohol until your concussion symptoms have cleared. Christmas Eve isn't until when, Wednesday? You should be good to indulge by then."

She leaned down and examined his cast, which was wrapped in alarmingly bright orange medical tape. His thumb was free, but the cast extended from under his elbow to just below his fingertips. "Looks good. Glad the fracture clinic technician was still here. Hours will be cut during the holidays, so they're working late."

Cole grimaced at the orange tape. "And hey, I can pick up extra work waving in planes on the runway."

She laughed. "Ask the nurse for a package of cast protectors for showering. They're shoulder-length gloves vets use to stick their hands inside cows. Take care!" With that, she disappeared around the next curtain.

Daniel was busy frowning at his phone again, and Cole didn't want to interrupt him. Soon after an attendant came with some paperwork, Cole was discharged. At least he didn't have to worry about paying for treatment. Now that he was an adult, he didn't take universal health care for granted anymore.

He cleared his throat. "Um, is everything okay?"

"Hmm?" Daniel glanced up. "Yes. Sorry—had to deal with a work thing. And—hold on." He put the phone to his ear. "Hi, Mom. Yes, like I said, he's totally fine." After a moment, he added, "Just a sec," and passed the phone to Cole.

He took it awkwardly with his right hand. "Hey, Claudia."

"Oh, you poor thing. How are you feeling?"

"I'm fine, really. It's great to hear your voice. The pictures of the resort on Facebook looked amazing. Are you having fun?"

"Having a blast, and it's wonderful to talk to you. Daniel's going to take good care of you."

Whether he likes it or not. "He's been great. I'm so grateful. I'd better let you go. Have fun and don't worry about me." He passed the phone back to Daniel, who listened again and uttered a few terse agreements.

When Daniel ended the call, he sighed. "All right. Guess we'd better get out of here. They'll need the bed for someone else judging by the shitshow in the waiting room."

Cole swung his legs around. He was totally fine. Then he stood. "Whoa."

In a blink, Daniel had hold of Cole's shoulders, his hands warm and strong, keeping him steady. "Careful."

Cole tried to smile. "Guess I am a little dizzy."

"Where's your coat? You can't go out in just a T-shirt." Daniel peered around the small area, keeping one hand on Cole as he reached for a plastic hospital bag. He held out the blue hoodie first, and Cole stuck his good arm through the sleeve.

Daniel's fingers brushed the nape of Cole's neck as he pulled the cotton over his left shoulder. A shiver ran down Cole's spine, and he held his breath as Daniel repeated the action with Cole's navy peacoat. He got his hand stuck in the ripped lining before putting his arm in the sleeve.

"Thanks," Cole said, his throat stupidly dry. Up close, Daniel smelled like woody, spicy tobacco, but not in a bad way. In fact, in a way that went straight to Cole's dick. His head swam as he turned, and he wasn't sure if it was the concussion or not.

Daniel Diaz is actually here. Touching me. I have got to be freaking dreaming.

Granted, the touch was a solicitous hand on his elbow like one he might give his grandmother, but Cole would take it. As they shuffled past the other curtains, Daniel paused by an elderly couple and asked the woman, "Can I get you anything before I go?"

She smiled, her blue eyes watery. "Oh, thank you, dear. But no, we're all right." She looked at Cole. "Is this your brother? Glad he's on his way home."

"Oh, he's not—" Daniel stopped abruptly and then said, "Thank you. You're sure you're okay?"

"Yes. Merry Christmas, boys."

They wished her the same before continuing into the hall. Cole asked, "Did you talk to her before or something?"

Daniel shrugged. "No." After a few steps, he said, "We'd better get going. We have to stop by your place and pack a bag."

"And then?" Cole's heart skipped. He'd been so stupidly in love with Daniel. His inner-thirteen-year-old was freaking the hell out.

"Then I guess you're coming on Christmas vacation."

Adrenaline surged through Cole, mixing with painkillers to send his head spinning. *Holy. Shit.* Christmas with Daniel. Maybe being a klutz wasn't so bad after all.

Chapter Three

PULLING UP IN front of Cole's three-story apartment building, Daniel was lucky enough to find a spot by the curb.

Cole said, "You can just wait in the car. I'll go up and grab my stuff."

Sighing inwardly, Daniel was already unbuckling. "Dude, you're not exactly steady on your feet. Last thing we need is for you to fall and hit your head. Again."

Cole opened his mouth, then snapped it shut. "Good point. I just don't want you to go to any extra trouble."

Too damn late for that. Daniel said, "Come on. I have to pack my own stuff. I'd like to get on the road before midnight." It was only just past eight, but still.

Daniel had agreed to look after him, so there was no point in Cole protesting. He reached over and pressed the button to release Cole's seat belt. He'd had to buckle him in too. The doctor was right—apparently they took using both hands for granted.

"Look, I'm sure I really will be fine. I can set the alarm on my phone for every few hours to wake me up."

Daniel raised an eyebrow. "And what? Is Siri going to ask you questions and judge your answers? I don't think the new iOS has a concussion app."

Cole rubbed his face with his good hand. "I just feel like such a dick intruding on your vacation with your boyfriend."

Daniel shifted uncomfortably. "Well, he's not my boyfriend yet." Justin was cute and lively, but would he really make good boyfriend material? Did they have a single thing in common aside from being gay and working at AppAny?

Chill. The whole point of this trip is to find out. And have some fun for once. CYC. He checked his phone, finding the lock screen still blank but for the stock image of a random cityscape. He'd texted Justin with the bad news that they'd have company, but no response yet.

"Is he waiting for you to pick him up? I'm sorry to delay everything."

"It's fine—he headed up this aft. And like I told you, there are four bedrooms. It's a big chalet, but it was the only one I could get last minute. Works out for the best. We can do our thing, and you can relax and whatever." *Won't be awkward at all.*

"Right. Okay. Uh… Well, if you're sure?"

He pushed the button to turn off the engine. "I'm sure. It's settled. End of discussion."

"Okay." Cole smiled tentatively. "You were always like that. Once you'd made up your mind, you were determined."

Daniel blinked. "You think so? I'm amazed you even remember me. You were just a little kid."

"Not that young. I was thirteen."

"Were you? I thought you were ten or something. Right, I guess thirteen makes sense since you're in grad school now." Cole had certainly grown up. He was only about five-six, but he had a tight, lean little body, like a swimmer or diver. His short hair was light brown, eyes blue, jaw square, and most importantly, he'd grown into his ears, which had seemed enormous when he was a kid.

Cole seemed okay as they walked into the building and he unlocked the lobby door, but Daniel stayed in arm's reach just in case and asked, "Where's the elevator?"

"There isn't one."

Of course. Normally Daniel wouldn't care, but considering stairs had made Cole their bitch once already today… "Tell me you aren't on the third floor."

Cole winced. "I'm not on the third floor?"

Wonderful.

Progress was steady, though. Cole really was being a trouper, and as he turned the last landing—right hand gripping the railing, Daniel beside him—Daniel said, "You're doing great."

Cole grinned, then stumbled, and Daniel caught him around the waist. "Whoa. Don't get cocky, kid." It wasn't quite a direct quote from *Star Wars*, but as he straightened up, Cole laughed.

"You still love those movies?"

"Sure. It's stupid, I guess." He could still imagine Trevor rolling his eyes at what he'd referred to as "Daniel's little sci-fi problem." He shifted his weight uncomfortably.

Cole blinked at him. "Why would you say that? Those movies are awesome. Did you see the new one when it came out last week? What am I saying, of course you did."

"Actually, I haven't yet," he said with a pang of regret. "Too much work to do before we closed the company for the holidays."

"Seriously?" Cole's thin brows shot up. "I'd have thought you'd be there opening day. I saw it on the weekend. *So* good. You're going to love it." He added, "At least, I think you will. Not that I know you anymore. Or that I ever knew you." His ears went bright red.

"Okay, well. Let's keep going. Carefully." Mindful of the cast, Daniel stood closer, his hand hovering over Cole's back. The stairwell smelled of nothing, really—stale air and concrete, which was better than the stench of piss that made itself home in many stairwells. But now the scent of Cole's sweat and the plaster from the cast filled Daniel's nose.

A strange protectiveness surged up in Daniel as he stayed close to Cole. It sucked being sick or hurt, and it was even worse being alone when you hurt. The previous winter, Daniel had sweat and shivered through a brutal flu, holed up in his room, too weak to even go downstairs for filtered water, refilling his glass at the bathroom sink instead. He'd even missed a day of work.

They reached Cole's apartment without further incident, and since it was approximately the size of a shoe box, it wasn't difficult to stay close to Cole in case of more dizziness. An unfolded futon took up most of the space straight ahead inside the door, and the little kitchen and bathroom stood off to the left.

The place was painted white, and some framed abstract prints that were likely from IKEA decorated two of the walls. A foot-high ceramic Christmas tree sat on a low coffee table, and there were lights taped up above the kitchen cabinets.

Cole said, "I know it's not much, but school's expensive."

"No, it's…nice. Your dad's not paying your tuition?"

"He did for undergrad. I want to do it all myself now. Really be independent, you know?"

"I hear you." Daniel eyed the only closet. The door stood open, and it held everything from a vacuum to shoes to clothes hanging from an adjustable shower curtain jammed up between the narrow sides. "Do you have a duffel or something?"

Cole did, and of course it was stuffed way in the back of the closet. Daniel pulled his tight slacks up a couple inches for room to move and got on his hands and knees, rooting around until his fingers closed over something that felt like a handle. The duffel bag—blue with the Toronto Maple Leafs logo—was worn but functional. Daniel crawled out and held it up. "Got it."

He'd left Cole leaning against the wall nearby, and Cole nodded and squeaked, "Great." His face was alarmingly red.

"Do you feel sick?" Daniel sprang to his feet.

"Nope! I'm good." He walked slowly toward a battered chest of drawers. A TV sat on top. Opening drawers with his right hand, he awkwardly pulled out a few T-shirts, a hoodie, a pair of jeans, socks, and underwear of the boxer-brief variety.

Daniel scooped the little pile into the bag. Just then, his phone buzzed.

Hey babe! RU on your way? Np about your bro. The more the merrier! Have surprise 4U, so hurry.

We're going to have so much fun!!!

Cole came out of the bathroom with a Ziploc bag of toiletries and asked, "Is everything okay?"

Realizing he was gritting his teeth at the way Justin used short forms for some words, Daniel unclenched. "Yep. It's all good." So Justin was informal in his texts. Most people were, and just because it drove Daniel crazy didn't make it wrong. He needed to loosen up. That was the whole point of dating Justin. Getting out of his comfort zone. CYC.

Still. Was it really so hard to type out three-letter words?

"I guess we should get going?" Cole asked.

Indeed they should. After the slow and steady trip downstairs, they got back on the road. Daniel lived in a new subdivision in Kanata, and half the streets were still under construction, the dark hulks of half-built houses standing watch. Daniel weaved around potholes made by the construction trucks and equipment.

Cole asked, "Is it noisy with all this being built?"

"I guess. But they don't work weekends, and I leave at six to hit the gym before the office. They're always done by the time I get home at night. I'm looking forward to all the mess being gone, though." He turned onto his street, strings of Christmas lights adorning some houses. There was also a massive, blinking Santa's sleigh where the little lawn would be in front of the house across the street.

They'd get sod put down in the spring, so currently their front yards were only dirt—now mud covered in wet snow. Daniel pulled into his short driveway and pressed the buttons for the house alarm and then the garage door.

In contrast with his neighbors, Daniel's only holiday decoration was a dark green wreath on the front door decorated with tasteful hints of silver. He'd never put up decorations inside at his condo, and hadn't done it at the house either.

"I'll go in through the garage. Too messy out front. Do you want to just stay in the car? I'll be quick."

"Yeah, cool. The seat warmer is making my butt way too toasty to get out. Do you rent this place?"

"No, I bought it last year. Moved in just before spring."

"Seriously, you have your own house? That's awesome."

Daniel shrugged and said a simple, "Thanks," but he flushed with pride. Only a few feet separated the houses in the cookie-cutter subdivision, but Daniel owned his own fully detached home before he was thirty. While Ottawa was nothing compared to the insane real-estate markets in Toronto or Vancouver, with the rising cost of houses, it was still an accomplishment.

He climbed the three concrete steps up from the garage into the house and unlocked the door. The alarm beeped twice in greeting, and he closed the door behind him and carefully removed his wet loafers. Normally he'd polish them immediately after wearing them in the snow, but they still had a two-hour drive to Mont-Tremblant.

Daniel flipped on the hall light and hung up his coat before hurrying up the stairs, his socks damp on the dark hardwood. He pulled his small suitcase out of the walk-in closet and eyed the racks of clothing, color-coordinated by black, gray, brown, and a few pieces of white. He chose several sweaters and slacks and a pair of dark jeans. Would he need his steamer?

Reluctantly deciding against it, he tugged off his tie and hung it in its place. While the office dress code was insanely casual, he'd always believed in dressing for the job you want. Sure, Martin wore tees or sometimes—Daniel shuddered—Hawaiian shirts, but

Daniel always dressed properly. He didn't wear a suit jacket, which was plenty casual enough.

He changed into a charcoal cashmere sweater and a pair of black jeans, then finished packing. Downstairs, he passed through the darkened living room into his open-concept kitchen. The walls in his house were painted a light gray, and all the furnishings and cabinetry were in black and chrome—although he did have a new dark purple rug in front of the black leather couch. CYC.

He opened the fridge and grabbed a couple bottles of water and bananas. Pam always teased him for keeping his bananas in the fridge, but he hated clutter on the gray quartz counters.

After zipping on his shin-high boots, he made two trips out to the vehicle, which was a car/SUV hybrid with a big open trunk space. He tossed his down parka in the backseat since he hated wearing bulky coats in the car. When he slipped behind the wheel, Daniel handed Cole one of the bottles. "There's a holder in your door. Doc said to stay hydrated."

"Right. Thanks. You know you really shouldn't buy bottled water." Still, he uncapped it and chugged half. "It's insanely wasteful. Not just the plastic, but—" He screwed up his face. "Sorry. You don't need a lecture."

"It's okay. You've gone green, huh? I guess as an environmental engineer, you kind of have to. Are you a vegan and all that?"

"God no. I'm way too much of a carnivore. And I love cheese. Sweet, sweet cheese. So to make up for my evil ways, I lecture unsuspecting people about disposable water bottles. You're welcome."

"Thanks. And hey, I recycle, for the record." Daniel touched the display screen on the dash. "Let me just give Trudy the coordinates."

"Trudy?" Cole chuckled. "You named your GPS?"

Daniel grimaced. "My friend Pam did, and it stuck. I was driving her to Costco and telling her about a woman I had to terminate at our office in Houston." He backed out of the driveway, ignoring Trudy's redundant directions for leaving the subdivision. "So I called her into the term meeting—"

"Wait, is that the euphemism for firing someone?"

"Yes. Anyway, most people cry and sometimes try to bargain, or there's denial. Definitely lots of shock, understandably. But once in a blue moon, we'll get a runner. Trudy stormed out and was cursing at the top of her lungs in the workspace. I went after her, hissing, "Trudy! Trudy!" I was afraid I'd have to call security to tackle her, but she calmed down. Anyway, I was telling Pam the story, and the GPS kept interrupting, so Pam declared it was Trudy's revenge."

Cole laughed. After a few moments, he asked, "Does it bother you? Firing people?"

A curl of dread wove through him, but Daniel shrugged as he turned onto the main road. "I don't enjoy it, but it has to be done sometimes. If profit margins go down, the company has to reduce spend and HC." He always felt sick to his stomach before a firing, but he had to do his job.

"HC?"

"Sorry. Head count. Also, if we acquire another company, we look for synergy opportunities. Weed out duplicated roles and try to consolidate business functions. Usually layoffs really have nothing to do with the staff members themselves. Which doesn't make it easier to take, I realize."

Daniel had often suggested that they could cut costs by not hiring executives who earn a quarter million a year for their ideas and didn't actually do the operational work, but for all of Martin's insistence on innovation, prestige still mattered. Daniel was the one who had to do the firing, so Martin got what Martin wanted.

"Do you have to do it often?"

"Several times a year, I guess. They send me to our other offices too. The one in Houston, and another in England. I don't get emotional, so I'm effective."

Pam's teasing voice echoed in his head: *It's because you're cold and dead inside. You really need to work on that.*

"Mmm."

Cole sounded sleepy, and Daniel glanced over after he checked his blind spot and accelerated onto the highway. They were heading back past Ottawa, then across the Ontario/Quebec border toward the Laurentian Mountains. Daniel said, "Go ahead and sleep."

"Sorry. I'm super tired all of a sudden." Cole leaned his head back, eyes drifting shut. He murmured, "Cars always put me to sleep. My mom said when I was a baby she used to drive me around the block and I'd be out like a light."

"Plus you have a concussion. Sleep. I'll wake you up in a little while to check on you."

Daniel put the satellite radio on low, the murmur of commercial-free Christmas carols keeping him company, along with the steady rhythm of Cole's deep breathing. It was strangely comforting that Cole trusted him enough to fall asleep while Daniel was driving. They hadn't seen each other in ten years, yet here they were. Life could be incredibly bizarre.

Flurries fell, a blanket of white over the fields, the temperature fortunately dropping. Daniel far preferred the frigid, snappy cold to the slushy mess around the freezing mark. The roads had been salted and were only a little icy, and there weren't many cars around. As Sarah McLachlan sang a melancholy yet pretty song about a river, the world seemed hushed and peaceful.

An hour and a half passed before Cole whimpered and moaned, lifting his head. "Fuck me. I think I'm going to be sick."

Daniel checked his blind spot and veered onto the empty shoulder. The amount of detailing needed to scrub vomit out of his interior was not something he wanted to deal with. He unbuckled Cole's seat belt before hopping out and running around to help him climb down, shivering in the cold, their breath pluming icily.

Cole took a few steps before bending in half and blowing chunks into the fresh snow. *Ugh.* Clearly Dr. Hanratty was correct about the nausea. Cole leaned his good hand on his knee, spitting and groaning. He seemed stable enough, so Daniel leaned back into the car to flip on the hazards and grab a box of mints from the glove compartment. He uncapped Cole's water bottle, handing it over as Cole straightened up with another groan.

"I haven't puked on the side of the road since high school."

"You partied in high school? Huh." Daniel rubbed his hands together and blew into them, stepping from side to side to keep moving in the cold. He brushed snowflakes off his sweater.

Cole swigged some water, sloshing it around his mouth before spitting it back out. "Nerds skimmed off the top of their parents' liquor bottles too."

"Ah, swamp water. I don't miss those days. Here, have a mint or five." He pulled the tin from his pocket and opened it.

"Thanks." Cole popped a few mints into his mouth and glanced around, moving his head gingerly. "Think it's okay to piss out here?"

The Audi's headlights cut through the night, but otherwise it was all dark. "Go for it."

Daniel stayed within arm's reach as Cole bent his head to unzip. Cole fiddled with his fly, cursing under his breath. "Fuck. I can't get the button."

"Oh. Um…" *Shit.* Well, he'd agreed to play nurse or whatever, so… "Here." Daniel stood in front of him, hoping the puking had definitely stopped. He couldn't see what he was doing, so he stooped and undid the button on feel and pulled down the zipper. He stood straight. "There."

Cole's sharp puffs of sour-yet-minty breath hit Daniel's throat where his sweater made a small V. "Thanks." Cole's voice was hoarse, probably from the cold night air. Not to mention the puking.

"Are you good now?"

"Uh…" Cole was tugging his underwear with his right hand, and he huffed, "Jesus, why couldn't I be ambidextrous?"

Daniel laughed awkwardly. *This isn't super weird or anything.* "Here, I'll just…" He pulled down Cole's underwear a few inches, his knuckles brushing wiry hair. Nerdy little Cole was definitely a man now. Cole's belly was taut and trembling, and more puffs of his quick exhalations warmed Daniel's skin.

Cole's laugh sounded strained. "I can pull my dick out. I hope." His fingers brushed Daniel's, and Daniel whipped his hands back. After a few moments, Cole said, "Are you into golden showers?"

"*Huh*? Oh, right!" He sidestepped out of the way. "Fire at will."

As Cole pissed into the snow, Daniel looked away, crossing his arms, debating whether to grab his coat from the back. Cole had to be freezing too in his hoodie. But soon enough, Cole said, "Can you just get the button? I managed the rest."

Daniel jolted at the sound of Cole's low voice. "Sure." He did it up, his numb fingers fumbling a bit, then he helped Cole back up into the passenger seat. Once he was settled, Daniel leaned across him to hook in the seatbelt.

Cole was motionless, and Daniel said, "You can breathe. I won't bite."

"No, I know." He laughed, clearly uneasy. "Thanks for your help. I'm sorry for the grossness and having to stop."

"Don't worry about it. We're almost there anyway."

When he was back in the car, Daniel flipped the seat and steering wheel heaters back on and swiped again at the snowflakes melting on his sleeves.

Cole said, "You've got some in your…" He lifted his left arm as if he was going to brush the snow away from Daniel's hair himself, then sucked in a breath. "Fuck. That hurts. Right. Broken hand."

Daniel brushed a palm over his head. "I'd think it would be hard to forget."

Cole wiped the snow from his own hair. "You'd think." He sighed. "Dude, I'm sorry you got stuck with me. You weren't planning on having a third wheel on your romantic vacay."

He bit back a surge of irritation. Beating a dead horse wouldn't change anything. "I wasn't, but shit happens. It is what it is. I made up my mind, remember?"

"I'm still grateful. This was a big ask considering we haven't even seen each other in ten years."

It was, but Daniel couldn't exactly leave Cole helpless. "For once and for all, don't worry about it. Besides, you know my mom is thrilled that we're 'reconnecting' as she'd say."

Cole smiled. "True. And…" He turned his head to look out the window. "I think it's cool too. Reconnecting."

Daniel didn't know what to say, so he went with, "Yeah," and turned up Kelly Clarkson singing very enthusiastically about a Christmas tree.

After another thirty kilometers, the warm glow of the village came into sight nestled at the bottom of the mountains soaring above. Cole sucked in a breath just as Trudy instructed Daniel to turn off the main road.

Cole said, "Wow. It looks like a postcard."

It really did. There was a cluster of colorful, mostly three-story buildings sandwiched together like gingerbread with fresh snow covering the roofs, a clock tower jutting up at one end of the village, and golden Christmas lights everywhere. Daniel had never really been one for the holidays, but it was gorgeous and welcoming.

Trudy directed them around the village and eventually onto a road that was surely dirt under the snow. It was a little icy, and he navigated the turns slowly.

"You have arrived at your destination."

The lights of the chalet glowed around the bend of a short driveway, and Daniel followed Justin's tire tracks, which were half-covered in the fresh snow. A minivan sat outside the chalet, and he pulled up beside it and turned off the car.

"Whoa," Cole breathed. "This place is gorgeous. All those windows!"

The two-story chalet had massive windows on both floors, and the listing had promised no neighbors for two kilometers on either side. Away from the lights of the village, it was too dark and cloudy to make out the view of the lake and mountains, but Daniel buzzed with excitement at the thought of seeing them in the morning. It really had been too long since he'd taken a vacation.

"It looks so peaceful," Cole added.

"It does." The owner had strung multicolored Christmas lights around the rail of the wraparound porch, and the effect was magical. Daniel opened the car door and stopped with one foot hanging out, baffled.

What was that thumping? A moment later he realized it was music. A tendril of unease unfurled. Huh. Well, perhaps Justin found techno relaxing? Daniel hoped it wasn't carrying over the frozen lake and disturbing anyone.

He grabbed his parka and put it on, leaving it unzipped as he walked around the car. Cole had managed to unbuckle himself and was standing there waiting with a frown, trying to shrug his good arm into his coat. Laughter and voices echoed. Voices.

Plural.

As Daniel's heart pounded in time with the bass, Cole said, "Uh, I didn't realize you were having a bunch of people up for a party?" His breath came out in frosty plumes in the frigid air.

"I'm not," Daniel managed to grit out, his jaw clenched. "Justin said he had a surprise, but…" But surely he knew better than this.

After helping Cole with his coat, Daniel marched up the walkway, which had likely been cleared that morning and was now covered by an inch of fresh snow. The wraparound porch had been cleared earlier as well, and he walked around the corner of the chalet toward where the hot tub sat in a sort of sunroom with glass doors that could be folded back, leaving it open to the elements but for the wooden roof.

Full beer bottles were wedged into the snow, empties discarded on their sides on the porch. Smoke drifted on the breeze—marijuana and cigarette. It was an eight-person hot tub—nice and roomy for two. Currently it held six goddamned people, including Justin, who realized with a joyful shriek that Daniel was standing there.

"Dan! Finally! Get your clothes off and get in here!" He stood, displaying his red Speedos, which hugged his package and showed off his muscled body.

The other occupants of the hot tub turned and waved, and Dan recognized them all from the office. A web writer named Melody—no, Melanie—squealed, "Hi, Dan!"

Justin spread his toned arms. "Surprise!"

As anger and awful, sticky humiliation spread through him, Daniel could agree it sure as hell was.

Chapter Four

*A*WWWKWARD.

Tension radiated so powerfully off Daniel that Cole was amazed the heat of his fury didn't melt the snow in a radius around him. Everyone in the hot tub looked to be in their twenties and in various states of wastedness.

The porch rumbled with the bass of the music coming from inside, the massive windows actually rattling. Cole's head pounded mercilessly. He just wanted to go to bed, but clearly that had to wait.

A redheaded guy glared at the Speedo-wearer, who was presumably this Justin, Daniel's maybe-boyfriend or whatever. In a Quebecois accent, the redhead demanded, "Justin, what do you mean, surprise?" To Daniel, he called, "You didn't know we were coming for the weekend?"

The Asian girl in pigtails who had greeted Daniel excitedly now exchanged worried looks with the blond guy she was cuddled up with. She shouted to Justin, "Did you seriously not tell Dan we were coming?"

"It wouldn't be a surprise if I did!" Justin splashed out of the hot tub, grabbing a terrycloth robe and shoving his feet in flip-flops, hopping around. "Brrr, it's freezing!"

No shit, Sherlock. Justin was blond and lean and had six-pack abs. He was objectively handsome, but *ugh*. He was clearly a douche and a half. Cole found it hard to believe Daniel was dating him.

As Justin approached Daniel, he batted his eyes. "Come on, Mr. Grumpy. Warm me up. You'll have fun, I promise." He reached out.

Thank the *lord*, Daniel held him back with a firm hand on Justin's chest. "I don't think so. Turn that music off. It's way too loud."

Justin rolled his eyes. "Oh, come on. Take that stick out of your ass already. We're on vacation! Let's party!"

Daniel's nostrils flared, and Cole thought he might be about to witness a homicide. Completely justifiable homicide. Pushing past Justin to the sliding glass door, Daniel disappeared inside.

Again, Justin rolled his eyes and asked Cole, "Has he always been so uptight?"

Before Cole could tell him to go fuck himself, the music was silenced. In the sudden quiet, the hot tub bubbled, its motor a low hum. Fat snowflakes drifted down, the Christmas lights wrapped around the porch railing casting a warm, colorful glow. The forest and lake beyond seemed utterly still.

A brunette with long, damp curls and a halter bikini top belched, then laughed uproariously, along with Justin and another hairy dude. When the laughter died down, she said, "Justin, get me another beer."

Cole left them to it, following into the house. Daniel had left his boots by the door, and Cole did too, closing the sliding door behind him. The chalet was gorgeous—a vaulted ceiling, exposed beams, light pine wood everywhere. An interior stone accent wall contained a fireplace, where logs smoldered. Two of the exterior walls were largely glass. The kitchen was down a short corridor to the left, just after a staircase that presumably led up to bedrooms in the rear of the house.

Red, green, and gold Christmas decorations sat on shelves,

garlands and lights wrapping the railing on the staircase. Two gold stockings even hung from the mantle over the fireplace. There was a fresh pine tree filling the corner past the fireplace. The tree was bare, but boxes surrounded it. Decorations, presumably.

Had Justin arranged all that? Cole glanced back through the glass at where Justin was taking a hit off a joint, apparently utterly unconcerned that Daniel was furious with him. Nope. Seemed highly unlikely Justin had done anything thoughtful.

On socked feet, Cole approached Daniel, who stood at the foot of the stairs, still wearing his parka. From behind, Cole couldn't see his expression, the hood of his coat blocking his profile as well. He was stock still, fists clenched.

It seemed stupid to ask if he was okay. Instead, Cole said, "You used to hate being called Dan." Also stupid, but he had to say something.

The sliding door opened behind Cole, admitting the three people who hadn't seemed happy with Justin's surprise. As they approached, wrapped in towels, Daniel said, "I still do. I hate being called Dan."

The Asian girl stopped short. "Shit, seriously? But everyone at work calls you Dan."

Daniel turned and shrugged tightly. "Martin calls me that, so after a while I stopped trying to fight it."

"Oh." She smiled nervously at Cole. "Hi. You're Dan's— Daniel's brother? I'm Melanie." She motioned to the blond guy, who had slipped an arm around her wet shoulders. "This is my boyfriend Paul, and that's Jean-Luc."

The redhead nodded. "Bonjour."

"Hey. I'm not really Daniel's brother."

Melanie blinked. "Sorry. I thought Justin said…"

"We were stepbrothers ten years ago," Daniel said. "Not for very long. Anyway, to answer your question out there, no. I had no idea anyone would be here but Justin."

Paul groaned. "I had a bad feeling about this. Didn't I say that, Mel?"

"You did, babe." Through the glass, the other girl shrieked in the hot tub, and Melanie huffed. "Fucking Louise. She and Mike are idiots, but I figured they'd be fun to party with. Of course I also thought we were invited. Justin said you were totally cool with us coming up just for the weekend, and then you'd have your romantic vacation after."

Daniel practically vibrated. "Safe to say the romance is off."

"We will leave in the morning," Jean-Luc said. "And take Justin with us, yes?"

"Definitely." Daniel shrugged out of his coat and marched to the closet tucked into an alcove before the passage to the kitchen.

Cole winced as he struggled out of his. Melanie said, "Do you need help? God, the last thing you needed was more drama, huh? How are you feeling? What happened?" She peeled Cole's coat off his shoulders.

"I'm fine. Thanks. I tripped and fell. I'm a massive loser."

"You are not," Daniel snapped. He exhaled and softened. "I'll get you some more water." He disappeared into the kitchen.

Melanie whispered to Cole, "We'll just leave you guys to it."

Paul asked, "Are the keys still in the car? I'll get your bags."

"I think so? It's a keyless car, but all Daniel's stuff is in there, so it should be unlocked if the keys are in his bag."

Cole gave them an awkward little wave and followed into the kitchen, grateful that not everyone who'd crashed was an asshole. Daniel stood by the fridge, as if he was going to open it and forgot what he was doing. He muttered, "I'm such an idiot. CYC my ass."

"See…what?"

Daniel rubbed his face. "It's too moronic to even repeat."

Cole hated seeing Daniel beating himself up. "Maybe it'll help to talk about it. It might stop you from drowning your boyfriend in a hot tub."

"Oh, he is *so* not my boyfriend and never will be. Which I *knew*, but I kept telling myself to get out of my comfort zone and try new things."

"I have to admit he doesn't quite seem like your type. Unless your type has become dickbags."

Daniel laughed harshly. "One could argue it always was."

Man, what had gone so wrong with Trevor? Clearly now was not the time to ask, so Cole said, "It's not your fault."

"Of course it is!" Daniel spun to face him, opening his mouth to say more and stopping short. "Are you okay?"

Cole realized he was grimacing, the throb in his broken hand growing stronger, along with his headache. "Yeah. It just hurts."

"You need to rest. I know what to do, but I'll find a concussion checklist just in case." He pulled his phone from his pocket. "Crap, I need the wifi password. No service out here."

A young woman wearing a bikini with an open parka over it clomped into the kitchen. This was Louise, apparently. "The wifi works for shit. We're basically incommunicado out here."

Daniel barked, "Boots off in the house!"

Opening the fridge, she jumped, then looked down at her feet and back to Daniel. "It's not like it's your house. What do you care?"

"First off, it's rude to drip all over someone else's hardwood. Second, I'm the one paying for any damage, aren't I? Boots. Off. In. The. House."

"Okay, geez." Louise took a case of beer off the bottom shelf, heaving it up with a grunt and disappearing back outside.

"Fuck," Daniel muttered. There was a thick binder on the island that said *Welcome!* He flipped it open, presumably scanning it for the password. He tapped the screen and waited. And waited. "Shit. I can't check my work email if the wifi isn't connecting."

Cole refrained from reminding him he was supposed to be on

vacation now, since, to be fair, as vacations went this one sucked so far. Instead he asked, "Um, where should I sleep?"

Daniel rubbed his face. "You can take the master bedroom. I'll sleep on the couch or something."

Flip-flops slapping wetly, Justin appeared and gave Daniel a heavy-lidded look and sly smile. "Come on now, Grumpy. I thought *we* were taking the master."

"I thought we'd be here alone," Daniel snapped. "I thought a lot of things. Just in case it's not clear, whatever this was between us? Is done."

Eyes red from the pot, Justin rolled his tongue in his cheek and treated them to a textbook expression of bitchface. "Fine. I'll bunk in with Louise. You and your little brother can take the master." He turned on his heel and stalked off. *Slap-slap-slap.*

Cole couldn't believe the nerve of the asshole, but kept quiet. "If there's a king bed, I'm sure it'll be fine," he said, and not just because sharing a bed with Daniel was a wet dream come true after a decade.

"Right." Daniel exhaled forcefully. "Let's grab our stuff and check it out."

There was definitely a king bed—a mammoth that was almost as wide as Cole's living room. The duvet was a tasteful navy blue with faint pinstripes, the room decorated in brown and green accents. The same light pine hardwood seemed to run through the entire chalet.

Daniel took Cole's duffel off his shoulder and placed it by the long dresser with his suitcase. Then he gathered up Justin's things and threw them into the hallway.

Cole slipped into the bathroom, which was so big he almost had to go around a corner to spot the toilet beyond a shower stall and soaker tub. The long double vanity closest to the door was made of smooth granite. The tiles on the floor and shower were white and gray with navy accents, and every surface gleamed.

Bending over the near sink, Cole managed to splash water on his face with his right hand. When he stood straight, Daniel was there behind him, waiting with a towel. Heart thumping, Cole gave him a little smile. "Thanks." He dried his face. "I just want to brush my teeth and go to sleep."

"I'll get your stuff," Daniel said, returning shortly with Cole's battered and soap-stained toiletry bag. "Here, let me help you…"

Turning and leaning his butt against the counter, Cole lifted his good arm, concentrating on breathing evenly as Daniel stood close and peeled off his hoodie and tee, then undid his jeans. They pooled at Cole's feet, and he kicked them free before Daniel could kneel. Because if Daniel kneeled in front of him, Cole would spontaneously come in his underwear.

While Daniel went to grab Cole's PJs, Cole reached down with his right hand and stripped off his socks. Daniel returned with the plaid red and blue flannel and said, "Easier if you go shirtless, right?"

"Uh-huh." Cole's nipples were tight peaks even though the bathroom was warm, the floors heated beneath his bare feet. He stepped into the plaid flannel pajama bottoms, holding his breath as Daniel tied the drawstrings into a loose bow. "Thanks."

Cole turned back to the sink, unsurprised to glimpse in the mirror that his blush crept all the way down to his sternum. He managed to unzip his bag, but after a few attempts at uncapping the toothpaste with the tube wedged against his hip for leverage, he gratefully handed it to Daniel, who'd been waiting and watching.

Cole tried to laugh. "I really am helpless."

"Anyone would be. I'm sure you'll get the hang of stuff in the next few days." Daniel took out Cole's toothbrush and turned on the cold water to wet it before neatly squeezing a line of paste onto the bristles.

The next few days.

Pulse skittering, Cole shoved the toothbrush in his mouth, trying to hide a burst of giddiness that temporarily eclipsed the pain. In the morning, Justin and the others would leave, and it would be Cole and Daniel alone for a whole week.

A whole week when absolutely nothing romantic will happen, so slow your roll.

Cole rinsed, spitting into the sink and talking himself out of getting carried away. Surely nothing would ever happen between them, but still. Just being friends would be amazing.

While Daniel disappeared back into the bedroom, Cole managed to tug down his PJs and undies enough to piss on his own. *Victory!* He left the bathroom light on for Daniel, stopping short as he reentered the bedroom. Naked, Daniel faced the other direction as he bent over and stepped into black pajama bottoms that looked like they might be silk.

Thighs and buttocks flexing, he straightened, pulling up the pajamas, which sat low on his lean hips. A lamp on the bedside table sent warm light over Daniel's golden-brown skin, and Cole swallowed thickly, his throat gone dry.

As Daniel pulled on a white tee and turned, Cole hurried around to the far side of the bed closest to the door. He pulled back the duvet and carefully climbed in, praying his twitching dick would at least stay soft until he was hidden. It was so inappropriate to want him this badly when Daniel was only being kind, but he couldn't stop the desire heating his blood.

Daniel walked around the bed and put a tall glass of water on the side table. "Drink some of this. You'll note it's not in a plastic bottle."

Cole smiled. "Thanks."

"I'll wake you up in two hours and make sure you're okay."

He drank, then gingerly lay down and got settled on his back, trying to find just the right position so his hand didn't ache too much. The mattress was so wide he barely felt the dip when

Daniel got under the covers and switched off the lamp. There was about a foot gap between the dark curtains, casting just a little bit of light from outside.

The odd whoop and burst of laughter and chatter echoed up from the hot tub, but it was distant, the walls of the chalet clearly solidly built. From what Cole could glimpse through the window, it was still snowing and the moon had peeked through as midnight neared.

So. Here he was. In bed with Daniel Diaz. No big.

Amid the physical pain, his heart raced, skin tingling. He peeked at Daniel from the corner of his eye. Daniel was on his back too, staring at the ceiling. There were so many questions Cole wanted to ask, but now that he was in a big, fluffy bed—the mattress one of the awesome soft kinds like at hotels—he couldn't resist the undertow of sleep, his eyes closing as he gave up the fight.

"COLE. WAKE UP."

"Mmm." Cole groaned. He ached, and he just wanted to sleep. Why was there light? Who was he dreaming about? That deep voice was so familiar…

"Cole. Open your eyes."

He groaned. That voice sent a tingle to his balls. Almost sounded like Daniel. Where was that light coming from? Groaning again, he forced his eyes open, blinking up at someone who looked exactly like Daniel and—oh! It all flooded back with a jolt of adrenaline. They were sharing a bed at the chalet, and currently Daniel was right beside Cole on the mattress, leaning over him.

"What's your name?" he asked.

"Cole Smith. You're Daniel Diaz."

A smile tugged on Daniel's lips. "Yes, I am. I'm supposed to ask the questions before you answer. Where do you go to school?”

"Carleton, but my program is a joint thing with U of O. Can I have more water?"

Daniel leaned over him to get the glass, then helped Cole lift his head to sip. It was nuts to think that less than twenty-four hours ago, Cole had woken alone in his tiny apartment, ready for another day of research in the library.

Aunt Judy had invited him to spend the holidays with her family, but he hadn't wanted to blow his money on the flight to Winnipeg. So he'd opted to spend Christmas alone with his books and Netflix, and it was just *fine*.

But Cole had to admit it was a hell of a lot better waking up to his teenage fantasy in bed with him. He took another swig and shook his head when Daniel offered more water.

Daniel asked, "What are you studying?"

"Environmental Engineering. Specializing in water and wastewater treatment."

"Huh. That sounds really cool. You'll have to tell me about it when you're not concussed. How do you feel? Any dizziness or new symptoms?"

"I don't think so. Can I go back to sleep now?"

"Yep." Daniel rolled away and switched off the lamp, plunging the room into darkness.

"Wake up, Cole."

This time, Cole remembered where he was and why Daniel was there, a squiggly burst of excitement fluttering in his belly. He hurt, but it was wonderful to know he was safe and protected before he even opened his eyes.

Daniel's here. I'm okay.

Maybe it was crazy to feel that way when it had been ten years since he'd seen the guy, but he trusted Daniel. He wished he could burrow close and feel Daniel's arms around him.

That wasn't in the cards, so he pried his eyes open, blinking in the lamp's glare. Daniel helped him take two Tylenol and finish the glass of water, then drilled him on the basic facts of his life.

After, Daniel nodded and flicked off the light. "I'll set the alarm for three hours this time."

Exhaustion tugged dully at Cole along with the thudding pain, but he felt strangely awake. As his eyes became accustomed to the dark, he watched snow hit the narrow strip of visible window pane. Before he could talk himself out of it, he asked, "What did you mean before? About 'see why' something?"

In the hush, he wasn't sure Daniel would answer. Then Daniel replied, "Go back to sleep."

"I can't. Talk to me for a bit?"

Again, silence. Then after a few heartbeats, a sigh. Daniel rolled onto his back from where he'd been curled facing the window. He murmured, "It's an acronym. CYC. Change your cadence. I went to a stupid self-help seminar with my friend Pam. This ex-Marine wrote a book on it. Change your cadence—you know, change it up, do things differently. I figured I had nothing to lose by trying." He laughed scornfully. "Nothing but my dignity."

"Justin's the one with no dignity. You rented this amazing place for him and he takes advantage of that? Screw him."

Daniel was silent a few moments. "I just feel so stupid. I ignored all my instincts. Because of a *self-help* seminar."

"It could be worse. You could have joined a cult." Daniel's chuckle warmed him. *I made him laugh!* Cole added, "You could be wearing a toga right now or be preparing for the coming of our alien overlords."

Daniel laughed again. "I guess that's true."

"I've been told they'll be merciful. Mark me down as dubious, but willing to be convinced if the aliens look like Han Solo." He pondered it. "I guess all the humans in *Star Wars* are actually aliens, aren't they?"

"Of course. Anyone not from Earth is technically an alien. And I'm with you. Hot Han Solo aliens can stay." He was quiet for a few long moments. "Thanks, Cole. You grew up pretty cool."

I'm cool! Daniel Diaz thinks I'M COOL!

Cole cleared his throat. He wasn't thirteen anymore. He needed to rein it in. "Yeah. You too." He shifted to stretch the crick in his neck, wincing as pain shot up his arm, then back down again like a pinball machine of *ouch*.

Daniel was suddenly close, saying, "Are you okay?" In the darkness, Cole could just make out the gleam of his eyes and the concern clear in them. His belly flip-flopped. *He's only being nice. Don't read anything into it.*

Cole managed to smile. "I keep forgetting about my hand. Not sure how, since my whole arm throbs. On the bright side, I think my head hurts a little less. Or it's numb. Whichever."

"Right. Cool." Daniel scooted back to his side, and Cole told himself he was imagining that he was cold now. Still, he tugged up the duvet with his good hand.

Daniel said, "We should sleep."

"Mmm." Cole had so many more questions to ask, but his eyes were heavy, and he knew Daniel would be there in the morning.

Chapter Five

THE WEIRDEST THING about waking up in bed with his former stepbrother was how it didn't actually feel that weird.

Through the gap in the blackout curtains, pale light flowed into the room. On his side with his back to the windows, Daniel could make out Cole's slack face a couple of feet away on the huge bed. Cole had tried to roll onto his side a few times, hissing in pain before resettling on his back and falling asleep again. His head faced Daniel, and every so often he whimpered in his sleep.

The duvet had slipped down to his waist, but it was warm in the room. Cole's chest was smooth and surprisingly toned. His nipples were pinkish more than reddish—not that it mattered. Daniel didn't even know why he was thinking about it. He shook his head and reached over to gently tug up the duvet.

It was definitely surreal to be there with Cole. But not unpleasant. Daniel hadn't shared a bed with anyone since Trevor, platonically or otherwise. Cole was virtually a stranger, yet there was a level of comfort between them that must have been a product of living together years before.

He didn't remember much about Cole from the short period their parents were married. Daniel had known it wouldn't last, and he'd been eager to finish high school and get away. He didn't recall thinking much about Cole one way or the other.

But adult Cole was a good listener, and being holed up with

him was a refuge from Justin's assholery. Something about whispering in the dark during the night had dislodged a memory that kept playing through Daniel's head now.

The bathroom he and Cole had shared was sandwiched between their rooms with a door on each end. They'd kept the doors ajar, usually closing them when the bathroom was in use.

He got up to piss in the night, not needing to turn on the light as he padded to the toilet, and not bothering to close the doors. When he finished and tucked himself back into his boxers, a little voice called out.

"Daniel?"

He went to Cole's door and stuck his head through the gap. "Uh, yeah? You sick or something?"

In his twin bed under the Leafs posters plastering the walls, Cole sat up. "No. I just wanted to say I think you and Trevor are awesome. You're so brave."

Daniel blinked. "Oh." Shame burned his cheeks. He'd pretty much ignored the kid since their parents got together. "Um, thanks." He tried to think of something else to say, and went with, "You should go back to sleep."

It had been the night after Daniel had brought Trevor home for dinner and they'd announced they were gay and in love. Daniel could admit now that, deep down, he'd been hoping his mom and Cole's dad would freak out. It hadn't been about bravery at all, but a petulant desire to cause trouble.

Ugh. I was such an asshole.

His phone buzzed, and he reached over to touch Cole's good shoulder, barely grazing his skin. "Cole. Wake up." Cole murmured, and Daniel wriggled closer, reaching across to wrap his hand fully around Cole's shoulder. "Hey." He squeezed.

Cole opened his eyes with a start, tensing. "Huh?"

"Shh. It's okay." Daniel squeezed gently again, Cole's shoulder warm beneath his palm. "Time for your quiz. What's your name?"

He relaxed, yawning widely. "Cole Smith."

"Who's prime minister?"

"It better still be Justin Trudeau, or else I might welcome slipping into a coma."

Daniel chuckled. "How are you feeling?"

Cole groaned. "Okay, I guess. Can I have more Tylenol?"

"Sure." Daniel sat up and reached for the bottle and water he'd left on the nightstand. "What hurts? Still your head?"

"Yeah. It's a bit better, though. My hand is throbbing."

Daniel slipped his hand under Cole's neck and helped him swallow the tablets. Then he put a note in his phone of the time and dosage, adding in the dose from the middle of the night too. "One last question: How much of a douche was I to you when our parents were married?"

Cole blinked at him blearily, then rubbed his eyes with his right hand. "You were fine. Don't worry about it."

"Ugh. That means I was a *total* douche, doesn't it? Was I ever nice to you?" He curled on his side under the duvet.

After a few moments of silence, Cole said, "It's not like you were *mean*. You just ignored me most of the time. I get it. You were pissed you had to move into our house and change schools. But after you and Trevor got together and came out, you were less angry."

That sounded about right. The thought of Trevor's bright smile and shaggy blond hair were a dull knife between his ribs even after so many years. Especially when he remembered how thrilling it had been when they'd first kissed and made out in the locker room after one-on-one practice on the rink. Trevor had seemed perfect for him. It had been four years before Daniel realized how wrong he'd been.

"I'm sorry I wasn't nicer. And I'm sorry I didn't help you. You know, about being queer."

"But you did. It's because of you I figured it out." In the pale dawn light, Cole's cheeks flushed. "I mean because you came out and were so bold. So brave."

Daniel snorted. "Trust me, I wasn't as brave as I seemed."

"It took guts to come out in high school. You and Trevor were so out and proud and all that. Once you decided to do something, you did it all the way."

"I guess. I was terrified at first when we walked down the hall at school holding hands. But aside from a few jerks, everyone took it in stride. Even our parents did. My mom joined PFLAG, like, the next day."

Cole smiled. "That's Claudia for you. And yeah, my dad's been cool. My mom was great." His eyes took on a faraway, pensive look, but before Daniel could offer any clumsy sympathy, Cole rubbed his face and said, "Anyway. Don't worry about the past. You're more than making up for any douchiness now since I'm crashing your getaway. Although I guess I've got lots of company in the crashing department."

Daniel grimaced. "Indeed."

"I think you might have to schedule some term meetings in the new year," Cole teased.

"Now there's a tempting thought." The house was still and silent, but soon enough he could wake up Justin and the others and send them packing. "I'll let them sleep a little while longer, and then they're out of here."

"Yeah? I wasn't sure if you'd have second thoughts once you cooled off." He quickly added, "Not that you shouldn't be mad. Or that you should have second thoughts."

"Like you said, once I make a decision, I don't back down. They can go party somewhere else. Melanie, Paul, and Jean-Luc seem cool, but I still want them all gone."

"Uh-huh. Totally. So it'll just be you and me, I guess."

Daniel hadn't really thought about it. "I guess so." Strangely enough, the thought of spending the week with Cole sent a bloom of warmth through his chest. "Is that okay with you?"

"Of course!" Cole's voice was doing that squeaky thing. He cleared his throat. "I mean, yeah. Sure. This place is amazing. I can't wait to see it in the daylight."

"Speaking of which…" Daniel threw back the duvet and went to the window, tugging up his silk pajama bottoms where they'd slipped down to his hips and scratching his chest under his T-shirt. He pulled the curtains open, blinking into the light. For a moment, he stared in puzzlement at the unending wall of whiteness. Then his stomach dropped.

"Oh, fuck me."

ARMS CROSSED, DANIEL stood by the massive windows on the side of the chalet facing the driveway. Beside him, Justin shifted nervously and said, "I don't think the minivan will even make it to the road until the plow comes. Jean-Luc's mom only has all-seasons on it, not snow tires. Crazy, I know, but she hardly drives in winter, apparently."

At least Justin seemed a little remorseful in the light of day—and now that he was sober. He peered up at the sky, which still unleashed a steady snowfall. "It doesn't look like it's stopping any time soon."

Behind them, Melanie said, "My weather app says snow all day. A hundred percent chance. We might have to stay with you and your brother if we can't get out of here."

"He's not my brother," Daniel and Cole said in unison.

Cole joined them at the windows, still in his flannel PJ bottoms but with a green sweatshirt on now. It was roomy enough for his cast, the orange and white sticking out, his fingertips barely showing.

Jean-Luc approached. "I just called every hotel in Tremblant on the landline. They're all full."

Unsurprising since it was Christmas vacation. Daniel gritted his teeth. "I guess you guys are staying until tomorrow."

Jean-Luc said, "Thanks, Dan." He glared at Justin. "We really had no idea we weren't invited."

"It's Daniel," Cole said. "He hates being called Dan."

"*Merde*!" Jean-Luc shook his head. "I forgot."

Daniel gave Cole a little smile, then said, "It's okay. After a while, I stopped fighting it at work."

Justin sidled closer. "Should I call you Danny instead?"

"No." Daniel gave him what he thought of as a full Death-Star glare.

With a big sigh, Justin actually *pouted*. "I said I'm sorry. Are you going to be grumpy all day?"

Melanie said, "Dude, I don't blame you. But hey, let me wake up Paul and we can make breakfast. His French toast is to die for."

Daniel groaned. "Shit. I was going to head into the village today to buy food."

"No worries! Paul and I brought challah and maple syrup. And bacon, of course," she added eagerly. "And the cupboards have a lot of staples, and there are chicken fingers and burgers someone must have left behind. Jean-Luc brought a bunch of chips too. Oh, and there's a whole jar of popcorn, and plenty of oil. We definitely won't starve. I did a mental inventory last night. I really like food."

Daniel exhaled. There was no sense in being pissed at her when she was trying so hard to be kind. If she, Paul, and Jean-Luc were lying about not knowing they hadn't been invited, they were pretty good actors.

He said, "Cool. Thanks, Melanie. If you guys could make breakfast, that would be great."

"We're on it." She gave him a thumbs-up and scurried off.

"You know, we can still have fun." Justin slid his hand up Daniel's arm.

Jerking away, Daniel headed for the kitchen. "We're definitely never having *that* kind of fun again." His skin crawled.

Bleary, barrel-chested Mike, shuffling downstairs, muttered, "Never say never. Justin will do anything to win a bet." He ran a hand through his mop of brown hair.

Daniel skidded to a stop, his socks sliding a few inches on the wood. The sticky, itchy ball of mortification that had taken up residence in his gut the night before spread its fingers wide. He turned to face Justin, who was shooting eye-daggers at Mike at the bottom of the stairs. Cole and Jean-Luc watched from the windows.

Daniel gritted out, "What does that mean?"

With a careless roll of his eyes, Justin answered, "Louise bet me I couldn't bag you. I told her I already did in the parking lot, but she's dubious."

Icy rage slithered down Daniel's spine. "Bag me."

"You know, take that giant stick up your ass and replace it with my dick? Or you could fuck me." He waved a hand. "Whichever."

It had been a *bet*.

Just when Daniel thought he couldn't be more humiliated. His face burned, and he wished the hardwood floor would crack open and swallow him whole.

Mel and Paul descended the stairs, and Mel asked, "What's going on?"

Justin opened his stupid, ugly, hateful mouth, but then Cole said, "Daniel, I feel sick. Can you take me upstairs?"

"Oh, you poor thing!" Mel fussed over Cole as Daniel forced his feet to move. Left, right, left right. He grasped Cole's good arm and led him up the stairs, glad for the warmth under his fingers, ice and fire battling in Daniel's veins. From below, Justin snickered and voices murmured, and Daniel wanted to scream.

He didn't. He walked Cole back into the master bedroom,

closing the door behind them. Managing to keep his voice even, he asked, "Are you nauseous?"

"Yes, but only because of that piece of shit downstairs."

Daniel exhaled, the ice melting in a rush of gratitude, embarrassment still simmering. "Thanks for getting me out of there. God, you must think I'm pathetic."

Cole's thin brows drew together. "No, I think he's a massive loser. A ginormous one. Humongous. Monumental. Colossal. Mammoth." He seemed to ponder. "Whopping. Gigantic. Supersized loser."

A little laugh bubbled up, and Daniel took a deep breath. "Thanks."

"I play Words with Friends a lot."

Daniel's smile faded. "I don't know how I let myself get snowed by him."

"A snake like that? I bet he can be pretty charming when he wants to be. And it's easy to see what you want to see. Especially…"

After a few moments, Daniel asked, "What?"

"Especially if you're lonely."

He wanted to argue, even opened his mouth and sucked in air, but the denial wouldn't come. "I really am pathetic."

"No, he is. Do you want me to list some other synonyms to describe how truly lame that jerk is?

"It's okay. But thanks."

"You know, I think there's a *Star Wars* marathon on this week. They're showing the movies over and over on TBS." He nodded to the flat-screen TV on the wall across from the bed. "We could check out where they're at in the cycle."

It sounded like the best idea ever proposed in the history of the world. But Cole didn't need to shut himself away to keep Daniel company. "The doctor said you didn't have to stay in bed."

"But she didn't say I couldn't." He flopped back onto the

mattress, then grimaced. "Note to self: still need to ease into things."

Daniel propped up several pillows behind Cole, then turned on the TV. Cole said, "Uh, you might want to keep a pillow for yourself."

"Nah. Headboard's padded. I'm good. Are you hungry?"

"A little?"

There was a tentative knock on the door. Daniel answered it, finding Melanie biting her lip. "Hey. Is Cole okay?"

"Yeah, but I think we're just going to chill in here. He needs to rest, and I'm going to take care of him."

"Totally. I'll make sure we stay quiet downstairs. No music. We'll hang in the hot tub and stay out of your hair. If that's okay?"

"Of course."

Her face creased. "Jean-Luc said something about a bet? We really didn't know about that. I'm sorry, Dan. *Daniel!* Shit, I'm going to get that right. I promise."

"It's okay." He gave her a smile. "I appreciate you trying."

"Do you guys want breakfast? I saw some trays in the kitchen. We can bring it up."

"Thanks. That's really nice of you."

She shook her head, waving him off. "It's the least I can do to make up for that douche. Paul and I are done hanging out with him and his lackeys. Jean-Luc too. We're getting too old for this shit."

She quizzed him and Cole on their breakfast preferences, and Daniel shut the door again. He went to grab his phone from the other side of the bed. He asked Cole, "Is the light too much? Do you want me to close the curtains?"

"I think I'm good. My head really does feel better. I'll let you know if that changes."

"Cool. I think the symptoms can come and go with a concussion." He tapped his phone. "I'd Google it, but the wifi definitely isn't connecting."

He glanced down at his PJs. Normally by this time he'd have worked out, showered, dressed, and would be behind his desk. He tried to connect again. No dice. "It's so weird that I'm not at work right now."

"It's Saturday."

"Oh, right. Well, I'd be working at home."

"Also you're on vacation and your office is closed. Right?"

Familiar irritation sparked. "*Yes*, but there's always something to do."

Cole watched him impassively, apparently not intimidated at all. "Yeah, of course there is. And it'll get done after the holidays. The world won't end."

"I know, I know. I work too much. I care about what I do, okay? It's important to me."

Cole still watched him with a dubious expression. "Yeah, I don't care at *all* about my thesis."

"That's not what I mean."

"Then what do you mean?" Cole asked calmly. "That people who aren't workaholics don't care about their jobs?"

"No! I just..." *Don't have anything else.* "I'm just used to checking my email and staying on top of things so tasks don't pile up. That's all." It sounded weak even to him.

"Well, I guess you'll be CYCing on that front whether you like it or not." Cole smiled tentatively.

The tension released, and Daniel had to laugh. "I guess I will."

Cole nodded to the TV, where lightsabers clashed. "We're in luck. Episode three is almost over, so we're just in time for the movies that don't suck."

Daniel went around to his side of the bed, noticing Cole had put two of the pillows back for him. He got settled and looked at the screen. "Oh, I think Padme's about to die of a broken heart."

Cole huffed. "I hate that. I mean, she just had two babies who need her. And now she dies of a broken heart because of that whiny dickbag Anakin? She was tougher than that."

"*Thank you.* I hate that too."

"And don't get me started on Hayden Christensen's acting in these movies."

Daniel put on a vacant, flat voice, imitating the most famous cringe-worthy line of dialogue. "I don't like sand. It's coarse and rough and irritating and it gets everywhere."

Cole's face lit up as he burst out laughing. "Don't make me laugh too hard! I have a concussion, you know."

Yet as they ate French toast and bacon—Cole insisting his stomach could take it—and watched Princess Leia and R2-D2 huddle, Daniel wanted to make him laugh again and again so he could see the little dimple that creased his left cheek.

"IF YOU'RE HAVING second thoughts we can just stay in here all night," Cole said. "It's fine by me."

Daniel pulled a soft charcoal sweater over his head, tugging it gently to make sure it wasn't wrinkled. "I know, but I want to prove that he doesn't bother me. That I couldn't care less."

"I totally get it."

"You can stay here, though. Rest." Daniel secretly hoped Cole would come downstairs. He'd feel better not being alone. Not that he'd be *alone* with six other people, but… "Seriously, I can handle it."

Cole was still in his PJs and sweatshirt. "I napped enough for today. I'm still pissed I slept through the first half of Empire."

"We'll catch it when it comes around again tomorrow. Or the next day. No rush." They'd have the rest of the week together—a prospect Daniel found increasingly appealing. He could admit his mom was right—he should have reached out to Cole months ago.

The driveway had finally been plowed by an apologetic man in a pickup truck hired by the chalet owners, and the main roads had been cleared. Come the morning, he and Cole would be blissfully alone. Daniel had been awfully tempted to kick the others out the nanosecond the driveway had been scraped clean, but they'd been drinking.

He eyed himself in the long mirror standing in the corner, smoothing down his damp curls. He'd showered and shaved and splashed on cologne. Which was all profoundly stupid, but a spark of pride blazed.

"You look great," Cole said. "Let's do this. Show that dick what he's missing out on."

Head high, Daniel led the way, making sure Cole was okay on the stairs. The others lounged on the leather couches near the fireplace. They'd apparently had enough hot-tubbing for the moment and wore sweats and T-shirts. This was going to be just fine. He'd show Justin he wasn't bothered or hurt at all. He'd—

"Dare," Melanie said. "I guess."

Daniel's stomach dropped. He'd apparently be joining in a game of truth or dare. He couldn't retreat now that everyone had spotted him. With Cole at his side, he walked on and took a seat like there was nothing the matter at all. Nope. Nothing the matter here. Cold and dead inside and utterly unruffled.

"Hey!" Jean-Luc grinned. "Feeling better, Cole? You guys want beer?"

"Much," Cole answered. "Thanks. And no, I can't drink for a few days until I'm sure my head's clear."

"You're going to have to put up with Mr. Grumpy sober?" Justin winced. "*Vaya con dios.*"

Mike groaned. "Enough, dude. You lost the bet. Deal. Are we playing or what?" He gulped from his bottle of beer.

"I dare you to kiss me," Paul said to Melanie, who sat on the floor between the coffee table and the couch, leaning back between his knees.

She rolled her eyes and lifted her face for a peck. Then she said, "Cole, you want to go?"

Daniel was about to insist that Cole was under no obligation to play these reindeer games, but Cole lifted his cast and said, "I can't really do many dares right now. Truth, I guess."

Justin's blue eyes gleamed, his expression one of faux innocence. "Just how big of a boner did you have for Daniel when you were kids?"

Cole stammered, going beet red. Melanie, Paul, and Jean-Luc groaned, while Louise shrieked with laughter and Mike chugged more beer. Rage slammed through Daniel like a tidal wave. How *dare* Justin pick on Cole? Daniel had never been one for violence, but the idea of punching Justin's smug face burned.

He managed to contain it, gritting out, "Don't be ridiculous."

Melanie shook her head. "You're so gross, Justin."

Chugging his beer, Justin shrugged. "You're the ones who keep insisting you're not brothers."

"We're not! That doesn't mean we'd ever…" Daniel grimaced, furious denial surging. He and Cole would never get together! They weren't brothers, but it would still be inappropriate as hell.

Wouldn't it?

As Justin howled with laughter, images of being with Cole flashed through Daniel's mind. Kissing Cole, touching his skin, pressing their bodies together—

What the fuck is wrong with me?

Paul said to Justin, "I really don't know why you and your minions have to be such turds. Didn't I tell you, Mel? No hot tub is worth this."

Daniel's mind spun. He should have been horrified to think of Cole that way—or at the very least, unmoved. Yet his balls tingled, the fire of his initial denial transforming. It wasn't possible. He hadn't felt a connection to anyone in years, and now…with *Cole*?

He glanced at Cole, whose face was creased with what looked like pain. Pushing aside his confusion, Daniel asked him, "Do you need more Tylenol?"

Cole shook his head and dropped his gaze as Jean-Luc said, "My turn. Dare me."

Mike belched and suggested, "Strip naked, go outside, and make a snow angel."

"Is that all you've got?" Jean-Luc rolled his eyes as he stood. He took off all his clothes, leaving them in a pile.

Daniel tried desperately to focus on Jean-Luc's antics instead of the entirely inappropriate bolt of desire for Cole. It was crazy to feel that. He was just all worked up and confused because of Justin.

Right?

Everyone got up to watch from the windows as Jean-Luc skipped outside, and Daniel followed, forcing a laugh as Jean-Luc flopped into the snow, yelping as he flapped his arms and legs. Cole's smile was strained, and Daniel leaned close to him.

Be normal. Everything is normal.

He asked Cole, "Sure you don't need more Tylenol?"

Cole kept his gaze on Jean-Luc, who was now sprinting along the porch and back inside. "Nah. Thanks." His voice was even.

Everything's fine. Totally normal. Nothing to see here but the naked dude I work with.

Jean-Luc shook his body and hurried to the fireplace, apparently utterly unashamed by his nudity. He took a towel from Melanie and narrowed his gaze at Mike. "Your turn. Truth or dare?"

Only a fool would choose dare at that point, so of course Mike lifted his chin and said, "Dare."

Daniel had to confess he didn't mind at all when Mike had to shave off his chest hair, whining the whole time.

"HEY, BABE."

Daniel groaned internally at the kitchen sink where he was rinsing dishes. The others had gone back into the hot tub, and Cole had retreated upstairs to rest. Daniel just wanted to clean up and join him.

Because I want to make sure he's okay. Not because I want to jump him or anything.

Apparently he'd have to deal with more of Justin's bullshit first. He turned and affected a bored expression as Justin sidled closer, a gleam in his eyes, wearing only a towel wrapped around his hips and possibly his teeny-tiny Speedo underneath. Justin displayed his lean muscles and ripped abs, his chest puffed out like he was on a catwalk.

Daniel couldn't believe he'd ever found Justin anything but absolutely repellent. He was never CYCing to that degree again. Nope. His cadence was just fine.

His lower back jammed against the counter, and while he could have shoved Justin away, he didn't want to show that he was bothered at all. He waited to see what game Justin was playing now.

"You know, we could still have a lot of fun tonight." Justin dropped his hand to Daniel's crotch and squeezed.

"But we won't." He felt nothing but contempt. "I need to go up and check on Cole, so if you're done here..." He made a flicking motion with his hand.

Spine stiffening, Justin let go. Then his face twisted and he practically bared his too-white teeth. "Oh yes, go check on your precious Cole. Who is totally into you, by the way. I know you're retarded when it comes to sex, but—"

"Don't use that word, asshole."

"What, 'sex'? You really *are* a prude. You should know that when we hooked up in your car, I hadn't worked so hard to give a guy a blow job in…ever."

He shrugged. "Not my fault your technique is lacking."

Justin jolted as if he'd been slapped. "I'll have you know my technique is *legendary!*"

Ignoring that, Daniel's mind caught up to the rest of what Justin had said before. "And you've been smoking too much grass if you think Cole—"

"Would jump on your dick in a heartbeat if you let him? Trust me, Danny. You know, I could help you poor guys out. The three of us could have *such* a good time. Loosen up already."

Now Daniel did shove him away, jagged-edged memories of Trevor spinning through his mind. "Fuck you." Chest tight, he concentrated on keeping his voice even. *I'm cold and dead inside. I'm not supposed to get upset.* "You're leaving in the morning if you have to walk to town."

With that, he stalked past Justin out of the kitchen, the buzz of anger in his head blocking out whatever taunts Justin was hurling after him. At the foot of the stairs, he met Jean-Luc, who curled his lip scornfully as he glared toward the kitchen.

"We'll leave tomorrow for sure. We've all had enough of him. Well, maybe not Louise and Mike, but they can have him. You know, maybe we can hang out sometime in the new year? You're a good guy, Dan. *Daniel.* Sorry."

Daniel exhaled a long breath and gave him a little smile. "It's okay. And that would be cool."

Mel called from the doorway to the hot tub enclosure. "Guys, come taste this."

His muscles unclenching bit by bit, Daniel followed Jean-Luc over, hoping Justin would see how unbothered Daniel was. *That's me. Completely unfazed. Cold and dead inside.*

Mel held out a beer bottle, and Jean-Luc said, "We've tasted Moosehead before."

She rolled her eyes. "Yeah, but I added something."

Jean-Luc took the bottle and lifted it to his lips. His eyebrows shot up, and he took another sip. "Is that…maple syrup? It's actually good!" He held out the bottle to Daniel.

Raising his hands, Daniel said, "I'm good. That sounds disgusting."

Mel called, "Cole, how about you? Want to try my new beer recipe?"

Heart skipping, Daniel turned to see Cole about to go into the kitchen. Cole answered, "I still can't drink right now, but thanks!" He disappeared around the bend.

Shit, was Justin still in there? Daniel hurried after Cole. He wouldn't put it past Justin to—

"I tried to help you out, sweetie. I suggested we do a three-way, but Dan just isn't into you at all."

"I swear to God, if you don't shut your fucking mouth, you're sleeping in the snow," Daniel roared. Justin jumped, spinning around and shrinking back gratifyingly.

Justin lifted his hands. "Okay, okay. So touchy." To Cole he added, "Don't say I didn't try, sugar!" He skirted around the island and disappeared.

Cole stood frozen by the fridge. After a few beats, he asked, "Are you okay?"

Fists clenched, blood rushed in Daniel's ears. "Yeah," he bit out. "Do you need something? More water?"

Trevor's voice echoed through his mind: *Threesomes are hot. Come on, loosen up.*

Cole opened the fridge. "I wanted a little juice." He took out the OJ container.

Daniel hurried over to unscrew the cap and pour him a glass. Cole took it and said, "Thanks. I'll just…" He motioned toward the stairs with an awkward wave.

Nodding, Daniel followed. The sooner he went to sleep, the sooner morning could come and Justin would be gone.

Chapter Six

INHALING AND EXHALING forcefully, Daniel shook his head, leaning against the closed bedroom door. "I can't believe I ever thought for a second I liked that guy," he muttered. "*Threesome.* He should get together with Trevor."

Cole had been about to switch on the lamp, but he froze, hand in midair. Would Daniel talk to him, or should he leave him be?

Daniel snapped up straight as if just realizing what he'd said. He strode toward the bathroom. "I'm going to have a shower. You need anything?"

"What happened with Trevor?" After a few moments of silence, Daniel hovering in the bathroom doorway, silhouetted by the light beyond, Cole added, "I know you don't want to talk about it. But maybe you should?" Cole was definitely curious, but there truly seemed to be a well of pain there that hunched Daniel's shoulders and haunted his eyes.

Daniel turned and leaned against the door jamb. His face was in shadow. Cole sat on the end of the bed facing him. Giving him some distance, but listening. Waiting.

After what felt like an eternity, Daniel quietly asked, "What do you remember about Trevor?"

"Hmm. Well, after you and your mom moved in with us, you had to switch schools. You joined the hockey team and met Trevor. You guys hung out a lot. Then that one night you brought him to dinner and came out. School ended, and you both went to Western in the fall. Claudia moved out just before Thanksgiving, and even though I saw her sometimes, I never saw you again. Until now. Obviously."

Cole wiped his palms on his flannel PJ bottoms. He wasn't sure why he was nervous—it was Daniel's story to tell.

Daniel crossed his arms, the warm light from the bathroom outlining his left side—broad shoulder, then narrowing down to his slim hip and long leg. "Right. So things with Trev were great for a few years. I was so in love with him. I felt like… Like he really *got* me. We could finish each other's sentences. That kind of shit. You know what I mean?"

"Theoretically. I dated guys in university, but I never felt like that." *Never felt the way I do for you.*

"It's a real rush. Like I said, everything was great. At least I thought it was." He was silent a few moments. "We had an apartment off-campus. Never lived on campus. In our fourth year, there was a big dorm party Trevor wanted to go to. We usually hung out at the pub and stuff, so it was weird that he was so insistent on going. But I wanted to make him happy, so I went."

Cole realized he was holding his breath. He exhaled and murmured, "Okay."

"Anyway, we got pretty loaded, and it was fun and all. I was ready to go home and crash, but there was this guy Trevor knew. Alex. Alex said he had vodka in his room, and Trevor wanted to do a couple shots. So I went."

"To make Trevor happy."

"Yeah." Daniel swallowed audibly, a sort of click in the stillness of the room. If the others were making noise, it didn't penetrate the walls. The curtains were drawn, and it was like they were in a little cave.

Cole felt like he had to whisper. "What happened?"

"God, it's so stupid. You're going to think it's nothing and that I'm a massive drama queen. Maybe I am."

"No, of course—"

"Long story short, Trevor wanted to have a threesome with Alex. I said yes, because he wanted it. It was fine. And I figured Trevor would get it out of his system, and we could just go back to normal. To being…us."

Cole winced. "But that didn't happen."

Daniel's laugh was humorless. "Nope. So we had more three-somes. We went to a bathhouse. Trevor wanted sex with all these random people, and I just *didn't*. And it's not like there's anything wrong with that." He groaned. "I probably sound like such a judgmental asshole. Threesomes and anonymous hookups and all that are totally great for other people. If it floats your boat, go for it."

Was that a question? Should I answer? "It's not really my thing either. But yeah, to each their own and all that." Cole could sense Daniel's laser gaze in the darkness. He still leaned in the doorway, his face shadowed.

After a few moments, Daniel asked, "Are you just saying that to make me feel better?"

"No! I mean, I get turned on by hot guys, and I've had some bathroom hand jobs and stuff. Fucked some guys on the first date. But I want more than that now." *I want you. I've always wanted you.*

"I know most people can get super turned on by strangers, but I never have. When Justin pursued me and blew me, I really wasn't that into it, but I wanted to make him happy." He snorted. "And I was trying to CYC. So he sucked me and it was fine and everything. I…" He shook his head. "I'm sorry, you don't want to hear all this crap. I should save it for my shrink. Or actually get a shrink first, I guess."

"No, I want to listen. I mean, if you want to tell me. No pres-sure."

Daniel's intent gaze made Cole's skin go hot. "I don't know why I'm unloading all this."

"Because Justin's dickishness stirred up a bunch of feelings?"

"I guess so. I'm supposed to be cold and dead inside."

"Wait, what? Why is that?"

Daniel waved his hand, cutting through the light from the bathroom. "It's a joke I have with my friend Pam. How I can be…stoic a lot of the time. And…a workaholic."

Cole kept his tone light. "Admitting it is the first step."

"Yeah, yeah," Daniel grumbled, but there was no heat to it. After a few moments, he said, "I don't know what's wrong with me. I'm usually much more…contained."

A thrill whipped through Cole that he was peeking beneath the mask. "It's okay to come undone sometimes."

"I guess. Lucky you, huh? We haven't seen each other in ten years and now you get a front-row seat to my nervous breakdown. I'm a workaholic freak who doesn't like casual sex the way I'm supposed to."

"You are *not* a freak. Fuck anyone who says you're *supposed* to like anything."

"But I'm missing some element that other people have. Especially guys. It's like, I'm supposed to want to go clubbing and have orgies, and I just…don't."

"There's nothing wrong with that. I have a friend who's demi, and there's nothing wrong with her."

"Demi?"

"Demisexual. Basically she's only really attracted to someone if she cares about them."

Daniel pushed off the wall, taking a step toward the bed. He stopped. "I didn't know there was a name for that."

"Oh yeah, there's a name for everything now."

"Huh." He came to sit on Cole's left. "I didn't realize that was a thing. But it's not as if I'm not attracted to people. I mean, I can appreciate a good-looking guy. Admire his body and think that he's hot. I like looking at Chris Hemsworth and his abs. But I don't want to *actually* bang him. Not that that's the only thing standing between me and Chris Hemsworth."

Cole laughed. "I know what you mean."

"So do I fit this demisexual thing?"

"I don't think there's only one right way to be demi. It sounds like you might identify with it, but I can't tell you yes or no. That's up to you. I can ask my friend Julia if she has links to any good blogs if you want?"

"Thanks. That would be cool." Daniel was silent a minute as they sat there, and Cole could practically hear his mind working. Then Daniel blurted, "I really like sex! I'm not a prude."

"I know. I believe you. It's okay. It really is." He could not think much more closely on Daniel and sex, his belly tightening with a bolt of desire. He ached to hold Daniel close and comfort him, but part of him—the part that had been horny for Daniel for years—wanted so much more.

Rein it in, asshole. Not now. Not that there ever *will be a right time, but it definitely isn't now.*

"I can't believe I'm talking about this." Daniel rubbed his face. "I really am losing it."

"I think we should all be talking about it more. It sucks that we feel this pressure from society to conform. Like, all gay men are supposed to be promiscuous? Fuck that. Gay men are not the Borg. No one is. Everyone gets to be who they are."

"This demi thing is blowing my mind. I thought I was weird all these years."

"Well, you are, but not because of this." As soon as the words were out, Cole cringed internally. Was joking really the right approach?

But Daniel snorted and said, "Yeah, yeah," as he elbowed him. Cole sucked in a breath, pain radiating from his upper arm down to his hand. "Shit!" Daniel exclaimed. "Are you okay?"

He pressed his lips together, inhaling. "Mmm-hmm." Opening his mouth, he blew out the breath, relaxing. "It's just all a little sensitive. I'm okay."

"You sure?" Daniel's hand hovered over Cole's shoulder, as if he was afraid to touch and hurt him more. Cole was dying to tell him to go ahead, but he resisted.

"Yep." Time to focus back on Daniel. "So, about Trevor. Obviously you guys broke up in the end. What went down? Unless you don't want to talk about it anymore."

Only an inch separated them, and Cole wished he could rest his palm on Daniel's thigh. Just to ground him. But even if Cole's hand wasn't broken, he wouldn't do it anyway.

The image of Daniel's face after Justin's taunts about them hooking up was seared into Cole's mind. Wide-eyed shock and fury, and a grimace of what had to be disgust. Daniel had made it clear he was outraged at the mere idea, and Cole wasn't about to cross any lines—especially given the story Daniel was telling. Sounded like crossing lines was Trevor's specialty, and Cole would *not* be that guy.

Daniel was still silent, and Cole added, "Seriously, you don't need to tell me."

"I…" His shoulders relaxed a fraction. "I guess it's good to talk about it. I know you won't go blabbing. I trust you."

Cole's heart skipped, and he watched Daniel's profile from the corner of his eye, the bathroom light on his face. "I trust you too."

When Daniel looked at him with a tiny smile tugging at his lips and a dark curl hanging over his forehead, Cole thought his heart might swell too big for his body and explode. As a kid, he'd been in love with Daniel yet hadn't really known him. Or known what love really was. Maybe he still didn't, but his gut told him this was it.

Which meant he was royally screwed.

Daniel turned his head back to stare off toward the bathroom, his gaze unfocused, and Cole looked forward as well. He waited. There was something more to the story—something he had a feeling was going to make him hate Trevor Chartrand with every fiber of his being.

When Daniel spoke, his deep voice was steady. "So I went along with the threesomes and stuff because I figured if Trevor needed that, then I'd do what it took to make him happy. Satisfied. We still had sex just the two of us, and I didn't feel like anything had changed there. Then I found out Trevor had been hooking up with guys behind my back pretty much since we went away to school."

"That asshole!" Cole cleared his throat and lowered his voice. "Sorry."

"Don't be. He is an asshole. He cheated on me for years, then figured if he brought me into experimenting with other guys, I'd be converted or something. Like I'd see that monogamy isn't possible. That it's only for straight people. That kind of bullshit. He made it my fault, like…" Dropping his head, Daniel's voice went husky. "Like there was something wrong with me. For a long time, I guess I thought there was."

Forgetting his cast, Cole reached out abortively. With a grunt of frustration, he got up and sat on Daniel's other side, taking hold of his shoulder. "There is *nothing* wrong with you. Trevor's an asshole and he can go fuck himself."

Daniel's eyes gleamed in the half-darkness, and he swiped at them, laughing. "But how do you really feel? Don't hold back."

Cole laughed too. "I could go on. There are some extremely colorful expletives I could use."

"Thanks, man." He took a long breath and blew it out. "I haven't really talked about all that stuff. Sorry for dumping it on you. I'm supposed to be taking care of you, not the other way around."

Cole squeezed his shoulder. "I'm not a kid anymore." He smoothed his palm behind Daniel's neck, longing to run his fingers through the ends of the soft curls. Instead he slapped him on the back like a buddy would and dropped his hand. "We can take care of each other."

Shattering glass echoed up from downstairs, followed by Mel screaming, "For fuck's sake, Justin!"

In unison, Cole and Daniel huffed. Cole said, "Speaking of people who can go fuck themselves."

"Indeed."

They sat in silence for a minute. There was so much Cole wanted to say, but he didn't know where to start. Instead, he said, "I feel kind of gross. I don't think I'm ready to attempt a shower yet with this thing, but I think a sponge bath is in order. Can you help me?"

Daniel blinked at him, mouth opening and closing. "You want me to give you a sponge bath?"

"No!" Cole's cheeks went hot, and he was glad it was probably too dark to see his blush. "I just mean if you could unscrew the bottle of body wash and help me take off my sweatshirt? I tried earlier and almost strangled myself." He forced a laugh that was too high-pitched.

"Oh, right. Totally!" Daniel sprang up and hurried into the bathroom.

Cole followed. "Sorry to be a pain."

"No, not at all!" Daniel kept his head down as he turned on the taps at the sink. "Do you want to just do it here with a washcloth or whatever?"

"Yeah. That's great."

In the mirror, Cole could glimpse the faint rosy hue on Daniel's cheeks. Clearly Daniel was embarrassed after his confessions, and Cole wanted to say something to reassure him, but would probably just make it worse. He went to the floating shelves on the far wall and picked out a facecloth from the piles of plush, navy-blue towels.

Daniel had plugged one of the sinks and apparently squeezed in half the bottle of body wash given the mountain of bubbles forming. He turned to Cole and motioned with his hand. "So you need help with stuff?"

Cole dropped the facecloth on the counter by the filling sink. "Thanks. If you can just..." He held his right arm up over his head, holding still as Daniel pulled up the hem of Cole's sweatshirt, his fingertips brushing Cole's ribs.

It's okay. I don't need to breathe.

His pulse thudded, and he stayed absolutely still as Daniel freed his right arm, eased the sweatshirt over Cole's head, then peeled it down his left arm over the cast as though he was dealing with fragile glass. They were only a couple inches apart, and Daniel's breath skimmed over Cole's face.

Gripping the sweatshirt, Daniel looked up, and Cole's lungs spasmed as he exhaled sharply, going lightheaded. Daniel's parted lips trembled the slightest bit, and emotion shone from his beautiful hazel-brown eyes. Cole scrambled to identify what the emotion was, because for a moment he'd thought it was lust.

And that was impossible.

He croaked, "Are you okay?" Daniel was probably just freaking out after revealing so many truths about Trevor and everything.

Backing up, Daniel nodded. He folded the sweatshirt and placed it on the counter, his gaze skittering away. "You good now?"

"Uh-huh. Thanks." He'd become adept already at tugging his

PJ bottoms up and down. Yep, he was *great*.

When Daniel closed the door behind him, Cole sagged against the counter. It was decidedly less great that Cole was falling hopelessly in love, especially since—barring some kind of Christmas miracle—there was zero chance of his feelings being returned.

Chapter Seven

THE MINIVAN'S TAILLIGHTS glowed red, sunlight glinting off the metal roof before it disappeared around the bend. Cole joined Daniel at the windows, and they sighed in unison, then laughed. Daniel's belly somersaulted. They were alone.

"Hallelujah," Cole said. He was still shirtless, his PJs hanging low on his hips. Daniel stared at the hair under his navel, leading down below the waistband.

Forcing his gaze up, he asked, "How are you feeling?"

After yawning and arching his back, Cole nodded. "Pretty good. I slept way better without you waking me up every two hours."

Daniel smiled. "You know what? I slept way better not having to wake you up."

"Huh. What are the odds?" Cole scratched his stubbly cheeks, smiling. While Daniel usually shaved religiously, he'd decided to let it go too. CYC and all that.

They stood in blissful silence, taking in the snow-capped trees soaring toward the blue sky, the Laurentians rising across the lake to the right.

Daniel had woken to find he'd drawn close to Cole in the night, only a few inches between them on the big bed. Those same inches were all that separated them now, their shoulders almost brushing.

He still couldn't believe he'd confessed the truth about Trevor—about himself—to Cole. Maybe he should have been embarrassed to tell those things, but he'd felt…safe. Something about Cole comforted him in a way he didn't understand. His instincts told him Cole had his back.

Maybe it was because they'd known each other before, but Daniel had never met anyone he trusted so quickly—not even Trevor. Cole hadn't judged or ridiculed him. He'd stood by his side for the whole ugly retelling of it. Now the tug toward Cole grew stronger by the minute. Did Cole feel it too, or was he simply being a good friend? Brotherly, even?

Daniel wished he could text Pam: *After being cold and dead inside for six years, I might be coming back to life. Send help.*

He thought about what Cole had said about it being okay to come undone sometimes. That was what it felt like—an unraveling, all his tightly coiled and controlled emotions spilling out in a hot mess. Apparently he was CYCing all over the damn place, whether he liked it or not.

"What do you want to do first?" Cole asked.

Daniel took a breath and forced away his crazy thoughts. *I'm good. Everything's fine. I'm still me. I'm in control.* He kept his tone light. "Honestly? I know it's a waste of water, but drain and refill that hot tub."

Needing something to do with his hands, he rolled up the sleeves of his black Henley. Before he'd dressed, he'd ridiculously debated between his shirts and which went better with his jeans, as if he was going on some kind of *date*.

"After Justin, that water is a biohazard. I'll allow it. You do that, and I'll see if I can make some one-handed breakfast. Oh. Maybe we should call Claudia? She's probably worried if she's texted with no replies."

"Shit! You're right." He grabbed the cordless, then paused, looking at the number pad. "I'll have to get her number from my cell. The only one I know by heart now is my own. And 911."

Cole laughed. "Same."

Once Daniel had the number, he waited for his mom to pick up. It went to voicemail. "Hey, Mom. It's me and Cole. We're calling from the chalet's landline since we're not getting any wifi or cell service. We're good. Cole's feeling a lot better. Enjoy Mexico. Love you." He hung up and said to Cole, "Okay, hopefully that'll hold her and she won't call back every day to check on us."

"I have my doubts, to be honest."

Daniel laughed. "Same."

Once the hot tub was refilled with the cover back on, the water slowly heating, Daniel joined Cole in the kitchen, the wood cold beneath his bare feet. "What have we got?"

"Frozen blueberry waffles a previous guest left behind and a desperate need to go grocery shopping. Can you unscrew the maple syrup bottle? I tried, but it's sticky." He rubbed at his belly where he'd likely been trying to brace the bottle, then licked the pad of his index finger, his pink tongue darting out.

When he met Daniel's gaze, Daniel jerked, realizing he'd been staring.

"Are you okay?" Cole asked.

"Uh-huh. Here." Heart thumping, he came around the island and opened the syrup, busying himself straightening up the kitchen as the waffles toasted.

"Maybe we could decorate the tree."

"Huh? Oh, right." Daniel had forgotten the fresh Christmas tree standing in the living room. "You want to?"

"Sure. Why not?" Cole smiled crookedly, jumping a little as the waffles popped up, then blushing.

Daniel cut Cole's waffle for him, and they ate while two more toasted. It was all so strangely domestic and should have been uncomfortable and weird, but somehow…wasn't.

After breakfast, they opened the boxes of decorations—colorful balls and glittery ornaments of all shapes and sizes. The chalet owners had left a hand-scrawled note on the top box:

You said you celebrated Christmas, so we thought you'd enjoy a tree with all the trimmings. Happy holidays!

Cole pulled out strings of neatly stored, colored lights that were wrapped around plastic frames to keep them untangled. "These hosts really thought of everything, huh?"

"They are getting a five-star review, that's for sure. Well, aside from the wifi, but maybe that's for the best."

He still experienced a bolt of panic when he thought of not being able to check his work email, but Martin had made it clear everyone was to take a break. Blah, blah, work-life balance.

Look at me. Balancing like a mofo.

As Cole attempted to unwrap the lights with his right hand, sticking out his tongue adorably in concentration, Daniel resisted the urge to offer help. Instead he went to the stereo, preemptively turning down the volume knob before pressing power so he didn't blow the speakers. Fucking Justin. Daniel hadn't been so glad to see the back of someone since…

Well, no. Despite how it ended with Trevor, part of Daniel would always love him. He wasn't sure he ever wanted to see him again, but he couldn't hate Trevor. Justin, on the other hand… He thought about going back to work in January and groaned.

"Hmm?" Cole was still intent on the lights, spreading them out on the pine floor.

"Just thinking that I wish I didn't have to see Justin again at work. We have an open concept, but at least the designers are on another floor."

"I'm just saying, I think a term meeting is in his future."

Daniel laughed and poked at the stereo. "He's not in my group, so it's not up to me. But yeah, not really looking forward to seeing him again ever."

"So, wait—you don't have an office? It's all open?"

"Luckily for me, my VP insisted HR have enclosures since we have to have confidential meetings with staff. The offices are all glass-fronted, but I'll take them over working in the ball pit."

"Ball pit? Like for kids?"

"People literally sit in there with their laptops. I can't even." He pressed another button, and low music sounded. "Ah. The satellite radio works, at least. No cell network or wifi, but I'll take Sirius." After hunting around, he tuned it to a holiday station, where Elton John invited them to step into Christmas. "Is this too lame?" he asked Cole.

"Two queers decorating a Christmas tree to Elton John? I think it's perfect."

As they wrapped the lights and hung ornaments, Daniel did too.

WHILE COLE FINISHED hanging silver foil icicles with painstaking precision, Daniel did a grocery run, and the day somehow passed by in a blink.

They sprawled on the couch and watched the original *X-Men* that night by the light of their newly decorated Christmas tree, eating the macaroni and cheese with Panko topping that Daniel had made. He'd figured macaroni would be easy enough for Cole to manage on his own, and he was right.

The Christmas lights outside matched the tree, glowing blue, green, yellow, red, pink, and orange. Fresh snow drifted down beyond the wide walls of windows, and Daniel stoked the wood fire, managing to keep it going all evening.

Cole nodded off before the end of the movie, and Daniel considered leaving him on the huge couch with a blanket. But in the end, he gave him a shake, and they shuffled upstairs and into bed.

It wasn't until Daniel was almost asleep, Cole breathing deeply beside him, that he realized neither of them had thought of Cole moving to one of the other bedrooms.

THE NEXT MORNING, Cole was stir crazy and asked to see the village, so they joined the crowd along the main street, a pedestrian thoroughfare jammed with high-end boutiques, restaurants, and various shops. The ski hills rose in the distance, little people zigzagging their way down, the chair lifts ferrying skiers to the top in a constant loop.

The colorful buildings sandwiched together in Mont-Tremblant were strung with golden Christmas lights that also ran over the street. Bells jingled, a Santa ho-ho-ho-ed and posed for photos with bouncy children, and a caroling group sang "God Rest Ye Merry Gentlemen," dressed in matching red hats and gloves.

The temperature was just below freezing and the wind calm, so it was perfect weather to stroll along and watch the holiday bustle under a cloudy sky. Daniel kept close to Cole just in case he felt dizzy suddenly.

No other reason. Nope.

He pointed at a patch of ice on the sidewalk. "Watch out for that."

Cole stepped carefully around it. "Thanks. You know, I probably shouldn't remind you, but I'm shocked you're not glued to your phone."

Daniel stopped. "Huh. I didn't even think about it." He realized he hadn't the day before either when he'd come for groceries. The only thing on his mind had been getting back to Cole and making him dinner.

Pulling out his phone, he checked the network. "Yeah, I have three dots." He hesitated, staring at the screen, which was crowded with notifications. Then he turned it off and resolutely put it back in his pocket.

Cole whistled softly. "Look at you CYCing."

They started walking again, and Daniel said, "Sergeant Becky would be proud."

"Sergeant Becky? Seriously? You have got to tell me all about that sometime." He pointed. "Hey, there's a little movie theater. And look what's playing."

Daniel's heart leapt as he spotted the poster in the window of the old-fashioned little cinema. "But you already saw the new *Star Wars* movie."

"I'll totally see it again! If I doze off, no harm, no foul. Come on, let's check the times."

"You sure you don't mind?"

Cole tugged on Daniel's sleeve. "I'm sure." He scanned the sign. "It's on in French right now, but English is in forty-five minutes. Perfect. Let's go to that chocolate store. We'll have popcorn and candy for lunch because you know what? We can."

Half an hour later, Daniel juggled two large tubs of popcorn—butter layered in the middle as well as on top—and his cola. Cole held his own pop, with the bag from the chocolate shop hooked over his good arm.

Cole asked, "Where do you like to sit?" They were the first ones in the theater, which only had eight rows, but a nice-sized screen.

"The back? I hate people kicking my seat."

"Oh my God, *same.*"

"And there are always too many people in the middle. People are so annoying."

"I'd high five you right now if either of us had a spare hand."

By the time the lights dimmed for the previews, the theater

was only half full, most tourists in town likely still on the slopes. A *thwack* made Daniel jump, and Cole whispered, "Sorry. Terry's Chocolate Orange?"

He unwrapped the foil and passed Daniel a segment. Their fingers met, and Daniel's breath stuttered before he reined in the wayward burst of *want.* He shoved the chocolate into his mouth.

I really am having a nervous breakdown.

Yet despite his confusion, peace filled him. As the John Williams theme played and the iconic yellow text crawled up the screen, bringing them up to speed on the galactic goings-on, he grinned to himself, happier than he could remember being since the early days with Trevor before it all went to hell.

That life felt a blessedly long time ago and far, far away. Daniel was here with Cole now, and he didn't want to be anywhere else.

"THAT BITCH HAS got to be hot enough by now," Cole said. "It's been more than twenty-four hours."

"A hundred degrees. Perfect, according to the guidelines." Daniel straightened from his crouch by the control panel on the side of the tub. "We can change into our suits and—shit. I didn't bring mine." He slapped his forehead. "I'm such a moron. Who rents a house with a hot tub and doesn't bring their trunks?"

"Oh. It never crossed my mind. I didn't really know where you were bringing me, in my defense. And I was recently concussed." Cole stood by the sliding door into the house. They hadn't opened the glass doors around the hot tub yet. "I mean… We can just go naked, right?" Cole's cheeks went rosy as though he'd gone back out in the cold. "It's only the two of us. But if it's too weird…"

"No, it's fine. Of course." *Yep, it's fine! Not a problem at all!*

We'll just get naked. No big. Pulse racing, Daniel scoffed. "We probably saw each other naked a bunch back in the day."

Cole smiled faintly. "A few times, I think."

"We need to cover your cast too. Just in case. There are a couple of bathrobes and slippers in the closet in our room that Justin fortunately didn't find." Daniel led the way, pausing to make sure Cole was okay on the stairs.

Everything is fine. Nothing to see here. I am not going to lose it.

He laid the robes on the bed and stripped down, keeping his gaze firmly on the floor. Belting the soft terrycloth robe around him, Daniel turned to find Cole still in his jeans.

"I was just thinking we should cover my cast before I put on the robe." Cole's cheeks were still awfully red.

"Good plan." When Daniel had Cole's arm encased in the plastic glove to his shoulder, he eased up an elastic band to hold it in place. "And just think, you could examine a cow after."

Cole's laughter puffed across Daniel's face. "I'll pass."

"Should I get your jeans?"

Adam's apple bobbing, Cole nodded. "Thanks."

Daniel was only going to pop the button for him since he seemed able to manage the rest, but found himself on his knees, peeling down Cole's jeans and helping him step out of them. He gazed up to find Cole's chest rising and falling rapidly.

Don't look at his dick. Even though it's right there, do not look.

Pushing to his feet, Daniel busied himself while Cole worked down his boxer-briefs and wrapped the robe around his shoulders. Cole asked, "Ready?"

Not at all sure of the answer, Daniel nodded regardless.

In the kitchen, he grabbed two plastic wine glasses from a cupboard marked: *For hot tub use.* In his, he poured merlot; in Cole's, OJ. He tucked both bottles under his arm in case they wanted refills.

Cole waited by the sliding glass door. "Thanks. Sorry, I would have taken off the cover, but I don't know if I can drag it with only one hand."

"It's cool. It's surprisingly heavy. You can get the door though."

Cole pulled it back with a flourish, and soon Daniel had stowed the cover, set their drinks in the cup holders, and slid away the far wall, giving them an unimpeded view of the white-capped mountain peaks beyond. The sinking sun glittered like diamonds on the snow of the lake, unbroken but for the odd snowshoe tracks. The wind remained calm.

"Okay." Cole eyed the tub. "Let me just…" He kicked off his slippers. "Cold, cold!" After whipping his robe off his shoulders and onto a wall hook, he went to the hot tub and threw a leg over it.

Naked. Totally naked.

Daniel really tried not to peek at Cole's long, uncut dick hanging from a trimmed thatch of dark hair, his balls low.

He really, *really* tried.

Cole held out his good hand to Daniel. "Um, can you…"

Spurred into action, Daniel took his hand, keeping him steady as he climbed onto the nearest seat, then down into the center of the hot tub.

They were holding hands, and it was warm and slightly sweaty. Daniel almost didn't let go when Cole reached the corner seat on the right side of the tub, where he could sit and rest his left arm along the back.

But he did release Cole's hand, and his voice was almost normal as he asked, "Okay?"

"Yep. Think I'm settled."

Daniel hung up his own robe, kicked off his slippers, and climbed into the seat in the left corner, sinking under the hot water with an involuntary sigh.

Cole grinned. "Feels great, huh?"

"It does."

"The view is amazing too."

Daniel watched Cole. "It is."

As night fell, the Christmas lights around the porch automatically came on, the tree glowing from inside too. There was something absolutely perfect about being in steamy water while the air was frosty and crisp.

Plus, now that Cole was covered in bubbling water to his chest, his pinkish nipples barely showing in the rhythm of the current, Daniel could relax and stop having inappropriate thoughts.

In three, two, one…

What was the matter with him? He gulped his wine, the dry, fruity aftertaste tingling on his tongue. He had to stop thinking about the way Cole's thighs had flexed when he'd climbed in. How warm and strong his grasp had been holding onto Daniel. How gorgeous his cock was, and how Daniel wanted to suck him and find out what kind of sounds he made when he came.

Fuck. Me.

He had to think about *anything* else, because he was getting hard beneath the frothing water. It didn't make any sense. First off, he was supposed to be taking care of Cole, not perving on him. They were sort-of brothers, but no, not really at all.

Still, Cole was younger. And injured. It was wrong. Daniel was supposed to be responsible and trustworthy. When he made director, Martin had told him one of the reasons was because he was so coolheaded. Even-keeled.

So why was he capsized and flailing around?

Also it had only been *days* since he'd met Cole again. He shouldn't be feeling this attraction at all, but certainly not so quickly. This was completely new territory.

He drained his glass, then reached over the side to where he'd left the bottle and refilled it. His skin felt itchy and too-small to contain him. Somehow he'd been scraped raw and vulnerable, this new desire for Cole exposing him and shattering his usual containment.

He ran through a list of hot actors he enjoyed looking at. Yet even if Chris Evans, Chris Hemsworth, *and* Chris Pratt had all magically appeared naked in the hot tub with them, Daniel would only have eyes for Cole.

"You okay?"

Blinking, Daniel forced a smile. "Uh-huh!"

"You looked kind of panicky. Are you getting overheated?"

Yep, but not in the way you mean. "I was just thinking about work. All the stuff I'll have to do in January."

Cole gave him a stern look. "No work. My thesis isn't going to write itself, but we are on vacation. Let's worry about all that shit when the time comes. It'll still be there. I promise."

Daniel had to laugh. "You're right. It will."

"But we should make sure we don't get too hot. With the cold air, I think it can be misleading."

He nodded and sipped his wine. Or guzzled it, whichever. After the second glass, he was still half-hard. Cole shifted, and his foot brushed against Daniel's, shooting sparks straight to his balls. Breathing in quiet little pants, Daniel watched Cole sip his orange juice, then lick his lips.

Cole's mouth was on the narrow side, and it glistened after the flick of red tongue. What would it be like to kiss him? To slide his tongue inside? What kind of sounds would Cole make? Would he moan and whimper?

Fuck, Daniel was going to come without even touching himself.

Then somehow he opened his big, dumb mouth and said, "I really want to kiss you."

Eyes wide, Cole stared at him, his glass of OJ halfway to his mouth. "Uh... Huh?"

Fuck, fuck, shit, piss, fuuuuck. "Oh my God. I'm so sorry. I don't know what's wrong with me. I..." He scrambled for some kind of explanation. Two glasses of wine were hardly enough to make him tipsy, let alone drunk. "It must be the heat after all."

"Wait. You want to kiss me? That's what you said. Right? I'm not hearing things?"

Daniel wanted to sink beneath the steaming water and hide, but he answered, "Yes. Cole, I know this is..." *What? What* is *this?*

"I'm in." Cole nodded emphatically.

"You...really?" A couple of feet separated them in the hot tub, and they stared at each other. Daniel's dick swelled, fire in his veins. Shock, lust, and a flare of joy bubbled together.

Cole slid over and straddled him, leaning his cast on the side of the hot tub beside Daniel's head. Steam rising all around, they groaned as their cocks met. Daniel was thrilled to discover Cole was hard too.

He flattened his hands over Cole's back, touching the flexing muscles there. Cole's tight little body was deliciously heavy, his knees snug around Daniel's hips.

"Holy shit. Is this weird?" Daniel asked, his mind spinning with too many thoughts to capture.

Cole shook his head. "I'm been dreaming of this since I was thirteen."

"Okay, *now* it's weird." He tried to focus on the man in his lap and not imagine that jug-eared little kid.

Cole laughed. "Shut up." Lips parted, his gaze flicked down to Daniel's mouth and back up again. A drop of water slipped down Cole's forehead, and Daniel raised a hand to brush it away before it could fall into Cole's eyes.

"Daniel, can I kiss you now?"

He could only nod, sucking in a shaky breath as Cole leaned down and met his mouth. It was soft at first, a tentative exploration, their lips parting with little tender kisses. One hand on

Cole's waist, Daniel slid the other into Cole's hair, cupping his head and threading his fingers into the short, steam-damp strands. The hot tub hummed, heat enveloping them.

He was *kissing* Cole.

Their noses bumped, and they laughed. A rush of giddiness swirled through Daniel like the bubbling water. It had been since Trevor that he'd kissed anyone, and now he was grateful Justin had been more interested in blowing him to achieve his conquest. Daniel had forgotten just how wonderful it was to taste and tease and share breath. Affection swelled in him.

They deepened the kiss, tongues meeting, stubble rasping. Cole tasted like orange and a hint of chocolate, and Daniel chased the sweetness, running both his hands up and down Cole's back, dipping lower to his ass.

Cole rocked his hips, gasping as he lifted his head, his eyes searching Daniel's. "I love that you're hard for me."

Holding Cole's ass, Daniel arched up, groaning. "I was afraid I would come just thinking about kissing you."

Cole dived for his mouth, thrusting his tongue inside, licking and sucking like he wanted to swallow Daniel whole. They jerked against each other, cocks rubbing in the water. Panting, Cole reached back with his right hand as he leaned heavily against Daniel.

He muttered, "Grab my ass. Spread it."

Daniel was only too happy to follow instructions, but... "We need a condom."

Cole licked across Daniel's mouth. "Not for this. Trust me." He lifted up on his knees and reached back to position Daniel's cock between his cheeks, then squeezed as he lowered down.

The friction was incredible. Daniel moaned, keeping hold of Cole's ass and thrusting up into the narrow cleft. Cole leaned closer, pressing their chests completely together and hooking his chin over Daniel's shoulder. His cock was stiff between them, and it rubbed against Daniel's stomach as they strained together.

Daniel was on fire and *alive,* his unraveling complete. He gripped Cole's ass as Cole writhed against him. Sparks ignited from Daniel's nipples and dick, from every inch of him that Cole touched.

"Fuck," Cole muttered. "I want your cock inside me so bad. But I can't wait. Need to come."

Daniel could only groan, his balls tight. The heat of the water, Cole's body, and the squeeze of his ass cheeks was too much. Daniel's orgasm tore through him, and he thumped his head back as he emptied in spasms, Cole rubbing against him in a frenzy.

The pleasure filled every pore, so much more intense than it was when Daniel jerked off. He trembled.

"That's it," Cole moaned. "Oh fuck, I'm so close. I want you so much."

Pushing one hand between them, Daniel took hold of Cole's cock in the water, stroking and pulling back the foreskin, swirling his thumb over the head. Cole cried out, shaking, and Daniel was pretty sure he was coming.

He squeezed Cole's ass with his left hand, encouraging him to ride it out, jerking him until Cole slumped in his arms, his face against Daniel's neck, mouth open and teeth grazing skin.

Their chests heaved, and Cole lifted his head, pupils blown as if he'd gotten high off some leftover pot. The sun had set, but the Christmas lights shone beyond him. Steam rose in the cold air.

They stared at each other, panting. The hot tub shut off, the cycle finished. Their breath thundered in the sudden quiet.

Had they just made a massive mistake?

Cole grinned. "Guess we have to change the water again before we go."

Relief whooshed through him. Daniel could only hold Cole close and kiss him tenderly as the moon rose over the snowy mountains, joy making itself at home in his heart after so many years gone.

Chapter Eight

"Tampons, Tums, sunscreen, baby shampoo…" Crouching in his fluffy white robe, Daniel rooted around in the cabinet under one of the sinks in the master bedroom. It was full of random supplies presumably left by other guests.

"How did you not bring condoms and lube on a romantic getaway?" Cole fidgeted and tried not to pace. If they had to go back to the village to stock up, so be it. Because he was getting fucked by Daniel as soon as humanly possible.

Daniel's voice was muffled as he leaned farther into the cabinet. "Justin said he'd take care of it since I was working late all last week."

"I think it was a Freudian thing. Deep down, you knew there was no way you were fucking that asshole. Literally."

Laughing, Daniel leaned back. "Touché. And ah-ha!" He held up a box of condoms. "Victory."

Desire simmered through Cole, tugging at his groin. *I'm getting Daniel Diaz's cock. I must be freaking dreaming.* "Check the expiry."

Daniel scanned the box. "We're good."

And they *were.* They'd gotten off in the hot tub, and then laughed and kissed. Daniel had made grilled-cheese sandwiches, which they'd eaten in their bathrobes, leaning against the island in the kitchen. It all felt so natural.

They were *good.*

"Let me see if there's any… Holy shit. This place really does have everything." He held up the lube, then touched Cole's right hand. "Cole?"

"Huh? Yeah, that'll work."

Daniel's forehead furrowed. "Are you feeling okay? You seemed kind of spacey there."

"No, I'm great." Cole brushed back a curl from Daniel's forehead. "Just thinking about how crazy this is. How right this feels. You and me."

But now Daniel's frown deepened. Shit, maybe Cole had said too much. *Stupid!* He was going to scare him off. It's not as if they were a *couple* after screwing around in a hot tub.

Daniel stood, leaning beside him against the vanity. He ran a fingertip over the shell of Cole's ear, sending a shiver down his spine, Cole's heart thudding. "But what you said, about wanting it since you were a kid… Is that true? Like, you had a crush on me or something?"

"A massive crush. I told you the other day that you helped me realize I was gay. That wasn't just because of the example you set by coming out. It was because thinking about you gave me a twenty-four-seven boner."

Still holding the box of condoms, Daniel laughed. "You have a way with words."

Cole exhaled. Maybe he hadn't freaked Daniel out too badly after all. "And I'm not a kid now. Obviously."

Daniel gave him a sly look. "Yeah, I noticed." He tugged at the belt on Cole's robe, then sank to his knees in front of him. He looked up under his thick eyelashes. "Can I…?"

"Oh hell yes. Suck me."

"You're kind of bossy." He grinned. "I like it."

Before Cole could respond, Daniel leaned in and nuzzled around the base of his cock, sliding his hands around to take hold of Cole's hips under the open robe. Leaning back against the vanity, Cole gripped the edge of the counter with his good hand.

Gazing up with his beautiful hazel eyes, Daniel licked a stripe from the base of the shaft to the tip. Cole could only moan, his dick pulsing with need.

Daniel was tentative at first, kissing and tasting, sucking on the head and gazing up at him. Cole had the feeling he wanted approval, so he smiled and murmured, "That feels amazing. You're so good at this."

From what Daniel had told him the night before, it had probably been years since he'd last done this, and while he was a little clumsy, it was already the greatest blow job in Cole's life because it was *Daniel* on his knees for him.

Daniel's pretty eyelashes fanned over his golden-brown cheeks as he sucked harder, taking him in deeper, his hand circling the base of Cole's dick, tongue exploring and teasing the foreskin. His breath catching, goosebumps broke over Cole in waves.

He wished desperately he had two usable hands. He let go of the counter, hoping Daniel's grasp on his hips would be enough to keep him on his feet as his knees shook.

Threading his fingers into Daniel's curls, Cole cradled his head and asked, "Are you hard?"

Looking up, his full lips stretched around Cole's cock, Daniel sucked hard before he pulled off with a wet smack that echoed deliciously off the tile. Sitting back on his heels, he tugged open his robe to show his thick, meaty cock curving up, straining and flushed red. The glistening head peeked out from his foreskin.

"Fuck, you're beautiful. That's so good." Cole caressed Daniel's head. "I can't wait to get that inside me." Heart galloping, he asked, "Do you like rimming? When I first saw it in porn, I thought about you doing it to me. I—" He sucked in a breath as Daniel spun him around, grabbing for the counter with his good hand and ignoring the flare of pain in his left.

Daniel hauled up Cole's robe and spread his ass, and Cole bent over the counter, parting his legs wider. He panted, "I'll take that as a *yessss*."

He groaned as Daniel licked up and down his crease, toying with his hole before pushing into it. The counter dug into Cole's belly, and his head thumped against the mirror, but he moaned, "Don't stop. More."

Hot exhalations washed over Cole's tender flesh. Daniel leaned back a few inches and spit before burying his face between Cole's cheeks, licking into him and eating his ass. Legs jerking, Cole's breath steamed up the mirror. His dick leaked, and he cried out, never wanting it to end, but also desperate for more.

"Fuck me. Please. I need your cock."

Cole moaned when Daniel gave him a parting kiss on his hole, watching in the mirror as he stood behind him. Their gazes locked, and Daniel said, "On the bed."

Cole was happy to get fucked anywhere Daniel wanted to do it. Nodding, he followed into the bedroom, tugging off his robe, swearing when the sleeve got caught on his cast before he could toss it aside.

"Careful." Naked now too, Daniel caught Cole around his waist, bending to brush their lips together. He whispered, "I don't want to hurt you."

Cole's heart glowed as brightly as the Christmas lights. "You won't." He backed up and turned to knee-walk onto the bed before flattening out on his back. "Can you put a pillow under my cast?" He stretched his arm out so his hand would be well free of their bodies.

Daniel did as he asked, then kneeled by Cole's feet, waiting and seemingly uncertain. He'd brought the condoms and lube, and Cole said, "Get yourself ready. Stop worrying." He rubbed his foot over Daniel's thigh. "I promise I'll tell you if anything hurts. Okay?"

"Okay." Daniel gave him a little smile that made Cole's heart clench.

After rolling on the condom, Daniel slicked himself, biting his reddened lip with a little moan. Cole spread his legs and lifted his knees, offering himself. Fuck, he *loved* cock, and knowing that he was actually going to have Daniel's made his head spin. He groaned, his dick jumping as Daniel pushed a slick finger into him.

"Uh-huh, I'm ready. I'm *so* ready." Cole grasped at Daniel's shoulder with his right hand, tugging him closer. "Fuck me." He shoved his tongue in Daniel's mouth, tasting the musky hint of himself.

When Daniel inched into him, gritting his teeth, his nostrils flaring, Cole bore down, urging him deeper, loving the burn as Daniel stretched him open.

"Fuck, Cole." Daniel's arms quivered where he held himself up.

"I know." He lifted his tailbone and hooked his legs around Daniel's waist. "Harder. I need it. I know you won't hurt me. Orgasm is the best medicine for a fading concussion and broken bones."

The burst of Daniel's laughter puffed across Cole's face. They kissed messily as Daniel rocked into him, settling into a rhythm, filling Cole completely.

"Never thought I'd have this again," Daniel mumbled. He gasped as Cole tightened his inner muscles around him, snapping his hips and really *pounding* him now.

Cole could have died happy, being plowed by Daniel Diaz. The real thing was so much better than even his most detailed fantasy. He couldn't have truly imagined the salty taste of Daniel's sweat on his tongue, the way he whimpered, red lips parted, staring into Cole's eyes as if nothing else in the world existed.

And it didn't. It was only the two of them, gasping and kissing and fucking.

When Cole came, he painted his chest without his dick even being touched. Daniel pressed against the perfect spot inside him, and Cole spurted until he could only quiver and moan, his balls emptying.

He squeezed around Daniel's cock. "I want you inside me forever."

"Oh!" Daniel whipped his head back, spine arching as he came. He collapsed onto Cole, panting against his cheek in warm gusts, their skin sticky and slick.

Cole kept his legs wrapped tightly around Daniel. Maybe it was crazy, but forever sounded about right.

Chapter Nine

"ARE YOU SURE you don't want to go skiing? I don't want to hold you back." Cuddled on the couch, Cole trailed his fingers up and down Daniel's arm. Christmas Eve had dawned cloudy with snow in the forecast, and Cole would be content to stay exactly where he was, but guilt that Daniel was missing out nagged.

They'd spent two days fucking every which way they could imagine with the limitations of Cole's cast. His ass was pleasantly sore, and his jaw ached from sucking off Daniel for ages that morning, edging him and not letting him come until Daniel had begged so prettily.

"I've actually never gone skiing before. I'd probably end up in a cast to match yours."

Cole laughed. "They must have a lot of other activities."

"Hmm. Maybe there's something we can do together." Daniel shifted Cole's feet off his lap and stood to reach for a brochure sitting on the coffee table. He sat back down, and even though Cole had bent his legs, Daniel took his feet and pulled them across his lap again, warm and secure.

He opened the brochure. "Let's see. Alpine touring—looks like we'd be hiking with ski poles, so that's out. Biking, cross-country skiing, downhill skiing, dogsledding, ice climbing—hell no—tubing, skating…" He flipped the pages. "I don't think any of these are broken-limb friendly. Oh wait! We could go on a sleigh ride."

"Tempting as that is, I think I'll pass. Maybe we should just head into the village and restock on food? Get some milk and cookies for Santa tonight. Ohhh, and eggnog."

"Eggnog?" Daniel scrunched up his face.

"Have you actually tried it?"

"Well…no. Not since I was a kid."

"A-ha! I'll get the stuff for my mom's secret recipe. You'll be converted, I swear." He thought of her with a familiar pang of grief, sharp, then dull again before fading into the background and never quite going away.

"Okay. I'll try it."

"Speaking of moms, what do you think Claudia's going to say? About us? I think she'll be good. Right?"

"Well, she already loves you, so yeah. I think she'll be jazzed. Once she gets over any weirdness. What about your dad?"

Cole pondered it. "He probably barely remembers you at this point, so I can't see why he'd care."

Daniel laughed. "True enough." He tossed the brochure back on the table and slid his hand along Cole's shin under his PJs. "I really don't mind just chilling instead of hitting the slopes. I haven't relaxed like this in…" His brow furrowed.

"No, don't frown! Stop thinking about it. You frown too much."

"I do?" Naturally, Daniel frowned.

"Yeah. I mean, you can do whatever you want to do. You just seem like you're anxious a lot. Stressed."

Daniel toyed with the hair on Cole's leg. He smiled softly. "I guess I am." Then he blinked and jerked his head, as if taken aback. "I haven't thought about work at *all* today! Huh. That's so weird."

"Well, don't start now." Cole sat up and drew him close for a kiss, rubbing his thumb over the stubble on Daniel's cheek. "Let's resupply, then we can hibernate until it's time to go home."

He wasn't sure what would happen to the happy little bubble they'd constructed when they went back to real life in Ottawa, but Cole chased the worry away. They'd take each day as it came.

SHIVERING, COLE JAMMED his right fist deeper into his pockets. "The wind chill has got to be minus thirty." His nose hair was stiff, little frozen icicles lining his nostrils. His fingertips tingled where they peeked out from his cast.

Daniel stopped short as they hurried from the parking lot toward the main area of the village. "Don't you have gloves?"

Cole held up his cast. "This presents a challenge."

"But your other hand!" Daniel stripped off his right glove and passed it over.

"Now you'll be cold!"

"I'll put my hand in my pocket. Come on. This way we'll each have one warm hand, at least."

Cole tried not to smile too much. "Okay. Thanks."

After stocking up on some alcohol and what was likely way too much food, they stowed the groceries in the car and headed back to the main street to grab takeout. Cole squinted at the red sign toward the end of the pedestrian street. "Is that a BeaverTails down there? I could really go for some warm sugary goodness."

"I'm not sweet enough?" Daniel gave him a cheesy wink.

"As sweet as you are, there's something irresistible about fried dough."

Daniel grinned. "You want to pick some up while I hit Coco Pazzo for our lunch?" He nodded to the nearby restaurant. "It says on the awning they do takeout. Unless you want to sit down and eat?"

"Nah. There will be other people there. At the chalet, it's just you and me. And the hot tub." He waggled his eyebrows and lifted his gloved hand for a high five.

With a laugh, Daniel slapped his palm. "Sounds like a plan. You have any allergies or stuff you don't like? Maybe you should come look at the menu. It'll probably take a while for them to make the food, so you'll have time to go after. Oh, we should get more challah from that bakery."

"I'll grab it on my way. And I'm easy. Get whatever you want for lunch. How about you? Anything you don't like? And there might be nuts in the pastries." He didn't remember Daniel having allergies, but people could develop them.

"I'm easy too."

"I know, but do you have any allergies?"

Daniel's laughter followed Cole on the wind as Cole hurried down the street. The golden Christmas lights strung across the pedestrian street and around poles shone merrily in the cloudy dullness. Salt crunched underfoot, and giant green and red wreathes decorated the streetlights. People bustled around, excited chatter and children's voices ringing in the air.

A little girl in a puffy blue snowsuit squealed in front of a store window displaying a massive dollhouse with various holiday scenes acted out inside by toy humans, mice, and what looked to be beavers. She pointed and laughed, her parents grinning.

Cole paused to take in the display too, and was about to hurry on when he spotted something inside the store beyond the dollhouse. Heart skipping, he pushed open the door, sighing in relief at the blast of warm air.

The shop carried home furnishings and knickknacks, and had a large selection of holiday decorations. Cole peered up at the top of a Christmas tree, excitement zipping through him. It was absolutely perfect. He didn't care how much it cost—Daniel had to have it.

A saleswoman approached, and Cole pointed to the tree topper and said, "Sold."

After buying the pastries and bread, he tucked the tree topper box in the bottom of the bakery bag. He tried to wipe the smile off his face as he rejoined Daniel inside Coco Pazzo's small takeout area, which was wonderfully warm and smelled of tomatoes and garlic and everything delicious.

"What?" Daniel asked.

"Huh? Nothing. I'm just happy."

Daniel frowned, but Cole could tell he was putting it on. "Are you sure you're not concussed again? What's your name?"

"Cole Smith, and I'm having the best Christmas ever. Maybe except for the one year my mom took me to Disney World." He pretended to ponder it. "Nope. Sorry, Mickey. This is the best."

Daniel's cheeks creased. "Me too. I still can't get over how surreal this is. In a good way."

"It really is." Cole's nose was thawing in the warmth, his cheeks tingling. His stomach rumbled, and he took off his glove and managed to open the BeaverTails box, tearing off the corner of one of the long, flat pastries that were shaped in rounded rectangles.

He held out the dough for Daniel. "I figured we can share. I got maple, classic cinnamon and sugar, and this one. Nutella."

With a low groan, Daniel took the sweet, sticky goodness, licking his lips. Cole had a piece too, and as he licked his fingers, Daniel watched with hooded eyes, leaning closer.

A woman cleared her throat. "Charcuterie platter, calamari, trotta affumicatta, gnocchi with gorgonzola, two lamb shanks, and the spaghettini con anatra."

Boggling, Cole asked Daniel, "Did you invite Justin and the gang back?"

"I figured leftovers wouldn't go astray. And I wasn't sure what you liked."

"So he got everything," the woman agreed cheerfully. "You boys have a merry Christmas."

Cole managed to wait until they were back in the car before launching himself at Daniel for hazelnut-chocolate kisses.

COLE NUZZLED THE back of Daniel's neck, his breath ticklish, stubble rough. "Merry Christmas," Cole whispered, pressed up behind him. He had put on his flannel PJ bottoms, and they rubbed softly against the curve of Daniel's ass.

"Mmm."

"Did I wear you out last night, sleepyhead?"

A bolt of pleasure shot down Daniel's spine at the memory of Cole riding him, his thighs flexing and cock bobbing, managing better than they'd expected, leaning his good hand against Daniel's chest and leaving imprints of his fingernails. Daniel couldn't remember ever having so much *fun* during sex as he did with Cole.

He opened his eyes, blinking at the dull light that shone in, clouds filling the slice of sky he could see through the parted curtains. "Is it snowing?"

"It is. Santa had his work cut out for him last night. Perfect day to stay inside by a roaring fire. But apparently fire building is a two-hand job, so time to get up."

Turning his head, Daniel gave him a kiss. "You really are bossy. I still like it."

Naked, Daniel shuffled into the bathroom to piss and wash his face before pulling on his silk PJ bottoms and a sweatshirt. Cole had gone back downstairs, and the aroma of brewing coffee wafted up.

On the stairs, Daniel breathed it in deeply, admiring the view of the fresh snow through the wide windows and the Christmas tree that—

He stumbled on the last step, catching himself, then walking slowly on bare feet toward the tree, which was lit up in all its glittering glory. The star that had sat atop it was gone. Daniel blinked up at the replacement.

It was *Yoda.*

With a *glowing green lightsaber.* Green-skinned Yoda wore a sandy-brown robe with a white robe over top. His wrinkled face was wonderfully detailed, and he held up the lightsaber on a diagonal.

"Merry Christmas, and may the force be with us."

Daniel spun around to find Cole biting his lip, clearly trying not to grin, scratching at his bare chest. Daniel looked back at the tree, then Cole. "How? When? Where?"

"I spotted it yesterday when I went to BeaverTails. I thought a Yoda tree topper was something you needed in your life."

"I do. I absolutely do." He'd needed so many things in his life and hadn't realized *how* much. "Thank you." He pulled Cole into a hug, leaning down to kiss his cheek.

Cole's body fit perfectly in Daniel's arms. It had been too long since he'd been able to just hug someone for longer than a greeting with his mom or Pam. He inhaled deeply, smelling soap, a hint of pine, and *Cole.*

"I'm melting," he murmured.

Cole leaned back. "Is it too hot in here? Do you not want to start a fire?"

"No, I mean…" Daniel ran his thumb over Cole's bottom lip. "I was frozen inside, and now I'm melting all over the place. This is crazy, right? The other shoe is going to drop any second."

"Nope." Cole inched closer, stepping lightly on Daniel's feet with his icy feet. "No shoes here." He wriggled his toes and slid his good arm around Daniel's waist. "Although I think the fire is a good idea. Right after you kiss me again."

With a smile, Daniel followed instructions, and soon he had the kindling sparked, rolled newspaper flaming and catching the log. Cole brought him coffee, and they sat cross-legged on the fake fur rug in front of the hearth by the Christmas tree, sipping from their mugs.

"You know what we should do today?" Cole asked.

Daniel swallowed his mouthful of rich, bitter coffee. "What?"

"This. Plus the hot tub and maybe a couple movies. Italian food leftovers. Oh, and fucking." Cole nodded seriously. "Definitely more fucking." He knee-walked to the tree and reached beneath it, pulling out the bottle of lube.

Daniel didn't know the last time he'd laughed so much as he had the past few days. His shoulders shook, and he pressed his hands around his still-warm mug. "What about a condom?"

Reaching up, Cole plucked a foil wrapper from the tree. "There are a few more hidden in there. Santa believes in safe sex." He caught the edge of the wrapper between his teeth, picked up the lube, and shuffled back to Daniel.

Daniel took the condom, his stomach swooping like he was riding a rollercoaster at Canada's Wonderland. "What do you think about fucking me this time?"

Cole's breath shuddered, his lips parting. "Yeah? You're up for that?"

"You're the one who'll have to get it up." He laughed at his own stupid joke.

Cole grinned. "Oh, I assure you that won't be an issue."

"What about your hand? How should we…"

"Hmm." He glared at his cast, then scooted closer, running his palm over Daniel's thigh, fingers soft on the silk. "How do you like it?"

Daniel knew he was blushing, his skin going hot down his sternum. "However we can make it work." It had been since Trevor, and the idea of having Cole inside him had his heart drumming.

"But if you had to choose?" Cole stroked Daniel's leg and licked his lips, watching him intently. Cole was so confident with sex, and it made Daniel's dick swell.

"On my hands and knees," he murmured. "You behind me."

"Uh-huh." Cole nodded, capturing Daniel's lips in a hard kiss. "That sounds A-plus."

He sucked in a breath. "But your hand?"

"I can balance. Let's do this." Cole slid his hand over Daniel's growing cock, rubbing him through the silk. "You want to come on my dick?"

Nodding, Daniel pulled him close for another kiss, pushing his tongue into Cole's mouth. Heat radiated through him, his head spinning with lust—with the need to get closer.

"Get naked," Cole commanded, and Daniel scrambled to obey. Still in his pajama bottoms, Cole sat back on his heels, his Adam's apple bobbing as his gaze skated over Daniel's body.

Goosebumps rippled across Daniel's naked flesh, and he waited on his knees, facing Cole.

"When I have full use of both hands, I'm going to rim you and finger fuck you until you're begging for me. But for now, get yourself ready." He nodded to the lube.

Blood rushing in his ears, Daniel squeezed the cool gel onto his fingers. The fluffy rug was soft under his knees as he reached behind to push a finger into his ass. The fire flickered to his left, Cole in front of him, the Christmas tree's colored lights glowing over Cole's skin.

Daniel couldn't stop the groan that slipped out as he impatiently shoved his finger inside, his hole burning as it stretched. "Fuck," he muttered.

With his good hand, Cole squeezed himself through his PJs. "Feel good?"

"It will." He grunted, squeezing in another slick finger.

"Don't hurt yourself." Cole's brow furrowed.

"Uh-huh." Dropping onto his left hand, Daniel twisted his wrist, pushing past the burn. He kept his head up, meeting Cole's avid gaze.

"Fuck, I wish we had a dildo. Look at you. You're so hot. And you want *my* cock." Cole shook his head like he couldn't believe it. His chest rose and fell quickly, his nipples peaked and flushed red.

Moaning, Daniel pulled out his hand and spread his discarded sweatshirt on the rug. He crawled over and grabbed the condom. Cole sat up on his knees and let Daniel tug his PJs down around his thighs, freeing his leaking cock.

In a warm gust, Cole exhaled sharply as Daniel rolled the condom onto him. His right hand landed on Daniel's shoulder, fingers digging in. Daniel slicked a ton of lube over the condom, and they kissed messily with little moans.

Daniel broke the kiss, his throat dry. "Fuck me. I want you so much. Need you."

Cole's pupils were blown dark. "You've got me. Turn around."

On his hands and knees, Daniel gripped his sweatshirt with slick fingers, making sure it was spread under him. He reached back with his left hand, pulling on his ass cheek as Cole did the same with the right.

It took a few tries, but then Cole had the slippery head of his cock nudging at Daniel's hole. Grunting, he held onto Daniel's right shoulder and pushed.

The air punched out of Daniel's lungs, pain sharp in his ass, Cole's cock feeling impossibly huge. Opening his mouth, he sucked in little gasps of air and shoved back, more than willing to take the discomfort to be filled. He hadn't realized how much he'd needed this.

"Oh, fuck. You're so tight." Cole's fingers dug into Daniel's shoulder as he inched inside. "Tell me if it's too much."

"Don't stop." Daniel's arms and legs quivered, sweat dampening the nape of his neck. "I want this. Want you. Trust you."

For a few moments, Cole didn't move, and his hand loosened, stroking Daniel's shoulder. Then his soft lips pressed to the knobs of Daniel's spine.

Daniel whimpered. "Please."

After another tender kiss, Cole gave it to him, finally pushing past the ring of muscle and slamming all the way home, his balls bouncing off Daniel's ass. They both cried out, and Daniel stared at the white fake fur rug.

He was so full he was afraid he'd split apart, but soon enough his body adjusted, and Cole began rocking in and out. Not much at first, then harder and harder until he was fucking Daniel relentlessly, their skin slapping, slick with sweat, the fire blazing beside them.

It blazed in Daniel as well, the stretch better than he remembered it. The sensation of fullness and brushes against his prostate revived his hard-on, and he could only moan and grunt, forming actual words too difficult.

Cole's rhythm stuttered. "Fuck, I'm going to come. It's too good."

"Do it," Daniel growled. He squeezed around Cole, who held his shoulder hard enough to bruise as he thrust a few more times before jerking and moaning.

Gasping, Cole folded over Daniel's back. "Fuck," Cole muttered, lips wet against Daniel's spine.

Since he was on his hands and knees, Daniel couldn't touch himself, and his dick strained. Cole couldn't touch him either, apparently hanging on for dear life with his good hand. Daniel whimpered low in his throat.

Panting, Cole lifted off, awkwardly rolling onto his right side on the rug. "On your back." He urged Daniel to flip over and said, "Feed it to me." He bent over and latched his mouth onto Daniel's cock.

It was so wet and hot and *good*, and Daniel groaned and shoved his hips up, only needing a few thrusts before his balls drew up and he came. The pleasure seared white hot, shuddering through him as he emptied into Cole's mouth.

Cole swallowed as much as he could, and some of Daniel's spunk dripped from the corners of his lips. "Oh fuck," Daniel groaned. He reached up and caught a few drops with his fingers, and Cole licked and sucked them clean too.

Chests heaving, they looked at each other and laughed. Careful of his cast, Cole snuggled close, draping his left arm over Daniel's belly. "Merry Christmas to us."

"God bless us everyone," Daniel agreed.

"It's even better than I imagined." Cole sighed contentedly, kissing Daniel's nipple. "And I imagined it a lot over the years. In so many ways."

In the colorful glow of the Christmas tree, snow fell beyond the huge windows. The fire crackled beside them, and they were quiet. Peaceful. Daniel traced the bumps of Cole's spine. "It shouldn't be this easy."

"Hmm?" His warm breath teased Daniel's chest hair.

"This, I mean. You and me. We just met—well, again. But it's only been days. How can it feel so right? Have I just been alone for too long?"

"Hey!" Cole poked him in the side with his finger.

"I didn't mean it like that." Daniel laughed. "Obviously you're amazing." He kissed the top of Cole's head.

"It's true. If you were just desperate for anyone, you'd still be with that douchecanoe."

Daniel shuddered. "I'm so glad you're a klutz."

"It has never come in more handy." Cole snorted. "Get it?"

They laughed, shaking in each other's arms. Daniel sighed. "It just feels *right* with you. I can't explain it."

"Maybe it's a Christmas miracle. But, you know, my aunt and uncle got together super quick. They had lunch with some mutual friends. I can't remember why. But at one point, Aunt Judy left to use the bathroom, and Uncle Steve said, 'That's the woman I'm going to marry.' And he did. Been together decades and have three kids. They just knew it was right."

Daniel swallowed over the sudden lump in his throat. Even with the warmth of the fire on his skin, a shiver ran over him. "Do you think this is right? Us?"

Cole nuzzled his stubbly face against Daniel's pec. "I think it really could be. I guess we'll find out."

"I guess we will." He stared up at the distant beams of the cathedral ceiling, grinning. A log sparked, and he glanced at the fireplace. Then he jolted, realizing the stockings were now full. "Wait, you bought stocking stuffers too? I didn't get you anything!"

Cole shrugged. "It's all stuff from around the house. Spoiler alert: I know you were eyeing those Tums."

Laughing, Daniel took Cole's face in his hands and drew him up for a kiss. Or two. Or five. Ten, perhaps. Catching his breath, Daniel murmured, "Next year, I'm going to get you everything you could possibly want for Christmas."

Eyes bright, Cole grinned. "Next year, huh?"

When Daniel thought of his future now, yep—there was Cole. "Definitely."

"I'll drink to that. Hey, the doc said I should be good by now to 'indulge,' as she put it. Let me pour eggnog Mom-style while you stoke the fire." Cole carefully sat and pulled up his pajama bottoms.

Smiling to himself and gazing up at Yoda every so often, Daniel pulled on his own PJs and hurried out for more logs, which were stacked under a tarp beyond the hot tub on the porch. The flames leapt again by the time Cole joined him with two small glasses full of thick, off-white nog.

"So, her secret recipe was mixing eggnog with Amaretto. Maybe calling it a 'recipe' was a stretch." He handed over a glass, and they clinked.

Daniel took a sip. "Mmm. I love it!" Actually, it was cloyingly sweet and he didn't really like the texture of cream, which was one of the reasons eggnog had never been his favorite.

Cole's gaze narrowed. "You're so full of shit. But thank you for trying it." He leaned in for a soft kiss.

"Anything for you," Daniel told him, and he knew it was true.

Epilogue

A year later

"COLE, YOU'VE BEEN such a wonderful influence. There's actual *color* in this house!" Claudia exclaimed. "A real Christmas tree!" She fingered the fresh pine needles.

Cole couldn't resist saying, "There's debate about whether real or artificial has more environmental impact, but we decided to support a local business instead of buying something plastic shipped from China."

"And you can't beat that smell." She inhaled deeply. "Your Yoda angel is a hoot."

"Thanks. We like it." The other ornaments were a mix of *Star Wars* and traditional sparkly balls and snowflakes. The colored lights glowed and silver icicles shimmered. Brightly wrapped gifts spilled out under the tree, too many to be contained.

"Oh, and I love the purple rug," Claudia added.

From the office down the hall, Daniel shouted, "I'll have you know I bought that rug before I met Cole! Well, before I met him again."

Cole laughed. "But I'm responsible for the burgundy tea towels in the kitchen." He'd moved in with Daniel that summer, and it felt like they'd been together forever. Life was super weird sometimes, but in the best way.

He asked Claudia, "Are you sure you don't want anything to eat?"

"No, no. The dinner on the train was surprisingly good. I'm so glad I splurged on first class." She winked and ran a hand over her perfectly coiffed brown curls. "I'm worth it."

"You definitely are. You look amazing, by the way."

She practically glowed. "Thank you, sweetheart. I tell you, I owe it all to Pilates. And Pierre."

Claudia's newish boyfriend had already gone up to bed, but Cole lowered his voice anyway. "He's very handsome."

"Isn't he?" She beamed. "I think he might be the one."

"I hope so." He really, really did.

"Are your aunt and uncle settled?"

"Yeah. It was a long day flying from Winnipeg with the delay connecting through Toronto." Shrieks of laughter echoed up from the basement, and Cole grinned. "I'm sure the kids will be awake way too late playing video games, but they're all set with their sleeping bags."

Cole hadn't expected Aunt Judy and Uncle Steve to take him up on his invite to spend the holidays in Ottawa, but it was awesome to have family around. With Daniel's friend Pam and her girlfriend coming for dinner the next day, they'd have a full house.

"Christmas Eve is meant for staying up late," Claudia said. "The little bastards have so much sugar in them they won't need sleep."

Laughing, Cole took his buzzing phone from his pocket and read the screen. "My dad says hi, and merry Christmas."

She smiled. "Well, tell Bill the same right back. You know, your father's a real piece of work, but if I hadn't made the mistake of marrying him, we wouldn't have you in our lives." She took Cole's chin and kissed his cheek. "I love you. Sleep tight and dream of lots of sugarplums."

"You too."

Once she was upstairs, Cole flicked off the kitchen light and went to drag Daniel away from his desk. As soon as he walked into the little office, Daniel said, "I know, I know. I'm coming."

Not yet, but you will be. Cole stood behind Daniel's chair, teasing his curls and peeking over his shoulder at the paperwork on the desk. "What can't wait until the new year? The office closed today at noon, didn't it?"

"Uh-huh." Daniel's pen scratched over the paper. "I implemented a new staff information form and said they had to be filled out before Christmas. Just living up to my end of the bargain. I'm almost done."

"Hey, have you heard if Justin has found a new job yet?"

Daniel glanced up, trying not to smile. "Not yet. Turns out when you lie about your qualifications and are crappy at your job, it's hard to find a new position."

"Couldn't have happened to a better asshole."

As Daniel chuckled and went back to the form, Cole rubbed Daniel's neck and said, "You're not supposed to work on our anniversary week."

"It's a whole week now, hmm?"

"Yep. It's a new thing."

Daniel grinned. "You know what? You're right—this can wait." He straightened the papers and left them in a neat pile on the side of the desk. "Let's go celebrate. Quietly."

"And unlike last year, I have full use of both my hands. And I know how to use them."

"I am well aware." Daniel pushed back his chair and stood, kissing Cole soundly and holding him close. "I love you."

"Love you too. Maybe next year we can go back to Tremblant. You, me, a hot tub."

"It's a date. We'll alternate. One Christmas with the fam, one Christmas at our private chalet." He tugged Cole around the desk and into the hall. "Oh, wait. I need my charging cable. Want to make sure I can take pictures tomorrow morning."

"I'll grab it. Go on up."

Cole ducked back into the office, flipping on the light. Behind the desk, he unplugged the cable from the laptop port. Then he glanced at the form Daniel had been filling out.

A line caught his eye before he went back upstairs, grinning the whole way, his heart full.

In case of emergency, contact: Cole Smith; domestic partner; 343-555-555

THE END

Santa Daddy

KEIRA ANDREWS

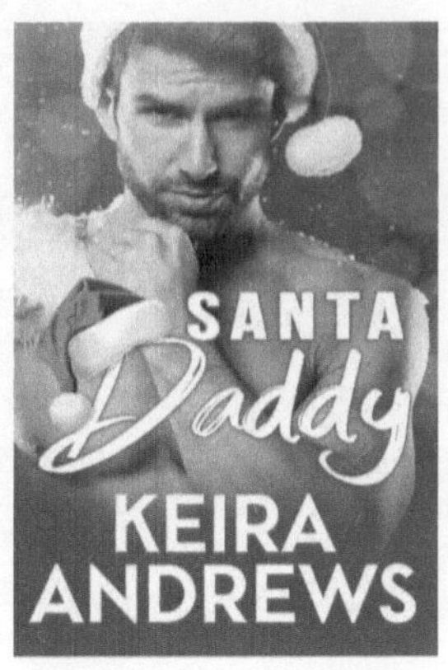

Acknowledgments and Dedication

Thanks to Anara, Mary, DJ Jamison, and Leta Blake. This one's for everyone who loves the holidays as much as I do. Fa la la la la! <3

Chapter One

MALL SANTAS WEREN'T supposed to be hot.

Heart thudding from his run through town, Hunter stopped short inside the storage room, the back door to the parking lot slamming shut behind him with a gust of frigid air. He blinked at the vision standing in front of him like a mirage amid the stacks of dusty boxes and crates.

Was he still asleep? Was this a fever dream? Because mall Santas were supposed to be old and kind of short and schlubby. It was the law of the universe or something.

Yet this Santa—probably mid-forties and wearing shiny black boots, red velvet pants with fuzzy white cuffs, and a matching red velvet coat hanging open—was something out of a *Details* lumberjack photo shoot or one of those fireman calendars Hunter's mom got every year that he used to secretly jerk off to as a teenager.

A white tank top stretched over Santa's broad, muscular chest, dark hair peeking out the top of the cotton, his nipples hard and skin a warm olive. His short hair and full, trimmed beard were way more pepper than salt, but the scattered silver highlights were crazy sexy. He had to be at least six-two and towered over Hunter, arching a dark eyebrow.

Please ask if I've been naughty or nice.

"About time."

Hunter blinked at him, his porno fantasy evaporating as he tried to catch his breath. "Huh?"

"You're late," Santa accused gruffly.

"Oh. Right." A burst of anxiety froze out the sizzle of lust that had warmed Hunter's veins. "I know, sorry." He panted softly, pulling off his wool hat. His hair fell over his forehead, and he pushed a strand out of his eye. "I overslept."

Santa stared at him as if he was profoundly stupid and/or pathetic. "It's almost noon."

What are you, my father? Hunter squirmed with embarrassment. He despised being late, but he couldn't turn back time now and erase the last twenty minutes. He hadn't *intended* to stay up until almost four playing *God of War*, and then he'd set his alarm for ten p.m. instead of a.m. because he was a tool.

He knew this—he didn't need inappropriately hot Santa to remind him. Mall Santas were also supposed to be jolly and kind, not judgy assholes. He rolled his eyes. "Whatever. You're not my boss. And where's Mr. Tremblay?"

"Broke his hip."

"Oh. Shit, that sucks." Old Mr. Tremblay had been Pinevale's mall Santa for as long as Hunter could remember. "Um, I'm Hunter. Hunter Adams." A couple hours north of Toronto, Pinevale wasn't so small that he knew everyone in town, but Hunter definitely would have remembered seeing this guy around. Where on earth had John found him?

"I'm Mr. Spini."

A first name was apparently unforthcoming. Who did this guy think he was? Hunter was twenty-three, not some kid. Before Hunter could say as much, John Singh bustled in through the mall entrance beyond the boxes, pushing wire-rimmed glasses up his nose and wearing an incredibly ugly reindeer sweater with fuzzy antlers. In his fifties, he and his husband, Desmond, lived a few blocks from Hunter's mom. He was short, stout, and always in a hurry, but was usually smiling. Not now, though.

"Hunter! Finally."

"I know, I know. Sorry." Hunter's face went hot as he shrugged off his backpack and pulled out the ridiculous candy-cane tights. Keeping his head down, he unlaced his boots and stripped off his jeans, goosebumps spreading over his skin in the chill of the storage room, the floor freezing. As he tugged the tights over his boxer briefs, he looked up and met Santa's gaze, which swept down Hunter's body.

"What?" Hunter shoved his socked feet into the too-tight black slippers with toes curved inward and golden bell on the ends. He muttered, "I look lame, I know."

Not all of us can look unfairly hot in these costumes.

Santa said nothing as John handed him the padded belly, long white beard, and red velvet hat with white trim. "Final touches."

Hunter buttoned the green velvet jacket that barely covered his ass and junk, the fluffy white cuffs landing two inches above his wrists. The seams were snug around his shoulders, and he couldn't really lift his arms. Last time he played elf was his senior year of high school, and he hadn't realized how much he'd grown in five years. He'd been a late bloomer, although usually he still felt like that pimply, bony kid.

"Good thing this is the last year for Santa's Village." Not that he'd be desperate enough to be an elf again next year. He was getting a real job in January if it killed him. A job that didn't require a humiliating costume.

Then he felt like a dick and quickly added, "I just mean because the costume's too small on me now. It sucks that the mall's closing." Even though it was the Mall That Time Forgot and was super depressing.

John had been the mall manager for ages, and he'd been a good boss. When Hunter had emailed him on the off chance he had seasonal work, he hadn't been thinking of playing elf again, but beggars couldn't be choosers and all that. He'd been lucky John had given him the job at all.

John waved his hand. "No offense taken. Gotta move with the times. Did you hear they're putting in a Marshall's and an Outback Steakhouse? And the old grocery store on Lake Street is shutting down and a big one's going here. It'll be box stores: Treeview Plaza instead of Treeview Mall. The new owners are keeping me on to manage, so I'm good. Security, snow removal—there's still a lot to coordinate." Sweat beaded on his brown skin, and he swiped a hand over his forehead. "It's a sauna out there—the heater's stuck on high."

Hunter shivered. "Yet it's freezing back here."

John grimaced. "Same in my office and the bathrooms, but obviously there's no sense in paying to fix it. The last day is December thirty-first, and then they're tearing this old dog down and rebuilding come spring. But first we need to give this mall one last Christmas to remember. Right, team?"

Santa buckled the wide black belt around his fake belly, his long white beard obscuring the lower part of his face. He muttered, "Why did I agree to this?"

"Because you're a good friend who's doing me a favor at the last minute. I'll find someone else for next weekend, I promise. Plus all the money's going to buy toys for kids and turkey dinners. With the factory closing down this summer, it'll be a lean Christmas for a lot of folks. So that's why you agreed to this, for the record."

Santa only grumbled under his breath in response, jamming the hat on his head.

"Wait. *All* the money?" Hunter's stomach dropped. "Are we not getting paid?" After three unpaid internships in Toronto since he'd graduated university and still no actual jobs, he'd come home early to Pinevale for the holidays to live in his old bedroom and play mall elf one more time. At least he'd be getting minimum wage—or so he'd assumed.

"No, no!" John clapped Hunter on the shoulder. "You'll be paid. But Mr. Tremblay had offered to give up his salary this year and donate it to Toys and Turkeys—that's what we're calling the fund. Nick followed suit."

"Oh." Hunter glanced at Santa—this Nick Spini, who watched him with a disdainful sneer.

Shit. Was Hunter being selfish? Doing eight-hour shifts Saturday and Sunday for two weekends would give him money for presents for his mom, sister, and his new niece. He'd been hoping to find some other seasonal work during the week since Pinevale wasn't big enough to warrant a full-time Santa's Village, and with the tiny, ancient mall closing, there wasn't enough demand for pictures with Santa for more than the two weekends.

Granted, he'd spent the majority of the last four days since he'd taken the Greyhound home playing video games and eating Doritos instead of job hunting, but he'd just wanted to not think about the mess of his life for a little while. The internship he'd just quit had expected twelve-hour days just like the other places, and he was burned-out.

Familiar acid flooded his belly. Before Hunter could explain that he needed to make money for working after more than a year of interning for "experience" and "connections" and to "get his foot in the door"—only to have said doors slammed in his face as soon as he tried to actually earn a living, Nick said, "Can we get this over with?"

Instead of calling him out for being a bag of dicks, John only laughed. "That's the holiday spirit. Come on, Grinch. Time to grow that heart. I know you're not used to being around people, but just think, What would Eric have said and done? Then do that."

Nick huffed, and Hunter couldn't tell if he was pissed or kind of laughing? Wondering who Eric was, Hunter grabbed his elf hat and followed Nick out of the storeroom after they stashed their stuff in an old staff locker. His eyes were drawn to how the red velvet stretched across Nick's wide shoulders. He was a mountain of a man.

They made their way over the ugly brown brick floor, a weird cobblestone that was probably done in the seventies before there were accessibility laws. Half the stores had closed already, and although John had hung wreathes and garlands on the brown brick walls, Treeview Mall was clearly in its death throes.

It was windowless, low-ceilinged, and one story in a square horseshoe shape, like a time capsule of ugly seventies design. The handful of old men who spent hours a day in the tiny food court area with only two greasy food options—Roy's Burgers or Donut Time—watched silently as they passed, paper coffee cups in front of them. The peppy strains of "All I Want for Christmas is You" played through the mall's speakers, Mariah's voice echoing on the cobblestones.

The women who worked in La Belle Style, the old-lady clothing store that was sticking it out to the mall's bitter end, gathered in the doorway as they passed. "Hunter!" Mrs. Buckingham called. "Don't you look adorable!"

He gave his mom's friend a weak smile, cringing as he felt hundreds of eyes on him as they reached the line of families, restless kids exclaiming in excitement at seeing Santa. The kids squealed and cried, "Santa!" and Nick jolted before waving at them as if remembering *he* was Santa.

Tugging down his green jacket, Hunter felt like a bigger loser than usual as he followed in Nick's wake. Hunter was five-eight, so not *super* short or anything, but he was a scrawny kid in comparison. He was blond and could barely grow a beard, and Nick was teeming with hair and muscles and manliness. Which was weird for Santa Claus, but he was working it, definitely catching the attention of the moms waiting in line in front of

Santa's Village.

Hunter supposed elves weren't supposed to be manly, but the merry *ding!* of the golden bells on his shoes with each pinched step didn't do anything for his self-esteem. Not that he was planning on picking up guys at the mall—he was hopeless in that department. Still, he felt as gangly as he had back in high school.

The village was an ancient gingerbread house sort of thing that had seen far better days, but John had strung it with tons of colored Christmas lights and garlands to cover how faded and decrepit the painted plywood was.

Nick settled himself on a wide bench. The line of people were roped off at the end of the fake candy path that wound through little snow-sprayed Christmas trees, so at least in the village there was a bit of breathing room. Hunter was surprised there was such a sizable crowd, but there wasn't much to do in Pinevale.

He frowned at the bench. "No throne thingy?"

John shook his head. "The whole sitting-on-Santa's-lap thing is inappropriate these days." He pointed to the bench, which had a backrest. "This way the kid can sit beside Santa, and there's room on both sides if siblings want to come up together."

"No one's sitting on my lap," Nick growled.

Hunter rolled his eyes. "You realize you have to be nice to the kids, right?"

Nick only stared at him above his fake white beard. His eyes were a steely gray flecked with yellow, and it was *really* annoying how hot he still was even though he was apparently a dick.

John clapped his hands, putting on a big grin. "Okay, show-time!" As he led Hunter back down the path, he whispered, "Nick's a grump, but his bark is worse than his bite."

Hunter wanted to ask how John knew him, but there wasn't time. "If you say so."

"Trust me. Okay, you remember how it goes? I take the money from the parents, and you ask the kids their names and escort them to Santa." He peered around. "Where's our photographer... There she is."

"Hey, guys!" Courtney Campbell joined them with a smile, her dark ponytail swishing and a big camera around her neck. She was in her forties and ran Pinevale's little photography store. She wore jeans and a snowman sweater, and it didn't seem fair that she didn't have to dress up. "Hunter, didn't expect to see you pulling on the candy-cane tights again."

Well, I'm almost twenty-three, I can't get a real job, I'm freeloading off my sister in TO, I have a shit-ton of student debt, I honestly hate working in an office, I'm still a virgin, and I have no clue what I want to do with my life, so why not make the humiliation complete by being a mall elf again?

He managed to smile. "Yeah. Me either."

"Hunter's doing me a favor," John said. "I had to beg, but he agreed."

Hunter gave him a grateful smile for the lie. "It's no problem."

John winked at him and turned to the line of people. "Sorry for the delay, folks! Rudolph got a flat!" The crowd laughed agreeably, and John murmured to Hunter, "Fa la la la la!"

Gah la la la la was more like it, but Hunter slapped on a smile, trying to choke down the worry about money and his future and what he'd do after the holidays. His mom would let him stay as long as he wanted, but what was he going to *do*? What did he even *want* to do?

He'd gotten an English lit degree because that's what he was good at, and it was useless in the real world aside from ticking off the requirement of most companies to have a BA in *something*. He couldn't even get an entry-level job, and he'd worked his ass off at those internships.

His gut twisted, pulse kicking up and his breath catching. Fuck, he just felt so out of control.

"It's Santa!" a little girl squealed, jerking Hunter back to the present. His life was an aimless shit-show, but at least he had *a* job to do. He took a deep breath and pulled on his green elf hat, the white fuzzy brim already too hot on his forehead. No matter. Even with a grumpy, brawny, stupidly sexy Santa to put up with, he was going to be his best elf self. With bells on—literally.

Chapter Two

SITTING ON THE too-hard bench, Nick watched as Hunter reached to straighten his elf hat. His green jacket rode up, giving Nick an excellent view of his perky, rather spectacular ass. He was quite pretty, what with his golden hair wisping over his forehead, a round face and pink lips, freckles on his nose, and deep blue eyes. Too bad he was apparently one of those spoiled millennials who showed up late and only cared about money.

Hunter looked to be in his twenties and probably still lived at home. By his mid-twenties, Nick had been working full time for years and owned a truck and a house. It hadn't been easy, and he'd worked his way up, learning about forestry and eventually tree farming. He hadn't expected anything on a silver platter. People of all ages these days seemed more entitled than ever, and Nick had no patience for any of it.

Well, Hunter wasn't Nick's business, or his problem. He was playing Santa for two days, and two days only. When the usual Santa had fallen that morning, John had called in a panic, and considering John and Desmond were Nick's only friends, he'd given in. So this weekend he'd have to deal with people whether he liked it or not.

He thought of John's instructions: What would Eric have said and done?

As Nick watched Hunter lead a little redheaded girl along the path toward him, he had to smile to himself, hearing Eric's voice—low, with a mischievous hint to his Scottish brogue.

I'd say you're being a miserable grouch and that you need to remove the stick from your ass, stat. That's my professional medical opinion.

Of course Eric was gone, so what did he know? But no, he was right, and Nick made an effort to smile genuinely at the girl, who clung to Hunter's hand. Maybe Nick's smiling skills were rusty, since Hunter said to her, "It's okay, Jessica. Santa's really friendly, I promise." He shot Nick a pointed look, eyebrows raised as if daring Nick to prove him wrong. Okay, perhaps there was a bit of sass there, not just eye-rolling millennial petulance.

Nick cleared his throat, pitching his voice a little higher and softer than usual, mimicking the way Eric had spoken to young children. "Hi there, Jessica. It's wonderful to meet you. Do you want to sit down and tell me what you'd like for Christmas?"

As Jessica hesitantly told him about wanting a sled and some kind of doll that was probably the latest fad, Nick nodded and smiled and pretended he knew exactly what she was talking about. From the corner of his eye, he was aware of Hunter watching, and when Nick glanced at him while he and Jessica shifted for their picture, Hunter's cheeks went red, and he hurried back down the candy path.

The picture was taken as Hunter brought up the next kid, and Nick smiled and nodded to the steady stream of children coming to sit with him. He also tried to ignore Eric in his head.

Admit it—the kids are adorable. You don't hate this. Especially with the sexy elf eye candy.

Eric had always called him on his shit, and eight years after his death, his voice in Nick's head was a familiar comfort. It wasn't *real,* of course, and it wasn't always there. But Eric would show up once in a while, usually when Nick needed a swift kick in the ass.

Yes, sometimes Daddy needs the spanking.

He snorted out loud, and Hunter, who had brought up another girl, glared and hissed, "What are you laughing at?" His fair cheeks flushed red, and when he had the girl seated, he tugged at the hem of his green jacket. Clearly, he was uncomfortable in the too-small costume, but he also seemed anxious and jittery in his own skin. Any traces of sass vanished, replaced by a flash of raw vulnerability.

Nick instinctively wanted to reassure him, but before he could, the little girl was providing detailed evidence of her being very, *very* good and deserving of soccer cleats and a princess dress with puffy sleeves she really, *really* wanted so, *so* much.

The stream of kids seemed unending, and Nick's ass was numb and his entire body uncomfortably damp with sweat by the time John closed off the line and put up a sign saying they'd be back in half an hour. Nick's cheeks actually hurt from all the smiling, and he couldn't wait to take off the beard and hat.

While John grabbed them lunch, Nick and Hunter retreated to the storeroom. As soon as they were inside, Hunter rounded on him and snapped, "Seriously, could you stop laughing at me? I feel ridiculous enough already in this costume."

Nick blinked in surprise. "I wasn't." He dropped his gaze over Hunter's body. Yes, the costume was comical, but those lean legs were enticing in the tights, and the way the green jacket just skimmed the bulge of Hunter's package... "There's nothing wrong with the way you look." He'd meant it to be reassuring, but it had come out decidedly flirty.

But Hunter rolled his eyes, his arms crossed tightly. "Yeah, right. Now you're just messing with me."

He bit back a surge of irritation. This was exactly why Nick spent most of his time with his trees and his dog. People were so much damn work. He clamped down on his urge to soothe. "If you say so."

"I just..." Hunter clenched his jaw. "Forget it." He swiped off his hat with attached ears, running a hand through his damp hair, sweat glistening on his forehead. "Jesus, it's hot out there."

"That we can agree on." Nick tried to unfasten the long beard, which fit with a string around his head that hooked together at the side, but the hook seemed to be caught in his hat by his ear. He tugged, but it was no use. "Can you give me a hand?"

After a beat of silence, Hunter pointed to himself and asked, "Me?"

"I don't see any other elves here." He motioned to his ear. "The hook's caught."

"Oh. Right. Um…" Hunter neared as if he was afraid Nick would bite.

And goddamn if that didn't rattle the cage of Nick's inner dom.

Tentatively, Hunter tugged on the snag, his knuckles brushing the corner of Nick's jaw. Nick watched from the corner of his eye as Hunter frowned and said, "It's really tangled somehow." He leaned closer, going up on his tip-toes, the bells on his shoes dinging softly. He wavered, and Nick took hold of Hunter's waist with one hand to steady him.

Hunter sucked in a breath, a tremor rippling through the firm muscles under Nick's palm. "These shoes are too tight," he mumbled. "Hard to get my balance."

"Take your time." Nick spread his fingers, wondering what Hunter's body would feel like naked.

Hunter stuck out the pink tip of his tongue as he concentrated on the hook. "There." He lifted off the hat, and the beard mercifully came free as he stepped back and Nick let go of him.

The fake beard made his real hair itchy, and Nick rubbed at his face. "Thanks." He unbuckled the thick black belt and dropped it to the concrete floor with a thud before stripping off his coat and padding. His white tank top stuck to his skin, and goosebumps spread over him in the chill of the room compared to the heat out in the mall. He tugged at the scooped neck of the cotton, tempted to peel it off, but he'd only have to put it back on damp.

When he looked up, a new shiver ran through him—one that had nothing to do with the temperature. Hunter was staring at Nick's chest, his full lips parted, a shine glistening as if he'd just licked them. He jerked his gaze up to Nick's, his Adam's apple bobbing. "Oh, um… You're welcome." He spun away with a decidedly guilty expression on his pretty face to go along with the lust.

Despite himself, Nick's balls tingled, and as John opened the door, Nick found himself flushing as well even though nothing had happened. Hunter stared at his feet, and silence stretched out. Holding a bulging paper bag and cardboard cup holder, John looked between them with arched eyebrows.

"How are my Santa and elf holding up?"

They nodded and assured him they were great, and the three of them sat on overturned crates, John fortunately carrying the conversation as they ate, telling them all about the plans for Toys and Turkeys.

After Hunter excused himself to go to the washroom, Nick asked, "What's his story?" before he could stop himself, barely even waiting for the door to shut. He huffed at himself in his mind. He did not have time to give a shit about anything but his harvest, and here he was in a Santa suit finding himself intrigued by a mall elf half his age.

John sucked cola through a straw. "Hunter's a good kid. Single mother. His father took off when he was a baby, I think. His mom's Pam Adams; she's a nurse at County. Probably knew Eric, come to think of it. Hunter worked for me when he was in high school. Went to U of T and graduated last year, but I think he's having trouble getting a job. Seems like he's floundering."

"Probably because this generation expects trophies just for showing up."

"Always the cynic." John shook his head with a mix of exasperation and affection. "It's not so easy for them, you know. Cost of living keeps going up, but salaries sure don't. It was easier for our parents, harder for us, and harder still for them. There aren't the jobs there used to be, at least not for decent money."

"Fair point." Nick popped a fry into his mouth, savoring the salty grease.

"I was reading about how new lawyers have to take the paralegal jobs because they can't find anything else. I wouldn't want to be starting work now, I tell you." He motioned with a fry. "But you know, I'm glad at least it's better for them coming out. Hunter did it when he was seventeen, which still wasn't *easy* in Pinevale. Took courage. He's always been high-strung, and he was pretty shy back then; I don't think he had a lot of friends."

"Really? With that face?" *And that ass?* Despite himself, Nick imagined the lovely *smack* his palm would make against that perky backside. Eric's teasing voice filled his mind.

Well, you do think today's youth needs more discipline.

John smiled slyly. "You like what you see, eh? I thought so."

"What? No." Nick scoffed. "He's half my age."

"And? As you can see, he's all grown up now. Back then he was covered in zits. Very awkward. He's still self-conscious, I think, despite looking like he does. Not that I would look."

Nick laughed. "You're married, not dead. I'm sure Des looks too."

John chuckled. "Yep. Do you ever watch that *Riverdale?* Archie is much more attractive than he should be."

"I've seen it listed on Netflix. I'll check it out."

"Netflix? So you mean you don't just sit around out there in the woods brooding and writing poetry and other Byronic pursuits?"

Nick tossed his wadded-up napkin at him, trying not to smile. "Shut up."

"But really, you're out there alone so much of the time. You really are becoming a hermit, and you're only, what? Forty-six? Are you hooking up, at least?"

"Sure, once in a while." Nick shrugged. "I go to the club in Barrie. It's fine." It had gotten a little boring, if he was honest. In a rural area, pickings were slim, and he hadn't found anyone who wanted a daddy or whose needs could satisfy him. Although he and Eric had only been five years apart in age, Nick had definitely been Daddy in the bedroom, and they'd both found it incredibly fulfilling.

But Nick hadn't assumed the role in years now. For him it was about more than just play-acting—the satisfaction came in that genuine need and surrender, giving them both peace. In his sporadic hookups over the years, he'd never met anyone with that certain vulnerability he was drawn to. Maybe he should have tried harder to meet more men, but it was so much damn work. Simpler to lose himself in the solitude and dependable rhythms of the farm.

"And do you ever bring someone out there to the Fortress of Solitude?"

Nick ate another fry. "You and Des come for dinner every month"

"We don't count."

He shrugged. "I have a dog. She's much better company than people."

"As wonderful as Ella is, she does lack certain qualities that people possess."

"I know. That's why she's perfect when she's not chasing squirrels and getting sprayed by skunks. But you'll be delighted to hear that I'm going to have to hire an extra hand to cut down trees this week. The demand is late this season after that warm spell at the beginning of December. I'll be behind after taking time out to play Santa."

John grimaced. "I'm sorry to put you out. I really do appreciate you stepping up at the last minute—especially considering how much you hate people, and particularly crowds of them." John winked, but his smile faded. "And I don't mean to nag. We worry about you all alone out there as the years go by. We just wish—"

Hunter returned, skidding to a halt as John and Nick looked at him. In the silence, he fidgeted and defensively asked, "What?"

Such rough, skittish edges Hunter had, and Nick wondered what it would take to calm those jitters. Which was *ridiculous.* He had no time to be intrigued by some pretty young man, so he said dryly, "Don't worry, we weren't talking about you." He looked away dismissively.

"Actually, you're just the man Nick needs!" John clapped his hands, grinning. "He was saying he needs help on the farm next week, and I know you're looking for more work. It's the perfect solution."

Nick glared at him, not sure whether the bolt of adrenaline coursing through him was dread or anticipation. "I was going to ask Bill Chang."

"I think he's in Florida," John said. "Hunter, you're free during the week, right?"

Hunter eyed Nick uneasily. "Yeah, totally. Uh, what kind of work is it?"

John said, "Nick owns a Christmas tree farm. Off ninety-three, out near Thorny Creek. All by his lonesome." To Nick, he asked, "You need help chopping down and that kind of stuff?"

Well… Maybe there was no harm in giving the kid a chance. "Yes. It's hard, sweaty work—and not the kind from wearing silly costumes in an overheated mall." He'd meant it as a joke, but Hunter shifted from foot to foot, crossing his arms. Not defiantly—defensively.

Hunter said, "Oh, okay. I don't know if I'm strong enough?"

The urge to guide and show him just how strong he could be rose up in Nick, a hunger he knew he should ignore. "If you don't think you can do it, I'll find someone else." He shrugged carelessly, yet he hoped Hunter would meet the challenge.

Yes, there was something about him—the spirited insolence paired with uneasiness, that self-consciousness like he truly didn't realize how beautiful he was. He seemed to be a jumble of contradictions, but Nick supposed he was too. He found most people exhausting and preferred solitude, yet he was drawn to Hunter.

"I can do it." Hunter nodded as if convincing himself, drawing up straighter, his tights leaving nothing to the imagination. "Definitely."

"There you go!" John opened a box of doughnut holes and ate one with gusto. "Santa and his elf! What could be better?"

Chapter Three

OMG IS IT true you're back in the tights???

Hunter smiled as Shelby's text flashed on his phone's screen Monday night, and he paused his game and stretched out on his mom's old leather couch. Shelby had been one of his few friends in high school and a fellow mall elf back when John could afford to hire more than one.

Hunter wished desperately that she was still in Pinevale, or at least Ontario. She'd gone to UBC and had landed a job at a hip yoga company in Vancouver. He was thrilled for her, of course. Maybe a little jealous that she seemed to have her life figured out, but at least ninety-five percent thrilled.

He typed back:

I hope my temporary return to elfhood isn't the biggest news Pinevale's gossip network has to offer.

Shelby responded:

I'm afraid so. Although I also hear Santa's some super hottie? Do tell. And poor Mr. Tremblay. He was always so nice.

Hunter filled her in on what he knew about Mr. Tremblay and his broken hip. Then he added:

Santa was hot, yeah. He owns some Christmas tree farm way out of town? He was kind of a dick, tbh.

Which hadn't stopped Hunter from seeing visions of Nick's chest in that white undershirt, his chest hair poking out, arms thick, nipples so…lickable.

OMFG, that hot guy who lives in the woods? I met him once when my mom went to talk to him about getting trees to sell for the Girl Guides. I was only thirteen or something, but I definitely appreciated that whole lumberjack vibe.

Hunter replied:

Yeah, he's still got that going on. He waited for Shelby's response.

You know, I think he might be gay now that I think about it? You should get on that. Tell him you've been very, very naughty.

He sucked in a breath, excitement sparking. Nick was gay? Well, he was apparently friends with John—not that John didn't have straight friends. But it was irrelevant anyway. Hunter laughed out loud and said to himself, "Even if Nick Spini's gay, he thinks I'm an idiot. And even if he didn't, I'd never get a guy like that." Before he could respond to Shelby, she sent:

And don't give me that crap about you not being hot enough. It's like you look in the mirror and still see yourself in grade ten. You're gorgeous. You realize most dudes are totally intimidated by you, right? And this is why you're somehow still a virgin despite being a walking wet dream?

Hunter barked out a laugh and replied:

Sure. If you say so.

He could imagine her impatient huff as she typed:

I'm telling you. Remember when we went out last summer when I came home? I know you're nervous and insecure, but it comes across like you're not interested. So you go home alone when everyone in the bar wants to bang you. Also, I maintain that Brett Leblanc wanted to do you even though you were still in your awkward phase.

He winced thinking of star hockey player Brett, who'd teased him and called him gay so much that Hunter had finally stood up to him and said he was, and if Brett didn't like it, he could kiss his queer ass. That had amazingly shut up Brett and anyone else who might have had an issue with it.

Hunter had already been honest about his sexuality at home, but he'd never planned to come out at school. It had turned out shockingly okay. He wished he could bottle the confidence he'd had in that moment and apply it to the rest of his life. Maybe he just needed to get really angry for it to come out. So to speak.

Seriously, you're a babe. It's time you got out of your own way. And don't roll your eyes.

Laughing, he stopped himself, although his eyes were halfway there. He typed:

Okay, okay, I'm gorgeous. Now fill me in about that new guy you're seeing.

He didn't tell Shelby he was going to Nick's farm the next day to work. It would probably be a disaster, and he didn't want to have to tell her later that he'd failed. Every time he'd had a job interview and had been sure he'd get it, having to tell Shelby and his family that he hadn't gotten the job after all had been more and more embarrassing.

After they finished texting, Hunter put down his phone and watched the lights on the fake tree in the corner of the living room shine on the glittery ornaments. He said out loud, "I'm gorgeous," then scoffed.

He was fine. Not too short, a little skinny, but not as bad as he used to be. His face had cleared up aside from the freckle situation, and he had okay blond hair. He'd definitely planned on having so much sex in university, but he'd always held back for some reason. He'd never been able to really let go and trust another guy, and then he'd started to feel extremely self-conscious about still being a virgin. Now here he was caught in a vicious cycle.

He closed his eyes, letting one of his favorite fantasies unspool. It was only images, really—a beefy man being in charge, Hunter being penetrated hard or maybe even spanked. All the control and worry taken from him so he could relax and be free. Be fucked and taken care of. He'd watched plenty of porn, and he was always drawn to the hairy doms.

His cock stirred, and he rubbed it with the heel of his hand through his track pants. In his fantasies, the man taking control was always older, although Hunter had never had the guts to try it in real life. He was terrified he'd be laughed at, and he'd probably get it all stupidly wrong anyway due to the whole virgin thing.

He should just man up, install Grindr, find some guy, and get his first time over with. Rip off the Band-Aid. It wasn't like he didn't *want* to have sex, but he'd built it into a mountain in his mind. He'd been too chickenshit to put himself out there for too long.

The idea that Nick was gay popped back into Hunter's head. On Sunday, they'd done another long day in Santa's Village, and Nick hadn't said much aside from giving him gruff instructions on coming out to the farm on Tuesday. But Hunter could have sworn he'd caught Nick checking out his ass more than once. That he'd felt…*something* in the air between them in that freezing storage room. He'd clearly made a shitty first impression on Nick by being late, and he was determined to prove himself.

He laughed out loud, shaking his head. Nick probably couldn't have cared less, and it was all in Hunter's pathetic virgin mind. Still, his thoughts drifted back to Nick. *Was* he gay? Had he actually been checking out Hunter's ass?

He was probably staring because I looked so stupid and lame in that costume.

But there was nothing wrong with playing what-if, was there? He shifted on the couch, the leather squeaking. Hunter imagined Nick with other guys, and he was going to be full-on jerking off in a minute. If Nick was gay, did he have a boyfriend? Husband?

Would he go for a younger guy?

Hunter's breath caught, and he shoved his hand into his track pants, gripping his cock as the floodgates opened and the fantasy took over. He imagined himself over Nick's knee on that bench in the mall, getting spanked as he cried out, Nick totally in control, holding him down, not letting him wriggle, showing him how to do everything—

The engine of his mom's Ford Focus rattled as she pulled into the driveway, the garage door vibrating as it rolled up. Hunter shot to his feet, turning in a circle before he sat back down, grabbed a throw cushion and plonked it on his lap, and picked up the game controller. He started playing, the sound of battle hopefully drowning out his panting.

"Hi, sweetie!" his mom called as she opened the door.

From where he was on the couch in the living room at the front of the house, he couldn't see her yet in the foyer, but he could feel the blast of arctic air. "Hey!"

She stuck her head around the corner and pulled off her toque, a dusting of snow falling to the tiles. Her hair was blond like his, and it was coming out of the bun she wore for work. "Did you have a good day?"

"Uh-huh. I made dinner. It probably sucks."

She pursed her lips. "I was just going to ask what that wonderful smell was. I'm sure it'll be delicious, and thank you." She took off her coat and boots, her purple scrubs wrinkled underneath. "I'm going to have a quick shower." She glanced at the TV. "Are you winning?"

He'd just gotten seriously injured because he was paying more attention to his mercifully flagging boner, but Hunter nodded and gave her a smile before she disappeared down the hallway toward the bedrooms. Their single-level house had three bedrooms and two bathrooms, and a finished basement that was mostly used for storage now that Heather and Hunter had (mostly) moved out. There was a nice little yard out back with a corner vegetable garden in summer. It was home.

In the beige kitchen, the worn linoleum chilly under his bare feet, he stirred the chili in the slow cooker, inhaling the cumin and other spices. It wasn't fancy, but it hit the spot. He turned on the oven to heat up the crusty bread. The kitchen wallpaper was a rooster design, and every time his mom watched HGTV, she talked about tearing out the old brown cupboards and doing a back-splash and new flooring and an island. But while she was lending Hunter money to make his monthly student loan payments, she couldn't afford it.

His stomach tightened. He'd been so sure he'd be able to find some kind of job during the six-month grace period for loans after graduation. He'd worked serving tables all through university, but it had been too much with the long hours the internships had demanded and commuting to his sister's condo in suburban Mississauga.

At least the companies had paid his transit expenses, which they'd made seem very generous. Hunter was willing to pay his dues, but at a certain point he needed actual freaking money.

"I can hear you worrying from down the hall," his mom said as she entered the kitchen, her slippers flapping on the tile. Her flannel PJs were covered in sleeping cats, and her wet hair hung over her shoulders. She kissed his cheek. "Don't worry, be happy."

"Are you going to start whistling that song?"

She twisted the top off a bottle of red and pulled down two glasses. "Probably." She handed him a glass. "Vino for your thoughts."

He took it and sipped the oaky, spicy wine. "The usual. That I can't get a real job, and I'm going to end up living in your basement until you kick me out."

"Good thing I'd never kick you out." She winked, the lines around her eyes crinkling as she smiled. She was fifty now but still super pretty. Hunter's father was a douchebag and moron for leaving her since she was the best. Hunter had been a baby when his father took off, but they'd been well rid of him. She'd dated a bit over the years but said she was single and happy now.

Still, Hunter couldn't help but feel guilty that both he and his older sister had moved out. Was his mom lonely here on her own? She never complained about it, but then again, she'd never let him hear her complain about anything that mattered.

"And your sister won't kick you out either, for the record."

He sighed. "I know, but… It's bad enough I've been freeloading off Heather since I graduated. She and Rick have been amazing, but they have the baby now. She doesn't want her little brother taking up the room that's supposed to be the baby's. It's not fair that they have to have the crib and everything in their room. I can't go back in the new year. I need to find another place. Give up on landing a real job and go back to waiting tables. I made good money."

"Mmm." She sipped her wine, leaning back against the counter. "You talk a lot about getting a 'real' job. Is being a server not a real job?"

"No, of course it is. I just mean, like…" He rubbed his face. "After university, you're supposed to get, like, a *grown-up* job. A career."

"And you want your career to be in marketing and communications?"

He shrugged. "I have an English degree, and I can write. I don't want to go to teacher's college because the only reason I'd want to teach is to get summers off, and that's a shitty reason. So if I want to work in business, communications makes sense."

"But do you want to work in business?"

He shrugged again. "I want to make a decent salary one day. It doesn't feel like there are a lot of options. I don't love working in an office, but most people don't, right?"

She sipped her wine and took bowls from the creaky cabinet. "Do you have to work in an office to have a 'real' job?"

"Well, it depends. Obviously you work in the hospital, and that's a real career. But what am I going to do with an English lit degree if I'm not working in some kind of office?"

"Do you have to *do* something with it? Is it not valuable in and of itself?"

Hunter stuck his hand in an oven mitt, flinching from the wave of heat as he took out the bread and dropped it on the cutting board. "You're very philosophical tonight."

"I am, aren't I?" She laughed and pulled him into a hug. "Just give it some thought. You realize there are plenty of people older than you who are still living with their parents and have no idea what to do with their lives, right? It's common these days." She pulled back with a frown. "But you're always so hard on yourself. And unpaid internships should be illegal."

He shrugged. "They're supposed to be, but the companies find loopholes. If you complain, you can guess who's *not* getting a job there in the end."

"It's BS, is what it is. You've more than paid your dues. So don't stress, honey. It's the holidays. You'll figure it all out."

When? What if I don't?

Hunter nodded and smiled, shoving away the worry. "You're right."

"Always." She winked.

They ate in front of the TV as usual, watching a recording of whatever procedural had been on recently. As his mom fast-forwarded through commercials, she asked, "So what's this job you lined up for tomorrow?"

Lust flamed through him thinking of his little fantasy earlier, and Hunter took a mouthful of chili and shrugged. But she paused the TV and waited for him to swallow. He cleared his throat. "I'm helping at a Christmas tree farm. The guy's a friend of John's? Nick Spini."

"Oh! Nick." She smiled. "Huh. I haven't heard that name in years."

His heart skipped. "You know him?"

"No, not really. I worked with his partner, though. Dr. McKinnon. Eric." Her smile went sad and distant. "Such a lovely man. Always had a smile for you even after a double shift. It was incredibly tragic, what happened."

Hunter toyed with his spoon, his chest tightening. "What happened?"

She stared off into the distance. "A boy fell through the ice on Swiss Lake, and Eric was driving by. He stopped and tried to save him, of course. Called 911 before he went onto the lake, but more of the ice gave way, and the water was just too cold. They'd both drowned by the time police arrived."

"Wow." So Nick *was* indeed gay or bi or whatever, but Hunter couldn't feel happy about it after hearing *that*.

"Nick was devastated, as you can imagine. He disappeared, more or less. I actually forgot about him." Tears glistened in her eyes, and she shook her head, focusing on Hunter again. "Isn't that sad?"

"It's not your fault. When did it happen?"

She swiped at her eyes. "Let me think." After a few moments, she said, "Must be seven or eight years ago now. Yes, eight, I think." A tear slipped down her cheek. "Poor Nick. How could I have not thought of him at all in so long?"

"From what I gather, he's kind of a hermit out there with his trees?" Hunter slid closer on the couch, putting his arm around her shoulders. "It's okay. Please don't cry."

Sniffing loudly, she half-laughed. "Oh, don't mind me. I swear, these hormones are making me an emotional wreck these days. Peri-menopause needs to shove it. Hard."

Laughing, he kissed her cheek and inhaled the fresh scent of her herbal shampoo. "Those hormones don't know who they're messing with." He paused, then added, "I love you, Mom."

"Well, aren't we just a couple of saps tonight? Thank you, honey. You know I love you too." She patted his knee. "And I'm so glad to hear you'll be spending time with Nick."

"Yeah. Hopefully it'll be okay? He's not much of a people person, I guess. But John got him to fill in as Santa, and he was actually really sweet with the kids." It had been incredibly sexy seeing him listening to the kids like their requests were all he cared about when Hunter knew he was probably bored shitless. "He said to come tomorrow since he needed today to be alone. You're sure it's cool for me to take the car on your day off?"

"Yep. I'm doing nothing tomorrow but reading my romance and relaxing. The duke is about to realize that the new stable boy is actually a young woman on the run from a dastardly viscount."

"Ohh, the plot thickens. Has he been confusingly attracted to this stable boy?"

She laughed. "Indeed he has."

"Good times."

"How about another glass of wine while we finish our dinner? Which is delicious, by the way. And don't say it was easy and shrug off the compliment. It's *delicious*. Thank you for making it. Now go get me more wine."

Hunter grinned. "Yes, ma'am."

He poured himself another glass too since it was still early. Later that night, he was going to set three alarms and make sure he was at Nick's bright and early and ready to impress. And he was *totally* going to jerk off to fantasies of sitting on Nick's lap and being very, very naughty.

"NO, NO, NO!"

The tires couldn't grip the hidden patch of ice, and as the road curved, there was nothing Hunter could do but cling to the steering wheel and brace as he slid into the ditch.

His heart pounded in his ears as he jolted to a stop, the car now tilted alarmingly, passenger side down and lodged deep in a snowdrift. The seat belt dug into the side of his neck. For a few frantic breaths, he didn't move. At least the airbag hadn't gone off and punched him in the face.

An old Bryan Adams song about Christmastime blared from the radio, and Hunter jabbed it off with a trembling finger, muttering, "Yeah, not so much magic in the air right now. But I'm okay." His voice was thin and unconvincing. He moved his limbs, and nothing seemed broken. He might have a few bruises from the seat belt, but nothing major.

"I'm okay," he repeated. And now he was stuck in a ditch in the middle of nowhere, and he was going to be late. "Fucking fuck!" He pounded the steering wheel, his leather gloves muffling the blows.

It was still dark, and he'd never been on the route that led to Nick's farm. The headlights illuminated more snow falling amid the shadowy trees looming around him, the narrow road curving out of sight. In the rear view, the high snow bank he was stuck in glowed a ghostly red above his taillights, only a void beyond. He panted harshly, twitching with the lingering adrenaline spiking through him.

Driving out toward Nick's, he hadn't even seen another vehicle in the last half an hour. He'd turned off the paved county road at least fifteen minutes ago, and Nick's driveway, which seemed pretty long on Hunter's navigation app, should have been within a couple kilometers. He grabbed his phone from the holder attached to the dashboard and blinked at the screen, the red band at the top sending a bolt of icy panic through him.

Searching for signal

"No! You have to have a signal!" He shook the phone, as if that would help somehow. "Fuck!" Gripping the phone, he closed his eyes, trying to breathe.

He was leaning down to the right, and if not for the seat belt holding him in place, he would have crashed into the passenger side when the car had slid into the ditch. But maybe if he gunned the engine, he'd be able to drive up and out? Highly unlikely, but he had to try.

"Okay. Come on, Jacques. You can do it." His mom had ironically named her car after an old Canadian racecar driver, and Hunter called on every spirit of Christmas and racecar drivers and justice in the universe as he eased on the accelerator, letting the tires grip before he gave it more gas.

The car shuddered and moved about an inch, the engine revving and the tires spinning uselessly.

"Damn it, Jacques!" He pounded the steering wheel and closed his eyes, wishing more than anything that this was a terrible dream. He muttered to himself, "Okay, think. You can handle this." He laughed harshly. "You *have* to handle this."

He opened his eyes and turned off the engine, silence setting in. First he had to call Nick to let him know he'd be late. Cringing, Hunter remembered Nick's sneer when he'd shown up late that first morning. That had totally been his fault, but this wasn't!

Surely Nick would understand. He was grumpy and gruff, but he'd been sweet with the kids, and John and his husband were friends with him. It was horrible what happened to his partner, and Nick was probably a great guy.

He'd understand.

Hunter tapped his screen with the special touch pad of his glove, acid flooding his stomach as he stared at the complete absence of bars. His voice sounded high and tight as he talked to himself. "Okay, I'll get out, and I'll find a signal. It's fine."

He shoved his door open, pushing against gravity. Bracing himself, he undid his seat belt, grunting as he climbed out. His side of the car was pointed up, and he had to jump down a couple feet to the ground, his boots sinking into the fresh snow up to his knees, his jeans instantly wet. Fuck, he should have worn his snow pants.

Dumbass!

There had been a bit of snow falling in town when he'd woken, but nothing remarkable. He should have known the farm would be in the snow-belt. It was amazing how the wind patterns, presence or absence of lakes, and the rise and fall of the land meant there'd be a couple inches of snow in one area and three times that not far away. His weather app had called for more snow later in the day, but it was falling heavier and heavier, the blowing wind reducing visibility.

Hunter held up his phone, walking in a circle through the growing drifts of snow. It was still dark as midnight, and his phone glowed in the gloom. He stood in the middle of the road, joy seizing him as a bar appeared.

"Yes, yes!" He jabbed at the screen, opening his contacts, where he'd put Nick's number in under "Santa Nick." He connected, putting the phone to his ear. His hat was in the car, and he brushed thick snow from his hair, his ears already stinging. The base temperature was actually not far below freezing—perfect conditions for damp, snowman-making snow—but the windchill was killer.

"Hello?" Nick answered.

"Hi!" Hunter's pulse raced. "I'm so sorry. I'm going to be late."

There was a huff of irritation. "It's six-fifty-two. You have eight minutes."

Humiliation ripped through him, and Hunter felt small and stupid even though he wanted to argue that he wasn't that far away and he would have been there on time, if not early despite the unexpected conditions. "I'm sorry. It's just that—"

"It doesn't matter. This was a mistake. Don't bother coming."

"Wait! I—this—" Hunter tripped over his words. "Let me

explain. My car's in the ditch."

Silence.

Blood rushed in Hunter's ears. "Hello?"

Nothing.

Jerking the phone away from his ear, he stared at the home screen. The single bar was still there. Had Nick actually *hung up* on him? "Are you serious right now?" he yelled at his phone. He wasn't sure if he was more furious or hurt. He shouldn't have cared if Nick liked him or wanted his approval, but…he did. Which was pathetic.

After pacing back and forth, he stopped and inhaled deeply. It hadn't been nostril-hair-freezing cold out when he'd left, but the wind was whipping up steadily as a storm apparently moved in. "Okay. Mom has CAA. Just have to call them. No problem."

He heaved open the car door, bracing himself on one knee so he could lean in and reach the glove box. He was blocking the overhead light, and he rooted around, feeling for the thick plastic folder. When he had it, he grabbed his wool hat and scarf, crawled back out, and closed the door. "Okay, emergency assistance," he mumbled, programming the number into his phone and saving it. "Here we go."

As soon as he got a signal again.

After fifteen minutes of slogging up and down the road, keeping the car in sight while jumping, praying, and waving his phone around, Hunter had to declare defeat. The sun was coming up for what it was worth—which wasn't much in the gloom of the forest, the wind definitely awakened and bringing down the temperature. The blowing snow stung Hunter's cheeks and eyes, his nose icy.

Back in the car, he belted himself in and turned on the engine to warm up and think for a minute. He rubbed his hands briskly in his gloves, waiting for the heat to kick in. Someone was bound to come along. He wasn't *that* far from civilization. Surely other people lived down this road, not just Nick. He hadn't seen any tire tracks in the snow, but that didn't mean anything. People would be going to work and coming along.

Definitely.

He jabbed at the radio, switching it to the local news station. The announcer's voice filled the car, her tone serious. "—snow squall warning is in effect, with the forecasted weather activity arriving hours earlier than expected and with far greater intensity, including winds gusting over seventy kilometers an hour by late morning. The OPP warn that they expect to enforce road closures on several routes in the area, including—"

Hunter's heart sank as she listed off road names, including the main county road he'd turned off. The odds of anyone coming along would plummet along with the visibility. "Fuck me," he muttered, fear beginning to drag icy fingers down his spine.

The vents had started shooting warm air, and Hunter peeled off his gloves and held up his bare hands. At least he wouldn't freeze if he had the engine on sporadically—

Gasping with a burst of true panic, he twisted off the ignition and shoved at the door to get out. He stumbled to the ground, scrabbling around to get his footing, his hands still bare. Another patch of hidden ice sent him sprawling flat out, heavy snow in his face. He finally got to his hands and knees, then to his feet, his legs shaking.

He peered around the back of the car, and sure enough, the tailpipe was completely stuck in the snowbank and blocked.

"Yeah, getting carbon monoxide poisoning is not going to help," he muttered to himself, remembering the story he saw on the news about how deadly gas could build up in a snow-bound car in under two minutes with the engine on. A mother and kids had died the previous winter, and it had happened crazy fast.

Pulse galloping, he inhaled the cold air deeply, jamming his fists in the pockets of his ski jacket. He felt okay—not sleepy or confused. He hadn't smelled any gas in the car, but of course carbon monoxide was odorless, so that didn't mean jack shit.

Would I even know if I'm confused? Am I thinking clearly?

He kept breathing deeply, turning his back to the wind and leaving the door open to air out the car. When he was as certain as he could be that he was in his right mind—the decision to come work for Nick Spini notwithstanding—Hunter opened the trunk, snow from the drift up to his waist.

There was cat litter to help the tires grip, a first aid kit, some bungee cords, the spare tire and jack, and a wool blanket. No shovel, so he couldn't dig out the car. He pulled out the blanket and wrapped it around his shoulders before going back into the front seat, sitting there for a minute out of the wind.

He tried to get a signal again, but it was no use. Even if he was strong enough to push the car out of the ditch, he needed someone behind the wheel putting on the gas. The only way Jacques was getting free was probably with a tow truck. Hunter climbed out, the thud of the door closing muffled in the snow.

It was silent in the trees aside from the growing howl of the wind and his own harsh breathing. What if he sat in the freezing car and no one came? He'd be out of the wind, but…

Hunter peered down the empty road behind and in front of him and listened, holding his breath. Nothing. No distant engines. No signs of rescue. He hadn't passed anything on his way from the county road, and it was a hell of a long walk, especially if the county road would be closed. Nick's farm had to be closer. It was the last place Hunter wanted to go, but it was preferable to freezing to death.

"I can't believe that asshole hung up on me," he announced to the forest. "Asshole!"

His shout was lost on the wind. The fact that he actually was in danger of freezing was an icy fist in his chest, and he had to keep panic at bay. He could follow the road and hope Nick's drive had a sign. At least he'd be doing something instead of just waiting and hoping.

Because what if no one came by for hours? It was very possible no one would. If he waited and *then* made a try for Nick's, he'd be in worse shape and trapped in even more snow. No, he couldn't just sit there.

The car alarm made a cheery little chirp as he pressed the lock button, leaving Jacques behind as he trudged toward what he hoped was the lesser of two evils.

Chapter Four

"ELLA, LEAVE THE damn squirrels alone!" Nick shouted into the wind as she barked. Visibility was crap, but that was beagles for you. Her nose could whiff out a squirrel, skunk, or raccoon kilometers away even if she couldn't see them. She always seemed disappointed when Nick didn't want to hunt them with her. At least they didn't have many bears around this far south, although a few had been spotted that summer.

He pushed up the fuzzy brim of his red trapper hat, which attached under his chin and protected his cheeks. He couldn't see anything beyond twenty feet in front of him. The weatherman hadn't called for a damn blizzard, but those fools were always wrong—especially with global warming making the weather more unpredictable than Nick could ever remember it. But blizzard or no blizzard, he had to harvest.

He fired up the chainsaw again, felling another tree from the grid of six- and seven-foot Fraser firs that were ready for market. Picking up the tree with his thick gloves, he shook it to get rid of any dead needles, his muscles aching already, and it wasn't even ten a.m.

Nick hefted the tree over to the baler, the engine on the round, red machine still running under the tarp he'd strung. He fed the tree into the baler's mouth, and it came out the other side wrapped in twine and ready to be stacked.

Ella was still barking at something back toward the house, her smallish brown-and-white body tense. Nick squinted through the snow. They were in the first acre closest to home, not far along the access road. He'd have to plow again with the pickup before he could get the flatbed truck down to load the trees, and the way the storm had taken hold, it would probably be tomorrow. He was used to doing everything himself—regularly working fourteen-hour days from spring through to Christmas—but it would have been good to have another pair of hands.

Too bad the sexy elf had proved unreliable after all.

He laughed at his foolishness. *Sexy elf.* Nick should have known better than to ever agree to hire him. Showing up late was apparently his MO, and Nick had zero tolerance for that shit, snow or no snow. Hunter should have left earlier and made sure he made it by seven a.m. sharp.

Nick should have known not to…what? Get his hopes up? He grunted, scowling to himself. He was better off on his own, and he'd just have to work harder. He'd already shipped out thousands of trees, but demand was high now around the fifteenth of December as busy people hurried to play catch-up and get their trees. The local nursery had asked for more than usual. Why had he agreed to play Santa and waste so much time?

"Yes, I'm being a grouch, Eric," he said to the trees, his words swallowed by the wind. He wasn't in the mood to hear the echo of Eric's teasing in his mind.

Ella had gone farther back up the access road, and her barking grew more agitated. Nick squinted again but couldn't see anything, Ella disappearing. Instinct told him it wasn't a squirrel or skunk, so he whistled for her and turned off the baler, covering it completely.

Letting Ella in first, he climbed into the pickup, driving slowly through the wall of white, the plow attached to the front of the truck clearing the way. As he neared the house, a dark smudge appeared, and he slammed on the brakes, the pickup jolting.

"Who the hell—" His heart skipped. It had to be Hunter, and Nick couldn't fight the pulse of eagerness at seeing him again. He realized he was smiling, for fuck's sake. With a grumble at himself, he wiped his expression blank. He'd told Hunter not to come, and that should have been the end of it. This was a distraction he didn't need.

He climbed out, Ella racing ahead, and called, "I told you to forget it!" before stomping over. "Why—" He halted a few feet from Hunter, blinking at him, Ella nosing around Hunter's knees.

Hunter was covered in snow. It topped the pom-pom on his dark woolen toque and the blanket wrapped around him, and dusted across his red, wind-raw face, his eyelashes actually white. He shook, his teeth chattering.

Nick looked beyond him and asked, "Where's your car?"

"In a ditch a few kilometers before the turnoff for your road." Hunter's voice was thin in the howling wind, his breathing labored. "I tried to tell you, but you hung up on me."

Fuck.

Despite the wind's bitter chill, shame and pure disgust at himself heated Nick's face and neck, bile in his throat. It was true—he had hung up before Hunter could explain his lateness. Christ, that had been hours ago! In the snow squalls, Hunter could have easily lost his way and frozen out there. Hell, he looked close to it now. Nick knew better than most how quickly nature could be fatal.

Shoving away the jagged, razor-sharp memories, he asked, "Are you hurt?" He took hold of Hunter's arms as if he'd be able to feel injuries.

Hunter shook his head. "Sorry to bug you. The OPP is closing roads, and I kept trying to get a signal, but it won't connect."

Nick shepherded him to the house. "Don't be sorry. Come on."

Inside, Nick flipped on the overhead light. Usually the big

window in the open living room and the kitchen window off to the right beyond the little foyer and closet provided plenty of natural light, but in the blizzard, the house was dim. It did feel warm, at least, even though Nick kept the thermostat low and hadn't lit a fire yet.

On the wide mat inside the front door, he eased the snow-crusted blanket from around Hunter, who shivered. Nick tossed his own heavy work gloves and hat into the corner and tried to shoo away Ella, who lingered curiously, sniffing their rare guest eagerly as Hunter toed off his boots before easing free his gloves and snow-crusted hat and scarf. His fingers trembled as he pet Ella's head, and then he struggled with the zipper of his ski jacket.

"Here." Nick unzipped it for him and pulled it free of Hunter's arms, hanging it on a wall hook. Damn it, he should have listened when Hunter had called. He'd been far angrier than the situation called for, and now guilt clawed at him. He yanked off his own boots, then his waterproof pants and jacket, and the fleece he'd layered over a plaid flannel shirt and thermal work pants. "How long have you been here? Why didn't you come inside right away?"

Hunter only watched him warily, shuddering, hugging himself.

Nick realized he'd sort-of *yelled* the questions. He cleared his throat and added more calmly, "I just mean that it wasn't locked. I would have wanted you to come in."

Ella pushed eagerly against Hunter's legs, and Nick snapped his fingers and pointed to her dog bed in the kitchen corner. "Ella, go. Now." With a single bark of protest, she did.

"I thought you'd probably kill me if I broke into your house," Hunter whispered hoarsely, his teeth clacking.

More shame flowed through him, digging into corners with sharp teeth. Nick nodded. "I can see why you'd have that impression. Jesus, you're frozen. Are you sure you aren't hurt? You didn't hit your head?"

"No," he rasped. "I wasn't going fast." He added, "I know how to drive in the snow!" as if he was waiting for Nick to accuse him of recklessness.

"I'm sure you do. We have to around here, especially with storms like this blowing in with hardly any warning. Then when we do get warnings, there will only be a couple centimeters of snow and it's nothing."

Brow creased, Hunter looked up at Nick as if trying to figure out a puzzle. "Yeah."

"Let's get you warmed up." He thought of Eric's old first-aid lessons. "If you have hypothermia, warm water could bring on arrhythmia, so a hot shower's out."

He put a hand on Hunter's tense shoulder and guided him to the thick rug by the couch in the living room. The wooden house had been built in a rustic cabin/chalet style, with a vaulted ceiling and the second story hallway open along the back with a bedroom on each side. It was decorated simply, although Nick had splurged on the thick navy-blue rug in front of the stone fireplace.

He guided Hunter there and gazed down at him, suddenly aware of how small Hunter was. Yes, Hunter was shivering from the cold, but Nick suspected he was also cowering because Nick had been judgmental and cruel when he'd hung up on him.

Making an effort to soften his tone, Nick said, "Those jeans look wet. How's your sweater? You should take them off. I'll get you some other clothes. Hold on."

After a long moment, his eyes wide, Hunter nodded.

Nick dashed upstairs for a sweatshirt, flannel PJ bottoms, and thick socks. Hunter was shivering where he left him. Keeping his gaze averted, Nick helped him undress. The green sweater was damp around the collar and wrists, and any wetness was the enemy to warmth.

Nick lifted the soft material over Hunter's head, trying to

ignore how deliciously red Hunter's nipples were. He knelt to tug off Hunter's socks, which were damp either from sweat or snow getting in the tops of his boots. Hunter grabbed Nick's shoulder to keep his balance, his hand shaking.

Peeling the cold, snow-wet denim down Hunter's legs, Nick's fingers brushed pale hair, and he wondered if the hair around Hunter's groin was as blond before forcing his focus back on first aid.

He left Hunter in his gray boxer-briefs, tearing his eyes away and helping him into too-big PJ bottoms and sweatshirt. He tugged the drawstring on the pajamas tight, knotting it so they'd stay on Hunter's slim hips.

He knelt with the soft, black wool socks. "Here you go."

Hunter held onto Nick's shoulder again, fingers sharp and trembling. Nick brushed his ankles as he pulled up the socks for him. He stood to grab the thick red fleece blanket folded on the back of the brown leather couch and wrapped it around Hunter's shaking shoulders.

"Are you thirsty?" Nick asked. At Hunter's nod, he went to the kitchen and poured a glass of room-temperature water from the pitcher on the counter. Ella whined softly, and she looked back at Hunter, clearly longing to meet him properly. Nick squatted and scratched behind her ears before giving her a kiss. "In a little while. Stay." He tossed her a treat, which she gobbled down as always.

Hunter was still standing where Nick had left him, apparently not wanting to sit. He took the water gratefully, gulping from it. Nick stayed close by in case Hunter's fingers were too shaky to hold the glass, but he seemed able to manage it.

Kneeling on the stone hearth, Nick struck a long match and held it to the twisted newspaper shoved under the waiting logs and kindling. Every morning in winter, he prepared the fireplace so it was waiting to be lit when he came home.

Then he took the empty glass from Hunter and set it on a wooden side table. Hunter's lips weren't blue, which was a good sign, and his winter gear had seemed good quality. Still, he'd been out in the growing blizzard for too long. Nick's driveway off the dirt road was a long walk in good weather, let alone snow squalls with deep drifts and that biting wind.

Knowing skin-on-skin was best for reheating, Nick rolled up his flannel sleeves and blew into his hands. "We should make sure you warm up enough. Better safe than sorry, right?"

Hunter blinked, clutching the blanket around him. "Uh…okay?"

"We'll start with the trunk and move out toward the extremities." He tried to imagine he was a doctor like Eric had been, professional and detached as he slipped his hands under the blanket and sweatshirt, wrapping them around Hunter's ribs, ignoring Hunter's little gasp and the way his blue eyes flared dark. That wasn't desire. No. It was cold, or shock.

"Oh!" Hunter laughed shakily. "You mean… Right. Um, thank you?" He had a habit of making statements into questions.

Nodding, Nick rubbed up and around Hunter's back, warming his trembling flesh. When he swept one hand over Hunter's stomach, Hunter jolted and swayed, grabbing onto Nick's shoulder. Their eyes locked, and *shit*.

Hunter was going to be a complication in Nick's perfectly ordered life. No doubt about it.

Dropping his head, Nick concentrated on rubbing warmth back into Hunter's torso. He had to face that he'd been so angry when Hunter had called that morning because he'd been so pathetically disappointed. While he'd felled, baled, and stacked grids of spruce from one of the back acres the day before—when he should have been reveling in being alone after two solid days of people—he'd looked forward to seeing Hunter again. Looked forward to getting to know him. Teaching him.

He'd let himself be…excited.

In the eight years since Eric, Nick had fucked other guys, but few more than once, and he'd rarely been *excited* about it. And there was no guarantee Hunter even wanted to fuck him, although Nick's instincts insisted he did. Hunter intrigued him with his flashes of spirit and anxious, jittery energy. There was something about him Nick wanted to soothe. He *craved* it in a way he hadn't in a long time.

He'd planned out how he'd teach Hunter about harvesting—how he'd show him how strong he really was. When Hunter had called, Nick had felt like the biggest fool and hadn't listened. Christ, he'd actually endangered the young man's life because of his own pride. He brought his hands up over Hunter's blanketed shoulders, looking down into his wary blue eyes.

"I'm sorry," Nick said. "I should have listened to you when you called. What happened with the car?" He took hold of Hunter's arms, pushing up the cotton sleeves and rubbing, wanting to feel skin again. The fire burned steadily now, the musky smell of burning wood tangy in the warm air. Hunter had stopped shaking and chattering, and was likely just fine now, but Nick didn't drop his hands.

"Um, I hit some ice," Hunter said quietly. "I wasn't speeding, but I skidded right into the ditch. After you hung up, I lost the signal, so I couldn't call CAA. And I couldn't get the car out alone."

"I really am sorry." And he was. He squeezed Hunter's hands gently, chafing his fingers. "You're sure you weren't hurt?"

He nodded. "It was just…" Now a tremor rippled through him. "Kind of scary."

The shame flared. "I can imagine. That wasn't an easy walk."

"I figured if I was going to die, I wanted to tell you that you were an asshole first."

There was a beat of silence aside from the crackling fire warming the air. Hunter sucked in a breath, his eyes big as he opened and closed his mouth. He looked stunned at his own words, his fingers trembling now as he added, "I—I… What I mean is…"

Instead of a burst of anger, Nick had to laugh—a loose, joyous eruption. "Honestly, more people should probably tell me that. I deserve it."

The apprehension that had darkened Hunter's face transformed into a smile that lit up his blue eyes and creased his freckled, ruddy cheeks. He laughed, a little giggle of delight and release that was utterly charming and genuine. He looked so young and intoxicatingly beautiful, his golden hair a mess from his hat.

Ella barked impatiently, and Hunter jumped, laughing nervously. "She's cute."

Nick grunted and muttered, "She's lucky she is," but he smiled at her fondly. "She thinks I'm hogging you." He whistled softly and nodded, and Ella rocketed over, practically flying, brownish ears flapping and her nails skimming over the wood floor. "Ella, this is Hunter."

Laughing, Hunter dropped to his knees on the plush blue shag rug, the blanket slipping off his shoulders to pool around him. Nick's old Banff sweatshirt hung loose on Hunter, the wide neck low over his collarbones. Nick had the absurd urge to stroke his thumb over the knobs of bone.

"Hey, girl. Nice to officially meet you." Hunter scratched behind her ears, and she licked his chin eagerly before flopping over. "You want tummy rubs, huh?"

Nick watched them, a strange sensation swelling in his chest.

That sensation is actual happiness at the company of another human, for the record. You're not having a heart attack or stroke, I assure you.

Nick smiled wryly to himself at Eric's imaginary comment.

Hunter scratched Ella's belly. "She's awesome."

"Yes. She is." She was splayed on the rug, in absolute heaven, completely innocent and guileless. Sometimes Nick loved her so much he could barely stand it.

He cleared his throat. "Did you want to use the land line to call anyone?"

"Oh. Right." Hunter withdrew from Ella almost guiltily and stood. Ella rubbed against his calves. "Um, I'll call CAA and get out of your hair? Unless you wanted to do some work?" He glanced at the window.

Nick squinted at the swirl of white. "Not happening today." He frowned. "And I'm not throwing you out. I just thought your mother might be worried."

Hunter sucked in a breath. "Shit, she probably is. That would be awesome if I can call."

"Of course."

It occurred to Nick that it was time for breakfast, his stomach growling. He usually only drank black coffee in the mornings before returning from the trees for a hearty brunch.

He asked Hunter, "Are you hungry?"

Hunter's face lit up, and *goddamn*, he was pretty. "Starving."

"Bacon and eggs sound good?"

"Definitely. Are you sure… It's just that—" He shook his head. "I might have inhaled a little carbon monoxide, so maybe this is all some fever dream since you're being weirdly nice now? I'm probably actually unconscious and near death in my car knowing my luck."

Nick had to laugh—and once again, it felt *good*. "This is real, I assure you." Hunter's joke registered with a tug of concern. "Are you serious about the carbon monoxide?"

"Yeah, I had the engine on for a couple of minutes and the tailpipe was definitely blocked, but then I realized and got out of the car fast."

"Good boy."

He'd said it without thinking, the words flowing naturally. Nick was about to apologize in case it came across as condescending, which truly hadn't been his intent. But the words died as he watched the way Hunter's breath caught, his body rippling, tongue darting out to lick his lips.

Oh yes, look at that, Eric murmured in Nick's mind. *He likes it. He wants to be a good boy for you.*

Nick had felt horribly guilty about wanting sex after the fog of grief had slowly lifted in the first few years after Eric's death. But over time the Eric in his mind had encouraged him. While the grief would never fully leave him, it had ebbed and flowed and transformed as the years passed.

Before he knew what he was doing, Nick stepped close to Hunter, who watched him like a deer in headlights. Nick said, "It's been hours, so I'm sure you're fine. But let me take a closer look to check that your pupils aren't dilated."

"Oh. Okay." Hunter stared up at him as Nick leaned in.

The pupils in his lake-blue eyes looked normal, or at least not massive the way they would if something was amiss. The wind-burned red on Hunter's face had faded, and the pink tinge to his skin looked like healthy warmth now—or arousal and embarrassment, not carbon monoxide.

"Looks normal." Nick tried to think of the other symptoms. "You haven't been dizzy or drowsy? Sick to your stomach?"

Hunter shook his head, still staring up at Nick. Their bodies were only a few inches apart, and it wasn't simply heat from the fireplace Nick felt coursing through him. He blurted, "Lips."

Adam's apple bobbing, Hunter rasped, "What?" Then he licked said lips, making them glisten again.

Nick managed a smile. "Cherry red lips. That's another sign." His gaze dropped to Hunter's mouth, and he clenched his fingers to resist the urge to touch. "Yours are more pink. I think you're safe." He forced his eyes back up to Hunter's, his skin prickling at the clear desire shining from those blue depths.

"Okay." Hunter nodded. "Thank you. I think I'm good. Unless my dying brain is just being generous by letting me enjoy this fantasy."

A spark of anticipation flickered through Nick. "Fantasy?"

The blush in Hunter's cheeks darkened now, and he fidgeted, trying to laugh, his gaze dropping. "Oh! Just, you know. Um, being warm?" He motioned to the fire before dropping to the rug to pet Ella again, much to Ella's slobbery delight. Hunter still didn't look up at Nick as he added, "And having a sweet dog to pet. Also bacon. Bacon is amazing."

"It is," Nick agreed, trying not to smile.

Oh yes, this pretty boy wants you. No doubt about it. What a shame you're trapped here together in such terrible weather with nothing else to do...

Nick could imagine the light in Eric's brown eyes and his mischievous laughter. Nick's own smile faded, one of the other things Hunter had said nagging. "I really am sorry about earlier, and if I wasn't overly friendly to you at the mall. I don't..." He exhaled noisily. "I'm generally not great with people, but I don't want it to be 'weird' if I'm nice."

Hunter did look up then, his eyes widening. "Oh, I didn't mean—"

"No, don't apologize. I was an asshole, as you said." He impulsively added, "Will you let me make it up to you?"

"Um, well..." Hunter took a shallow breath, his voice going hoarse, his hand frozen on Ella's back. "How?"

The possibilities were endless, and images of Hunter naked and writhing under Nick's hands and tongue flashed through his mind. He was able to keep his tone light. "I'll start with bacon. Go ahead and use the phone to call whoever you like."

He escaped to the kitchen, his socked feet sliding a bit on the wood. He put the cast-iron pan on the range before turning on the gas, the flame making a satisfying *whoomp*. From the corner of his eye, he watched Hunter unzip his cell phone from his jacket pocket, Ella at his heels.

Nick couldn't help but listen as Hunter returned to the couch and called someone from the old phone on the side table. He was talking to CAA from the sounds of it.

"*Tomorrow*? Wow. Okay, yeah. Do I have to call back, or... Uh-huh. Yeah, I'm pretty sure I know where it is on the road."

Hunter spoke more, giving directions. Nick found himself smiling over the sizzling bacon, Ella eagerly rubbing against his legs, the lure of food drawing her into the kitchen.

Clearly Hunter should stay the night. It would be a foolish, unnecessary risk for Nick to attempt to drive him back to Pinevale in his pickup, and if the roads were closed it was pointless.

Hunter would just have to stay. It was as simple as that.

Chapter Five

O F COURSE HUNTER staying the night was a *terrible* idea, but Nick couldn't seem to do anything but grin to himself as Hunter hung up with CAA.

"I assume you got all that? They are way over capacity. Said they'll come tomorrow and tow the car back to my mom's house, or a garage if it's damaged. So…"

Nick took the carton of eggs out of the fridge, glancing over to see Hunter watching him with apprehension and an unmistakable flicker of eagerness. Nick said, "So you should stay the night. I have a guest room. You'll be safe here."

Hunter bit his lip. "You really don't mind? I don't want to be a pain." Nick could almost see the insecurity and self-doubt flood Hunter's mind. "I'm sure I can figure something out. Maybe I can—"

"You can stay." He repeated, "You'll be safe here. And welcome. All right?"

"Yeah? Okay, cool."

"How do you like your eggs?"

"Huh? Oh! Uh, over-easy?"

"Is that how you like them? You don't sound sure."

"Yes." He laughed nervously. "Over-easy, please."

"Done." Nick returned to the pan and grabbed the bacon with tongs, plopping the strips on a paper-towel-covered plate while shooing Ella away.

He realized with a pang that Hunter would be the first man to sleep over since Eric's death. A few had come over for sex, but Nick had never considered having them stay. Granted, there was a raging blizzard, and he couldn't exactly turn Hunter out.

Of course he heard Eric's teasing brogue in his mind on cue.

You want him to stay, and the blizzard is very convenient, isn't it? He's a beautiful boy. Why shouldn't he stay? You've been a lonely grump far too long, my love.

Nick couldn't argue that he'd been alone a long time. He hadn't thought of himself as particularly lonely, but… Regardless, he shouldn't get ahead of himself.

John had said Hunter lived in Toronto, and this would obviously only be a holiday fling—assuming *it* even happened. Hunter might end up sleeping in the guest room after all. He was staying a night—not moving in.

Hunter's voice came from the couch as Nick cracked the eggs into the greasy pan. "Hey, Mom. Yeah, it's crazy, huh? Is it bad in town?" He was silent a few moments, then he said, "Wow. Way more snow than they were calling for. It's a blizzard out here. And I'm fine, but—" He sighed heavily. "*Mom.* I just said I'm fine. Would you let me finish? The car slid into a ditch, but I'm not hurt. I don't think there's any damage to the car, but I'm not positive. CAA said they'll get it tomorrow and tow it to you." After a pause, he said, "I'm not hurt at all, I promise. Yeah, I'm going to stay the night. Uh-huh. He's really nice."

Nick gave him a dubious smirk as he grabbed the sourdough loaf from atop the fridge. Hunter said into the phone, "Okay. Love you too, Mom. Walk carefully tomorrow." He hung up.

"'Really nice' is a generous assessment," Nick noted.

Hunter shrugged. "It's like with the kids. You were actually sweet with them in the end."

"Hmm." He flipped the eggs. "Am I being sweet with you

now?" He hadn't meant it to sound suggestive, but somehow it had.

Hunter shifted on the couch, looking a little flustered. "I dunno. I guess?"

Guilt still nagged. "You really could have ended up in a bad way this morning. I didn't realize a storm was blowing in."

"It's okay, really."

Nick put two slices of bread in the toaster. "I don't know if I deserve your forgiveness."

"Well, you have it." There was no question in Hunter's tone, and when Nick glanced over, Hunter nodded seriously. "Don't worry about it anymore. I'm fine, and you're making it up to me, remember?"

Their gazes held, silence in the house but for the fire crackling and eggs sizzling. Nick nodded slowly. "I will." *Oh,* he was going to make it up to Hunter all right. He was going to—

The toast popped up, and they both jerked before laughing. Nick quickly slid the eggs from the pan onto plates before they overcooked, and put down two more pieces of bread in the toaster.

"Can you grab a couple place mats and cutlery? In those two drawers." He nodded toward them. "We can eat by the window." His round dining table of sturdy oak and four matching chairs sat by the wide expanse of glass.

Feet silent in the big socks Nick gave him, Hunter padded over to the kitchen. He gave Ella—clearly torn between him and staying near the bacon—more rubs and set the table, humming a carol. "Joy to the World," Nick thought. He rarely heard Christmas music nowadays—although he'd gotten his fill at the mall—but he found he liked Hunter's gentle hum.

Nick fetched the butter crock and brought their plates and toast to the table, putting the plates on the cork-backed place mats, which depicted forest and lake scenes painted by the Group of Seven.

After tossing Ella a piece of bacon, he pointed to her bed and snapped his fingers. She went, gobbling down the meat. She'd be giving them puppy eyes, but Nick didn't let her beg by the table. If she was good, she'd get another bacon strip when they were finished.

As Hunter sat, he seemed to realize he was humming and broke off with a guilty expression. "Sorry. I can't get Christmas music out of my head."

Nick smiled. "Peril of the job. Orange juice? Or I can put more coffee on. I don't have any tea." Being a Scot, Eric had drank it daily, but Nick had never taken to it.

"Juice is awesome, thanks." Hunter slathered butter on his toast and dipped it into an egg, smearing the yolk around. "Mmm. This is perfect."

Nick got their juice and sat across from him at the round table. They ate in comfortable quiet, the wind howling, trees barely visible through the whiteout. The fire roared, keeping them toasty while Mother Nature raged, and the meal was salty and hearty. It really was perfect. Nick couldn't recall the last time he'd felt so…*peaceful* in someone's company.

Eventually, Nick said, "John mentioned you came out in high school. Impressive."

Hunter shrugged, swiping with his tongue at a dribble of yolk in the corner of his mouth. "My one moment of bravery. I got so pissed with the teasing I couldn't take it anymore. My friend Shelby thinks the bully was probably in the closet. Maybe she's right."

"That's often the way it seems to go. And I'm sure there's much more bravery in you. Don't sell yourself short."

Hunter scoffed. "I doubt it."

Ignoring that, Nick asked, "Then you went to U of T?" He took a bite of warm, buttery bread.

"Yeah, for the all the good it did me. If you want to know about the arbitrary nature of rule itself in Arthurian legend, I can tell you all about it. Not much good in the real world. But I always sucked at math and science—my brain just doesn't work that way, you know? So I got my English degree, and now... I don't know. I figured marketing and communications since I'm a pretty good writer. I've had three unpaid internships—doing mostly promo type of stuff. There don't seem to be any actual jobs. It's a little depressing."

Nick remembered his judgment of Hunter wanting to be paid for being an elf and felt like an ass. "That's frustrating. Although I don't think education is ever useless. I never went to university, and I wish I had sometimes."

"Yeah, I guess. I just feel like..." He toyed with a strip of bacon, picking it up and shredding off a piece. "I should be getting a real job, like in an office. But I don't think I really want to. I mean, I know most people don't like their jobs, but the whole nine-to-five thing in the city? My soul was being sucked out already. But obviously I need to suck it up."

"And be miserable?" Hunter's uncertainty and turmoil made Nick want to reach for him. He kept hold of his cutlery. "Don't make yourself unhappy doing something you believe you 'should.' There are plenty of things people think *I* should do. But I know myself."

"Yeah, I mean, you're so..." Hunter waved his hand. "Confident and stuff." He chewed the bacon and asked, "Do you enjoy your job?"

"I do, yes. Always have."

"What's it like? I know you cut down the trees to sell in November and December, but what about the rest of the year?"

"January and February are quiet. I still check on the trees regularly, so I keep busy. Spring is planting season, of course. Have to watch the late frosts here. Then the warmer months are filled with weeding and insect-management. Also shearing to make sure the trees grow in the right shape."

Hunter frowned. "What do you mean?"

"Douglas firs are generally a natural cone shape that people want for Christmas trees, but I still have to keep an eye on them. Scotch pine needs regular shearing, though."

"Huh. I guess I thought Christmas trees just…grew like that."

"Not in the perfect shape, I'm afraid. My job would be a lot easier if I didn't have to shear and guide them."

"How many trees do you have?"

"About seventy-five thousand on fifty acres."

Hunter's eyebrows shot up. "Whoa. That sounds like a lot."

"It's big enough. There are massive operations that would dwarf my farm, and smaller ones as well. It's a lot of work for one person, but I manage. I'm used to long days."

Eric's voice piped up with: *Yes, because if you're a workaholic, you don't have time to think about how lonely you've become out here.*

"Wow." Hunter scratched at his neck, and Nick's eyes dropped to his collarbones before he forced his gaze back to his plate. "Do people come and cut their own trees?"

"Hell no." Nick grimaced at the thought. "I sell to nurseries and stores. Last thing I want is people tramping around here with axes they don't know how to use."

Hunter chuckled. "Fair enough. I remember going to some place when I was a kid, and we made a wreath."

"Mmm. I sell greenery for that. Wreaths are good business. Does your mom do a tree?"

"Um…" Hunter winced.

Nick had to laugh. "Don't tell me she has a fake tree. You know those things will sit in a landfill forever."

"I know! If it's any consolation, it's the same old tree we've had as long as I can remember." He peered around. "For a Christmas tree farm, there is a distinct lack of holiday decoration."

Nick hadn't really thought about it. "I suppose there is. Doesn't seem worth it when it's just me and Ella. She'll probably try to eat everything anyway." He thought back to something Hunter had said earlier. "Where's your mom walking to tomorrow? You mentioned it on the phone. Sorry for eavesdropping."

"It's okay—hard not to hear when we're in the same room. She works at the hospital, and it's close enough to walk since she won't have the car back."

"Ah." Distant memories of Eric and that gray brick building flitted through his mind. "What's her name? John mentioned it, but I can't recall."

"Pam Adams?"

"Hmm. I don't know if I ever met her." He realized Hunter might not understand what he was talking about, but before he could explain, Hunter nodded.

"I think once or twice? She remembered you. And…him, obviously." Hunter glanced toward the fireplace. "Is that… Is he with you in that picture?"

The rustic wooden mantel was an old railway tie, and there were a few framed pictures atop it. "Yes. Eric." Nick looked toward the photos across the room even though he'd seen them a million times. "That was on my birthday one year. Long time ago now."

The memory was faded, a summer barbecue at the cottage of a friend Nick hadn't spoken to in years. He'd drifted away from almost everyone, and if not for John's stubbornness, he wouldn't know any of the old group anymore.

"He had a great smile."

Nick smiled himself, bittersweet memories filling his mind before receding. "He did. He was brilliant, although he struggled to believe that sometimes. His parents were harsh." They hadn't approved of his homosexuality either, and Nick was glad they were back in Scotland and he'd never had to deal with them.

"What about your parents?"

"I never knew my father. My mother died years ago now." The distant ache of her loss was familiar and bittersweet in its own way. "Lost touch with the rest of the family over the years. My brother lives in BC. We email once in a while."

Hunter was quiet a moment. "I didn't know my father either. It sucked, but it was what it was. My mom's amazing, and so's my sister."

Nick went to the fireplace and tossed in a couple logs, sparks spraying. He nodded to the mantel and the other silver-framed pictures. "The golden retriever's Max, and that's John and Desmond with me and Eric in that one shot."

"I've never actually met Desmond, but I'm sure he's great. John's always been awesome to me."

"They're good friends. Stubborn friends, luckily for me." From her bed in the kitchen, Ella whined. Nick laughed. "Want to give her that last piece of bacon? Unless you want it."

"I could never deprive her." Hunter went and knelt by her bed, and she licked his face while he laughed, the sweet, low sound echoing through the house. He stood and grabbed the bacon, Ella practically leaping up to the counter.

Nick should have scolded her, but he didn't as Hunter fed her, still laughing. Instead, Nick said, "She lives to eat."

The phone rang, and Ella barked. Nick shushed her as he went to pick up the receiver by the couch. He still had an old wired phone since cordless receivers didn't work in power outages, and in an ice storm electricity could go out for days. "Hello?"

John's deep, cheerful voice filled his ear. "Nick! How's it going out there? Thought I'd check in on you."

"We're fine. Getting a lot more snow than expected but still have power. Can't complain."

"We, huh? Wasn't sure if Hunter would make it. How's he working out?"

"We can't do much until the storm passes, but…" He cleared his throat. "I'm sure he'll be a hard worker. For now we're snowed in."

John's laughter boomed. "You're fucking him already, aren't you?"

"What? No!"

"Oh, don't try to deny it. I know you too well, my friend. If you haven't tapped that fine ass yet, you will soon."

Nick grumbled, "Whatever."

"Well, that works out for me, because I have another favor to ask."

"No. Whatever it is, no."

"There's one more weekend of Santa's Village. There's buzz around town about hot Santa. You're such a recluse, and people are curious. And if you and Hunter are fucking, I'm sure you won't mind spending more time ogling him in his tights."

He wanted to deny the ogling, but couldn't with Hunter listening—and because it would be a lie. "I have too much work."

"May I remind you that it's for charity? Think of the children."

"You're a son of a bitch, you know that?"

"Yep. You and Hunter enjoy yourselves. See you Saturday!"

"Yeah, yeah." Nick hung up and turned back to Hunter. "Well, I guess we'll be teaming up in Santa's Village again this weekend."

Hunter grinned. "I guess John really can get you to do something you don't want to."

Nick chuckled. "Yes. One of the few." He smiled over at Ella. "And her, of course."

Hunter toyed with the frayed seam on one of the sweatshirt's cuffs. "I guess we really are snowed in, huh?"

"Seems that way." Anticipation skipped through him as Hunter neared to stand before him on the blue rug.

Hunter asked, "What should we do?" He peeked up at Nick through his thick lashes. Was he trying to be…seductive? Nick honestly couldn't tell, but he hoped so.

Of course the best thing to do would be to put physical distance between them. Stay professional. Avoid complications.

Eric's voice echoed again before Nick banished it.

Oh, however will you pass the time? The poor lad still needs warming up, surely…

Nick heard himself say, "I promised I'd make it up to you. Being such an ass earlier."

Hunter stared up at him, his lips parting. He scratched his neck, tugging down the low collar of the baggy sweatshirt. Before Nick could shove his hands in his pockets, he was reaching out and brushing his thumb over the knob of a collarbone. Hunter sucked in a little gasp.

Nick pulled his hand back. "I'm sorry. I shouldn't have done that. That was inapprop—"

Hunter lunged, kissing him forcefully, his arms looping around Nick's neck and tugging him down. He'd apparently found another moment of bravery inside him, and Nick felt strangely proud of him.

The kiss was clumsy—but, *oh*, the hunger in it fired Nick's blood. He opened his mouth, urging Hunter's lips to part so their tongues could meet.

The sweatshirt bunched up under his hands, and Nick stroked Hunter's back, stopping at the cotton of his underwear even though he wanted to rip them off, the PJ bottoms sliding low on Hunter's hips. Ella barked, butting against their legs.

Moaning as he gasped into Nick's mouth, Hunter rubbed against him, actual static electricity sparking on the flannel of Nick's shirt. Hunter yelped and jerked back, laughing. Nick smiled, and they both laughed at Ella by their feet, barking and confused by what exactly her master was doing.

Nick snapped his fingers and ordered her back to the kitchen. "Bed. Now." She hesitated, barking softly and looking between Nick and Hunter. Then she obeyed, still tense and giving them a decidedly judgy glare.

Laughing softly, Hunter ran his palms over Nick's pecs with awe. "Oh my God, did I really do that? Is this really happening?"

Nick held Hunter's waist. "Do you want this to happen?"

"Yes." He nodded vigorously, meeting Nick's eyes.

"You're feeling all right?"

"Uh-huh," Hunter breathed, his arms snaking around Nick's waist as he thrust his swelling cock against Nick's hip. "I could have died out there, and I don't really know what I'm doing, but I'm positive I want to do this. I need…" He panted softly, licking his lips. "I need to get out of my own way." He stared up at Nick, his expression open and vulnerable. "Will you help me? Please?"

Nick slid a hand beneath the sweatshirt, teasing one of Hunter's nipples. Hunter shivered as Nick circled rhythmically with his thumb. "You need to get out of your own way?"

Tensing, Hunter dropped his gaze. "That must sound stupid. It's something my friend Shelby says, and—never mind."

There it was, that anxious self-doubt that Nick instinctively wanted to calm. He could practically hear Hunter berating himself, and he wanted to take control and give him the freedom to stop worrying. To help ground him. He pressed his palm over Hunter's thudding heart.

Hunter was still doubting and tense. "I need… I don't know what. I'm such a mess."

"Maybe you need a daddy." As Nick said it, it felt *right,* and goddamn, he wanted this. More than he'd thought.

Hunter stared up at him, his eyes widening as he whispered, "What?" He looked truly shocked, his hands jerking on Nick's waist before dropping, his fingers twisting anxiously.

Damn it. Nick had gone too far. "Never mind." He stepped

away, though his body protested, his cock demanding friction and his hands eager for more skin. "I need to…" He cast about for tasks. "Stoke the fire and let Ella out."

But Hunter reached for him, snagging Nick by his belt. "Wait." He looked down at his hand, as if surprised to see it grabbing onto the black leather. Brow creasing, he licked his lips. "Did you mean…"

"It was inappropriate. You're probably still in shock from the accident." This was the part when Nick would gently ease Hunter's fingers from his belt and walk away.

Any second now.

Hunter stepped closer, the rug thick beneath their feet. Nick gripped with his toes in his wool socks instead of walking away like he was supposed to.

Yep. Any second now. Walking away. He'd gone too far.

"So you *did* mean like…" Hunter blinked up at him. "Like *that*?"

Lust hung thick in the air with the husk of their breathing and a spray of sparks in the fireplace as a log shifted. Nick couldn't look away from Hunter's hopeful blue eyes, glowing with such innocence and desire.

Then Hunter dropped his hand and head, shoulders hunching. He crossed his arms like a shield. "Never mind. I'm an idiot. The cold obviously affected my brain. I shouldn't have kissed you."

Sighing in silent relief, Nick took Ella outside, cooled off, and he and Hunter spent the rest of the day with polite distance between them as they watched movies. The next day, Hunter went home, and Nick returned to his solitude, so busy with work he barely had time to think of anything, let alone the narrow escape he'd made from an enticing complication he didn't need in his life.

Well.

That would have been the smart thing to do, but Nick couldn't bear the defeat in Hunter's voice—how the tremor returned as he stared at his feet, looking unbearably fragile.

So instead of walking away, Nick said clearly and confidently, "Yes. That's what I meant." When Hunter's head whipped up, his eyes wide again, Nick held his gaze and asked, "Have you ever had a daddy?"

Hunter swallowed, his Adam's apple bobbing. "No," he whispered. "But I want one."

Chapter Six

*O*H, HOW HE wanted a daddy.

Hunter could barely breathe, afraid he'd break the spell if he so much as moved an inch. He stared up at Nick, who watched him with his gray eyes hooded and intense. Unflinching.

Obviously Hunter had heard the term before—like leather daddies or whatever—but he'd never quite understood until right *now* that *this* was what he'd craved for so long. "I don't… I don't know what…" Fuck, he wanted to climb the mountain—and the man—but he didn't know how to start.

Nick stepped close, brushing a hand over Hunter's head and sending a sweet shiver down his spine. "It's all right. I'll show you."

Hunter still wasn't sure how he'd gotten the nerve to kiss Nick. Another bold impulse seized him at the intense way Nick's gaze swept down over Hunter's body with what really, really seemed like desire. The clothes were baggy, and Hunter tugged off the sweatshirt and then the PJs, not even needing to undo the drawstring since they were so big. He worked his feet out of the socks on the rug.

Now he was standing in his gray boxer briefs, breathing hard. "I know I'm too skinny, and not all buff like—"

Nick pressed a finger to Hunter's mouth. "You're beautiful." Then he bent and kissed him, and Hunter thought his heart might explode.

Ella's barking echoed, and she raced over, circling them in agitation. They broke apart, laughing. Hunter knelt on the rug and petted her. "You're a real cock-blocker, huh, girl?"

"Ella," Nick said. "Time to go out."

She leapt to obey, her tail wagging as Nick walked to the front door. A swirl of snow and arctic air blew in, and Hunter wallowed in the warmth of the fire to his right. He'd been cold as hell after his slog down Nick's incredibly long road, but now a fever sizzled through him. Being touched by those big, calloused hands was everything he'd ever dreamed of.

It was beyond surreal, kneeling there in his undies on Nick's rug. How was this actually happening? Nick had been such a dick, hanging up on him, but then he'd seemed concerned and caring, his touch so calming and strong.

I really hope I'm not actually dead and imagining all this. Although if I am, this must be freaking heaven.

Still kneeling, he watched Nick walk—no, *prowl* back to him. Nick's arms were hairy where he'd rolled up the sleeves of his plaid shirt, and with his full beard and dark, silver-sprinkled hair—not to mention his muscles—he was every inch a *man*.

I am getting out of my own way if it kills me.

Hunter's throat was dry, and he probably needed more water, but he wasn't moving. He waited, breathing shallowly, feeling the need to say something. He went with, "It's not dangerous for her to be out in this weather?"

"No, she loves the snow. She won't go far, and she can sniff her way back blindfolded. She'll play for hours in the barn watching the birds in the rafters if I let her."

"Cool. Yeah, that's…cool." *Oh God, I'm actually going to have sex.*

Nick tilted his head, watching Hunter closely. "Do you really want to do this?"

Taking a deep breath, Hunter said, "Uh-huh." The fire

warmed his skin, but goosebumps still shivered over him. He tried to joke. "It's a little late to back out now."

Nick frowned. "It's never too late to change your mind and say no."

"Oh, I know! I didn't mean…" Shit, he was screwing this up, like usual. He stood and approached Nick. "It was a stupid joke."

Not touching him yet even though Hunter was inches away, Nick nodded. "All right. If you ever want to stop for any reason, just say so."

"Right. Okay." God, it was so embarrassing that he was a virgin. Not having done anything kinky or whatever before was one thing, but was Nick really going to want to have sex with someone so clueless?

Before Hunter could say anything else, Nick leaned closer, running his rough palms down Hunter's back to the top of his ass. He whispered, his breath a hot gust, "Do you need a daddy, Hunter?"

Dick hard again in an instant, he clung to Nick's waist. "Yes." The sensation of Nick's flannel shirt against Hunter's nipples was so sexy, but he was dying to feel that hairy chest.

"Are you a good boy?"

Oh my God. Hunter was going to jizz in his underwear. "I try to be."

"Hmm. So you're a bad boy sometimes?"

Hunter rubbed against him, feeling Nick's hardness through his work pants and wanting that cock inside him. In his mouth, his ass—Hunter didn't care. He just wanted to be owned. "I'm so bad sometimes."

"Do you need discipline?"

"Uh-huh."

Nick slapped Hunter's ass. Hard. "Good boys answer properly."

"Yes." Hunter nodded, a thrill shooting to his balls at his own words as he added, "Yes, Daddy."

With a rumbling groan, Nick kissed him, his tongue surging against Hunter's. He tasted of orange juice and pine, or maybe that was the scent filling Hunter's nose as Nick took him in his arms, almost lifting him off his feet. His kiss was commanding, and Hunter whimpered into his mouth, desire burning through him, any hint of chill eradicated.

Nick's thick beard was wonderfully rough against Hunter's face. They kissed until his head spun, his lips tingling, Nick's tongue exploring and teasing. Hunter clung to him as he gasped for air, spit stringing between their mouths. Nick ran his thumb over Hunter's lower lip, his flinty eyes dark.

"I want you naked."

Nodding, Hunter shoved down his boxer briefs and kicked them free, his cock springing up. Despite his earlier bravery, he would have agonized over whether or not to take them off, and when. It was a glorious relief to have Nick in charge.

Nick dropped his gaze over Hunter's body, and Hunter shifted, wishing he could read Nick's mind. Was he too skinny? His cock was uncut and fairly long, and he'd always thought it was a decent size? He wished he had more chest hair, though, and—

"You really are beautiful." Nick took Hunter's face in his big hands and kissed him softly. "You don't have to worry about anything. Do you trust Daddy?"

"Yes," he whispered. Maybe it was crazy since they'd just met, but he did trust Nick. He thought of him in that Santa costume and the way he'd been so kind and patient with the children. The sweet way he was with Ella and how he'd taken care of Hunter.

Nick kissed him again, and Hunter tasted a hint of the salty, wonderfully greasy bacon. Nick had actually *cooked* for him. Hunter's mom had worked such long hours, and he and Heather had often made do with sandwiches or whatever. Nick cooking for him had made him feel comforted in a way he couldn't really explain.

"You'll be safe here."

Nick's calm command eased the tension in Hunter. He gasped as Nick tweaked his nipples.

"On your knees like a good boy."

A thrill zinging through him, Hunter did as he was told. Nick towered over him, still in his work pants and plaid shirt, and it made Hunter's dick throb to be naked at his feet. He didn't know what to do with his hands, and he fidgeted with his fingers, waiting for Nick to tell him what he should do.

Nick brushed back Hunter's hair, which was probably an ugly mess after having a hat on for hours. "Hands behind your back. Don't move them until I say you can."

Hunter clasped his fingers behind him.

"Very good." Nick traced Hunter's lips before pushing his thumb inside.

Hunter circled it with his tongue and sucked, pride flushing through him when Nick's nostrils flared with desire.

"Do you want to suck Daddy's cock?"

With his lips still wrapped about Nick's thumb, Hunter nodded, moaning. *God,* how he wanted to suck that cock. Nick pulled his thumb free and unbuckled his belt. He eased the leather free of its loops, dropping the belt to the rug with a soft thud. As Hunter watched eagerly, still half-convinced this couldn't be real, Nick released his erection, his pants hanging open on his hips.

He was cut, flushed red, and *big.* His cock was thick, his hairy balls hanging heavy. Throat dry, Hunter waited, his fingers gripping together behind him so he didn't accidentally reach out to touch. He burned to take that meat in his mouth, bury his face in Nick's dark pubes, and give himself over to it.

But Nick didn't seem to be in any rush. Looking down at Hunter with a little smile, he unbuttoned his plaid shirt, starting at the bottom where his cock poked out. He brushed his fingers over his thick shaft, and Hunter couldn't have looked away for all the money in the world. He watched each button be loosed, his heart a drum as Nick's stomach and chest were revealed, hairy and strong and *perfect*.

Hunter didn't even realize he'd moved to take himself in hand, pleasure rippling through him until Nick barked, "No." He softened his tone as Hunter jerked his hand away from his dick. "No touching yourself unless I give you permission."

"I'm sorry, Daddy." He clasped his hands behind him again. "I didn't mean to."

"I know. That's a good boy." Sliding the plaid shirt down his back, he freed his arms and let the flannel fall to the rug. His impressive cock stood, his dark pants still on his hips. He ran his fingertip over Hunter's mouth. "Don't move. And especially don't touch yourself."

Hunter bit back a groan of frustration, watching as Nick tossed another few logs on the fire, staying out of spark range on the hearth. Then he went upstairs, and Hunter craned his neck to see, careful not to shift too much.

Nick disappeared into a bedroom at the end of the exposed hall, and Hunter held his breath, listening. The rug was soft under his knees, and he flattened his feet and sat on them.

Anticipation zipped through him. Sure, he was nervous, but it was like a puzzle piece had finally slotted into place. With Nick, kissing and touching felt right, like Hunter was made for it. He'd lusted after Nick the moment he saw him half-dressed in that Santa suit, and maybe he should have been afraid to give himself to a virtual stranger, but he wasn't.

"Maybe you need a daddy."

Balls tingling, Hunter's hard cock twitched. He clenched his hands behind him. No matter how much he wanted to jerk off, he was going to obey—and that gave him a flush of pleasure all its own. The fire roared to his right, his skin wonderfully warm.

He ached to be touched and filled, and he definitely was staying the fuck out of his own way for the first time. He wanted this. *Needed* it. And he trusted Nick to give it to him. He didn't have to worry. Nick would take care of him.

John wouldn't be friends with a serial killer, right?

He laughed under his breath. His instincts told him he was safe, and he was going to listen to them for once, refusing to let anxiety whirl up like a tornado. Staying in place, he looked around the main floor. The wide window along the side of the house was before him, the round rustic dining table and chairs sitting in the dim light. Through the glass, there was only white, and Hunter couldn't tell if it was cloudy sky as well as snow.

To the left, he peered into the kitchen. There was a big island with a couple of stools, and the cupboards were dark wood. The only thing on the counter aside from a coffeemaker and toaster was a mug. Ella's bowls were on the floor on the left side of the island, the fridge to the right. There were only a couple of magnets on the fridge, as opposed to the colorful mishmash Hunter's mom had.

Nick's house was neat and orderly, but it did look lived in. The brown leather couch looked soft, the cushions on the right side especially worn, the huge leather ottoman dipping a little on that side. Navy and dark green throw cushions were tossed aside to the left.

To his right, the massive TV over the fireplace was dark. He peered up at the thick, rustic mantel. There were no stockings hung from it yet, and it made Hunter sad to think that there wouldn't be. He'd always loved the ritual of decorating with his mom—baking sugar cookies and sipping fresh hot chocolate, listening to her jazzy holiday CDs on the old stereo.

He peered at the three framed photos on top of the mantel, going up on his knees and squinting. Eric had been handsome— short brown hair with a curl to it, a lock hanging over his forehead. He was laughing, and he looked at Nick with a glowing smile. It was awful to think of him dying in an icy lake, trying to save a doomed boy.

In the photo with Eric, Nick was smiling too, and he was younger—the silver not highlighting his dark hair yet. There was a lightness in his expression that made Hunter's heart clench. He wanted to know him. He'd never felt an attraction like this before. He wanted to know *everything*.

The floor creaked above, and Hunter jerked back into position, sitting on his heels again, not looking as Nick crossed the hall and slowly descended the stairs. His pulse raced. He wasn't sure what Nick had done up there. Had he brought something back?

As Nick stood in front of him again, Hunter stared at his huge cock, mouth dry. It had softened a bit, but was still thick and flushed, jutting out. Hunter thought about leaning forward and licking it…

"Did you touch yourself?"

Focusing, Hunter shook his head. "Not even a little."

Nick chuckled. "Good boy."

He didn't need to touch himself for another powerful wave of pleasure to roll through him. He watched as Nick eased down his pants and black briefs, stepping out of them and kicking them aside. He stood before Hunter, legs slightly spread, in all his hairy, masculine glory, like a lumberjack god from a wet dream.

"Fuck me," Hunter mumbled, not meaning to speak aloud.

Taking his cock in hand and giving it a few strokes, Nick stepped even closer. He traced Hunter's cheekbones with the shiny tip of his dick. "Later. If you're a good boy."

Hunter shuddered with lust, a thrill tingling through him all the way to his toes. "I'll be so good."

"I know." He circled Hunter's lips with the head. "Do you want to suck this?"

"Yes." It was barely a whisper. "Can—*may* I?"

"Such good manners. You may. Keep your hands behind your back."

This is actually happening. I'm doing this.

Before his brain could have second thoughts and get in his way, Hunter opened his mouth and swallowed Nick's cock into his mouth, taking in as much as he could and sucking like his life depended on it. Nick groaned, and it was music to Hunter's ears.

He'd never blown anyone before, but he mimicked what he'd seen in porn, pulling back to lick along Nick's swelling length, tracing the bulging vein with his tongue. He was actually sucking another man's cock. He was *doing* it. Lust scorched through him.

His nostrils flared as he tried to breathe, his rhythm probably clumsy and haphazard. He licked and sucked, peeking up at Nick, who watched with lips parted, his chest rising and falling rapidly. His eyebrows were drawn near in a little frown, and he spread his hand wide over Hunter's head—not pushing or pulling, but guiding. He slowly began to thrust, fucking Hunter's mouth.

"That's it. Such a good boy for daddy."

Hunter moaned around Nick's dick, his own leaking and so hard he was about to come without touching it at all. He wanted to choke on Nick's cock until there was nothing but the ache in his jaw and the throbbing flesh filling his mouth. He could taste the salty musk of precum, and he craved more. But it was so hard to breathe, and he coughed, pulling back, his eyes watering.

Nick caressed his head. "It's okay." He dropped to his knees, stroking down Hunter's arms, easing his hands from behind his back and holding them. Not too tightly or loosely, but securely. "When you said you didn't know what to do…" He tilted his head, watching Hunter closely. "What exactly did you mean?"

Hunter swallowed hard, squirming with embarrassment. He could feel spit dribbling from the corner of his mouth. Was he so bad at blow jobs that it was that obvious? "I've never done very much. Kissed a few times, and made out or whatever at a party. That's it." He dropped his eyes, his face hot. "I'm, like, a virgin?"

Nick made a breathy sound that was maybe a sigh, and Hunter's skin itched, acid spinning in his stomach. "I'm sorry. It's pathetic. I don't know why I haven't done it yet. I get too…knotted up, you know? In my head, I mean." He tried to laugh. "It's lame."

Nick lifted Hunter's chin with his finger and stared into his eyes, that gray gaze so certain. "It's not lame. There's nothing wrong with taking your time."

His heart leapt. "You mean… You don't mind?"

"*Mind?*" He shook his head again, smiling softly. He leaned in and brushed their lips together, murmuring, "Baby, I don't mind at all. You're doing so well. I'm very proud of you."

Hunter's chest swelled with emotion as Nick kissed him for real now, their tongues meeting, his hands roaming down to Hunter's ass, their knees pushing together on the rug. Then Nick pushed to standing, hauling Hunter with him, almost off his feet.

He asked, "Do you want me to fuck you?"

Head light, Hunter nodded. "Please." He wound his arms around Nick's waist and rubbed a cheek against his bearded neck. "Please fuck me, Daddy."

Nick exhaled heavily, stroking down over Hunter's ass and squeezing. "You need my cock, hmm?"

"*Yes.*" He vibrated with need, eager and nervous all at once, but not going back.

Nick kissed him deeply, sucking on his tongue, and Hunter wondered if he could taste his own cock. Then Nick spread the forgotten blanket on the couch and sat in the middle, urging Hunter to straddle his powerful legs. Hair tickled Hunter's inner thighs, and he rocked, spreading his fingers over Nick's chest, raking his nails through the coarse fur there.

There was a bottle of lube on the couch cushion beside them, along with a foil-wrapped condom. After slicking his fingers, Nick reached behind Hunter and circled his hole, the pad of one finger teasing. He watched Hunter closely as he pushed the finger barely inside.

"Do you ever do this to yourself?"

Panting already, Hunter nodded. "Sometimes." With his knees on the couch next to Nick's hips, he gained leverage and rose up a few inches so he could push down on Nick's finger.

"So naughty," Nick murmured with a smile, pressing another slick finger inside without warning.

Hunter gasped, tensing before lowering down again, loving the burn as Nick's fingers penetrated him. "*Oh*," he murmured. It had never felt like this when he'd fingered himself. The angle was so much better, his ass stretching open. Their cocks were hard, butting against each other with teases of friction.

"You're going to be so tight around my cock. Going to make Daddy come so hard."

Flushed with pride, Hunter squeezed his ass, ignoring the pain. "Yes."

With his other hand, Nick teased Hunter's nipples, pinching and rolling them until they stung wonderfully, oversensitive and rigid. He continued stretching Hunter's ass, the sensations rippling through Hunter until all he could do was moan.

Finally, Nick withdrew his fingers, and Hunter whimpered at the loss. Nick kissed him long and slow and wet. "Don't worry, baby. You're going to be so full you'll think you might break. But you won't, I promise. I'm here. I'll take care of you."

He urged Hunter up higher on his knees, and Hunter clung to Nick's shoulders as Nick rolled on the condom and slicked it with more lube. "Here you go. Take my cock like I know you can."

Hunter sank down, fumbling to get the head lined up with his hole. Running his palm over Hunter's back, Nick murmured, "Slow and steady. Don't hurt yourself." He quirked a dark eyebrow. "Trust me, I'm not going anywhere." He helped nudge his cock against the opening of Hunter's ass.

With a shaky laugh, Hunter tried to relax against the intrusion. "You're so big," he blurted, the burn intense.

"You can do it. I know you can." He watched Hunter with such confidence.

Hunter took a deep breath and blew it out, screwing his eyes shut and hanging onto Nick's shoulders as he bore down. His thighs trembled, the stretch bringing tears to his eyes as he impaled himself on Nick's cock. Then it was like something gave, and he groaned as he sank all the way, letting gravity help.

"Look at me."

In a daze, Hunter obeyed, opening his eyes. Nick stroked his spine gently. "Good boy. You feel incredible." He reached down to run his fingers around the rim of Hunter's stretched ass where they were joined. "How does it feel to have me inside you?"

"Full." Hunter laughed, shaking his head. "I can't believe this is happening. I didn't expect this when I woke up this morning."

Nick's chest rumbled with laughter. "Me either. Yet here we are." He caught Hunter's mouth in a kiss, then whispered against his lips, his beard tickling. "You're beautiful." He took hold of Hunter's hips and thrust up. "So sweet and tight for Daddy."

Hunter could only cry out as Nick speared him again. He let himself relax—well, as much as he could with a massive cock splitting him open—giving himself over and letting go. He started to lift and lower, finding Nick's cadence. That wonderful cock stretched and filled him deeper than he'd thought possible.

Pleasure obliterated the pain, and Hunter's cock strained, desperate for friction. But he kept his hands digging into Nick's broad shoulders since Nick had told him not to touch himself. He realized the cries and moans filling the air were his, and a pulse of embarrassment at how shameless he sounded squirmed through him. He snapped his mouth shut.

"No." Nick dug his fingers into Hunter's hips. "Let me hear you. You're a slut for my cock, aren't you? *Aren't you?*"

"Yes!" Hunter admitted, releasing another high cry as pressure hit his prostate just right.

"Don't be ashamed. You're gorgeous." Nick thrust up harder now, pulling Hunter down in a rough rhythm. "Made for this. Made for my cock."

Sweat glistened on Nick's forehead and in the hollow of his throat, and Hunter leaned down to lick it, the salt tangy on his tongue. Sweat gathered on his own skin, the heat from the fire on his back—heat *everywhere.* He was going to explode with it, his muscles shaking as he pleaded, "Please."

"You want to come, baby?"

"Yes," he croaked. "Need to."

"Do you think you've been well-behaved enough for Daddy to let you come?"

Hunter nodded so hard his jaw clacked together. With a smile, Nick wrapped his hand around Hunter's dick, twisting and tugging. "Come like a good boy."

After only three strokes, Hunter did, spraying Nick's chest with jizz. Seeing the white globs land there on the dark hair made Hunter come even harder, and he squeezed convulsively on Nick's iron cock inside him as he shot again, his cries echoing in the rafters.

He clung to Nick, panting as Nick fucked up into him, groaning as he came as well. Hunter wished there was no condom and that he could feel the wetness of cum inside him.

The tension finally released, and Hunter slumped, Nick holding him close and caressing his fevered skin, murmuring, "Such a good boy."

Panting softly against his neck, Hunter kissed him. "Thank you, Daddy."

Mall Santas weren't supposed to be hot, and they also weren't supposed to be sexy lumberjacks who fucked you within an inch of your life and made you crave more. It seemed like days ago that Hunter had been stuck in the ditch and freezing his ass off trudging through the blizzard. Now he was safe and warm, and freaking *finally* no longer a virgin. Nick's softening cock was still inside him, and it was amazing.

He'd never considered whether Christmas miracles were real, but Hunter decided he was definitely a believer.

Chapter Seven

ELLA WASN'T QUITE barking or growling, but pacing at the bottom of the stairs and making a low noise of discontent—followed by a full-on whine. Nick ignored his urge to go back down and give her another kiss and treat as he and Hunter approached the bedroom door just before nine p.m.

"Aww," Hunter said. "She doesn't want to be left behind."

"She knows she's not allowed upstairs. It's only because you're here, and you're her new favorite person in the world since you've been indulging her all day with belly rubs."

Hunter seemed pleased by that, a bright smile on his face. "I'll miss you too, girl," he called. "I'll see you in the morning." The sweatshirt hung off him, and he'd rolled the sleeves up over his wrists. One had slipped down now, and he toyed with the cuff, glancing at Nick nervously.

A *virgin.*

Nick would never have guessed it given how gorgeous Hunter was, and that he was out of university. How had he not had sex before today? He'd begged so prettily, and Nick had wanted to ease him through it—make it as good as possible for a first time. He was confident he'd succeeded, and for his part, he'd had the most powerful orgasm he could remember in a long time.

"Let me just give her one more minute." Hunter hurried back down the stairs, tugging up the too-big PJs, Ella yelping with joy and licking his face as he knelt to pet her, laughing as she slobbered on him. Nick watched with a smile.

He and Hunter had spent the rest of the day watching movies, and Nick had to admit they'd...*cuddled*, Ella heavy on their laps on the couch being spoiled rotten, the fire crackling and mindless gun battles on TV.

It had been the most relaxing day Nick could remember in ages. There had been no more daddy/boy talk—he preferred to keep that roleplaying for sex and not have it bleed into everyday life. Some people enjoyed a twenty-four-seven dom/sub dynamic, but Nick liked a more equal balance.

Not that he and Hunter would have a routine or *life* together or anything even close. Christ, they'd barely met—it was still day one. This would be a temporary diversion. Hunter might not even want to have sex again—although Nick really hoped he did. Nick hadn't initiated anything else, and although they'd sat close on the couch, Hunter snug under his arm, they'd only kissed briefly.

On the threshold of his bedroom, it struck Nick again that Hunter was the first man to spend the night since Eric's death. He hesitated for a heartbeat as Hunter's footsteps thudded softly back up the stairs toward him, then he pushed the door open all the way and switched on the overhead light.

He'd fucked other men in the bed—which was a new one he'd bought a few years prior. It was beyond foolish to make a big deal of the fact Hunter would be sleeping there.

"It's nice," Hunter said, following tentatively and peering around. He shut the door, chuckling as Ella's indignant bark of protest echoed.

"Thanks. It's comfortable." Nick looked around at the king-sized bed in a rustic wooden frame to the right, matching side tables with dark orange glass lamps, a tall dresser, and multicolored throw rugs on either side of the bed.

Hunter motioned to the framed artwork—Group of Seven

prints of windswept trees. "Those are pretty." He approached the window opposite the door and pulled aside a dark curtain. "Oh, there's a river! I think." He cupped his hands around his eyes. "Not much moon tonight with the clouds, but at least the snow has stopped blowing."

Nick flipped off the light so they could see better before joining him, their arms brushing. He burned to pull Hunter close and touch him all over, but since Hunter couldn't just leave, Nick refused to make him feel obligated. "Yes, it's a small river. Cuts through this corner of the property."

"Do you skate on it?"

Nick hadn't skated in years, and never on this particular river, but the thought of anyone out on the ice gripped him with a pulse of fear that sucked the air from his lungs.

He managed, "No," and sounded normal enough that Hunter didn't seem to notice anything amiss, still peering out the glass at the faint curve of the river hugging the clearing, dark forest beyond.

"It's beautiful. I can't wait to see the trees." He looked up at Nick. "Assuming you still want my help."

"Yes." He was relieved to be back on solid ground, shoving away thoughts of icy water. "I'll teach you to use the baler. There's a lot of work to catch up on." He was looking forward to it, and undeniably glad Hunter wouldn't be vanishing come morning.

"Is it cool if I shower before bed?" Hunter asked. "I usually do."

"Of course. I'll get you towels. The bathroom's in there." He nodded toward the en suite, turning on the overhead light before grabbing towels from the linen closet in the hall. He ignored Ella's huffs before shutting the bedroom door again.

"Whoa," Hunter said when Nick joined him in the bathroom. "That's a hell of a shower."

"I suppose it is," Nick agreed with a smile.

The tile was slate gray, the spacious shower extending across the rear of the bathroom with multiple jets embedded in the walls and overhead. Double sinks in an off-white vanity with a wide mirror were to the right, the toilet to the left.

Christ, Nick wanted to tug Hunter under the jets and kiss him until they couldn't breathe, but… Although Hunter had begged to be fucked—and it had been incredible—it had all moved so fast, and the responsible thing was to put on the brakes.

"Enjoy it," Nick said, passing over the towels.

"Um, yeah. Thanks?"

Nick nodded and closed the door behind him, giving Hunter privacy. He stood by the window and heard the water turn on after a minute.

A *virgin.*

Nick hadn't been with a virgin in… Jesus, possibly decades. On one hand he felt incredibly old, but it also filled him with a tenderness he hadn't experienced in a very long time.

He'd been telling the truth when he'd said he didn't mind that Hunter was a virgin. How could he *mind* that Hunter had been so eager to gift Nick his body, being his good boy with such pure passion?

After the sex, Hunter had been warm and pliant in his arms, pressing wet little kisses to Nick's neck and nuzzling against his beard. Nick would have been content to stay there for hours, but he'd cleaned them up, and they'd gotten dressed. He'd wanted to give Hunter time to process what they'd shared.

Now they were going to sleep together, and Nick felt strangely out of his depth.

A *virgin.*

Had he been considerate enough? Did Hunter want to have sex again? He had to leave the ball in Hunter's court no matter how much he wanted to march into the bathroom, sweep him into his arms, and kiss him for hours. He had to get a grip.

Fucking him was one thing. More than that was off the table. It had to be.

Why? I know I'm a hard act to follow, but you've been brooding alone in the forest for long enough.

Eric's voice stubbornly filled his head. Nick wanted to argue with it, which was surely a sign that he *had* been brooding alone too long.

He's a breath of fresh air. I like him. And you like being daddy again. Don't deny it—you were always a terrible liar.

It was true. And Hunter had so much innocent need. It called to Nick, to instincts deep within him. Eric hadn't been young and insecure the same way Hunter was, but he'd questioned himself more than he should have.

Because he'd had to be in such control at the hospital, he'd craved submission and freedom from being the one in charge. After a stressful shift, he'd come home and beg for it, wanting to be a bad boy who had to be spanked. Nick had reveled in giving him the peace and release he'd needed, finding his own soul-deep pleasure in it.

"Nick?" Hunter called.

Closing the box firmly on memories of Eric, Nick cracked the bathroom door, steam flowing around him. "Do you need something?"

"Can you come in?"

Heart leaping and cock definitely on board, Nick entered the bathroom, the air thick and humid, the mirror fogged over. Hunter had opened the glass door to the long shower stall. Christ, he truly was beautiful—his pale skin flushed, nipples starkly pink, slim muscles slick and dripping, his uncut cock half hard and oh-so tempting.

He held out a bar of soap, his lip caught between his teeth. "Can you wash my back?" He lowered his head, water-darkened hair hanging over his forehead. A little shudder rippled through him, and he looked up, squaring his shoulders. "Please, Daddy?"

It was music to Nick's ears, and he was already unbuttoning his plaid shirt as he asked, "You're sure?"

"Oh, yeah." Hunter nodded. "I'm sure."

"I don't want you to feel obligated because you're staying over."

True confusion creased Hunter's face. "I don't think that word means what you think it means."

Nick's laugh warmed his chest, lust firing through his veins. "Well, you're the English major, so you'd know." He stripped off his clothes and joined Hunter in the shower, taking the soap and putting it back in its tray for the moment.

Because right now, he needed both hands to haul Hunter against him, Hunter going up on tiptoes and grabbing Nick's face, pushing his tongue into Nick's mouth. That little spark of independence and confidence was exactly what Nick had been yearning to see, and he let him take control of their kiss.

When they were gasping for air, Nick took the washcloth and dragged it down Hunter's back to his ass. He murmured, "Spread your legs."

Hunter eagerly did, and Nick gently probed with the cloth. "Does it hurt very much?"

"A little. About what I'd expect after having something that big up there."

Chuckling, Nick skimmed his fingers up and down Hunter's crack, the need to touch drumming through him steadily. "Did you like being fucked?"

He nodded eagerly. "I loved it."

Nick kissed him. "Such a hungry little slut, hmm?"

"Yes, Daddy."

A curl of lust simmered through him to hear those words. Nick hadn't realized just how much he'd missed that dynamic, and Hunter had taken to it like he was born for it. Beautifully submissive but spirited and vibrant. He made Nick's blood sing—

which was dangerous, since Hunter was surely going back to Toronto after the holidays, and Nick was content in his solitary life, and—

With a burst of irritation at himself, he cut off that line of thinking, giving Hunter another slow kiss. They'd just met. He should simply enjoy being together for the time being. Santa and his elf having a holiday fling, and that was all.

"I never realized—" Hunter broke off. He swallowed hard, meeting Nick's gaze. Water dripped from his nose, the hot shower spraying from above and around them. "I've always been attracted to older guys, but the whole daddy thing?" His chest rose with a sharp breath. "It turns me on so much."

"Mmm." Nick slid a hand between them, stroking Hunter's cock. "Does it make you hard to call me Daddy and be my good boy?" He could feel it did, the flesh in his grip throbbing.

"Fuck, yes." Hunter laughed before smirking. "I guess Freud would have a field day with me wanting a daddy since I grew up with a single mom."

"Probably. But I didn't have a father either, so Freud can fuck off." He ran his hands over Hunter's ass, rubbing their cocks together. "Can you feel how hard you make me when you call me Daddy?"

"Yes," Hunter breathed. "Yes, Daddy." He rubbed his cheek against Nick's before leaning back and asking, "What do you want me to do, Daddy?"

"Hmm." Nick pondered it.

"I'll do anything." His brows drew together, and Nick could practically see his mind spinning with what "anything" might entail.

"You don't have to worry about that. I'll take care of you. You don't need to worry about anything."

"Right." He exhaled, his face smoothing out. "Thank you."

Nick swept his tongue into Hunter's mouth with command.

Hunter moaned, reaching up to clutch Nick's shoulders, rutting against him eagerly.

Nick wasn't sure how long they stood under the hot water, locked in an embrace as they kissed until their lips were swollen and Hunter's face had to be raw. Nick kissed his red cheek tenderly and whispered, "Let's go to bed."

Their skin was still damp, towels abandoned on the floor in the bedroom when Nick pulled back the duvet and urged Hunter onto the mattress. He left one of the orange glass lamps on low, and it was almost like firelight on Hunter's pale skin.

As much as Nick wanted to bury himself in Hunter's tight heat, he didn't want to hurt him. Instead, he said, "I'm going to eat your ass. You've been such a good boy, and you're going to come so hard with my tongue inside you."

Hunter shivered, nodding. "Yes, Daddy." He glanced around at the mattress he was kneeling on. "How should I...?"

"On your hands and knees for me. That's it. Now on your elbows. Good. Rest your cheek on the pillow." Nick crawled onto the bed behind him, barely resisting reaching out to grab the round globes of Hunter's gorgeous ass. "Now bring your arms back. That's right. Hold yourself open for me."

Hunter's fingers trembled, but he obeyed beautifully, reaching back for his ass cheeks and spreading them. "Like this, Daddy?" His cheek and shoulders rested on the bed.

"Yes. That's perfect, baby." Nick leaned in, blowing a cool stream of air, watching Hunter's hole twitch. Then he huffed warm air over it, and Hunter moaned.

With Hunter holding himself open, on display, Nick teased with a fingertip and his breath, giving him the occasional hint of his tongue—just brief, wet touches. Hunter's cock strained, and Nick eased it back toward him between Hunter's legs until he could suck the head.

Hunter cried out. "Yes! Please, Daddy. Please."

Nick swirled with his tongue, swallowing the musky, pearly drops of precum. Hunter's hands shook where he still held himself open, and when Nick let go of his cock with a wet smack, he said, "You're being such a good boy."

"I thought you were going to rim me," Hunter blurted. "Please, I need…"

Nick swallowed a chuckle and put on a stern voice. "Now you're being a bad boy. I promised I would, but you have to be patient. Or I won't let you come at all."

Hunter gasped. "No! Please. I'm sorry, Daddy. I'll be good."

"I know you will." He stroked Hunter's quivering legs, drawing soothing circles with his thumbs over the tender skin of his inner thighs. "I'll take care of you."

Hunter exhaled loudly. "Thank you."

Nick's own cock was like steel, but he had to take care of Hunter before he tended to himself. Taking pity on him—and himself—he covered Hunter's hands with his own and spread him as wide as possible before licking from his balls to the top of his ass.

Crying out, Hunter jerked. "Oh God."

He was deliciously responsive, and knowing Nick was the first man to ever taste him was like drinking fine Scotch, a smooth burn that fed Nick's hunger. He circled his tongue around Hunter's hole before finally licking into him.

As Hunter's cries of pleasure echoed off the wooden rafters, Nick ate him out, licking and kissing and nipping, burying his face in that sweet ass. He knew his beard was rough against the tender flesh, and he used it as a counterpoint to the wetness of his tongue and softness of his lips.

When he reached down and fondled Hunter's balls, hair bristling his palms, Hunter seized up and came without his cock being touched. Nick licked him through it, pride swelling in his chest. Hunter was almost crying with the pleasure, and he probably would have toppled over when he was finished spurting onto the sheets if not for Nick holding him up.

Nick eased him onto his side and then his back, and Hunter looked up at him in a daze, panting through his mouth, his face red. "Oh my God," he murmured. His gaze dropped to Nick's rock-hard cock. "Can I taste you, Daddy?"

Nick groaned, surging forward to straddle him and feed him his cock. He fucked Hunter's mouth, careful not to go too deep, knowing it wouldn't take much.

Sure enough, he came before long, gripping the headboard with one hand, petting Hunter's damp hair with the other as he spent himself, milky semen dripping out of that pretty mouth. Hunter struggled to swallow, and Nick pulled out, milking himself and letting the final drops paint Hunter's flushed cheeks.

He and Hunter were wet and messy, but Nick gathered him close and kissed him, tasting himself and whispering, "Daddy's so proud of you."

Eventually, he cleaned them up and turned out the light, Hunter smiling at him with shy, dazed pleasure. Nick curled himself around Hunter's smaller body and tried not to think about how right it felt having him in his bed.

Chapter Eight

"I S THAT YOU, sweetie?"

"Hey, Mom!" Hunter called back as he untangled his scarf from his mom's massive wreath and closed the front door, dropping his keys on the little table in the foyer. His heart thumped as she appeared in the hallway from the kitchen. "I just need to pick up my elf costume."

Be normal, he reminded himself.

Wearing purple scrubs and slippers, she came to hug him. Her hair was knotted up, which meant she was going to work soon. "I feel like I haven't seen you in weeks!" She gave him a squeeze, smelling faintly of sweet lemons.

He laughed and hugged her back. "It's only been a few days."

"Nick Spini's been working you hard, huh?" She stepped away, grinning.

Hunter knew she didn't mean anything else by it, but despite his best efforts, his face went hot, the blush spreading to the tips of his ears. He tried to sound normal. "Yeah, it's been great. Muscles I didn't even know I had are sore."

Oh yeah, terrific work on not making this sound sexual.

It was true, though—along with his wonderfully sore ass, Hunter's body ached pleasantly from the three days of manual labor. He quickly added, "I know how to use a baler now, and chop down a tree with an axe. It's really cool."

Tilting her head, a little furrow between her brows, his mom smiled. "That's great, honey."

He bent to pull off his boots. "Yeah, I never thought of myself as outdoorsy or, like, good at doing that kind of physical stuff, but it's been really satisfying."

Not making this sound less sexual, you dumbass!

His face was burning as he straightened up. "Anyway, it's been cool. How are you? How's work?"

"I'm good. Work's busy, as always." She was still watching him quizzically. "I'm glad you're enjoying spending time with Nick."

"Yeah, like I said, the work's been good. There's so much to do."

"Mmm. There must be, since you've stayed out there four nights in a row now."

Nick had driven him home Wednesday to pack clothes and toiletries, and Hunter had told his mom it would just be easier to stay at the farm since he didn't have a car. Which was true! Sure, it also meant he could spend the nights in Nick's bed and be fucked until he was blissfully exhausted.

Hunter brushed past his mom. "Yeah, like I said, there's been a ton of work. Now I'd better hurry and get over to the mall. Nick's waiting in his truck. John convinced him to be Santa again." He laughed—too high-pitched—and escaped down the hall to his room.

He grabbed the cursed elf costume, closing his eyes for a moment and breathing deeply. The past four days had been beyond his wildest dreams. He truly did enjoy the work. They'd put in long days, and Nick was all business when they were out among the trees.

Well, *almost* all business. Butterflies flapped through Hunter's belly as he remembered how Nick had kissed him fiercely at the end of the work days when they'd climbed into the pickup truck.

As soon as they were in that cab, the leather seats freezing, Nick always hauled Hunter close as if he'd been dying to touch him again. Then they fogged up the windows, Ella barking outside, demanding to be let in.

And once they'd returned to the house each day…

In the doorway of his room, Hunter closed his eyes, shivering in delight. It was like he'd been on rations before, and now he was glutting himself at an all-you-can-eat sex buffet. He grinned with a giddy thrill as he thought about Nick and how gentle and patient he was while also being dominant and perfectly demanding.

Daddy kink was *so* Hunter's thing. Lust spiked at the thought of how he'd been able to give up control and relax and be taken care of in a way that soothed…well, his *soul*.

Laughing aloud at how corny he was being, Hunter hurried back to find his mom hadn't budged, and now her hands were on her hips. Her eyebrows lifted. "You and Nick Spini?"

His heart dropped. "Huh?"

She just watched him, eyebrows still about to disappear into her hairline. There was a stray piece of tinsel caught in her hair, probably from one of the red-and-gold garlands wrapped around the bannister heading downstairs. He reached out and plucked it free, letting it drift down to the floor.

"Tinsel," he said. "Anyway, I've gotta run."

She didn't move a muscle, her gaze unwavering.

Sighing, Hunter shrugged, willing himself not to blush again and failing, heat burning his cheeks. "I guess?"

"Well. You and Nick Spini. He's a lot older than you." She watched him evenly, her voice calm as she crossed her arms. She didn't seem mad, which was good. Although sometimes she would go horribly quiet when she was really furious.

"Yeah. It's cool, though. I…" He shrugged again. "I really like him."

"Mmm." She still stared like she could see right into his mind in that way moms had. "He's been good to you?"

"Yes," he answered without hesitation. "He's great. I thought he was a jerk at first, but he's not at all." Hunter tried to find the right words. "He's so…"

His mom laughed softly, shaking her head. "Dreamy? You should see the expression on your face. You look like he hung the moon, the stars, and all the planets to boot."

Relief that she wasn't too mad flowed, and Hunter laughed too. "Do I?"

"You do." She sighed. "I can already tell that it's not going to matter what I think."

His smile faded. "Of course it does. I can understand why you wouldn't be thrilled."

"You've never really had a boyfriend before. At least not that you ever let on."

"He's not my *boyfriend*. We just met." Although the idea of Nick being his boyfriend made Hunter want to grin, his heart dancing. "And no, I've never really dated anyone before. I was too…in my own way."

She laughed ruefully. "I can understand that." Taking a big breath, she blew it out. "Okay. I don't love that he's so much older than you, but you're a grown man yourself now. Even though you'll always be my little boy." She glanced toward the closed front door. "He's waiting outside? Maybe I should go say hello."

Hunter groaned. "*Mom*. Not right now, okay? We have to get to the mall."

She sighed noisily. "All right. You're off the hook for now. Are you coming home tonight?"

"Yeah." Although he ached to think of spending the night away from Nick, he did want to catch up with his mom. "I'll get takeout, and we can have a late dinner when you're home from work."

"That sounds lovely."

He smiled tentatively. "I know this is unexpected. For all of us! It's just been…" A little bubble of joy escaped him with a laugh. "It's been amazing."

She smiled back. "I distantly remember that feeling. Infatuation can be a glorious thing. And you're an intelligent young man. I trust your judgment, and that you'll always stay safe."

"*Yes*," he muttered, rolling his eyes.

Laughing, she kissed his cheek. "I'm still your mother. Always going to nag."

"I know." He kissed her back, then pulled her into a hug. "Thanks for being so cool, Mom. I'm really, really lucky."

She squeezed him tight. "I love you, sweetie. If Nick Spini hurts you, I know how to make it look like an accident."

He laughed and pulled back. "Let's hope it doesn't come to that. Oh! You're working the night on Christmas Eve, right? And Heather and Rick are coming Boxing Day?"

"Yep. They're spending Christmas with Rick's parents."

"John and Desmond invited us for dinner on Christmas Day. I figure since you'll be sleeping until the afternoon, it's kind of perfect." John had apparently guessed there was something going on between Hunter and Nick, and he was delighted by it, much to Hunter's relief.

"Well, that would be lovely." She gave him a knowing look. "And will Nick also be in attendance?"

"Yeah." Hunter tried not to smile, but that giddy joy bubbled through him again.

"I look forward to it. And not only so I can grill him." She winked.

"Thanks, Mom. You really are being awesome about this."

"Well, you're an adult." She inhaled deeply and blew it out. "I'd ideally like to lock you in your room and chase away Nick Spini with a shotgun, but since that's not an option, I'm going to be chill. Ish. Now you'd better get going. The kids are waiting for Santa and his elf."

By Sunday night, Hunter was so ready to never, ever wear the damn candy-cane tights again. It seemed like everyone in Pinevale had come to the mall to see the sexy Santa, but the last stragglers had finally gone.

And now he and Nick could…what?

Hopefully pick up where they'd left off, but was Hunter getting ahead of himself? After spending the night alone, he'd missed Nick more than he'd thought possible, but the day had been so busy. John had been in the storeroom when Hunter had arrived that morning, so there had been no privacy. Hunter and Nick hadn't so much as brushed hands all day, let alone kissed or anything.

He itched to throw himself in Nick's arms once they reached the freezing storeroom, the cold air a relief after the sweltering heat of the mall. Yet he held back, watching Nick stretch his spine, his hands on his lower back and fake belly sticking out.

"Thank Christ that's over," Nick muttered.

"Yeah." *But what about us?* Nick hadn't said anything to make Hunter think he wanted to call it off—whatever *it* was—but Hunter's mind had spun all day, taking a little thread of doubt and whirling it into a massive ball of uncertainty that now lodged in his chest.

As Nick struggled to unhook the white beard, Hunter hurried over, his heart pounding. "Here." He went up on his tiptoes, déjà vu washing over him as Nick's big hands came around his waist to steady him.

As Hunter unhooked the beard and freed him from it, Nick murmured, "Thanks."

Still holding the beard, Hunter didn't move away, gazing up at Nick, who watched him with a little frown. Was he being crazy? He should just kiss him and—

John bustled into the storeroom, and Hunter tripped away from Nick, his heart thumping rapidly. "Hi!" he practically yelled.

John burst out laughing. "Don't worry, kid. I can handle a little PDA. He grinned. "I knew sparks were flying from the first day you two met. And don't give me that look, Nick. Let me enjoy being right."

Hunter tried to laugh. "I'm just not used to…" Fidgety and self-conscious, he stared at the bells on his shoes.

"It's all right." Nick smoothed a hand over Hunter's back and gently squeezed the back of his neck.

Hunter exhaled, the tension easing. "Okay."

He wouldn't do that if he didn't like me anymore. Right?

"This is really nice to see." John beamed at them. "Really nice. You two make a great couple."

"All right, all right," Nick groused, but he was almost smiling as he unbuttoned his Santa jacket to pull out the padding.

Hunter's heart leapt. *A couple.* Was that what they were? It was still too soon to really say, right? God, he had missed Nick desperately the night before. It was ridiculous since he'd slept alone his whole life, but his bed had seemed so cold and empty.

When he'd spent the nights at the farm, Nick's big body had curled around him, warm and comforting. Even when they'd shifted during sleep, Nick had always seemed to end up with an arm over Hunter's waist or nuzzling him close.

Had Nick missed him as much? The worry returned full force, despite Hunter's best efforts to chill the eff out. Maybe Nick had been relieved to sleep alone again. He'd told Hunter not to masturbate last night, implying that they'd be together again Sunday night. Hunter had totally disobeyed, the urge to think of Nick and get off simply too strong. But perhaps he'd also assumed too much?

Maybe Nick had had his fill, and now that they were finished with their duties at Santa's Village, this would be it. Maybe—

"What's wrong?" Nick asked, brow creased as he reached out to take hold of Hunter's shoulder.

"Nothing!" Hunter answered too quickly.

Nick's frown deepened, but he let go, and they both turned as John swore under his breath. Nick asked him, "Everything okay?"

John sighed. "I was hoping we'd be able to use the basement over at St. Mary's on Tuesday afternoon, but they're booked with childcare since the kids are out of school. We had plans for Toys and Turkeys to do a charity lunch: buy a hot dog and give a family a turkey this Christmas, but the original venue fell through. We've had all the food and soft drinks donated, but we need a big enough space. Thursday's Christmas Eve, so we planned a big final push for fundraising Tuesday to buy out what's left in the stores and get everything delivered. It'll be good for the local businesses too."

"The mall's already half empty," Nick said. "Why not here?"

John scowled. "Red tape with the property management office. I'd have to get a permit. There's no time for that."

The perfect solution popped into Hunter's mind, and he shoved away his worry about his relationship with Nick to focus on it. "Could you do it outside? You know, a winter wonderland thing? Hot chocolate and snowman-making contests. Crafts for the kids?" He glanced at Nick. "Maybe do a raffle, and the winner gets to cut down their own tree?"

Nick jolted at that, narrowing his gaze on Hunter. "No. Forget it."

"Why not? You have the space and the most winter-wonderland location possible. I know most people will already have their trees, but some leave it until the last minute, so the raffle could be a big hit. And I bet people would come from all over for a one-day-only holiday charity extravaganza on a Christmas tree farm."

"Yes," Nick agreed sourly. "The key word there being *people*." He looked to John, who grinned. "*No.*"

Hunter sighed dramatically, raising and then dropping his shoulders. "I guess the needy kids won't get toys or turkey on Christmas. Sucks to be them."

"Oh, for fuck's sake," Nick grumbled.

Trying not to grin, Hunter promised, "It'll be awesome. I'll plan it, and you don't have to do anything." And he would have an excuse to go back to the farm, one way or the other.

"Woo-hoo!" John high-fived Hunter. "Strong work, kid. This Grinch doesn't stand a chance with you around." He tapped his phone. "Okay, I've got to run now, but let's talk tomorrow and brainstorm activities." He winked at Nick. "Like he said, Hunter and I will work it all out, and you won't have to worry your pretty head about it."

Nick pressed his lips together. "I suggest you leave before I change my mind."

John backed away, his hands in the air. "I'm already gone. Security will be here in a few hours to make the rounds, but for now you're the only people left. When you go, make sure this door locks behind you, okay?" He pressed the metal bar on the storeroom door to the back parking lot, a gust of arctic air blowing in. "Toodles!"

"How did I just get talked into that?" Nick muttered.

Hunter almost said something cheeky about how Nick couldn't resist him, but doubt bit his tongue. What if Nick really was pissed? And *was* Hunter going back with him to the farm? Had he overstepped?

"What's wrong? You got your way—you should be thrilled." Having stripped down to his white undershirt, still wearing the Santa pants and boots, Nick looked just as he had when Hunter had first seen him.

Ignoring the bolt of lust, Hunter removed his green hat, his sweaty hair probably sticking up all over. He toyed with the hat's fuzzy white pom-pom. "Just wondering…. Am I coming back with you to the farm tonight? I mean, most of the work is done, right? So I wasn't sure if you wanted…"

There was only silence, and Hunter had to look up, his heart in his throat. Nick stared at him, his hands held up to his sides, puzzlement plain in his expression. Shaking his head, he said, "I thought we talked about it? You said you should spend a night at home, and then I assumed you'd be coming back." Something flickered across his face, his brow furrowing. "But if you don't want to…"

"I want to!" Hunter exclaimed too eagerly. He huffed out an embarrassed laugh. "I'm not very good at playing it cool, as you can tell. I really want to come back. You just never said it explicitly?"

A small smile tugged on Nick's lips. "So then you started getting in your own way."

Hunter had to laugh. "Exactly."

Nick closed the few feet between them, taking Hunter's face in his rough hands and kissing him soundly. Exhaling as they parted, Hunter looped his arms around Nick's broad back, grinning.

He likes me. He still likes me.

Nick said, "Since we're having Christmas dinner at John and Desmond's with your mother, I assumed it was clear that we're… Well, that we're continuing." He reached up to smooth a hand over Hunter's damp hair. "At least, I'd really like to continue. See where this goes." He grimaced. "I know you're going back to the city in January, but until then…"

"Uh-huh?" Hunter leaned into his touch. The thought of going back to Toronto filled him with dread, and he focused on Nick. The future could wait.

"Until then, I want to be with you as much as possible. Is that *explicit* enough?" Then he whispered in Hunter's ear with a warm puff, "I'll be more explicit from now on. *Very* explicit."

Shuddering, Hunter pressed against him. "That sounds good. Really good. So…" He peered up at Nick. "This is a thing? Between us? You're not sick of me or anything?"

Nick regarded him seriously. "Not at all. I missed you last night." He laughed softly, like he was surprised by it. "House felt too quiet. Poor Ella is bereft."

"Awww." His heart swelled. "I can't wait to see her. And I missed you too. I couldn't get to sleep missing you, so I had to—" He broke off, biting his lip.

Nick's dark eyebrows rose. "You had to what? Were you a bad boy, Hunter?"

Swallowing hard, he nodded. "I missed you so much. I couldn't resist."

"Mmm. But I told you not to touch yourself. How naughty of you." He ran a hand over Hunter's ass, not squeezing or slapping, but with…intent.

Desire firing through him, Hunter whispered, "I'm sorry, Daddy. Let's go home, and you can punish me."

Nick blinked, opening his mouth, then closing it. Hunter realized what he'd said—*home*—and was about to clarify when Nick swooped down and kissed him, taking his breath away with the commanding sweep of his tongue as he lifted Hunter clear off his feet.

Putting him down, both of them breathing hard, Nick muttered, "Yes. Let's go." Then he swore. "I forgot my thermos out there."

"I'll go with you." Hunter needed to touch, and he threaded their fingers together as they re-entered the deserted, sweltering mall. He realized it was the first time they'd held hands, and he grinned to himself, loving how big and rough Nick's hand was, and how secure his grasp.

The bells on Hunter's elf shoes dinged merrily, echoing as they hurried over the cobblestone brick. The lights were low in the stores that were left, but the strings of Christmas lights still shone around Santa's Village.

Nick bent by the bench, grabbing the thermos he'd tucked under it. The Santa pants hugged his ass. Standing on the curving candy path, Hunter's throat went dry. Fuck, Nick was so *gorgeous*, and Hunter's dick swelled at the promise of getting to be naked with him again soon. He pressed the heel of his hand against his junk, failing to bite back a little groan.

Turning to him, Nick's eyes went dark. *Predatory.* Hunter whipped his hand back, his breath catching. He waited, watching as Nick seemed to consider. Nick's dark hair was mussed after wearing the Santa hat all day, and the colored fairy lights caught the glints of silver on his head and in his beard. His dark chest hair shadowed the white tank top.

Then Nick's hands moved to the thick belt holding up the red velvet pants. He unbuckled it, and Hunter's pulse zoomed. Nick unzipped the pants and sat on the bench at the heart of Santa's Village, spreading his legs. His black briefs were visible in the V of his open pants, but he didn't expose himself fully.

"Come here," he commanded.

Glancing around the narrow strip of the deserted old mall, a thrill sang in Hunter's veins. John had mentioned the security cameras were broken, at least. "But someone might…"

"Come. Here." Nick raised an eyebrow. "Good elves obey Santa."

Hunter giggled nervously, his cock swelling thicker in his tights as he approached, his shoes ringing. He stopped in front of Nick and breathlessly asked, "Do I get to sit on Santa's lap?"

Nick wordlessly patted his left thigh, and Hunter perched on it, clasping his hands together. His too-short green elf jacket rode up, totally exposing the bulge in his tights.

Nick asked, "Have you been naughty or nice?"

"Um, naughty." He practically shook with anticipation, blood rushing south.

"Hmm." Nick spread his hand over Hunter's lower back, heavy and firm, his gaze focused on Hunter's with laser precision. "What did you do?"

"I jerked off last night. Thinking of you."

"Even though I told you not to?"

"Yes," Hunter breathed, excitement and nerves battling.

"Show me."

Hunter jolted. "What?" He glanced around. "You mean…*here*? Now? I can't!"

"Are you going to be a bad boy and disobey your daddy again?" Nick gripped Hunter's ass. "I'll have to spank you."

"That's not really incentive to be good," he blurted.

Nick's face creased with a smile, and he laughed softly. "Fair point." He breathed deeply, and his smile faded. "But I think I need to spank you anyway."

Without any further warning, he lifted Hunter by the waist, his muscular arms flexing as he turned him over his lap. Hunter squawked, scrambling for balance, bracing his hands on the side of the bench, his stupid shoes ringing as he dug in his toes to steady himself.

He sucked in a breath as Nick spread a hand over his ass, waiting until Hunter stopped fidgeting and had himself braced. Then Nick tugged down the tights and Hunter's boxer briefs to bare his ass.

At least it was warm given the heat of the mall, but Hunter still felt goosebumps spread over his exposed skin. The tights were caught on his junk in the front, tugging on his cock.

He waited, panting already. He dug his blunt nails into the wood of the old bench, staring at the plywood floor, painted in a candy-cane swirl. Was Nick going to say anything else, or was he—

Nick's palm came down, and Hunter yelped, jerking. It wasn't super hard—just enough to make a *smack* in the silence of the mall, the sound making Hunter's dick swell even more.

"Naughty boy," Nick chided.

Anticipating the next spank, Hunter held his breath. Then squirmed impatiently, his heart thudding. He whimpered, and Nick soothed his palm over his ass.

"Shh. I've got you. You don't have to worry about anything. Do you trust me?"

Hunter exhaled the breath that had gotten knotted in his throat. "Yes, Daddy."

"Good boy."

Nick's hand slapped down again, and again, alternating cheeks, and Hunter moaned, the anxiety melting, a sweet tension remaining as his arousal intensified. He was uncomfortable sprawled the way he was, yet that added to his pleasure at being under Nick's power, spread over his lap and held down.

It was *perfect.*

The smacks on his ass had him crying out, thrusting against Nick's lap and the answering hardness Hunter felt there. "Oh God," he groaned. The mix of pain and pleasure whited out his vision, and he squeezed his eyes shut, abandoning himself to it.

"Do you want to come?" Nick asked in a growl.

"Yes!" Hunter humped Nick's thighs desperately. "Please, Daddy."

"You were so naughty. I think you have to show me what you did first."

He opened his eyes, gripping the side of the bench and twisting his neck to look up at Nick. "Huh?"

"Bad boys need to learn their lessons." With strong hands on Hunter's hips, Nick lifted and turned him so Hunter sat on both his legs now, with his back against Nick's chest.

Fully exposed if anyone did appear.

Nick slid his hand over the front of Hunter's groin where his tights and underwear snagged on his straining cock, cupping him. "Show me," he ordered.

"Someone could come in! John might come back."

"Show me how you disobeyed me." Nick's tone was steely in his ear. "Push down your tights to your ankles. Spread your legs."

Holy shit, was he really doing this? Legs shaking, Hunter lifted to pull down his underwear and the damn candy-cane tights to the tops of the black shoes, the bells tinkling. "I... I don't..." Sweat rolled down his spine under his elf coat in the too-warm air.

It seemed so wrong to be doing this in Santa's Village, with Christmas lights and merry gingerbread and candy decorations around them. The bench where kids had told Santa their wishes. So wrong—which of course made Hunter's blood run even hotter as he spread his legs as far as he could, his throbbing dick standing free.

"Show me how you touch yourself," Nick ordered, his teeth grazing Hunter's earlobe.

Gasping, Hunter wrapped his right hand around his dick, automatically swiping the drops of precum from the tip and easing down his foreskin. "Oh, fuck," he mumbled.

He was doing it—he was jacking himself in the middle of Treeview Mall, sitting on Nick's lap in Santa's Village, Nick's hard cock nudging his ass.

"Fuck, I'm going to come so hard," he cried, arching up into his hand, his dick leaking and flushed dark red.

"You're so beautiful." Nick's whisper was hot in Hunter's ear, his hands rough as he gripped Hunter's hips. "You were a bad boy, but I'm so proud of you now."

Sweat dampened Hunter's neck, and he thought he might burst from the heat—Nick at his back and under him, the hot air of the mall, and the fire blazing through his body, centering on his cock and balls, which drew tight.

"You need it, don't you, baby?"

"*Yes*," he whined. He was so close. He strained, stroking himself faster, his gasps loud.

"Show me how good boys come for their daddies," Nick ordered.

Whole body tensing, the bells ringing as he flexed his feet and leaned back against Nick, working himself frantically, Hunter's cries were high and loud. He chased the orgasm that was just beyond reach, suddenly catching it, the pleasure exploding.

Shuddering on a strangled moan, Hunter came all over his green elf coat, spraying himself as white-hot bliss gripped him. It dripped down over his hand, and he milked himself, panting and whimpering as he relaxed, boneless in Nick's strong grasp.

He was butter against Nick's chest, which heaved with deep, excited breaths, his cock like stone under Hunter's ass. Nick picked up Hunter's sticky right hand, rasping, "Taste yourself."

Moaning, he obeyed, licking the earthy, salty fluid from his skin, dipping his tongue between his fingers, his balls twitching at how deliciously *dirty* it was.

"Can I taste you too, Daddy?" he asked breathlessly.

Nick groaned, urging Hunter to his feet and turning him. Hunter's legs were jelly, and he happily dropped to his knees between Nick's thighs, his shaking hands tugging Nick free. The red velvet pants were soft under his palms as he pushed Nick's legs open wider.

When he took Nick in his mouth eagerly, he imagined what they must look like: Santa in his village, a bare—and red—assed elf between his legs, sucking his big cock. It sent fresh lust rushing through Hunter, and he hummed around the hot flesh filling his mouth.

Nick's hands tangled in Hunter's hair. "So good. *Yes.* Good boy. Harder."

Hunter hollowed his cheeks, sucking like his life depended on it, and clumsily took hold of Nick's heavy, hairy balls with his hand. It was clearly the right thing to do, because Nick jerked, his cock choking Hunter as it swelled even bigger.

He came, groaning, his fingers tight in Hunter's hair. Hunter had to pull back, gasping and swallowing, spit and semen leaking from his mouth. Their eyes locked, and Nick sprayed the last bit of his climax on Hunter's face, hitting his cheek and wet lips.

"Fuck," Nick mumbled. He lurched forward and kissed Hunter messily, licking his splattered face and feeding the jizz to him with his tongue, the mingled taste of them both filling Hunter's mouth.

They parted, breathing heavily. Hunter glanced around, smiling. "Well, I guess Santa's Village went out with a bang."

Nick's laughter rumbled in his chest, a grin brightening his face. There was a white streak in his beard, and Hunter swiped at it with his finger and sucked it clean. "Am I on the nice list now, Santa Daddy?"

Nick chuckled. "Yes. Maybe I should keep the suit?"

"Hell yes."

"You realize you're keeping yours too. Santa needs his elf, after all." He ran his hand tenderly over Hunter's bare ass, the skin still hot from the spanking. Hunter wished he could see how red it was. Nick added, "No one else will ever get to see you in this costume but me."

Ever.

Thrilling at Nick's words, Hunter leaned up and kissed him, sucking on Nick's tongue before pulling back to whisper against his lips, "Only you, Daddy."

Chapter Nine

"ARE YOU SURE about this?" Hunter asked. "You've already donated your time in Santa's Village."

Dawn still streaked the cloudy sky orange over the horizon of snow-capped green, but Nick and Hunter were already out on a distant acre. Nick nodded. "I'm sure." He'd agreed, and it really was for a good cause.

Hunter bit his lip, his cheeks pink in the crisp, cold morning air. The pom-pom on his woolen hat bounced as he shifted boot to boot. "But I kind of forced you into hosting this fundraiser. I mean, you couldn't really say no."

"I tried," Nick noted dryly, but he didn't really mind.

You already can't deny him anything, can you?

Nick couldn't argue with Eric's sly observation. To Hunter, he added, "I hate to think of kids without a Christmas tree. John's worked his ass off to collect presents and food for these families. They need trees to put the toys under."

Hunter beamed at him like a heart-eyes emoji come to life, and Nick *had* to smile back. Hunter said, "You're really just a big softie, you know that?"

He's right, of course. Smart lad, and you should keep him around.

Grumbling with an exaggerated scowl, Nick fired up the chainsaw, cutting off the light, cheery sound of Hunter's laughter. He felled a Scotch pine that could have grown another year but was plenty big enough to fill a living room corner.

There was a ton to do before the fundraising event for Toys and Turkeys that afternoon, so they'd woken early. Nick had wanted to stay snuggled under the covers with Hunter warm and sweet in his arms, kissing Nick's chest and neck, his hair sticking up adorably. But he had to plow a makeshift parking lot in the small field to the east of the head of his driveway after they dealt with the trees.

Hunter heaved up the tree and put it through the baler, and they fell into a rhythm that was already shockingly familiar. Hunter had taken to the work like a fish to water, and pride flowed through Nick as he watched Hunter stacking a few baled trees.

Hunter glanced up when he was done. "What?" He smiled uncertainly. He breathed a little heavily, puffs of air clouding in the cold.

"Nothing." Nick turned to the next grid, sawing through the trunk of another pine.

The thing was, after the holidays this would all be over. Nick would be back out on the land on his own. Ella barked in the distance, as if to remind him he wouldn't be completely alone. He just hoped she hadn't discovered a skunk den.

He sighed to himself as he sawed another tree. After so many years of solitude, it was ridiculous that he didn't want Hunter to leave. That the thought of a quiet January and February—months when he didn't work as much and caught up on reading, watching TV, and generally hibernated—filled him with dread.

You've been alone too long and you know it, my love. He fits with you. Birds of a feather, like the song goes.

Nick argued with Eric in his mind, which was insane since it wasn't actually Eric. He argued that Hunter was too young, and surely he'd want to go back to Toronto and date other men and live his life. Not be stuck in the middle of nowhere with Nick.

Eric calmly refuted the arguments, and Nick couldn't get "Sleigh Ride" out of his head, humming it under his breath and sneaking glances at Hunter.

It had snowed again, and they stood in it up to their knees aside from the space he'd plowed for the baler. The boughs of the trees were heavy with fluffy, slightly wet snow—perfect for making snowmen. It was five degrees below freezing, and the wind was calm, the perfect winter weather. Cold enough not to be slushy, but not biting and unpleasant.

Turning off the chainsaw, Nick called, "Do you want to chop down the last one?"

Hunter's face lit up. "Yeah? Okay." He brushed dead needles from his gloves and neared. He'd learned the axe well, although it was tough work since he was slight. Nick handed him the chainsaw.

"Whoa." Hunter held it uneasily. "Heavy."

"Safety's obviously the most important thing," Nick said, taking him through the ins and outs, Hunter listening carefully and nodding.

When Hunter felled the tree with the chainsaw, he whooped with joy, making sure to turn the machinery off properly and engage the safety lock. "I did it!" He put down the chainsaw on a tarp spread on the snow.

"You did." Nick grinned at him, spreading his legs and digging in when Hunter threw himself into his arms.

"Thank you." Hunter kissed him. "For everything. I never thought I'd be good at stuff like this."

"You're very good at it." Nick nipped his jaw. "This, and…other things." He'd tried to maintain a businesslike manner when they were out on the farm, but what the hell. "We'd better load up these trees and get back to the house. John and Des will be here soon to help set up."

"I hope it'll go okay." A furrow appeared between his brows.

"Maybe I should have—"

"It's going to be perfect. Trust me."

Exhaling, Hunter nodded. "I do." He smiled softly, kissing Nick again, and Nick held him close, deciding they could take a few more minutes.

THERE WERE SO many people.

Nick leaned against the barn, the inside of which was off limits to visitors, a no-entry sign tacked to the sliding door. The many, many visitors had started arriving at eleven sharp, and somehow, they just kept coming as the afternoon wore on.

That's a good thing, remember?

"Yeah, yeah," Nick muttered to Eric's teasing voice. But it *was* a good thing, and though he'd needed to escape the crowd for a few minutes, he was undeniably pleased.

Hunter and John had planned an incredible event in only two days. In the open space near the barn, they'd set up a dozen folding tables and chairs lent by one of the local churches. They'd decorated the tables with garlands and hung the barn door with a massive fresh wreath strung with red ribbon. Nick had cut the big boughs for the wreath and other hanging decorations.

Des was judging the hourly snowpeople-making contest, and children laughed and shrieked, snowballs flying. Adults stood in clumps, chatting and sipping coffee, cider, or hot chocolate. The propane barbecues roasted a steady supply of hot dogs and chestnuts, and families sat at the tables eating eagerly.

John had borrowed a portable sound system to play carols, protected under a tarp from the gentle flurries that had started around noon as more clouds had moved in. The weather was meant to stay calm, though, and Nick hoped the weather report was correct this time.

What, you don't want to be snowed in with all these people? Eric teased. *Just Hunter. Can't say I blame you.*

Still, Nick had to admit it was nice seeing people so happy and festive. He'd talked to folks he hadn't seen in years, even some old friends who'd come at John's invitation. They'd ohhed and ahhed over Hunter, and Nick had found himself making dinner plans, only half-reluctantly.

The raffle to cut down your own tree had proved a big success. They'd drawn one winner earlier since people were coming and going, and would do another soon. It had actually been all right to take the winner onto the farm and show him how to use the axe to chop. Hunter had come along, beaming.

And of course Ella was in her element, ecstatic over so many new people to meet and all the attention she was getting. Nick watched her with a smile, his gaze then finding Hunter. His smile deepened, warmth filling his chest.

At a table, Hunter leaned over craft supplies—Styrofoam balls, spray paint, glitter, and macaroni—helping a little girl make a tree ornament. He was patient as the girl fumbled, and though Nick was too far away to hear what he was saying, he knew Hunter was being kind to her.

He couldn't tear his eyes away. He wanted Hunter too much. Not just in his bed, but…all the time. Which was *ludicrous* since they'd known each other barely more than a week.

We knew after the first date. Do you remember? Eric asked.

Memories wheeled through Nick's mind—the coffee date that had become lunch, and then dinner at another restaurant, then drinks, then back to Eric's house for a night of sex. They'd been inseparable after.

Perhaps this is just how it goes with you. Hunter's practically moved in already, and you don't want him to go anywhere. Do you?

Boots crunched in the snow, approaching, and Nick pushed away the thoughts and Eric's imaginary voice, tearing his gaze from Hunter, who clapped as the girl held up her macaroni creation.

Nick focused on a woman who neared the barn. She was perhaps a little older than he was, small and golden-haired, a little plump in a puffy red ski jacket, her cheeks pink under a hat with reindeer antlers. When she smiled tentatively, he knew, recognizing the shape of her mouth.

"Nick? I don't know if you remember me."

He stood up straight, pushing away from the side of the barn. "Pam, isn't it?"

"Yes." She glanced over at Hunter. "You and my son have been getting to know each other."

"We have," Nick agreed, trying to keep his voice even. He was forty-six goddamn years old, yet he felt like a schoolboy picking up his prom date with a cheap corsage in his sweaty hands. Not that he had ever done that. He'd gone to the prom with a lesbian friend.

"He's quite taken with you," Pam said. "To be honest, I don't know how to feel about it."

"Neither do I."

She laughed. "I appreciate the honesty."

He shoved his gloved hands in the pockets of his dark coat. "I never planned on this. Or expected it. Not in the slightest."

"I believe that." She brushed a snowflake from her nose. "I haven't seen him this happy in… In a long time. He's been so anxious and unsure of what to do with his life."

"Yes. I suppose he should go back to Toronto in the new year. Give it another go."

She frowned. "I suppose. But I'm not so sure."

Despite himself, Nick's heart skipped. "No?"

"He's been so hung up on what he *should* do. Get a 'real' job in an office. Even if it makes him miserable." She looked over to where Hunter now chatted with an adult couple, gesturing animatedly toward the acres of trees that extended off into the distance. "He's really enjoyed the work here."

"He's a fast learner."

"You seem to give him confidence. That's a big point in your favor."

Nick chuckled. "Good to know."

Her smile faded. "I just don't want my son's heart to get broken. I know you suffered a great loss with Eric. He was a wonderful man."

Throat suddenly thick, Nick nodded.

"Please make sure you know what you're doing. Don't make promises you can't keep. I've been on the receiving end of that. I don't want it for Hunter. If this is only a Christmas fling, that's fine—just make sure he knows that. If you can't give him more, be upfront. That's all I ask."

Nick nodded again and cleared his throat. "Fair enough."

She smiled. "All right. I'll see you for Christmas dinner, I understand? I look forward to it."

"Me too."

As she walked away, a little tug of panic bloomed. *Did* he know what he was doing? More than just fucking Hunter, he was practically living with him already. Having Christmas dinner with his mother.

He'd told Hunter he wanted to continue on with whatever it was between them, and he did. But what *was* growing between them? It was happening so quickly. Was Nick making promises he couldn't keep?

The carols and shrieks of laughter and all the *people* were entirely too much now, and he escaped into the dark cold of the barn, closing the door firmly behind him. It smelled of pine and earth, faint light filtering in through gaps in the wood.

The last thing he wanted was to break Hunter's heart—or his own.

Chapter Ten

INHALING THE COLD night air deeply, Hunter ran after Ella behind the house toward the river, his legs straining in the drifts. She barked around the rubber chicken in her mouth as if to complain he was too slow, racing back to drop it into the unbroken snow at his feet. Laughing, he threw it again, and she bolted off in pursuit.

He was wonderfully exhausted and a little too full of leftover hot dogs. The fundraiser had been a huge success, and Hunter felt stupidly proud of himself. Of course John had done a lot of the work, but Hunter had planned the crafts and stuff for the kids, and everyone had seemed to have fun.

Well, perhaps everyone but Nick, who had been broody and quiet that evening. He'd been friendly enough to people earlier, but all the interacting had clearly worn on him. Hunter's mom said she and Nick had "had a little talk," which was so mortifying he hadn't gotten up the nerve to ask Nick how embarrassing she'd been.

Nick hadn't been *overly* grumpy during dinner, but he hadn't said much, seeming preoccupied. Hunter had shut up and let him watch the episode of the latest superhero show they'd cued up on Netflix.

Ella slid to a stop at his feet, and Hunter whirled and threw the rubber chicken again. This time, it sailed across the frozen water and landed on the ice near the far side, a wind tunnel created by the nearby tree line having driven most of the snow on the river clear. But Ella skidded to a stop, whining by the edge.

Hunter laughed and called, "Come on, go get it!"

But she wouldn't budge, so Hunter carefully tested the ice and slid onto it, his arms out for balance. The small river likely wasn't very deep, and it felt frozen solid beneath his boots. He made his way across and bent to snatch up the chicken.

"Get off the ice!"

Hunter whirled around, his heart jumping, wheeling his arms to stay on his feet. Nick's voice had boomed in the peace of the night, and it took Hunter a moment to understand why Nick was shouting, stalking closer, inexplicable fury vibrating from him.

As it hit Hunter that Ella had likely been trained not to go on the ice—and that it was for a very particular reason—he gasped and slip-slid back toward shore, which was only ten feet or so, Ella barking from the edge.

Hunter was almost there when Nick grabbed him, lifting him practically off his feet. He felt like he was soaring the rest of the way to solid ground, landing with a thud, his hat falling off. Nick's eyes were wild, his bare fists gripping the front of Hunter's jacket. He was out in just his jeans and plaid flannel shirt, no hat or coat or any winter gear.

Their breath clouded together in sharp bursts. Maybe Hunter should have been afraid with Nick towering over him, but he wasn't. Not at all. He could see the raw terror beneath Nick's fury, and he grabbed around Nick's waist, holding on tight. "I'm sorry. I didn't think."

Squeezing his eyes shut, Nick shook his head, his fingers twitching where he held onto Hunter's coat, his whole body shaking. Hunter pulled him close, trying to hug him.

"It's okay," Hunter murmured. "Everything's okay."

Nick exhaled a mighty breath that sounded close to a sob,

collapsing against him. Hunter staggered under his weight but dug his heels into the snow. No way in hell he was letting go. He pulled off his glove so he could run his fingers through Nick's hair and feel him, the hot gusts of Nick's breath moist against his neck.

"I'm here," Hunter whispered. "It's okay."

But Nick shoved away from him. He swiped a hand across his face. His voice was hoarse. "No. I can't do this. I *shouldn't* do this. It's a mistake."

Now fear snaked through Hunter, ice down his spine. "What do you mean?"

Nick drew himself up, steel in his voice, like the standoffish, haughty man Hunter had first met in that storeroom. "This was a mistake, having you here. You should go."

"*What?*" He couldn't believe what he was hearing. "You don't mean that."

"I do. This never should have happened between us. Now go. And don't come back." He stomped toward the house, Ella whining and looking between them but following Nick with agitated barks.

Hunter stood motionless by the frozen river, his breath white puffs in the frigid air, his bare fingers tingling. After everything they'd shared, it was just over? He was supposed to leave with his tail between his legs because Nick said so?

Fuck. That.

With a growl, Hunter followed, his boots crunching in the snow. By the woodpile, Nick turned and stared incredulously as Hunter marched toward him. "I told you to go."

"No." Hunter stopped in front of him, squaring his shoulders. "First off, I'm not walking back to Pinevale."

Nick grimaced as if he hadn't considered that. "You can take the pickup. I'll get it another day. It doesn't matter."

"As long as I do what you say and leave you alone and never come back?"

Gaze on his unlaced boots, Nick nodded.

"That's not how this works. Not out here. You're Daddy in bed, and I'll happily do what you say. But you don't get to give me orders when we're not fucking. You don't get to decide things between us without even *talking* to me. In a snap of your fingers this is over? No. I'm not going anywhere."

"I told you, this was a mistake." Nick's jaw was clenched, but his voice shook. He still looked down.

"Why? Because you saw me on the ice and got scared something would happen to me? Because you care about me?"

Shaking his head, Nick backed up, hitting the stack of firewood. Ella whined again, tense by Nick's side. Nick's throat worked, his breath short. The front door of the house was standing open, and Nick snapped toward it. "Ella! Inside."

Reluctantly, she went. Hunter breathed hard, trying to figure out the right thing to say. He wanted to hold Nick again and tell him everything would be okay, but not yet. Ella followed Nick's commands always, but Hunter wasn't backing down.

"That river is frozen solid, and even if it wasn't—it's only, what, waist-deep? But it probably scared you seeing me out there because of what happened to Eric." Hunter was pretty sure it was the first time he'd said that name aloud. Nick flinched, looking up at the stars now, panting softly.

Hunter took a deep breath and continued. "I'm so, so sorry about what happened to him. I can only imagine what that was like for you. But I'm not going to let you push me away because you're afraid. You wouldn't be afraid if you didn't care about me, and I care about you too. I know we just met, but I'm falling in love with you."

Hunter's words hung in the air, and Nick lowered his head, facing him. "I can't do this again," he rasped. "I should never have... This is why I was alone. I can't love you and have something happen. I can't. Your mother said..."

Hunter cringed. "Oh God, what?" She'd always been so cool, but he was going to freak if she'd messed with Nick's head because she was overprotective.

"It wasn't bad." Nick cleared his throat, his fingers clenching and unclenching. "She doesn't want me to break your heart or make promises I can't keep. And she's right. I can't give you this." He motioned between them with rigid jabs of his hand. "*This* is too much. Already." He laughed hollowly. "I don't even know how it happened, but it's too much. Because I can't care and lose you. I can't go through that. Not again."

"We're all going to die. And I hope it's not for a very long time for either of us. But we have to live in the meantime." He had Nick cornered, which sounded stupid since Nick was twice his size, but Hunter stepped closer slowly. He reached out tentatively, taking Nick's hand and squeezing his trembling fingers. The toes of their boots touched, their white puffs of breath mingling again.

Hunter whispered, "I want you to love me. I want us to love each other. I want to stay here and work with you."

Nick clung to his fingers. "You want to stay? Not go back to Toronto?"

"Right. If you'll have me? I never thought of myself as out-doorsy or anything like that, but I love the fresh air and my muscles burning and being out here far away from cubicles and computers and rush hour. Have you ever ridden the subway at rush hour? If there's a hell, it's being crammed into a metal box with thousands of other people twice a day. I don't want to do it. Even if that means I'm wasting my degree or whatever, I don't want to work in an office. I want to know everything about trees and planting and harvesting—all of it. This is a real job, and I want to do it. Or at least try."

Nick blew out a long breath in a stream of white. "I want that too. The twelve- and fourteen-hour days are a lot. Maybe I've been too much of a workaholic. Having full-time help…a partner, would be good."

"They say work/life balance is vital." Hunter gave him a little smile.

Nodding, Nick exhaled again, his expression serious. "I'm sorry I was rough with you. Seeing you on the ice..." He took another deep breath and exhaled. "Please don't go out there, even if it's safe." He lifted a hand and stroked Hunter's cheek with cold fingers. "Is that unreasonable of me?"

"No. I can do that for you. It's an easy thing to do." He still held Nick's other hand, and he squeezed gently. "Can you do something for me?"

Nick stared down into his eyes, his own softening. "Anything."

Hunter smiled gratefully, joy making a tentative return. "Don't shut me out of important decisions. Like, you know, whether or not we should be together? That's pretty important. We're equals in this, right? Even if you're in charge when we have sex?"

He didn't hesitate, squeezing Hunter's hand. "Yes. Absolutely. Even if I'm an overprotective ass sometimes."

Hunter laughed softly. "I can handle that. I know you were scared. And I'm sure it won't be the last time we argue."

Nick's lips twitched in a smile. "I'm sure not. Especially if you're moving in."

His belly flip-flopped with excitement. "Is that what you want? I got snowed in, and now I'm staying?"

Smile growing, Nick said, "Yes. Maybe it'll end in disaster, but I want you to stay. I want you with me out there." He nodded in the direction of the trees before motioning to the house behind him. "And in here." He stepped close, pressing their bodies together and taking Hunter's face in both his hands. "In my bed. *Our* bed."

"I want that too," Hunter whispered. "All of it." His pulse galloped. "And I don't want either of us to have our heart broken. So let's not, okay?"

"Deal."

"Let's have a Christmas miracle instead and be happy forever." He went up on his tiptoes and kissed Nick then, trying to tell him everything he was feeling with the steady press of his lips. He wanted to work with him and live with him and love him. He inched back, looking up into Nick's moon-glow eyes. "Take me to bed, Daddy."

Hunter's feet went out from under him, and he gasped as Nick swept him into his arms and strode to the front door. Hunter's laughter bubbled out of him, echoing in the trees standing silent guard. He loved the sensation of being aloft and secure against Nick's body.

"You're not supposed to carry me over the threshold until we get married," he teased, then bit his lip. He was only joking, but would it scare off Nick?

Nick paused under the eaves. "This is the quickest way to get you naked in bed." He strode inside the open door with his own laugh and kicked it shut.

His arms around Nick's neck, Hunter giggled. "Can't argue with that logic." Ella barked, her tail wagging, and Hunter couldn't stop laughing as Nick carried him upstairs. "Ella agrees."

When they were naked together, the curtains open to the silver night, Hunter got on his hands and knees. But Nick turned him and drew him close, kissing him with a gentle, questing tongue. Nick tasted him until Hunter's head spun, then pressed him back against the mattress, his lips exploring every inch of flesh until Hunter could only beg for more.

Nick kissed his mouth again, and Hunter could taste his own sweat and desire. Nick was heavy on top of him, surrounding him, keeping him safe and cherished. Raising his knees to his chest, Hunter cried out as Nick entered and fucked him, stretching him to the breaking point, but never too far.

Epilogue

One Year Later

"HIGHER ON YOUR side!" Hunter called, and Nick raised his end of the banner, balancing on a ladder by the trunk of one of the bare maple trees at the entrance of the farm's long driveway. John was on another ladder by a tree on the other side. Snow piled up around the ladders, the sun peeking out of the scattered clouds and making the fresh snow glitter like diamonds.

In his parka, woolen hat, and work boots, Hunter stood in the middle of the curving country road as he peered up. Nick couldn't hear any vehicles approaching, but still. "Would you hurry up and get off the road?"

Hunter huffed a laugh and stepped closer. "Okay. It's good."

Nick and John climbed down, and the three of them stood back enough to peer up at the banner.

Toys, Turkeys & Trees Annual Holiday Fundraising Extravaganza

"This is going to be epic," John said. "I can't believe Hunter talked you into it again. But I also can't believe he convinced you to let people cut down their own trees this season."

Nick grumbled. "Me either."

Hunter grinned. "It wasn't so bad, and you know it."

"Maybe not." Nick tried to scowl but didn't succeed, and Hunter's grin brightened.

Along with working with Nick out on the farm, Hunter had taken on the marketing and communications for the business. He had ideas to grow revenue. One was to open the farm to the public for three weekends as the holiday season began at the end of November, letting people cut down their own trees and offering sleigh rides, hot chocolate and snacks, and wreath-making.

"Actually, the weekends were a huge success," Hunter added. To John, he said, "And he knows it."

"Oh, you've got this Grinch's number all right." John winked at Nick merrily, pushing his wire-frame glasses up his nose. "Before you know it, you'll be playing Santa again, Nick."

"Never going to happen." Nick glared. "*Never.*"

"But you were so good at it!" John insisted, laughing and raising his hands. "Don't worry, that rundown Santa's Village is no more." He checked his watch. "Okay, I've gotta run. Des, Pam, and I will be back tomorrow morning to help set up. Oh, and Tim and his new boyfriend volunteered to come early."

"My friend Shelby's in town, so she's coming to help too," Hunter said.

John exclaimed, "It's going to be even better than last year. I can feel it!"

"Yeah, yeah," Nick muttered, but he gave his friend a smile.

"Want me to drop you guys off back up at the house?"

Hunter and Nick shared a glance, and Hunter said, "I wouldn't mind the walk, actually." Nick nodded, and they waved goodbye to John as he climbed into his SUV and drove off.

In tandem, Nick and Hunter reached for each other, clasping their gloved hands as they ambled up the long, plowed driveway, curving through the trees for a couple of kilometers. Their boots crunched in the packed snow, breath pluming in the cold air.

"I haven't walked along here since that first time," Hunter said with a smile. "Hard to believe it's been a year."

Nick squeezed his fingers. "Time flies. This journey should be a little more pleasant."

"Let's hope so." Hunter grinned, his blue eyes sparkling as he gave Nick a quick kiss with cold lips.

Playing outside, Ella greeted them like conquering heroes when she spotted them approaching the house, and they indulged her in scratches and pets until they all went inside.

Hunter chided Ella when she tried to jump up and swipe at the end of a sparkly red, gold, and green garland that had come unstuck from around one of the wooden support beams in the kitchen.

Chuckling, Nick got out the tape and fixed the garland before flipping the light switch that powered the multicolored Christmas lights strung around the bannister and along the railing of the landing along the open second-floor hallway.

The switch also powered the Christmas tree dominating the corner to the right of the fireplace. As the colored lights gleamed, silver tinsel sparkled, a hodgepodge of old and new ornaments glittering. Wrapped presents to each other filled the space below the Scotch pine. They'd learned the hard way the previous week not to put anything under there if they didn't know what it was after an incident with Ella and a box of After Eights from a vendor.

It had been forever since Nick had actually had his own Christmas tree. Ironic given he farmed the things, and he found he loved the fresh scent that filled their home.

Home.

It really was a home again. It hadn't always been easy—he and Hunter definitely argued sometimes, although the makeup sex was…*remarkable*. As was all the sex, and he was looking forward to having a lot of it in the weeks to come.

With the hard work of the year done as Christmas approached

in a few short days, it was a relief. Once the charity event was over, Nick looked forward to relaxing in front of the fire with Hunter and Ella. Although he and Hunter—ninety-five percent Hunter— had somehow volunteered to host Christmas dinner, so there would be lots of cooking to do.

Lighting the stack of wood and kindling waiting, Nick smiled to himself. He'd cooked a lot more in the past year since Hunter was such an enthusiastic eater, so he didn't really mind. In fact, he relished it. Hunter liked cooking as well, and they often chopped and stirred together, listening to a podcast or audiobook, Ella at their feet hoping for them to drop something delicious.

Nick ran his fingers over the soft cotton of the three stockings hung from the wooden mantel, their names inscribed in curly gold script on the red material.

Nick, Hunter, Ella

There was an addition to the collection of framed photos as well—a selfie of him and Hunter, sweaty with their shears over their shoulders after a long day of summer work, satisfied smiles on their faces and wide-brimmed hats on their heads.

In the other corner of the living room, Hunter was humming to himself and fiddling with the old stereo. Then jazzy Christmas music flowed through the room, and Nick's heart clenched.

"Is that the Ella Fitzgerald CD?" he asked.

Hunter picked up the case. "Yep. *Ella Wishes You a Swinging Christmas*. There's a lot of her, actually." He laughed. "Oh! I just realized where our Ella got her name!"

Nick smiled softly. "Yes." He paused, then added, "Eric loved Ella Fitzgerald. I haven't listened to those old CDs in years."

Hunter's beautiful face creased. "Do you want me to turn it off?"

You'd better not. This is the greatest holiday album of all time. It deserves to be heard.

Nick smiled at Eric's voice in his head. He heard it less frequently these days, but once in a while Eric would appear with a piece of wisdom. To Hunter, Nick said, "No. It deserves to be heard. Thank you for finding it."

He turned back to tend to the fire as the wonderful smell of burning wood filled the house along with Ella's smooth, jazzy Christmas tunes. Hunter went upstairs, and Nick was humming when he heard him return, the steps creaking.

"I found something else," Hunter announced.

Nick turned, his breath stolen and desire sparking like the kindling in the fireplace. Hunter stood on the bottom step wearing the old elf costume. After a year of manual labor, the green jacket was an even smaller fit, and he'd left it open over his bare chest. The candy-cane tights were obscene, hiding nothing. His feet were bare, and the green velvet elf hat and fake ears sat on his head.

Hunter held up a bundle of white-trimmed red velvet. "Santa, I've been a very naughty boy."

"Oh, I *know* you have." Nick crooked his finger, love and lust filling him completely, making him whole.

Their Ella barked in the kitchen, Ella Fitzgerald crooning about birds of a feather as Hunter and Nick met by the hearth with hands and mouths, hearts soaring.

THE END

Where the Lovelight Gleams

BY KEIRA ANDREWS

Dedication

To Rachel and Lisa for celebrating Christmas in July
with Ryan and Cary.

Chapter One

CHEST HEAVING, RYAN slammed the door behind him and leaned against it. "I should've just kept my big mouth shut," he muttered. "He's never going to like me the way I like him. God, I'm such an idiot!"

Pounding footsteps preceded a forceful knock. Ryan waited, breath lodged in his throat.

Cary's voice rang out. "I know you're in there. Open the door! Please."

Ryan ran a hand through his hair, then took a deep breath and blew it out. Trying to appear utterly calm, he twisted the doorknob and stepped aside as Cary rushed in.

"Didn't you hear me calling?" Cary was slightly breathless, his brow furrowed.

"No." Ryan tried to smile. "Sorry. Do you need something?"

"Do I..." Cary shook his head incredulously. "What I *need* is for you to talk to me. I heard what you said to Dara."

Blood rushed to Ryan's cheeks, and he laughed, although it came out as more of a squeak. "Oh that? I was just kidding around."

"Kidding around." Cary didn't sound convinced. "So you're *not* in love with me?"

"I..." Ryan swallowed, his throat suddenly dry. "It was a

joke."

"A joke." Cary stepped forward, backing him up against the closed door.

Ryan jerked his head in a nod.

Cary was now less than a foot away. He was a few inches taller, and his broad shoulders tapered down to a narrow waist, his body muscular yet lean. Short light blond hair swept up from his forehead, and his green eyes were intense as he watched Ryan. This close, Ryan could see the flecks of gold in Cary's eyes, and his heart skipped a beat. *God, he's so beautiful.*

"That's too bad, because I've been in love with you for months."

Ryan's eyes widened. "But that's…impossible."

"Shut up and kiss me."

With that, Cary closed the gap between them, taking Ryan's face in his hands as he pressed their lips together. Their mouths opened as they kissed passionately. Ryan's pulse raced, excitement skipping up his spine as he yanked Cary against him, their bodies—

"Cut!"

Cary broke the kiss and stepped back. He looked to the director. "Go again?"

The director nodded. "Good kiss. But give me a little more on the 'I heard what you said to Dara' line." She focused on Ryan. "You're playing it just right. Great trembling in your hands. Just need to get some more sweat on your brow. You're supposed to have just run from the air lock, and it's a big ship."

As the assistant director called for makeup to bring their spray bottle, the crew prepared for another take. Cary grinned at Ryan, and dimples appeared in his cheeks. "Sorry, think I slipped a little tongue in there."

Yes, you did, and God I want more. Ignoring the desire thrumming through his veins, Ryan waved it off. "That was a good take." It was their fourth, and he'd hoped it would get easier as the day went on. Instead his yearning for Cary increased each time their lips met. Despite the twenty-five bored crew members watching, when Cary kissed him, everything else faded away.

After fantasizing about being with Cary for the past year, Ryan had told himself that the reality—even if it was fictional and not *real*—would be a huge disappointment. On-screen kissing was supposed to be awkward and uncomfortable and epically unsexy. And in Ryan's experience it always had been.

Until now.

He wasn't supposed to breathe in the citrus of Cary's after-shave and feel desire coiling in his belly. He wasn't supposed to notice how thick Cary's eyelashes were, and how the gold in his eyes matched his hair. His knees weren't supposed to go weak because Cary's kisses were warm and wet and tasted like honey and promised so much more.

"Let's just hope the network censors don't look too closely. I swear, straight couples can practically get naked on screen, but gay characters…" Cary shook his head. "Drives me nuts. Hey, did you hear anything more from that hate group who sent the nasty letters?"

"Nah. I think Tammy took care of making sure my mail is examined more closely. It's no big deal."

Cary huffed. "No big deal? You shouldn't ever have to hear that kind of garbage. You'll tell me if it happens again, right?"

"What are you going to do? Beat them up?" Ryan secretly loved Cary's protectiveness. He smiled and nudged Cary with his elbow. "Besides, now that they're finally putting Steven and Kishi together, you'll probably start getting your own hate mail."

Cary still frowned. "Yeah, but it's not the same. Everyone knows I'm not gay in real life." He scoffed. "No way a tough guy like my dad would ever have a gay son. No one would believe it even if it was true."

"Yeah." Ryan stopped himself before his brain went too far down the "what if" road. "By the way, your scales are coming loose a bit on your neck."

"Crap. I keep sweating them off."

As the makeup team sprayed fake sweat onto Ryan's forehead and touched up the purple scales crawling up the side of Cary's neck and across one cheek, Ryan breathed deeply. He reminded himself that none of it was real. Cary's declaration of love and his kiss that left Ryan buzzing—it was all for the cameras. Nothing more.

So he should stop remembering the press of Cary's body and how his firm muscles had felt beneath Ryan's hands. Ryan was in good shape himself, but he was positively ordinary next to Cary's golden handsomeness and toned, perfect body. Not too bulky, but just right. As Cary tipped his head to give the makeup artist better access to his neck, Ryan imagined kissing him there, sucking on the tender skin and—

One of the show's publicists approached, her heels clacking across the spaceship set. "How are we today, gentlemen?"

Ryan smiled. "Hey, Tammy. We're good."

"Excellent. The reporter from *Out and Proud* will be here in an hour. He wanted to see the kiss filmed, but as you know we're keeping the set closed. If anyone leaks this kiss before the episode, I will eat their lungs for breakfast."

Cary smirked. "And their balls for lunch?"

"Nope. Balls are for second breakfast." Tammy winked.

The director called out, "Places everyone."

Fake sweat artfully moistening his dark hair where it fell across his forehead, Ryan took his position to run into Steven's room once more. Part of him hoped the director would want dozens of takes, but he wasn't sure how much longer he could keep himself in check. He'd worn extra-tight briefs to keep from embarrassing himself, but his one-piece bodysuit costume didn't leave much to the imagination.

The second assistant cameraman clapped down the slate in front of the camera. "*Space Academy*, two-twelve, scene nine, take five."

Silence settled over the set, and the director yelled, "Action!"

As he ran and slammed the door once more, Ryan's heart pounded anew, and he couldn't help but look forward to Cary's next kiss.

AFTER LEAVING HIS TRAILER, Ryan almost walked straight into Tammy, who tapped a manicured nail on her watch. "You're five minutes late."

"Actually, I'm three and a half minutes late, but I had to go to the bathroom. Besides, actors are supposed to be late. And/or hungover."

Tammy laughed and tucked a red curl behind her ear. "You haven't reached that phase of your career yet. Talk to me when this show has garnered more than a cult following and you've made at least one successful slasher flick during hiatus."

Cary was already seated in a director's chair on the command deck of the set, which wasn't being used for filming that day. It was little more than a *Star Trek* rip-off, but there were only so many layouts of a spaceship that worked well for filming. Cary still wore his dark green one-piece costume, but the top half pooled around his waist, and he wore a white T-shirt.

It was a V-neck, and Ryan tried not to look at Cary's light chest hair poking out. He wondered for the hundredth time what it would be like to run his fingers through it and taste Cary's nipples and—

Never. Going. To happen.

With a smile on his face, Ryan sat in the empty chair beside

Cary and shook hands with the reporter seated across from them. Tammy lingered in the background by the space-thruster control station.

The chubby, middle-aged reporter smiled. "Hi, I'm Chuck Basilica from *Out and Proud*. Thanks for meeting with me today."

"I'm Ryan Drake. It's our pleasure," Ryan answered. He and Cary had done a ton of press for the show at the upfronts in May, and they had a system down pat. They'd alternate answering questions, share a few amusing anecdotes, and generally be their most humble, charming selves.

Of course now that their story line was heating up, the gay press was taking interest. Chuck didn't waste any time.

"Rumor has it the sexual tension between Steven and Kishi is going to move from subtext to text during February sweeps. You'll be the first gay human/alien love story on American network TV. Is this true?"

Cary answered. "Well, we're definitely exploring our characters in greater depth this season, and relationships between many of the cadets will be evolving."

"Hmm. That sounds like a yes to me." Chuck smiled.

Ryan smiled back. "All we can say is that fans should keep watching, because there's some great stuff coming up for Steven and Kishi."

"Fair enough. Now, were you both surprised at how quickly fans embraced your characters? Individually, but especially as a potential couple. There are quite a few 'Stishi' fansites out there."

"I think we were both surprised, and of course it's an honor," Cary replied. "I mean, we were just happy our little midseason replacement show got a pickup for season two, and that viewers took to it so passionately. We may not get the highest ratings, but the fans are extremely vocal and loyal. The best in the world. We feel so blessed to be a part of *Space Academy*."

"Let's talk about your careers for a moment." Chuck glanced

at his notepad. "Cary, of course you're part of a Hollywood dynasty. You were named after family friend Cary Grant, isn't that right?"

He smiled. "That's right. I only hope I can have a career half as incredible as his."

"Your father and grandfather made their mark in action and adventure movies, while you've focused more on drama and now sci-fi. Do you feel any pressure to live up to their legacy?"

Cary's smile didn't falter, but Ryan noticed the way Cary's jaw flexed briefly, his shoulders tightening. "Only in the best way. I'm so proud of Dad and Grandpa, and they've always been so supportive of me."

As Cary went on about his family, telling the public what they wanted to hear, Ryan put on his best listening face. He remembered the first little cast get-together at the exec producer's house one night in the Hollywood Hills. Ryan had gone outside to get some air and stumbled across Cary on the phone with his father.

"But, Dad, it's a good show. Plenty of movie actors are doing TV now. It's not the way it was before. It's a great part! I want to do it. Besides, I can't exactly turn down steady work."

Cary paused, and Ryan could hear Robert Holloway's raised voice through the phone but couldn't make out what he was saying.

Cary went on, "I want to make my own way. I can have a good career in TV. Maybe do some theater in the summers. I think it's worth a shot." He paused again. "Well, I'm sorry you feel that way, but I guess you're used to disappointment by now, aren't you?"

Ryan tried to back away without being heard but of course promptly tripped on the leg of a deck chair, sending it clattering.

Cary whirled. "Dad, I've gotta go." He hung up and eyed Ryan cautiously. "Hey. Look, if you could just forget you heard any of that..."

"Heard what?" Ryan raised his hands. "I didn't hear a thing."

The tension in Cary's face relaxed. "Thanks, man. Ryan, right? I think we have a couple of scenes together in the pilot."

"Yeah, we do. You want to run lines this weekend?"

Cary smiled, his eyes crinkling. "Absolutely."

Now, almost two years after they met, Cary was just about Ryan's favorite person in the world. Of course Cary was straight, and they'd never be anything more than friends. Which was totally fine with Ryan. Well, not *totally* fine. But he was working on it.

"And let's talk about *your* background, Ryan. You're from Toronto. How has it been adjusting to life in La-La Land?"

"I've lived here for a few years now. There are always great things about any city, and LA has so much to offer. It was a bit of a culture shock, but being close to the beach sure helps."

"You came out while you were still in Toronto performing in a local production of *Rent*. You mentioned having lunch with your boyfriend in an interview, and when *Space Academy* premiered, many bloggers and gossip sites picked up on the old article. Do you regret coming out so early in your career? Do you think you'll get pigeonholed?"

He'd expected the question, so Ryan resisted the urge to sigh long-sufferingly. He wished it didn't come up in every interview. "No, I don't regret it at all. I've been out since my senior year of high school. It's just who I am, and I don't think it's impacted my career negatively. I played a straight character in a movie during summer hiatus." He shrugged. "All I can do is give the best performances I can and hope to continue to have opportunities."

Cary interjected, his tone firm. "I think Ryan is an inspiration to other gay actors. And straight actors, for that matter. Someone's sexuality shouldn't matter in this day and age. He's an amazing artist and person."

Warmth bloomed in Ryan's chest. "I'm lucky that Cary and everyone here at *Space Academy* are completely supportive. I hope that we'll get to the point one day when it won't be a big deal anymore."

"I hope so too," Chuck replied. "So are you seeing anyone, Ryan?"

"No, there's no one special right now." *No one I can actually date, that is.*

"Cary, you've been seeing *Succubus High* star Amanda Walker for over a year now. Any wedding bells in the future?"

Cary chuckled. "We'll have to see. Amanda's a great girl."

Actually, Amanda's a high-maintenance pain in the ass. Ryan kept a pleasant expression on his face. It wasn't that he was jealous or anything. Okay, maybe he was. But Cary deserved so much more than her. He reminded himself that it wasn't as if Amanda Walker was the only thing standing between him and Cary. She was irrelevant. Cary was straight. The end.

"You guys are both twenty-five now. How does it feel to be playing high school students?"

Ryan chuckled. "Well, I don't think we're the oldest actors to play teenagers."

"With his big brown doe eyes and baby face, I think he'll be playing a high schooler for at least five more years." Cary laughed, eyes crinkling.

"But we love our roles," Ryan added. "High school—whether here on Earth or orbiting the fifth moon of the newly discovered planet Alida—is so rife with drama and potential for character growth."

Chuck's eyebrow popped up. "Ah yes. Such as discovering one's sexuality?"

Cary and Ryan shared a glance and a smile. Cary answered. "That is a common theme, Chuck. I think our fans are really going to enjoy our characters' arcs as this season continues in the new year."

Tammy cleared her throat. "I'm afraid we have to end things there. Ryan and Cary are needed back on set."

They said good-bye to Chuck, and Ryan checked his call sheet. The next scene was an "intimate moment" between Steven and Kishi. No kiss, but they'd both be shirtless and playing a particularly close game of *imperia*, a basketball-ish game. The scene was early in the episode, before their kiss, and Steven would be barely able to contain his attraction to Kishi.

Ryan took a fortifying breath as he headed back to set. He didn't think of himself as a Method actor, but he was certainly living and breathing his character's emotions these days.

WITH A SIGH, Ryan popped open a can of soda as he sat back on the couch in his trailer. He still had one more scene to shoot, and it was going to be a long day. As he picked up the TV remote, there was a knock on the door.

His heart stupidly skipped a beat when he found Cary waiting outside. "Hey, man! I'm wrapped. Just wanted to say merry Christmas and all that."

Ryan ushered him in and handed him a bottle of water from the fridge since Cary didn't drink soda. That was just one of the reasons he'd been featured on the cover of *Men's Health* and Ryan never would be. Ryan worked out and kept trim and healthy, but he wasn't a heartthrob like Cary.

"Big plans for the holidays?" Ryan asked. "Will you be with your mom or dad?"

"Neither. Dad's in Thailand shooting another sequel to *Blowing Shit Up*."

Ryan laughed. "Is this *Strike Back* part four?"

"Yep. The world's appetite for explosions and cheap one-liners continues unabated." He flopped down on the couch. "Besides, my stepmother's with him, and I can't deal with her. She seriously tried to give me parental advice at Thanksgiving."

Ryan sat beside Cary and swung his feet up onto the low coffee table. Most movie stars would sniff at his small oak-paneled trailer, but with a sofa bed, shower, toilet, and kitchenette, the twelve-foot space was luxury for Ryan. He still wasn't used to being waited on, and at first the trailer had seemed unnecessary. But for the long days of shooting, he was very glad to have it.

"Tell me you're exaggerating."

Cary took a swig of water. "I wish. No, it seems that in Janelle's twenty impressive years here on Earth, she's learned a lot. She was quite put out that I didn't want the benefit of her extensive knowledge when picking my hiatus project."

"Wow. Okay, so what's your mom doing for Christmas?"

"She'll be in Hawaii. I'd go, but Amanda booked us into a spa for a cleanse."

"A cleanse? For *Christmas*?"

Cary grimaced. "Yeah, nothing but lettuce and lemon water or something. Oh and pepper or hot sauce, I think. Yum. It's in the desert near Palm Springs. Lots of yoga and massage, at least."

"And *starvation*. No turkey? No stuffing? No cookies? It's just not Christmas without a ton of fattening food."

"Eh, it's no big deal." Cary shrugged. "I've never really had a real Christmas. Growing up, my parents were always getting married and divorced, and they vacationed in the tropics. A white Christmas and the family all together is just something I saw on TV."

Ryan's jaw dropped. "You've never had snow at Christmas?" He realized he was practically shouting and flushed at his overreaction. "Sorry. Christmas has always been my favorite holiday."

"The most wonderful time of the year? Well, you're Canadian, so it's understandable," Cary replied playfully. His smile faded. "Nah, Christmas was just never a big deal. I got presents and everything, but it's never been a big special day with walking in a winter wonderland and all that."

"I'm sorry." Cary seemed uncharacteristically melancholy about it. "Hey, you're more than welcome to join me and my family in the Great White North."

To Ryan's surprise, Cary's face lit up. "Really?"

The invite had slipped out, and he hadn't really been serious, but the thought of actually spending Christmas with Cary had Ryan's stomach flip-flopping. "Of course. I'm flying home tomorrow, and we're going up to our cottage on Friday. More snow than you can shake a stick at." He knew he should limit the time he spent with Cary off set, but... *But I can still look even if I can't touch.*

Again, Cary's smile disappeared, and he slumped back against the cushions. "Man, I wish I could, but Amanda will kill me if I try to back out of the spa. Besides, I wouldn't want to intrude on you and your family."

"It wouldn't be an intrusion at all. My parents keep saying they want to meet you. You're my best friend out here."

Cary's expression was unreadable. Pleased, maybe? "Really? Thanks, man. That's nice to hear. You know you're my boy too." He punched Ryan's shoulder lightly.

Ryan cleared his throat and pretended his whole body wasn't on fire. "Well, the invitation stands if you change your mind."

They smiled awkwardly at each other. Things had always been totally comfortable between them, but now that they'd kissed on set, Ryan felt on edge. If he relaxed, he was afraid he'd do something that would cross the boundaries without even thinking about it. Now any kind of touch barring a shoulder punch seemed too intimate. *He's not your boyfriend. It's all pretend.*

Their eyes met, and Ryan swore a current surged between them, shooting up his spine and then right down to his dick. Cary licked his lips, and they stared at each other in the silence. Ryan could feel the heat from Cary's body beside him on the couch, and

Cary seemed to be leaning into him.

A soft knock on the door was followed by a PA calling out, "Ryan? We're ready for you."

The strange mood broken, Cary drained his bottle. "See ya next year." He stood, then pulled Ryan up into a straight-guy hug, slapping his back with a thump.

"Right, see you next year. Merry Christmas."

As he walked to set, Ryan decided it was a good thing they had three weeks until they had to be back in the second week of January. Time to get this crush on Cary under control. Between work and their friendship, they had a good thing going, and Ryan was damned if he was going to mess that up.

Chapter Two

RYAN'S CELL BUZZED on the seat beside him as he pulled off the highway into Parry Sound's mall—which was more of a glorified plaza. He scanned the busy lot for a parking space and glanced at the display. His stomach somersaulted ridiculously, and he quickly pulled into a spot by the huge snowbank created by the snow plows at the edge of the lot.

He swiped his finger across the screen. "Hello?"

"Hey, man. It's Cary."

"Hi." *Say something!* "Um, what's up? Everything okay?"

"I kind of did something a little impulsive."

"Okay. What did you do?"

"I'm at Pearson right now."

Ryan blinked. The cold must have blocked his ears. "Pearson? Airport? In Toronto?"

"That's the one. I've been trying to get a hold of you for two days, but you never picked up."

"Shit, sorry. There's no service out on the bay." Ryan's heart thumped. *Cary's here.*

"You said the invite stood and some stuff happened and I really needed to get away. But you were probably just being polite, being Canadian and all, so I'll just catch the next flight home and—"

"No!" Ryan cleared his throat and took a breath. "Of course you're still welcome. I can come pick you up, but it'll take me about two hours to drive down to the airport." He checked his watch. They'd miss dinner, but shouldn't be back too late.

Cary chuckled. "Dude, I'm renting a car. Don't even think about driving back down here."

"But the roads are slippery. You're not used to the snow."

"I'll be fine. I went four-wheeling in Aspen once. Just give me the address and I'll GPS it."

Palms tingling, Ryan gave Cary instructions on how to reach his family's cottage on Georgian Bay, since there wasn't a street address. It was an hour outside of the booming metropolis of Parry Sound (population 6,191) on country roads that would be dark before too long. "Use your brights once you get off highway sixty-nine. Unless it's snowing and there's a whiteout, because the brights will just make it worse."

"I'll be fine, Ry. Don't worry, the California boy will go slowly."

"Let me give you the number for the cottage in case you get delayed. We have a landline."

When Cary had all the details Ryan could think of, they said good-bye and hung up. After pulling out his mom's shopping list, Ryan hurried toward the grocery store, his boots crunching on the salt in the parking lot. As he walked through the sliding doors, he caught a glimpse of his reflection and realized he was grinning like a fool, but he couldn't help himself.

"WHY DIDN'T YOU tell me sooner you were inviting a guest?"

Ryan's mom, Maureen, glared at him with hands on hips. Her glasses had slipped down her nose, and flour dusted her cheek. Her dark hair was starting to go gray, and with a festive red-and-green apron on over her plump form, she resembled Mrs. Claus just a bit. Her English West Country accent always came out more when she was agitated. "I've only made a casserole for supper!"

"Because I didn't know. I didn't think he'd actually come, but his plans fell through." Ryan hadn't allowed himself to speculate too much about what might have happened and what it meant for Amanda and Cary's relationship. "And a casserole is fine, Mom."

"Look at this place! You're helping me clean up, young man."

Gazing around at the tidy kitchen, Ryan's eyebrows shot up. "Oh yeah, Mom. It's a real pigsty."

"Go straighten up the living room. What does he like to eat? Is he one of those vegantarians?"

"It's just vegan, and no. He eats meat. You don't have to make anything special."

Leaving behind his grumbling mother, Ryan straightened up the wood pile by the large stone fireplace that dominated one wall of the living room. The cottage was an A-frame, narrowing at the top to a point, built with stone and wood and furnished in a style he thought of as "comfy country." Not fashionable by any means, but warm and welcoming, with a thick rug by the hearth on the wood floor and a soft couch against the opposite wall. Two armchairs and a love seat framed the couch and a wagon-wheel coffee table.

The main floor was decked out for the holidays, with garlands and wreaths and stockings hung by the chimney with care. The only thing missing was the Christmas tree, which Ryan was going to cut down the next day, December 23. He wasn't sure why it was family tradition to get the tree each year on that date, but it was.

Ethan and Amy zoomed by him on their way from upstairs to the kitchen. "I still don't get why there's no cable here," Ethan groused.

At eight and six, Ryan's nephew and niece already owned

more technological gadgets than Ryan did, yet it never seemed to be enough. But Ryan remembered his own complaints as a kid. Ethan and Amy were both dark haired and round faced—the spitting image of Lisa, and therefore Ryan as well. They always joked that Ryan could kidnap them and pass them off as his own.

"I'm boooooored!" Amy whined. "Can't we watch a movie?"

"Oh yes, it's a hard life, I know," Maureen replied. "You get one movie a day and you've used your allowance already. The cottage is for family time. You little devils spend enough time glued to your phones and TVs and computers. And if you're bored, I'll find you some work to do! Or I'll have to tell Santa you've been naughty."

As the kids continued to whine in the kitchen, pestering their grandmother for shortbread cookies, Ryan's sister came downstairs with a duster in hand. She pulled her long brown hair up into a ponytail and smiled slyly. "I hear there's a guest coming."

Avoiding Lisa's gaze, Ryan put another log on the fire. "Yeah, my friend Cary. From the show."

With a glance to the kitchen, where their mom was giving the kids jobs as her helpers, Lisa whispered, "I know exactly who Cary is, little brother. You guys did the kissing scene last week, hmm?"

"What? How did you know that?"

She rolled her eyes. "There's this thing called the Internet. A reliable source told TMZ that—"

"Ugh, I've heard enough. And Lisa, we're just friends."

"*Uh-huh*. But you want more."

Marching to the cupboard to pull out the vacuum, Ryan scoffed. "Why would you say that? He's straight."

"Why would I say that? Because you've been mooning over him for over a year! You may be an award-winning actor, but you're not fooling me."

Ryan rolled his eyes. "I'm not an award-winning actor."

"Teen Choice awards totally count, little brother. Even if it's for Cutest TV Heartthrob. You beat out some stiff competition for that title."

Barking out a laugh, Ryan jammed the vacuum plug into the wall and pulled out the cord. "We're friends. The end." He stepped on the button on the back of the vacuum, and it roared to life.

Lisa stepped close, still keeping her voice low. "He's going to have to share your room, you know."

Ryan swallowed hard. "There are two beds up there. It's no big deal."

"Sure. No big deal."

"Lisa, please. Just…don't."

She dropped her teasing tone. "I'm sorry. I promise I won't embarrass you in front of your friend. It's just that I've had years of practice, and it's a hard habit to break." She leaned up and pressed a kiss to his cheek.

Although she was five years older, Ryan had been taller since he was thirteen, much to Lisa's chagrin. He gave her shoulder a knock. "Okay, squirt."

"Hilarious. Come on, let's get this place clean—well, clean-er—while Mom keeps those two busy."

"Where are Dad and Tony?"

Lisa rolled her eyes. "Ice fishing. Where else?"

Ryan chuckled as he vacuumed the rug. Lisa's husband Tony and their father were two peas in pod when it came to fishing. "It was good of you to marry the son Dad always wanted."

"Bite your tongue, Ryan Patrick Drake!" his mother yelled back from the kitchen.

"Mom, I'm kidding!"

Ryan and Lisa shared a glance and burst out laughing. Lisa tugged on her earlobes, their old signal from childhood that their mom was listening. *Ears of a hawk*, Lisa mouthed, and they both chortled.

"What's so funny?" Their mom stuck her head out of the kitchen doorway.

Dissolving into giggles, Ryan and Lisa went back to their tasks. When they were finished, Ryan went up to his room to make sure it was neat and ready for Cary's arrival in—he checked his watch for the umpteenth time—forty-three minutes. Give or take.

The second floor housed his parents' master bedroom, two guest rooms, and the cottage's main bathroom with tub. There was a small toilet on the main floor, but everyone had to take turns showering on the second floor. Ryan clambered up the ladder to the third floor loft, which had been his room since he was a kid.

The ladder led into the middle of the room, which was the top of the A-frame structure. There was just enough room to stand along the center of the narrow room, with the walls slanting in on either side. To the left of the ladder was Ryan's single bed and small dresser under the window at the end of the room. There was a window on the other side as well, and an identical single bed and dresser.

When they were little, the bed to the right of the stairs had been Lisa's, until she turned twelve and deemed herself too mature to share a room with her little brother. Over the years cousins and friends had slept there. *Now it would be Cary.* Going over to his bed, Ryan flopped down, gazing at the familiar slanted walls and the old space-themed wallpaper. When it got dark, the glow-in-the-dark solar system stickers would appear.

Even though he made a very good salary now, his parents had refused his offer to renovate the old cottage. His father, Jack, had simply furrowed his brow at the idea, while Maureen had fluttered her hands and told him to save his money, because God knew an actor's income was never steady and *Space Academy* could be cancelled at any moment.

Ryan smiled to himself. No matter how many teenage girls put his face up in their lockers, his family always treated him as same old Ryan. At least they had let him pay for a new deck overlooking the expanse of Georgian Bay.

He just hoped Cary wouldn't feel too out of place. He grew up in mansions, and an old single bed in a cottage would be way outside his comfort zone. Not to mention Ryan's comfort zone. Sometimes he'd get hard just *looking* at Cary, let alone sharing a room with him. Seeing him undress. Hearing him breathing, knowing he was only feet away…

Groaning, Ryan stood. He needed a cold shower, but going out to the shed for more firewood would do the trick. He checked his watch. *Thirty-seven minutes.*

BY THE TIME CARY was seventy-four minutes late, Ryan thought he might vomit. Snow was falling, and clouds obscured the moon and stars. The snow wasn't heavy, but the roads would be slick, and Cary wasn't even used to much rain in LA, and—

"You're going to wear the carpet out." His mother handed Ryan a hot mug of tea. "He still had to rent a car, and if he's driving slowly, he's bound to take a bit longer than usual. He might have stopped for coffee along the way."

"I know, I know. But…he's not used to snow. Winter driving can be dangerous."

She patted his cheek. "Aren't you sweet to be so concerned about your chum."

As if on cue, footsteps thumped on the porch. Ryan raced to the door and threw it open. He sighed. "Oh."

His father's laugh boomed through the cottage from the small mudroom where they kept their boots and snow shovels. It wasn't insulated but helped keep out the cold from the main building when people were coming and going in the winter months. "That's a fine greeting from my only son." He held up a cooler. "We caught an even dozen, Mo."

Maureen took the cooler, laughing and squirming away as Jack tickled her. "Get those cold hands away from me!"

Tony followed and unzipped his coat. "Everything okay, Ryan?"

"Huh?" Ryan realized he must have been frowning. "Yeah, fine. My friend's late."

"Your friend?" Tony stooped so he didn't bang his head passing through the doorway. At six-five, he often had to watch where he was walking.

"Cary. From work."

"The cute one?"

Lisa cleared her throat from the couch, where she was supervising the kids' game of Candyland. Her eyes twinkled. "Should I be jealous?"

Rolling his eyes, Tony kissed his children and then planted a big one on his wife. "Babe, you know I don't swing that way." He glanced apologetically at Ryan. "Not that there's anything wrong with that."

Ryan laughed. "Let me guess. Maria's a fan?" Tony's teenage sister was always glued to Ryan's side at family gatherings, asking him a million and one questions about Hollywood. He tried to tell her it wasn't as glamorous as it seemed, but she was unconvinced.

"Think I can get an autograph for her? She's going to be so jealous when she finds out I spent Christmas with not one, but *two* TV stars."

Ryan glanced at his watch again. "Yeah. Sure."

He heard Tony ask Lisa, "What's up with him?" but Ryan didn't hear her response as he raced to the window. He could hear a vehicle approaching, and headlights flashed past as a large SUV pulled up.

Ryan took a couple of deep breaths as he put on his coat. Still his stomach clenched, and he was a pile of jittery nerves.

It's the same old Cary. Your straight friend. Get a grip.

In the mudroom, he yanked on his boots and then hopped down the few steps to the ground, closing the glass storm door behind him. He waved and approached Cary's rental. Cary killed the engine and opened the SUV door. "Is this a good spot to park?"

"Yeah, it's fine. Did you find the place okay?"

Cary got out and pulled Ryan into one of his patented back-slapping hugs. "Yep, your directions were good. Just took me a while to get out of the airport. Realized I'd better not show up at Christmas empty-handed, so I hit up the airport stores." He stepped back and spread his arms, displaying his hooded black parka. "Also bought my first winter coat. And Jesus, do I need it!" He shivered.

Ryan grinned. "You're not in Kansas anymore, Toto."

"So that makes you Dorothy, huh?" Cary elbowed him playfully. "Can you help me with this stuff?" He opened the back of the SUV.

"Holy crap! Did you buy out the entire airport?" There were at least a dozen shopping bags.

"Well, I wasn't sure exactly who was here, so I got a variety of gifts for different ages and stuff."

"You really didn't have to do that." Ryan's heart sank. "We don't have anything for you."

"Are you kidding? Letting me spend Christmas here is more than enough." He peered around at the snow-topped trees. "It's beautiful. Like something out of a movie."

"Boys! Dinner's almost ready!" Maureen's voice rang out from the mudroom door.

Ryan picked up as many bags as he could carry. "Okay, I guess you'd better meet the family. They can be a bit much when they all get going. And once we get into the eggnog, there's no telling how things'll turn out."

Cary grinned. "Sounds perfect." He reached out and squeezed Ryan's shoulder. "Thanks again for inviting me. You're…a great friend."

Ryan tried to ignore the sparks of desire he felt at Cary's touch, even through the layers of fabric. "Anytime." Snowflakes caught in Cary's thick eyelashes, and Ryan tightened his grip on the shopping bags, resisting the urge to brush the flakes away.

After they took off their boots in the mudroom, Ryan's mother ushered them inside. In the doorway, she drew a startled Cary into a hug. "Welcome! So lovely to have you, Cary."

"I…thank you, Mrs. Drake." Cary smiled.

She pressed a kiss to his cheek and pointed up at the bough of leaves and berries hanging above the door. "Mistletoe."

Ryan shrugged apologetically. "It's tradition."

Cary's eyes crinkled, and he gazed up. "That's awesome. I've only ever seen it in movies."

"You'd better come in, or I'll have to kiss you too." The words were out of his mouth before Ryan could stop himself. He stuttered. "I…um, here, let me get your coat."

Jesus, get a grip! Even joking about kissing Cary was a bad idea. He just hoped he wouldn't do something stupid and ruin their friendship by New Year's.

AS LISA SCURRIED around on her hands and knees, sniffing the corners of the living room, they all roared with laughter. She wiggled her nose and stuck her teeth out over her bottom lip.

"Bugs Bunny?" Tony asked.

Lisa glared as the sands in the timer ran out. "Rat race! That was a rat!"

"Ohhhh. Mom, that was smart," Amy said.

Pushing herself up onto her feet, Lisa laughed. "Thank you, sweetie. Too bad my team didn't think so!" She sat back on the couch next to Cary, shaking her head in mock sadness. "You'd think an actor would be better at this game."

"Hey, did I not act out *March of the Penguins* perfectly?"

"Okay, I'll give you that. The rest of you, get it together!"

They were divided into two teams, sitting across from each other with the wagon wheel coffee table between them. Ryan passed Amy the dice. "Roll a six, okay?"

Remarkably, she did, and she and Ryan high-fived. It was Jack's turn to perform, and he had to hum a song for their team to guess. Jack read the card, and his eyebrows disappeared into his hairline. "What's a Feist?"

"She's a singer, Dad," Lisa answered. "You won't know any of her songs, so take another card."

This one he did know, and as his dad hummed "I Wanna Hold Your Hand," Ryan glanced around happily. He'd had a few glasses of spiked nog—along with wine at dinner—and a pleasant warmth suffused his chest. His family had welcomed Cary enthusiastically, and Cary had fit right in, joking around and getting in on the family's playful bickering. As the evening wore on, Ryan couldn't remember the last time he'd felt so relaxed. So peaceful.

His mother quickly guessed the song, and then it was her turn to act out a clue. They all howled with laughter as she beat her chest and dragged her knuckles before swooning with a goofy smile on her face. "Monkey love!" Ryan called out.

His team won the game a little after ten o'clock, and they called it a night. As Ryan led Cary up to their room, his pulse increased. At the top of the stairs, he waved his arm grandly. "Welcome to the little-known Canadian cousin of the Ritz

Carlton. Sumptuous comfort awaits."

"This is so cool." Cary gazed around the room, a smile dimpling his cheeks. "I can just picture you here as a kid. It must be nice, having everything be the same. I grew up on movie sets more than anywhere else. Hotel rooms."

Ryan had brought up Cary's things earlier and placed them by the spare bed. Cary sat down on it, and the mattress creaked.

Ryan grimaced. "That mattress is years old. I hope it'll be okay."

"It's perfect, Ry." Cary grinned. "I'll just climb in with you if this bed isn't comfy enough."

Ryan's laugh was slightly manic. "Yeah, plenty of room over here." *Ha-ha.* "So the bathroom's on the second floor. There's a night-light down there, but be careful going down the ladder. When you're half-asleep you can end up on your ass."

"Will do." Cary stood and unzipped his small suitcase. "I usually sleep in the nude, but I guess I'll freeze my tail off if I do that." He pulled out a T-shirt and flannel pajama bottoms.

At the thought of Cary naked, Ryan turned away, desire shivering over his skin. "Yeah, gets a little cold up here." Keeping his back turned, Ryan quickly pulled on his pajamas.

Cary chuckled. "Are those…Christmas pajamas?"

Wait, did Cary just watch me undress? Ryan turned and held up his hands. "Guilty as charged. Santa brought them for me last year."

"Santa. As in, Claus?"

"Yeah, every year my mom gets us presents from Santa. Just silly stuff." He glanced down. "Like reindeer pajamas."

"Love 'em." Cary climbed into bed. "I think it's really cool that your family's so into Christmas and everything. It's nice."

"I never really thought about it. But yeah, it is." Ryan flicked off the overhead light and got into bed. As darkness settled in, the solar system stuck to the slanted ceiling above his bed glowed faintly. Ryan cleared his throat. "So…is everything okay with Amanda?"

There was only silence for a moment, and he thought Cary might have gone to sleep already.

"It's over. It just wasn't working out. We were fighting all the time."

Ryan tried to keep his voice somber despite the giddy whirl of joy whipping through him. "I'm sorry to hear it."

"Are you?"

Ryan's heart skipped a beat. Cary was across the room in the dark, and they couldn't see each other, which was a good thing since Ryan probably looked guilty as hell. "Of course!"

"Dude, it's cool. You and Amanda just never seemed to click."

"No. I guess not. But I'm still sorry. I know you cared about her."

"Yeah. I guess. We're just not right for each other. Wanna hear something crazy?" He paused. "I think she was jealous of you."

Ryan swallowed hard. "Of me?" He and Amanda had certainly never been friends, and he'd often felt the sharp edges of her piercing gaze when she visited the set. "That's definitely crazy. We work together. We're friends."

"She kept trying to convince me to quit the show. Never mind that I have a contract. She thinks our story line will hurt my career."

"Oh." Ryan couldn't help the stab of hurt. "But everyone knows you're straight. It'll be fine."

There was a long moment of silence. "Yeah. Anyway. Thanks for letting me crash your Christmas. 'Night."

Clearly Cary didn't want to talk about it any further. "'Night."

Silence descended, and Ryan closed his eyes. It was strange to be sharing a room with Cary—especially *this* room. It felt as if there was something hanging in the air, but he wasn't sure what.

After a while, Cary's breathing evened out, and Ryan burrowed deeply under the covers and drifted away. Visions of Cary danced in his head, with not a sugarplum in sight.

Chapter Three

"**S**O HOW DOES THIS work?"

Ryan turned off their laneway onto Shell Bay Road. It hadn't been freshly plowed yet, but his father's pickup could manage the new inches of snow. "Well, first there's a seedling, and it grows in the earth and—"

"Ha-ha." Cary rolled his eyes. "I mean how does it work to cut down a Christmas tree? Can you just walk into the woods?"

"I guess you could, but there's a tree farm not too far away." The sun blinked out from behind a cloud, and Ryan adjusted the shade.

Cary squinted. "Man, it's brighter than the beach with all this snow. It's nice, though."

"Especially when you don't have to shovel it. One of the best parts of Lisa having kids is that they get to do all our old chores." He cleared his throat. "Uh, not that I don't love the kids."

"Of course. Slave labor's just a bonus."

"Exactly."

They laughed, and before long Ryan turned onto a winding road cutting through the forest. Fortunately it had been plowed, but he still went slowly. The sun was mostly blocked by the tall trees, lending the area a slightly mysterious air. Ryan spotted movement on the left and took his foot off the gas. As the truck rounded a bend, dozens of eyes swiveled toward them in unison.

Cary gasped softly. "Wow. What are they all doing here?"

Ryan pulled over and shut off the engine. The deer all stood motionless, watching. "It's a feeding station. Must be because there's so much snow this year. Sometimes the local anglers and hunters group will feed them if they're getting too hungry. With global warming everything's all topsy-turvy."

"Wait, the hunters feed them? Aren't they just going to kill them?" Cary glanced around as if expecting men with guns to materialize from the forest.

"Not until hunting season next November. But yeah, it's kinda weird when you think about it."

"Kinda. But it's cool. I've never seen deer up close."

Ryan lowered his window, and the deer remained frozen. But after another minute, the animals began eating again. Cary took off his seat belt and slid closer on the seat, his warm breath puffing into the cold air. Ryan shivered, but not from the chill. Cary pressed against his side, leaning close to peer out the window.

"They're beautiful," Cary whispered. "I wish we could pet them. I know we can't, though." He was silent for a moment. "I hope they're fast runners and the hunters are lousy shots."

Ryan smiled. "Me too," he whispered back.

They watched the deer for ten minutes until another truck came, this one noisier and causing the deer to bound into the protection of the forest. Ryan put the truck into drive, and Cary slid back across the seat. Even with the window shut, Ryan felt chilled and bereft on his right side where Cary had been so close a moment ago.

Half an hour later, they struggled through knee-deep snow. Ryan had an ax slung over his shoulder, and he led the way. Cary had picked up top-of-the-line boots, which was a good thing since in LA he only ever wore flip-flops or sneakers.

"How do you know where we're going?" Cary gazed around at

the sea of trees. It was brighter at the tree farm, and Cary's hair gleamed golden in the sun. "They all look the same."

Ryan mock gasped. "The same? No, no. Among these trees is The One. The one true tree that I must find to bring home to my family. Usually it would be my dad accompanying me on this quest. But this year it's you who must prove your bravery, good knight."

Cary chuckled. "Are there Orcs in this forest? Because I didn't sign up for Orcs."

"You're a Portigan warrior. You can handle a few Orcs." Ryan changed course and went deeper into the trees.

"Too bad I left my warp blaster at home."

The snow crunched underfoot as they continued along, away from the families and other people looking for their own trees. The sun darted in and out of the clouds, but there was no wind, so even though it was below zero, it didn't feel cold. At least not to Ryan. Cary's cheeks were rosy in the chill.

"Are you warm enough? Here, take my toque." Ryan pulled off his woolen beanie hat and held it out.

"Your what?" Cary laughed. "It's okay, I'm fine."

"You're not used to this weather. Take it."

After a moment, Cary relented and slipped on the red hat. "Thanks. How do I look?"

Gorgeous. Perfect. Sexy as hell. "Fine." Ryan's voice sounded strange, and he cleared his throat. "My mom's probably knitting you your own as we speak, so I hope you like it."

Cary grinned. "I love it." After a moment, he stopped walking. "See something you like?"

Heart thumping, Ryan huffed out a strangled breath. "What?"

Cary waved his arm around. "The trees. You looked like maybe you spotted one."

"Right. No. Not yet."

Ryan started walking again and hoped the blush staining his

cheeks would be mistaken for a reaction to the temperature. He ducked around a particularly large pine, and then he saw it.

The sun beamed onto the thick snow-covered branches. Ryan could instantly imagine the tree strung with lights and garlands, his family's ornaments hanging from the branches and his grandmother's star beaming from the top. The tree was just the right height to fill the corner of the living room—not too big, not too small.

"Just right?" Cary asked.

"Yeah. You can tell?"

Cary smiled. "I can tell by the way you're looking at it. Come on, let's chop this sucker down."

They took turns with the ax, thwacking away at the trunk. Cary listened to Ryan's instructions and went about his task with a concentration that Ryan really needed to stop thinking of as adorable. As the tree fell, Cary grinned.

"Timber!" he called out.

They surveyed the tree, and Ryan couldn't stop smiling. Yep, this was the one.

"So…now what? Do those Orcs carry the tree back for us?"

"Usually old Mr. Barnes would help take the tree back and wrap it up, but I don't want to put him out. Think we can manage it on our own? We're pretty far out."

"As Angelo at the gym would say, this is functional training. Maybe I'll start a new fitness trend: hauling trees. Of course in LA they'd have to be palm trees."

"I think you're on to something there. You should tell *US Weekly*."

Cary laughed and picked up the trunk of the tree. "Stars: they're just like us! They haul Christmas trees through the snow."

Ryan grabbed on as well, and they worked in unison to drag the tree back to the farm's entrance. It wasn't easy work, and after a few minutes sweat moistened the back of Ryan's neck. He put the tree down and scooped up a handful of snow into his mouth. Cary followed suit, his brow furrowed as he tentatively placed some snow on his tongue.

"For the record, we should never eat snow if we're lost in the woods." Ryan put another handful into his mouth, where it melted refreshingly.

"Really? Why not?"

"You can get hypothermia. But I think we're safe here on Mr. Barnes's farm. Even if we got lost, someone would come by sooner or later."

"Huh. What else are you not supposed to do with snow?"

"Well, don't ever eat the yellow snow."

"Ha-ha. That much I know." Cary bent down and picked up another handful before packing it into a misshapen ball. "Should you do this?"

Before Ryan could react, the snowball smacked his face, and he sputtered.

"I've always wanted to throw a snowball." Cary grinned and backed up.

"Oh you asked for it, California boy!"

Laughing and shouting, they did battle, dodging behind trees and firing snowballs at each other. For a newbie, Cary had great aim. He launched a missile that Ryan had to dive to evade.

"Just like throwing out a runner at second!" Cary shouted.

"Except you missed! Need some glasses, huh?"

Back and forth they went, the tree forgotten as they dodged and ducked and hurled snowballs. They were both breathing hard by the time Ryan called for a time-out. "Okay, okay. I think it's safe to say you've got the hang of it. With all the cardio you do, I'll never beat you."

"So you're giving up?" Cary grinned.

"On snowballs? Yes." Ryan dusted off his parka and wet jeans. As Cary reached his hand out to shake, Ryan grabbed him and used Cary's momentary surprise to topple him into the snow. "But we have another tradition here. The snow job."

Before Cary could answer, Ryan ripped the red toque from Cary's head and crammed fistfuls of snow into his hair and down the back of his jacket. Cary squirmed and kicked, laughing so hard his breath hitched.

"Okay, okay. I surrender!"

Ryan straddled Cary's hips and pressed Cary's arms above his head in the snow. "You're an honorary Canadian now." His chest heaving as he caught his breath, Ryan smiled down at his friend.

Cary's face was wet and flushed, and a smile played at his parted lips. His tongue darted out, and Ryan couldn't look away. Desire thundered in Ryan's veins, and before he could stop himself, he leaned down and captured Cary's mouth with his own.

Although Cary's lips were cool, beyond them the heat of his mouth drew Ryan in uncontrollably. Their tongues tangled, and the fire in Ryan's veins shot straight to his cock. It felt so good, and he'd wanted it for *so long*. He breathed Cary in as Cary shook off Ryan's grasp on his wrists and grabbed Ryan's head and—

With a gasp, Ryan sat up and staggered to his feet. "I'm sorry! Jesus. I didn't mean to…"

Cary sat up in the snow. His hair was damp and mussed, and he took a shaky breath. "Ryan…"

Ryan raised his hands. "You don't need to say it. This was just…muscle memory." Shame burned in his gut. *How could I be so stupid?*

Cary blinked. "Muscle memory?"

"You know, from the show. From kissing you on set. I didn't mean to do it just now. You know I don't feel that way about you."

"Right." Cary's face was blank as he reached for the toque and put it back on. "Of course. I know."

Cary was probably in shock, and Ryan prayed he hadn't ruined their friendship. "Seriously, you don't have to worry. You're the last guy I'd want to be with."

As Cary got to his feet, he kept his eyes averted. His voice was tight. "I get it. It was just…an accident. Like you said—muscle memory." He brushed the snow off his jeans. "We should get the tree back."

Great. He can't even look at me. "Yeah. I hope…I don't want things to be weird. Especially with you staying here." *He probably wants to catch the first flight back to LA.*

"Do you want me to leave?" Cary's expression was still impassive, and his gaze was fixed somewhere on the horizon. His shoulders hunched.

"No! Of course not. You're my best friend. Can we just forget this happened?"

"Yeah. It's all good, man. Just like another rehearsal." He reached out his fist, and Ryan bumped it. Cary's lips lifted in a ghost of a smile before he picked up the trunk of the fallen tree and began dragging it. He kept his head down.

"IT'S *MY* TURN to put on the star!" Amy stamped her foot.

"Uh-uh. You did it last year. Moooom, tell her she can't do it!"

Lisa sighed and swallowed a sip of wine. "Ethan, can't you and your sister do it together?"

Maureen spoke up from the kitchen, where she was pressing shortbread dough into a glass dish and singing along to the jazzy Ella Fitzgerald Christmas album they listened to on repeat every year. "It is Christmas, after all. Santa would want you to cooperate with each other."

Grumbling all the way, Ethan and Amy climbed up on the stepladder. Amy wailed, "I can't reach!"

Tony hoisted her up. "Now you're taller than the tree!"

Amy giggled and reached down to straighten the star as her brother placed it atop the tree. "Lights!"

On cue, Ryan plugged in the cord in the outlet by the fireplace, and the whole tree lit up red, green, blue, pink, and yellow, with the bright white star the crowning jewel. "Ta-da!"

Everyone clapped, and Amy squealed as her father swooped her through the air in his arms. When Ryan stood, he caught Cary's gaze, but Cary quickly glanced away. Ryan's stomach churned, and he tried to hide a grimace as his mother passed out glasses of nog. She put her hand on his forehead.

"I've never seen you turn up your nose at my nog before!"

"I'm fine, Mom." Ryan took a gulp of the sweet, creamy drink. "See?" His mother always spiked nog with amaretto, and the almond liqueur burned pleasantly in Ryan's throat. Maybe a drink was just what he needed to forget what a complete moron he was. He concentrated on Ella's smoky voice jauntily advising on building a snowman in the meadow and calling him Parson Brown.

He was on his second glass when his mother brought in a tray of sausage rolls and settled onto the couch beside him. Cary was in one of the armchairs, and the rest of the family relaxed in various seats or on the thick carpet. The Christmas tree cast colored light over everyone's faces, and Ryan munched happily on a sausage roll.

Maybe everything would be fine. Sure, it had been a little awkward with Cary since…the incident. But Cary seemed okay, eating his sausage roll and talking to Ethan about the latest edition of *Halo*. It would be fine. He and Cary had been friends for a long time now—at least in Hollywood years—and it was just one stupid kiss. Cary had been nice about it, and they'd move past it. Yes, it would be fine.

"The other day I was waiting in Dr. Feinberg's office."

Ryan snapped his wandering mind back to his mother. "Is everything okay?"

"What? Oh yes. I was just getting a wart on my toe burned off."

Amy wrinkled her nose. "Ewwww!"

"Gotta go with Amy on this one, Mom," Lisa added from the other end of the couch.

"My point is that I was reading about that David Baker. You know, from those movies."

Here we go. "Oh right. Yeah, I heard he came out."

Maureen leaned in and stage-whispered, "And he's single!"

"Mom, I don't even know him."

"But you're both actors! Of course you know him. Don't you think he's handsome?"

"Maureen, give the boy a break." Ryan's father glanced up from the fishing magazine he was flipping through.

Ignoring her husband, Maureen turned to Cary. "Do you know him?"

Cary shrugged. "Not really. I met him once at the Golden Globes. He did a movie with my father."

"You see? Ryan, you should get Cary to introduce you. Cary, don't you think they'd make a lovely couple?"

"Yeah. Sure." Cary fiddled with his cocktail napkin, tearing it into neat strips.

"*Mom.* Enough. I know you mean well, but I don't need any help with my love life."

"Well, it *has* been forever since you've had a boyfriend," Lisa muttered.

"*Et tu, Brute?*" Ryan glared. Okay, it was true he hadn't dated anyone seriously in…well, since he met Cary. "I don't have time for a boyfriend. We work fifteen-hour days."

"But you don't work in the summer," Tony said. "And Cary has time for a girlfriend."

Ryan clenched his jaw. "How do you even know that?"

"Maria follows Cary's love life like it's a hockey pool." To Cary, he added, "That must be weird, huh?"

Cary shifted in his seat and shrugged, clearly incredibly uncomfortable. God, it was bad enough Ryan had crossed the line and kissed him—now everyone was going to start asking about Amanda. Ryan jumped in before anyone else could say anything. "Look, when I meet Mr. Right, you'll all be the first to know, okay?"

Jack cleared his throat. "Yes, I think that's enough grilling for now. It's Christmas, not the Inquisition."

Ryan's mother sighed. "I'm sorry, dear. I just want you to be happy. Isn't there anyone you're interested in?"

The memory of the dimples in Cary's cheeks and the warm taste of his mouth invaded Ryan's mind. "No! There isn't." He kept his gaze locked on his glass.

"Mom, I think we should go check on the roast. Kids, set the table, please." Lisa gave Ryan's shoulder a quick squeeze as she passed by behind the couch.

When Ryan dared to look over, Cary was reading one of Jack's fishing magazines. He was apparently engrossed, and didn't look up once until they were called to dinner.

TUGGING AT THE COLLAR of his ridiculous reindeer pajamas, Ryan tried to get comfortable in his narrow bed. He heard Cary climbing the ladder and debated whether to fake sleep. But Cary appeared before he could decide, and their eyes met. Ryan swore a current of electricity sparked in the air between them, but clearly he'd had too much eggnog.

Cary's hair was damp, and he gave his face another swipe with his towel before hanging it over the end of his bed. His T-shirt clung to his lean muscles, and Ryan thought about what Cary had said the night before about sleeping nude.

Stop. Danger. Retreat!

Ryan stared up at the neon solar system as Cary flicked the light off and climbed into bed across the narrow room. Ryan knew he should say something and was batting around ideas when Cary beat him to it.

"Hey, do you think your parents would mind if I call long distance tomorrow? I'll pay for it. I'd use my cell, but no service, so…"

"Sure. It's no problem. And you can give your folks our number in case they want to call. My parents won't mind at all."

There was a beat of silence. "Why would they call?"

"Oh. Tomorrow's Christmas Eve. I thought…but right, your family's not into Christmas." Ryan's palms itched, and he felt like an idiot. It was like every word out of his mouth made everything worse.

"No. Anyway, I'm going to call Amanda and apologize."

Ryan bolted up in bed and came extremely close to whacking his head on the slanted ceiling. "*Amanda?* But I thought…I mean, you said she wasn't right for you."

"I overreacted. I should apologize and try to work it out with her. I can probably move up my flight and get home for New Year's. It's her favorite holiday."

"Right. Sure. Yeah, you can use the phone whenever you want."

"Cool. Thanks."

As the minutes ticked by, Ryan stared up at the glowing planets and stars. He listened for Cary to fall asleep, but in the tense silence, he didn't seem to be sleeping either. Ryan cursed himself again. For a year and a half he'd kept his feelings in check, and in one careless moment of want he threw it all away.

Ryan couldn't blame him for being upset. Cary trusted him to be a good friend—not to put the moves on him. Especially when Cary was fresh off a breakup. Not to mention *straight*. He came for the holidays to relax and get away from it all, and Ryan had just made everything worse. He couldn't blame Cary at all for wanting to leave.

As the minutes ticked by, Ryan found himself wishing he could ask Santa for a do-over.

Chapter Four

"SEE HOW THICK that ice is? Tell your mother she's worrying for nothing."

Ryan nodded dutifully. "Yes, Dad. Although this is early to have the hut out. I can't remember the last time you fished in December. It's nice."

Next to him, Cary shifted on the wooden bench, his knee brushing Ryan's. Quarters were tight in the hut with Ryan, Cary, and Tony squeezed onto the bench. On the other side of the fishing hole sawed into the ice, Ryan's father sat back on his folding chair.

A fire in a metal drum kept the hut relatively warm, and of course the wooden walls and roof protected them from the wind. A chimney funneled the smoke from the fire outside and a gas lantern hung from a hook in the ceiling.

"Now I know it isn't much, Cary, but I've caught thousands of fish in this hut. Plenty of people today want all the mod cons, but all I need is a seat, a fire, and a hole in the ice for my pole."

Cary smiled. "It's great. I wish I'd been able to go fishing as a kid." He ran his gloved fingers over the rod and reel he held. "I love it out here."

"You're not too cold? It's a far cry from Malibu, I know." Jack smiled kindly.

Cary's lips were practically blue, but he shook his head. "I'm good. How many years have you had this place?"

"Hmm. I suppose it's almost twenty years now. Ryan was about five when we bought it. It was awfully run-down, but we fixed it up over the years. If Ryan had his way, he'd have built us a mansion, but it suits us just fine the way it is."

Ryan rolled his eyes. "I didn't want to build a mansion. I just wanted to help pay for the work on the roof. You know you can't put it off for another winter."

"And I won't. I'm retiring this summer, and I'll have plenty of time to do the work."

"Ryan said you work for the government. Are you looking forward to retirement?" Cary asked.

Jack grinned. "Am I ever. I've spent long enough as a civil servant. Have to spend some time catching fish before the bay dries up. Water levels keep going down and last year we barely had a white Christmas."

Ryan and Tony shared a glance. Jack could talk for hours about global warming and the water levels and the impact on the environment—and fishing.

Tony stood. "Well, I've had enough for today, fellas. I'll take the catch in."

Jack checked his watch and sighed. "I suppose we should call it a day."

"I just want to catch one more. Is it okay if I stay?" Cary asked.

"Sure. I'll stay with you," Ryan quickly replied.

His father chuckled as he stood and stretched his arms over his head. His hands brushed the ceiling. "I've never seen you so eager to fish, son. I used to have to drag you out here."

Shrugging, Ryan fiddled with his rod. "It's not so bad after all."

"I suppose you're older and wiser and can finally appreciate the finer things in life." Jack ruffled Ryan's hair, and Ryan ducked away with a laugh.

Ryan and Cary stood so Tony could squeeze by. Ryan's rod dipped with an insistent tug, and he quickly sat back down to reel in the fish while Cary lifted the bucket.

"You two okay to take out the lures? Just remember what I showed you," Jack said. "We'll take the cooler, and you can bring the rest in the bucket. Don't be too long. Your mother will have dinner on the table soon."

"Thanks, Mr. Drake. We won't be long."

"It's Jack, remember?"

Cary smiled. "Thanks, Jack." He stood as Jack and Tony left. When he sat back down, he left room between him and Ryan on the bench. "You don't have to stay if you don't want to."

Ryan shifted and let out the line on his rod a bit. "Do you want to be alone? I can go."

"Whatever. If you wanna stay, it's cool."

"Okay." Ryan hated the awkwardness between them. He and Cary had always been so comfortable with each other, and now Ryan had changed everything. He cleared his throat. "I have to say I didn't peg you for an ice fishing fan."

Cary bobbed his rod up and down and shrugged. "It's peaceful."

They sat in silence for a few minutes until the words that had been swirling through Ryan's mind spewed out of his mouth. "I don't think you should call Amanda."

Cary visibly tensed. "Why not?"

"You said it yourself. You two aren't right for each other."

"Yeah, well. Maybe I don't know what's right for me. I thought I did, but I was totally wrong."

Ryan frowned. "What do you mean?"

"Forget it." Cary kept his gaze on the hole in the ice where their fishing lines disappeared. He sighed. "Maybe I should just go. This is your Christmas with your family, and I just barged in."

"It's your Christmas too." The thought of Cary leaving was unbearable. "Besides, it's Christmas Eve. You wouldn't even be able to get a flight out."

"It's just…" Cary rubbed a hand over his face.

"What?" Ryan's throat scratched. He realized his hands were shaking, and not from the cold. He clamped his rod into one of the metal holders his dad had fashioned and gulped from a thermos of now stale coffee.

"Being here with you…it's hard."

Ryan's eyes burned, and he blinked rapidly, looking everywhere but at Cary. "I understand. I don't want you to be uncomfortable. If you want to leave, I guess that would be best."

"Sure. Okay. I'm sure Amanda will take me back. I could meet her at the spa. I'll get a flight somehow." Cary's voice was strained wire thin.

He had to say it. "I just think you deserve better."

"Why do you care?" Cary asked sharply.

Ryan blinked. "You're my friend. When I moved to LA, I lost touch with most of my friends from Toronto, and it's hard to meet anyone there who's real, you know?" He was babbling, but he couldn't stop. "I'd go to parties and bars, but it wasn't until I met you and started working on the show that I stopped feeling totally alone. You're not just my friend—you're my best friend."

Cary jumped to his feet and began reeling in his line. "Right. You've made it very clear, Ryan."

"What?" Nausea roiled in Ryan's gut, and he stood beside Cary. This was all going wrong. *Please don't hate me.* "If this is about yesterday—"

"Look, I get it." Cary finished reeling in his line and stared at the lure swaying back and forth. "I'm an idiot, okay? I thought… God, I denied how I felt for so long, but I actually thought there was something between us."

Ryan felt as though all the air had been sucked out of the hut. He gaped as his brain struggled to process. "You…us?"

Cary winced. "I'm sorry. Stupid, huh? I always thought we had a connection as friends, but…"

"But?" Ryan could barely get the word out.

"But once Steven and Kishi got together on the show and I got to kiss you…" He blew out a long breath, a miserable expression darkening his face as he closed his eyes. "I realized how much I want you. I thought you wanted me too, but you were just doing your job."

Cary opened his eyes again but kept his gaze averted. "You made it really clear yesterday that you're not interested. I imagined it, and now I've made things all weird and embarrassing. So I'll just leave, and we can go back to normal in LA and try to forget this ever happened. Okay?"

"You…feel…" Ryan's head spun violently. "For me?" Disbelief and hope and affection melded in his chest, and Ryan couldn't stop the incredulous laughter that bubbled up. "You *like* me?"

Cary leaned his rod against the wall and crossed his arms. The tips of his ears burned red. "I'm sorry. It's ridiculous, and you don't like me back and—"

"Oh my God, shut up and kiss me," Ryan blurted as he yanked Cary against him and pressed their lips together.

His hands tangled in Cary's hair, and Cary's mouth opened and their tongues met. Cary gripped Ryan's hips, and they tumbled against the wall of the hut, fortunately missing the fishing hole as the bench tipped over. The lantern swung wildly overhead, casting light and shadow over them.

Gasping in a breath, Ryan pulled back. "I must be dreaming."

"You said you didn't want me." Cary stared, face so open and vulnerable, his lip caught between his teeth.

Ryan could only laugh. "I thought you'd be *mad* at me. I thought you were straight."

"I don't know what I am. All I know is that I want you." He wedged his thigh between Ryan's.

Cary kissed him again, his tongue sweeping into Ryan's mouth as they rubbed against each other. They were wearing too many layers, and their hands were clumsy as they grabbed and stroked, desperate to touch, but not willing to stop kissing.

Ryan thought he might come from the taste of Cary's mouth alone, or from the breathy little moans that escaped Cary's lips when Ryan managed to get his hands on Cary's denim-clad ass under his parka. They ground together, both hard in their jeans.

As they rutted, they exhaled in stolen whispers between kisses.

"I've wanted this for so long. Want you so much," Ryan murmured. "I thought you'd hate me if you knew. Thought I'd ruin everything."

"I could never hate you." Cary kissed him again, his tongue sliding over Ryan's. "I was going crazy. Wanted you so bad. I jerked off in my trailer every day before our scenes so I wouldn't get hard when I touched you."

Moaning, Ryan gripped Cary's ass tighter and hooked a leg over his hip to get a better angle. *If this is a dream, I don't ever want to wake up.* His leaking dick was trapped in his jeans, and he was going to come in his pants like a kid, but he didn't care. "I never thought..." They rocked together, and Ryan's balls tingled. He brushed Cary's cheeks with his fingertips. "I can't believe you want me too."

They kissed again, and after a few more frantic thrusts, Ryan came, his legs trembling as the pleasure crashed over him. Cary sucked on Ryan's neck, his hips still seeking friction. Ryan sank to his knees and pushed Cary against the wall, a new desperation whipping through him like electricity through a wire.

He managed to unzip Cary's jeans. The parka was awkward and heavy and in the way, but Ryan just pushed it up as he tugged Cary's jeans open and pulled out his cock. It was heavy and red, the tip glistening. Ryan sucked it into his mouth and swirled his tongue around the shaft, savoring the musky taste and scent. He could do this all day.

Cary was practically whimpering, his fingers tight in Ryan's hair as Ryan worked him with his mouth. *I'm sucking Cary's cock. This is actually happening.*

"Ry, I'm gonna—" Cary's hips stuttered, and he cried out.

Ryan swallowed convulsively and milked every last drop of Cary's orgasm. Sagging against the wall of the hut, Cary caressed Ryan's hair and breathed heavily. There was a sheen of sweat above his lip, and Ryan got to his feet and kissed him soundly.

Cary pressed their foreheads together. "Feels so good with you." He took a deep breath. "So I guess I wasn't imagining it? You do want me?"

Ryan took Cary's face in his hands. "From the day we met." He ran his thumb over Cary's bottom lip. "Wanted to kiss you. Wanted…everything." He leaned in and—

"Boys!" Maureen's voice echoed distantly on the wind.

With another kiss, they reluctantly separated and straightened their jackets. Fortunately their parkas and layers would cover up the wet spots on their jeans and they could change before dinner. Ryan extinguished the fire and lantern and pushed open the door of the hut. The last flare of orange light from the setting sun splashed over Georgian Bay, reflecting softly on the snow.

"Wow." Cary joined him outside. He looked up. "Maybe we can look at the stars tonight. Can you see them from your room?"

Ryan's body thrummed with desire. He swallowed hard. "Yeah."

Cary met his gaze, the hunger in his own eyes clear. "I'm pretty tired from fishing. Think I'll have an early night."

Ryan nodded. "Me too."

"Are you coming?" Maureen called out, echoing across the frozen bay from the deck of the cottage about a hundred yards away.

Glancing at each other, Ryan and Cary actually giggled. Ryan called back. "Yes!"

They started back across the ice, slip-sliding in some places where the snow had been blown thin, laughter echoing in the stillness of the winter night.

IN THE END THEY had to sit through not only dinner, but Scrabble *and* Monopoly. As eager as Ryan was to be alone with Cary again, he was afraid everyone would know exactly what was on their minds if they tried to get away early. As it was he felt like everyone knew, even though no one was acting any differently.

"Go straight to jail and do not collect two hundred dollars," Ethan recited. With a groan, he moved his top hat to the jail spot. "This freaking blows."

As Lisa and Tony scolded Ethan for his language, Ryan glanced at Cary across the dining table and found Cary watching him. Cary quickly lowered his gaze to fiddle with his colored money. Ryan still couldn't believe this was actually happening. He'd been so horrified when he kissed Cary at the tree farm, but Cary had *wanted* it.

It didn't seem possible. Ryan had worked so hard to hide his own feelings that he'd somehow missed spotting Cary's. He had so many questions. Was Cary gay? When did he start feeling this way? Were they going to be a couple now?

"Uncle Ryan?"

Ryan focused on Amy, who sat at the head of the table. "Uh-huh?"

"Why are you so happy? You don't have any good properties. Not even a railroad."

"I know. But it's Christmas. Of course I'm happy." He kept

his gaze away from Cary. "I'm here with my favorite niece, after all."

Amy frowned. "I'm your only niece."

"What? Are you sure? Lisa, you don't have any other daughters hanging around? I swear there were a couple more."

Lisa pretended to ponder it. "Hon, what did we do with those other daughters?"

Tony stroked his chin. "Now that you mention it, I think we might have left them in Florida when we went to visit my folks in St. Pete's that winter."

"No you didn't!" Amy giggled. "I'm your only daughter."

Jack spoke up from where he lounged in his recliner by the fireplace beside the Christmas tree. "I do seem to recall some other little girls. I thought they'd been eaten by bears."

"No!" Amy shrieked, laughing and shaking her head.

Ryan's mom brought out a plate of shortbread from the kitchen and a tray of tea and hot chocolate. As everyone laughed and teased Amy, Ryan passed Cary his mug. Their fingers brushed together, and beneath the table, Cary pressed his foot against Ryan's. Even through their woolen socks, Ryan swore he could feel a spark.

Finally it was time for bed. The stockings had been hung from the mantel above the fireplace for days, but Amy still insisted on making sure they were all there—along with a plate of shortbread and a glass of milk. She peered at Cary, brow furrowed, and then back at the fireplace.

"Are you sure Santa will know you're here, Uncle Cary?" she asked. "He might get confused. We should put your name on your stocking."

Cary smiled. "It's okay, sweetheart. I don't have a stocking here. I'm sure Santa will leave me my presents at home in LA."

"Of course you have a stocking!" Amy seemed scandalized at the very thought that he wouldn't. "See?" She pointed to each stocking. "Gran, Granddad, Mommy, Daddy, Uncle Ryan, Ethan, and you. But yours doesn't have your name on it."

For a moment, Cary didn't say anything. He cleared his throat. "That's okay. I'm sure Santa will know." He turned to Ryan's parents. "Thank you. You didn't need to do that."

Maureen waved her hand. "Nonsense. Everyone needs a stocking at Christmas! I would have sewn your name on it, but I've been up to my elbows in turkey and breadcrumbs, and my darling daughter can't sew on a button to save her life."

"Because she works twelve-hour shifts at the hospital and chooses to pay people to sew for her," Lisa replied.

Maureen scoffed good-naturedly. "She says that as if I wasn't a nurse myself for thirty-five years."

"But you're superwoman, remember?" Lisa laughed and gave her mother a kiss. "All right, kids. Off to brush your teeth and go to bed, or you'll be on the naughty list."

As Amy gasped and headed for the stairs, Ethan rolled his eyes. "It's not like Santa's even re—"

"Really paying attention tonight since he's too busy?" Tony asked with a stern look. "Santa's a man of many talents. Now get going." Under his breath he added, "And don't ruin it for your sister."

"All right, all right. Sorry." Ethan followed Amy upstairs, with Lisa and Tony on his heels.

Jack stretched his arms over his head and yawned. "That's me as well. Ryan, do you and Cary want to do the honors?" He nodded to the plate of shortbread.

"Either that or I put them back in the tin. I'm stuffed," Maureen added.

"Sure. Cary and I can polish them off." Ryan kissed her cheek. "Thanks, Mom. Merry Christmas."

"Merry Christmas. Sleep tight."

As his parents got settled upstairs, Ryan turned off the rest of the lamps until only the Christmas tree was lit by the fireplace. Cary stood by a window nearby, the colored lights catching in his blond hair.

"It's snowing again."

Ryan joined him at the window and, with a quick glance at the stairs, wrapped his arms around Cary from behind. Although Cary was broader, Ryan felt as if their bodies fit together perfectly. He kissed the back of Cary's neck. "I feel like every Christmas wish I ever made just came true."

Cary put his hand over Ryan's and threaded their fingers together. "I never made any Christmas wishes, but I guess I got on the nice list this year."

They watched the snow drifting down outside, the Christmas tree behind them reflecting softly in the glass.

"I guess we have a lot to talk about," Cary whispered.

Ryan pressed kisses along Cary's neck, finding a place behind his ear that made Cary's breath hitch. "I guess so."

Cary turned in Ryan's arms. "But I don't wanna talk."

Ryan wasn't sure how long they stood there kissing. They explored each other's mouths slowly and deeply, and he was light-headed by the time he took Cary's hand and led him upstairs. Somehow they made it up the ladder to the third floor while still kissing, even if they ended up in a heap on the bedroom floor at the top.

They quickly pulled their clothes off and tossed their sweaters and jeans aside. The carpet was rather worn, so Ryan pulled down his duvet and spread it out before leaning back. Cary straddled his hips, and Ryan drank in the sight of Cary's bare skin in the cool moonlight. He ran his hands over Cary's chest and muscular shoulders, exploring every inch.

"You look like you've never seen me shirtless before," Cary blurted with a nervous laugh.

"Not like this." Ryan propped himself up on an elbow and slowly sucked one of Cary's nipples. "Not when I can *really* look." He sucked on the other nipple and drew his fingertips down Cary's spine before teasing the crack of his ass. He whispered against Cary's skin. "Not when I can really touch."

With a groan, Cary tangled his hand in Ryan's hair and crushed their mouths together. He lengthened out on top of Ryan and thrust against him desperately. "Want you so much, Ry."

The feel of Cary's lean, powerful body against his own from head to toes was intoxicating. Ryan spread his legs and urged him closer. Their cocks rubbed together, and Ryan trembled with a feverish want and *need*. Any minute now he'd wake up and this would all be a dream, but until then he clung to Cary.

"I don't...I don't know what I'm doing," Cary muttered. "I mean...I've never...with a guy. Not really."

"It's okay." Ryan forced himself to take a long, deep breath and stilled his hips, even though his throbbing dick protested vigorously. "We can go slow." What he really wanted was Cary's cock in his ass immediately, but he didn't want to scare him off.

Cary shifted a little of his weight onto his hip and reached down to wrap his hand around Ryan's shaft. He stroked tentatively.

Biting back a groan, Ryan thrust into the heat of his palm. "This works."

"You said once..." Cary took a deep breath. "Remember the wrap party for season one when we all got wasted and played truth or dare?"

"Vaguely?" It was difficult to concentrate on anything but Cary's hand on his cock. Ryan desperately tried to remember what he said in the haze of Corona and tequila shots but came up blank.

"You said you were a bottom." Cary took a deep breath and rushed on. "SoifyoulikeitthenmaybecanIfuckyou?"

Ryan laughed and took Cary's face in his hands. He kissed him hard. "I've wanted your cock inside me every day since our screen test."

Cary's cheeks dimpled. "So that's a yes?" He teased the slit of Ryan's dick with his thumb.

"Yes, yes, y—shit."

Cary froze. "What? Did I...?"

"I don't have anything with me." He cursed himself. "And I don't think Santa will leave condoms and lube in our stockings tonight."

"Oh." Cary relaxed and kissed Ryan. "It's okay. I brought some. Just in case."

Ryan's whole body tingled. *Just in case he could have sex with me.* "You must have been a Boy Scout."

Cary's smile was rueful. "Nope. I tried one year, but I missed half the meetings because I had to go on location with my dad."

"Well, you're going to earn a badge tonight. Probably a few different ones."

Chuckling, Cary hurried over to his suitcase. Ryan shivered without the heat of Cary's body, but soon enough Cary was back with a box of condoms and a tube of lube that looked like it came from Costco.

"You *definitely* came prepared."

On his knees by Ryan's feet, Cary flicked the cap with a grin and squeezed some lube onto his fingers. Then he paused, brow furrowed. "They never really do this part in the videos."

"So you've been watching gay porn?" The thought made Ryan's throat go dry.

"Uh-huh. I was curious."

How is this real life? "Did you like it?"

Cary nodded, his Adam's apple bobbing as he swallowed thickly.

His low voice sounding foreign to his own ears, Ryan asked, "Did you jerk off while you watched?"

Another nod.

Did you think about me? Ryan couldn't quite get his next question out. His throat was too dry.

"I imagined it was you," Cary whispered. "That I was fucking you."

Ryan spread his legs wide and brought his knees up, exposing his hole. He reached for Cary's hand. "Use your fingers. Open me up for your cock."

His breathing shallow, Cary nudged his slick fingertip into Ryan's ass, just barely. Ryan reached for Cary's wrist impatiently. "More. It's okay."

"It feels good?" Cary's gaze was locked on Ryan's hole as he worked him open with one long finger and then two. "God, you're so tight." He shuddered and jerked his straining cock a few times.

Ryan jerked his head in a nod, pressing his lips together to swallow his moans as Cary pushed into him. He spread his legs even farther, totally unselfconscious in a way he'd never been with anyone else before. "I do this to myself and pretend it's you," he confessed.

With a groan, Cary leaned over and kissed him. He wiggled a third finger inside Ryan. "Is it enough?"

Groaning at the delicious fullness, he nodded. "You now."

When Cary pulled his fingers out, Ryan couldn't help but squeeze at them with his ass, not wanting to let them go. Sitting back on his heels, Cary rolled on a condom and coated himself with another squirt of lube. His cock glistened in the moonlight, and his body looked like a marble statue. *So beautiful.*

Ryan's legs were already pulled up, but he spread them even more and lifted his ass as Cary lined himself up. Lips parted, Cary swallowed thickly.

"God, you're amazing. I wanna fuck you so hard."

Ryan's heart thumped so loudly he was sure it would wake his family. "Do it." He gripped Cary's waist and urged him closer, not able to bite back the moan as Cary finally inched inside him. Their eyes locked, and Ryan bore down, reveling in the burning stretch in his ass as Cary filled him.

"Ryan. God, this is…" Cary groaned as he filled Ryan to the hilt. His arms shook slightly where he held his weight. "Better than anything."

"It's okay. Let go."

Ryan wrapped his arms around Cary's shoulders and opened his mouth in a silent cry as Cary plunged in and out of him. Even though the attic room got chilly in the night, they were both sweating as they rocked together, kissing with open mouths and gasping softly.

Cary's inside me.

He could hardly believe it was happening. Cary was fucking him, his thrusts getting more and more chaotic as they got closer to the edge. He hoisted one of Ryan's legs over his shoulder and went even deeper, brushing against Ryan's prostate.

"There. *There*," Ryan cried out, before slapping a hand over his own mouth. There was no door on the attic room, but at least the closest bedroom to the ladder was the kids', and they would sleep through an earthquake.

"You feel so good," Cary whispered, eyes wide. "Wanted to fuck you for so long. Wanna come inside you and fill you up. See my cum dripping out of your ass…"

Ryan's balls tightened. "Fuck, yes." He imagined they didn't have to use a condom—that Cary could shoot deep inside him. "Harder."

His thighs flexing, Cary tried to hit the right spot again. When he did, Ryan could only close his eyes and ride it out. He snaked a hand between them and jacked his leaking cock, so close to the edge already.

"You're the best I've ever had. Knew you would be." Panting, Cary pushed even deeper. "So good."

Lips parted, Ryan teetered on the edge before another thrust from Cary sent him over. He splashed his chest, coming in long spurts that had his whole body trembling. He clamped down, and Cary threw his head back as he drove into Ryan's ass until he shook with release. Eyes closed and mouth open, his face was a mask of sheer bliss before he collapsed on top of Ryan.

Chests heaving, they lay in a heap until Cary rolled away and tossed the tied condom into the garbage can by Ryan's dresser. He rolled back and peered at Ryan with a frown. Tentatively, he reached down and skimmed his fingertips over Ryan's stretched hole.

"Was it…I didn't hurt you, did I?"

Shaking his head, Ryan drew Cary down for a gentle kiss. "It was perfect."

Cary's smile lit up his face. "It kind of was. You're…" He caressed Ryan's hair, brushing it back from his forehead. "You're amazing. The best Christmas present ever."

Ryan laughed softly. "You too." He grabbed his discarded briefs and wiped off his chest. "Hey, you want to look at the stars?"

Cary squinted at the window. "I think it's snowing too much to see them."

With a smile, Ryan got up and led Cary to his bed, bringing the duvet with them. It was a tight squeeze in the narrow bed, but they found a comfortable position with their legs tangled and heads together on the pillow. Cary laughed quietly as he noticed the glowing stickers stuck to the slanted ceiling.

"Thanks for showing me the stars," he whispered.

It was almost four o'clock when Ryan woke with a start and tried to inch out of bed. Cary blinked blearily, his arms tightening around Ryan. "Where are you going?"

"Santa needs to eat his cookies or I'm in big trouble in the morning."

"I'll come with you."

They pulled on their pajamas and tiptoed downstairs where the gentle glow of the Christmas tree waited. They ate the cookies and shared the glass of now warm milk, trying to see who could make the biggest milk moustache before kissing them away and creeping back to bed for a long winter's nap.

Chapter Five

"UNCLE RYAN! UNCLE CARY! It's Christmas!"

Ryan opened his eyes to find Amy at the side of his bed in the dark, her cheeks flushed and a reindeer antler headband holding back her curls. He was spooning Cary—and had been drooling on the back of his neck—and was very relieved they'd put on their pajamas. He felt Cary tense in his arms. Ryan cleared his throat and held Cary close. "Merry Christmas, Amy. What time is it?"

"Six thirty. Mom said if I woke her before seven the Ghost of Christmas Past would haunt me tonight. But you guys can come down and open your stockings! We're allowed. We got Silly Putty, and Ethan already lost his in the woodpile. Come and see all the presents Santa brought!"

"We'll be right down. Go help Ethan find his Silly Putty."

"Okay!" With boundless energy, Amy raced to the ladder and practically jumped down to the second floor.

Cary sprung out of bed and paced. "I'm sorry. I should have gone back to my bed. Do you think…will she say anything?"

Ryan waved his hand. "The only thing on her mind is what Santa left her under the tree."

Running his fingers through his disheveled hair, Cary exhaled. His pajama bottoms were low on his hips and his T-shirt rode up over his hard stomach. "Okay. It's not that I don't…you didn't seem to want to tell your family. Right?"

It was a great question, and Ryan wasn't sure how he felt. It was all so new, and he could hardly believe in the slowly dawning morning light that it hadn't all been a fevered dream. "Yeah, I guess we have stuff to talk about first. Are you…how are you feeling?"

Cary's lips twitched into a tentative smile. "Good." He reached for Ryan's hand and tugged him lightly out of bed and into a sweet kiss. He smoothed his palm over Ryan's ass. "Reindeer pajamas have never been so sexy."

There was a crash from downstairs, and Ryan reluctantly broke away from Cary. "I'd better get down there before they break something else. My mom's probably in the shower. She usually gets up around six to put all the presents under the tree and fill the stockings. Sorry, there's always a line for the bathroom."

"It's okay. It's nice, everyone being here together and not spread out over a dozen rooms. I like it." Cary traced Ryan's cheekbone with his knuckle and then leaned in and slowly licked a spot on Ryan's jaw near his ear. "I've wanted to lick that mole for so long," he murmured.

With a groan, Ryan stepped away. "Okay, we've got to get downstairs or I'm going to throw you down and have my way with you."

Cary's eyes twinkled. "That was definitely on my Christmas list."

"WHAT'S THIS?" CARY took his place at the dinner table and prodded the brightly wrapped cylinder by his plate.

Amy frowned. "It's a Christmas cracker."

Cary picked it up and peered into one open end. The cardboard tube was wrapped in shiny gold-and-red paper with both ends tied off near the middle. "What's it for?"

"For fun, I suppose," Maureen answered with a wink as she brought in the cranberry sauce and added it to the incredible spread of sliced turkey, stuffing, yams, beans, and crispy roasted potatoes on the table. "Considering how fond Americans are of fireworks, I'm surprised this tradition was lost."

"Here." Ryan picked up his own cracker by one end and held out the other to Cary beside him. "Put your thumb on the little stick inside. Now give Ethan the other end of yours. When we're all ready, then we pull at the same time."

Once they all had one end of a cracker in their hands, they counted in unison. "One, two, three!"

Loud *pops* filled the air as the crackers tore apart and the contents went flying. Ryan fished his toy out of the gravy with his spoon, slurping the tiny pinball game into his mouth to clean it off, much to the delight of Amy and Ethan.

Cary peered into his torn cracker with a grin and shook out the contents—a toy, a joke, and a purple tissue-paper crown. He unfolded it and put it on. "This is awesome."

Somehow Cary still looked incredibly handsome wearing a ridiculous paper hat. Ryan put on his red one. "Just wait until you hear the jokes."

"Why did the cow cross the road?" Tony asked, reading from a curled piece of paper. He waited a beat. "To get to the udder side."

They all groaned, and once they had on their hats, Jack retrieved the camera from the living room and stood at the end of the table. "Everyone say Merry Christmas!"

"Merry Christmas!"

Twenty minutes later, Cary rubbed his belly and shook his head. "My trainer's going to kill me, but that was the best turkey

I've ever had. How do you get the stuffing so perfect?"

Maureen sipped her glass of Pinot Noir at the head of the table near the kitchen, her yellow crown askew. "Years of experience. And thank you." She reached for the platter in the center of the table. "You're sure you don't want more?"

Cary raised his hand. "Thank you, but I couldn't."

"There's still dessert though, right?" Ethan asked. He spun the top that had come with his Christmas cracker.

"It wouldn't be Christmas without plum pudding and mincemeat pies," Jack said. He folded his orange hat beside his plate. "But I think we all need a breather first."

There were nods and murmurs of assent, and Ryan got up to help clear the table. Cary leaped up beside him and began piling plates. "Thank you again for an incredible dinner, Maureen."

She fingered the new pearl necklace she wore. "My pleasure, dear. Thank you for the wonderful gifts. They really are too much."

"It was the least I could do after you welcomed me into your home." Cary picked up a stack of plates and carried them to the kitchen.

"Don't be silly. Any *friend* of Ryan's is part of the family," Lisa said as she reached for more wine.

Tony deftly maneuvered the bottle out of her reach. "Come on, let's put on some coffee."

Ryan gave him a grateful smile as Lisa grumbled but followed Tony to the kitchen.

Once they finished coffee and dessert, they all flopped in the living room, too stuffed to do anything but watch one of the new movies Santa had put under the tree. Christmas dinner was always early, and by nine they were all in bed.

Well, his family was in bed. Ryan was pacing by his, waiting for Cary to finish in the bathroom. All day he'd had to keep his hands in his pockets to stop himself from reaching out to touch. It didn't seem real that he *could* touch Cary now.

"I like the new PJs." Cary stepped off the top of the ladder.

Ryan flushed. He'd stripped down to his white briefs while he waited. "Thanks."

"Guess I'm overdressed." Cary pulled his T-shirt over his head and kicked off his pajama bottoms. He wasn't wearing underwear. He switched off the light, but the moon was still bright.

Ryan's throat went dry as Cary stalked toward him. "That's a good look for you."

As he sank to his knees, Cary reached for Ryan's hips. He nuzzled Ryan through his briefs, taking deep breaths, his exhalations sending goose bumps over Ryan's thighs. Cary tugged down Ryan's briefs, and Ryan stepped out of them. His pulse zoomed, blood rushing in his ears as Cary closed his lips over the head of his dick.

His initial tentativeness, with little kisses and experimental swipes of his tongue, soon evaporated, and Cary sucked Ryan deeply. He bobbed his head back and forth, his lips stretched around Ryan's throbbing cock. As the blissful minutes passed, Ryan reached up to hold on to the slant of the ceiling, his legs shaking as he watched his fantasies come to life—Cary on his knees for him, saliva dribbling down his chin, his mouth so hot and tight and—

Ryan tugged on Cary's head to warn him as his balls tightened, but Cary just sucked harder, his cheeks hollowing. Ryan saw bursts of color as he pulsed into Cary's mouth, biting his tongue to stop his cries. He stroked Cary's hair. "Jesus. You're a natural."

Cary tensed and got to his feet. He swiped his hand over his mouth and wouldn't meet Ryan's gaze. "Thanks," he muttered.

Blinking, Ryan reached for him and cupped his cheek. "What just happened? Where did you go?"

Eyes still averted, Cary shrugged. "I don't know. Sorry."

"Come on." Ryan took his hand and urged him onto his back

on Ryan's bed. He straddled his thighs and stroked Cary's chest, teasing his nipples and the light hair sprinkled there. "You're beautiful."

Cary opened his mouth as if to argue, but Ryan cut him off by swallowing his cock. Cary was already hard and leaking, and Ryan traced the vein on the underside of his shaft with his tongue as he reached down and caressed Cary's balls and the sensitive skin behind them. He wanted to lift Cary's ass and bury his face there with his tongue inside, but Cary was already whimpering softly.

Lips stretched wide, Ryan watched as Cary came, his long eyelashes dark on his cheeks, ecstasy written on his slack face. Ryan swallowed as much as he could and licked up the semen that dripped out of his mouth. Cary had been gripping Ryan's shoulders, and now his hands fell away.

"God. I've never…it's so good with you."

Ryan stretched out and pulled the duvet over them. He rested his head on Cary's chest and listened to his heartbeat slow back to normal. "It's the best it's ever been." He skimmed his fingers over Cary's stomach and circled his belly button. "Better than I dreamed."

They were quiet, and after a while the rhythm of Cary's breathing began to lull Ryan to sleep. But then Cary spoke, just a whisper.

"Do you really think I'm a natural?"

Ryan opened his eyes, but kept his head resting where it was. "I do. Is that…okay?"

"When I was thirteen, my dad did that terrible movie—the one with the aliens that farted poisonous gas? Anyway, I had to spend the whole summer in New Mexico. It was so hot you could barely move."

"Uh-huh?" Ryan wasn't sure where Cary was going with this, but he waited quietly.

"The director's son was there too, so we hung out. His name

was Matt. We played video games and stuff. He was fifteen. He had an indoor pool at their rental house, and we'd spend hours in there goofing around. One day he dared me to go skinny dipping. So we did, and we were roughhousing and…I'm sure you see where this is going."

Ryan pressed a kiss to Cary's chest. "Yeah. Go on."

"We jerked each other off, and it felt so good. The furthest I'd been with a girl was second base, and this was like…heaven. We did it every day, just hand jobs. But I really wanted to kiss him, and one afternoon in the pool, I did." Cary went silent.

"What happened?"

"He punched me. Called me a fag. Said if I told anyone what we'd done together he'd tell everyone I was queer and get my father fired. I spent the rest of the summer by myself. I felt guilty every time I jerked off because I couldn't stop thinking about kissing Matt, or some other guy. It had only been for a second when I kissed him, but it wasn't like kissing girls. It turned me on in a different way."

Cary still sounded so ashamed, and it twisted Ryan's heart. He caressed Cary's stomach. "There's nothing wrong with that."

"I…I know. But I don't think my father would agree. I may be named after Cary Grant—and the irony is not lost on me considering the rumors about him—but my dad and grandfather are old-school Republicans. They'd freak if they knew about me. That I'm…whatever I am."

"Gay? You can say it. It won't bite."

"Maybe."

"But you can't say it out loud yet." Ryan wished it didn't make his chest ache hollowly. He wanted to sit up and see Cary's face but part of him was afraid to look.

"The thing is that I don't know if that's the right word. After Matt, I never went near another guy. I told myself it was a phase—just part of growing up. And I really thought it was. Or at least I convinced myself for a while. I've slept with a lot of women, and I liked it. I wasn't faking. I love tits and pussy."

"Okay." Ryan grimaced. "I can't relate, but there's nothing wrong with that. And you also like cock. Clearly."

Cary ran his hand down Ryan's back and over his butt. "And ass. And strong, hairy, male bodies. Cock is…fuck, it's amazing. So what does that make me? Bi?"

"I guess so." Ryan pondered it. "Is that how you feel?"

Cary was silent for a long moment that stretched out in the darkness. "Yes," he rasped. Clearing his throat, he added, "But I didn't want to admit it. I was afraid."

Ryan pressed a kiss to Cary's chest and held him tightly. "You don't have to be afraid anymore. It's okay. I promise."

"It wouldn't bother you if I'm bi?"

"I've never considered it until right this second, but…no." Ryan propped his chin on Cary's ribs and met his gaze. "I haven't been with a guy who was bisexual before. At least not that I know of."

Cary shrugged awkwardly. "I know it must seem weird to you."

"No, it's just different. There's nothing wrong with being bi. Obviously. Plenty of people are. Probably more than want to admit it, or who are afraid to, like you were. As long as you want to be with me, why should it matter? It's the way you are. And I want you." It was pathetically needy, but he had to whisper, "You want me too? Right?"

Cary ran his fingertip over Ryan's lips. "All the time. In every way. I've never felt like this about anyone."

Ryan sighed in relief. "I want to kiss you," he blurted.

A furrow appeared between Cary's brows. "Okay." He laughed softly. "I'm right here. Have at it."

"No, I mean I want to kiss you on New Year's Eve. I want to tell my family that we're together. I don't want to hide it. That was a stupid idea."

Cary was silent for a long moment. "Okay. Yeah. We can trust them."

Any lingering uneasiness flared into full-on panic and Ryan tensed from head to toe. "But it's not like we're going to be a secret if we're together. I'm out of the closet, Cary. I'm not going back in."

"I'm not asking you to!" Cary lowered his voice again. "I just want a little time to figure out who I am before I tell the world."

Ryan sat up, almost grazing his head on the sloped ceiling. "So what does that mean? Up here you're my lover, and back in LA we're just friends again? What happens in Canada stays in Canada?"

"That's not what I said." Cary clenched his jaw. "You don't understand. It's easy for you. Your family loves you the way you are. My family won't be like that. And can you imagine if the tabloids got a hold of it? I'm up for the new Michael Bay movie, and I can't afford bad publicity right now."

"Oh, so being my boyfriend would be bad PR? Thanks." Ryan's temper flared white-hot, and he clambered out of bed and jerked on his pajamas. A voice told him to calm down and not let this spin out of control, but it was lost in a flurry of hurt and fear. "I guess I'm good enough to fuck, but not date."

"That's not what I meant! I just want some time to figure things out. The public doesn't even know I broke up with Amanda yet. My parents don't know. I can't get off the plane at LAX holding hands with you."

"Fine. Maybe we should just stop all this until you decide what you want." Ryan crossed his arms and took a ragged breath. He wanted to shout it from the rooftops that he was in love with Cary—because he was, without a shadow of a doubt—and it hurt more than he thought possible that Cary wanted to wait, no matter how logical or understandable it might be.

Cary threw back the duvet and stalked over to the other side of the room. "Fine. If that's the way you want it."

"The way *I* want it?" Ryan's voice echoed too loudly in the stillness, and he winced.

"Well, if you want to stop, then we'll stop." Cary tugged on his pajamas and climbed into bed. He turned on his side and faced the wall.

After a few moments of impotent pacing, Ryan got back in his own bed. The sheets smelled of Cary, and he could still taste him on his tongue. As Ryan willed sleep to come, he blinked back tears and wondered how things had managed to get so messed up, so quickly.

Chapter Six

"GOOD AFTERNOON!" MAUREEN called out.

"Ha-ha." Ryan shuffled into the kitchen. "It's not even eleven. Besides, I'm on West Coast time."

"You've been here more than a week! And by that logic, Cary's on West Coast time, but he's been out with your father and Tony for hours. We're not going to have room in the freezer for all these bloody fish." She stood at the counter, cleaning the latest batch and separating them into freezer bags with an affectionate smile. "But it makes him happy."

"Mom…" Ryan wasn't sure what he could even ask. He'd woken with his stomach in knots, hating himself for fighting with Cary.

"Hmm?" She expertly filleted the fish, removing the bones and tossing them aside.

"Nothing. So fish for Boxing Day dinner?"

"Not on your life. Crown roast of pork, thank you very much."

"Gran! Are you ready to go yet?" Amy barreled into the kitchen.

Ryan tickled Amy. "Where are you off to?"

She giggled. "We're going to the Morgan's down the road to play. If Gran will ever finish."

"Gran will finish *you* if you keep talking like that," Lisa admonished. "You want to come along, Ryan? Greg and Kathy are up with the kids. Kids can play and we can have a nice grown-up lunch. Dad and Tony—"

"Are right here," Tony replied as he pushed open the front door. "We've worked up an appetite. Jack's waiting in the truck, so we'd better get moving, babe."

Ryan craned his neck to see beyond Tony into the mudroom. His heart was in his throat. "Where's Cary?"

"Still out in the hut. He's really taken to ice fishing."

"You should take him some sandwiches for lunch." Maureen washed her hands and wiped them on her apron. "He seems a little out of sorts today." She raised an eyebrow. "As do you."

Ryan busied himself with opening the fridge and poking around. "Huh? We're fine."

"Mmm-hmm."

Shrugging, he took a swig of juice from the container. "We're fine, Mom."

She sighed as she left the kitchen. "There's leftover turkey on the top shelf, and that sourdough bread you like is on the counter. And use a glass!"

Ryan concentrated on making sandwiches as the rest of the family got ready to go in a flurry of activity. Once the door shut behind them, he took a deep breath. *Okay. I can do this. Maybe it won't be so bad if we talk.*

The walk out to the fishing hut felt like it took a hundred years. The cloud cover that had brought a fresh foot of snow on Christmas had dissipated, and the sun was bright overhead. The wind whistled, and Ryan realized he'd neglected to bring his gloves. He clutched the lunch bag tightly with numb fingers, his stomach churning.

When he pushed open the door to the hut, his breath caught in his throat. In the lantern light, Cary was beautiful, his hair golden and cheeks ruddy, his lips a deep red. He met Ryan's gaze.

"Hi."

"Hi." Ryan closed the door behind him. It was fairly warm inside, but the fire was getting low. "I brought lunch. Thought you might be hungry."

"Oh. Thanks."

It was unbearably awkward, and Ryan handed Cary the bag and busied himself stoking the fire. Once he was finished, Ryan hovered by the fishing hole. "I can…if you want to be alone…"

"No, I should go. It's your…hut." He reeled in his line.

"I don't even like fishing. It's cool, you should stay."

"I need to call the airline anyway."

"Oh. You haven't done that yet?" Hope flickered to life.

Cary zipped up his parka. "Sorry. Your dad wanted me to come fishing. But I'll call now. I should go back to Toronto either way. I'm sure I can get a room by the airport even if I can't fly out for a couple of days. I've already imposed too much."

Ryan inhaled sharply. "Would you stop with the martyr routine already?"

"Whatever. Clearly you want me to leave."

"That's not what I said! Would you just—"

But Cary was gone, the hut door slamming in his wake. Blowing out a long breath, Ryan rolled his shoulders. They were both lashing out, and he wasn't even sure why. He slowly counted to ten silently and then followed Cary outside.

Cary wasn't there.

Blinking in the glare of the sun, Ryan held up a hand to shield his eyes as he looked over the expanse of ice between the hut and the cottage up on the hill. He saw movement to the left, and his stomach clenched. Instead of walking the way they'd come across the main part of the bay, Cary was taking a shortcut by a tiny inlet.

They called it the narrows, and in the summer boats had to lift their motors while passing through. With the falling water levels in Georgian Bay, soon it would be little more than rock, with the pond beyond it dried out.

"Cary!" His cry echoed in the winter stillness, and Ryan raced after him, boots sliding.

Cary stopped, but even as he turned, an ominous *crack* filled the air, and he just *disappeared.* Ryan's lungs burned as he ran, blood rushing in his ears. He battled the panic, and a voice reminded him that he wouldn't be any good to Cary if he fell in too.

As Ryan reached the narrows, he dropped down to his stomach to spread out his weight and slithered closer to the jagged hole. "Cary!"

The ice creaked as he got closer, but he dragged himself on. When he came within an arm's length, he met Cary's wide-eyed stare. Cary's face was barely out of the water, and his normally tanned skin was frighteningly pale. He made horrible gasping noises as he clutched at the sharp edges of the ice.

Fingers sliding, Ryan couldn't get any purchase. He unwrapped his woolen scarf and tossed it toward the hole. It stuck to the wet ice, and Ryan used it to inch forward. "Grab the end!"

Still gasping, Cary reached out.

"It's okay. I've got you."

For a moment that lasted a lifetime, Cary's head disappeared below the black surface.

"No!" Praying the ice would hold, Ryan squirmed closer to the hole and plunged his hand into it. The cold took his breath away, but he was able to catch Cary's hair. His fingers were hopelessly numb, but he forced his body to follow his commands and yank Cary back above the water.

Crack.

Another fissure in the ice appeared beside him. Ryan focused on Cary. "It's okay. Hold on to my scarf as tight as you can."

With trembling arms, Cary did as he was told, and Ryan backed up on his belly, knowing the ice around the hole wouldn't hold both of them. It fractured farther as he tried to drag Cary to safety, but he moved back, inch by inch, until finally, arms burning, he was able to pull Cary onto solid ice.

He reached for Cary's arm and dragged him along, not risking getting back on his feet until he knew the ice would be thick enough to hold them. When he was able to kneel, he drew Cary into his arms, gripping him tightly.

"It's okay. You're okay. Can you stand? We have to get you inside."

Jerkily, Cary nodded, and Ryan wrapped an arm around his back. They struggled to find their footing on the ice and plodded slowly toward the shore. Ryan's whole body felt numb and stiff— so he could only imagine how Cary felt.

Once they were back on solid ground, it took precious minutes to climb the stairs leading up to the cottage. Cary's body didn't want to bend, and he finally started shivering, which Ryan took as a good sign.

"Come on. You're a Portigan warrior. You can do it." Ryan's voice sounded strained and frightened to his ears.

Cary might have been trying to smile, but it was a grimace instead. Still, he managed to move a little faster, and they made it to the top of the stairs with Ryan pushing and pulling. The cottage had never looked so welcoming as Ryan maneuvered Cary inside the mudroom and yanked off their boots and jackets.

The fire had burned out, but it still felt wonderfully warm in the living room. Cary swayed on his feet, and Ryan gripped him as he peeled off Cary's wet clothing. After throwing down a blanket in front of the fireplace, Ryan eased Cary down and rubbed his icy flesh. The hospital was an hour away, and he needed to get Cary warm now.

He knew the best thing for hypothermia was body heat, so

Ryan stripped off his clothing and stretched out on top of Cary, his hands roaming. Cary shuddered helplessly, but after some of the longest minutes of Ryan's life, began to warm up.

"You're okay now." Ryan murmured as he stroked Cary's body. "I've got you." He examined Cary's body for signs of frostbite, but found nothing.

With jerky movements, Cary wrapped his arms around Ryan's back. Ryan stilled his movement, and they held each other until their ragged breathing slowed. Ryan hadn't realized how fast his pulse was racing until it returned to normal. He buried his face in Cary's neck and pressed kisses to the damp skin.

"I don't ever want to lose you," he whispered.

"Ry." Cary's voice was wrecked.

Ryan struggled to keep his voice steady. "I'm sorry."

"Me too." Cary's fingers tightened on Ryan's back.

Ryan wasn't sure how long they stayed in each other's arms. Finally he pulled himself away—much to Cary's obvious displeasure—to start a fire and grab another blanket from the rocking chair to pull over them.

The fire sparked to life, radiating warmth and flickering light over Cary's still-pale skin. Ryan rubbed Cary's chest. "Feeling better?"

Nodding, Cary closed his eyes. "So tired. It was…I couldn't move. My brain was screaming, but my body couldn't do anything. I thought…I've never been so scared."

"Shh." Ryan kissed Cary's chest and caressed his belly. "You're okay."

"Thanks to you." Cary stroked Ryan's hair.

As they kissed gently, Maureen's voice suddenly rang out from the mudroom. "What a fine mess to come home to. Ryan! Pick up after yourself for bloody once in your life!"

Ryan bolted upright, still sitting tangled in the blankets as Cary groaned. He kept a firm hand on Cary's chest, not wanting

Cary to move too soon. "Mom, wait!"

But she was already throwing open the door, and she skidded to a halt just inside the entrance, mouth open. Lisa, Tony and Jack stopped behind her, eyes wide.

"I can explain—" Ryan began.

"Well, this is certainly what we were all hoping for, but a little decorum would be appreciated. This isn't *Hollywood*, Ryan." His mother's face flushed brightly. She called out behind her, "Children! Stay outside for a minute!"

"It's not what it looks like."

"Of course not!" Lisa grinned. "Do explain then, little brother. We're all ears."

"Cary fell through the ice. I had to warm him up and—"

He didn't get a chance to finish in the volley of exclamations. Lisa and Maureen hurried over, all business as they examined Cary, poking and prodding. Ryan could only scurry out of the way with one of the blankets wrapped around him.

"I told you it was too early to be out on the ice!" Maureen scolded her husband.

"It was a foot thick!" Jack ran a hand through his silver hair. "I'm sorry, Cary. Is he all right?"

"Dad, it's not your fault. It's mine. I never told him not to cross at the narrows."

Amid the hubbub, Cary spoke up. "If it was anyone's fault, it was mine. But Ryan knew just what to do."

"How are you feeling, dear?" Maureen held Cary's wrist with one eye on her watch.

"Better. Like I could sleep for a week."

"Of course. Let's get you to bed." She shook her head. "This is why I say stay off the ice! You just never know. You could have both drowned," she muttered.

Holding the blanket awkwardly, Ryan crouched down to help Cary to his feet, keeping his arm around Cary's back. "We're fine,

Mom. Really. We just need to rest now."

For a moment, silence stretched out, and they all looked at each other. Tony cleared his throat.

"So…you sure there's nothing else going on? Because Maria's been saying for months that you two have, and I quote, like, amazing chemistry."

It was Ryan's turn to blush. He glanced at Cary, who studied the floor, a telltale dimple in his cheek.

"Ah ha! Finally!" Lisa bounced on her toes. "Told you, Mom."

"It seemed too good to be true! Oh Ryan. Cary's such a lovely young man and we're all thrilled—"

"Um, can we have this conversation when Cary and I aren't naked?" Ryan asked.

"That would probably be best, son." Trying to hide a smile, Jack clapped him on the shoulder as Ryan steered Cary toward the stairs.

"Can we come in yet? It's cold!" Amy cried out from the mud-room.

His family's laughter rang through the cottage, and as they made their way to the attic, Cary and Ryan chuckled softly. Ryan guided Cary to the guest bed and tucked him in. But Cary reached for him as Ryan backed away.

"Stay. I'm still cold. Need your body. You know, for the warmth."

"I guess if it's a medical necessity, I can't really say no." Ryan couldn't stop grinning as he snuggled in under the covers. "Now sleep."

Cary nuzzled Ryan, kissing him softly, his eyes already shut. "Okay."

THEY WOKE TO the smell of sizzling pork and what Ryan could

imagine were crispy roasted potatoes. His stomach growled, and Cary huffed out a laugh, his breath warm on Ryan's chest.

"I think dinner's almost ready," Cary murmured.

"You feel up to it? I'm sure my mom will bring up a tray."

"I think I'm okay." Cary stretched his limbs and turned onto his side, facing Ryan on the narrow bed. "Feel a lot better than I did earlier, that's for sure." His expression darkened. "I'm so sorry. I never meant for you to think that I don't want to be with you."

"Really?" Ryan's heart skipped a beat.

"Really." Cary kissed him tenderly. "I want you more than anyone I've ever known. It's just so new. My head is spinning. Up here it feels like we're in our own secret world. I can't help but be afraid of what will happen when we go back to the real one. I know I shouldn't be. I know I should be stronger."

"No, no." Ryan brushed back Cary's disheveled hair. "You *are* strong. I'm afraid too. Afraid you'll change your mind."

"I won't change my mind." Cary rubbed their noses together. "I want to be with you, Ryan."

"What if we get back and everything's different? And your father pressures you, and Amanda wants you back and—"

"She's the one who told me to come here." Cary drew away, a smile tugging at his lips. "She was always jealous of you. Finally she told me to just man up and admit I was in love with you."

Ryan's breath stuttered, and his voice squeaked embarrassingly. "Love?"

"Duh." Cary smiled and brushed his thumb across Ryan's bottom lip. "Of course I'm in love with you. Have been for a long time. Amanda pushed me to admit it."

"She's not so bad, really."

Laughing, they kissed, mouths opening and tongues twining. When Ryan pulled away a minute later, breathless, he pressed kisses all over Cary's face—cheeks, forehead, chin, the tip of his nose.

His stomach was all butterflies in the best way. "In case it wasn't clear, I love you. I'm sorry I pressured you. I know you need time before we tell the world."

"So you understand? It's not that I don't want to be with you, or that I'm ashamed of you. God, I could never be ashamed of you. You make me want to be a better person. A better man. I'm so proud to be with you. To be wanted by you. But the idea of coming out before I fully understand who I am? It really scares me."

"I don't blame you. I was being selfish. Insecure."

Cary held him tightly. "I'm with you. Being bisexual doesn't change that. You're the only one I want to be with. The only one I want to kiss at midnight when the ball drops. Or on Boxing Day. Whatever the hell that is." His eyes crinkled at the corners.

Ryan's own laughter was like a balm. "It's clearly a day when...I have no idea, but Canadians get the day off work, so it's awesome. Definitely kissworthy."

"Assuming you still want to kiss me, that is."

Ryan felt as though his body was filling with helium and he could just float away. "I guess that would be okay. Maybe we should give it a try. Make sure we have our form down for New Year's."

"Good idea. Rehearsal." Cary cleared his throat and leaned back to mime a clapperboard with his hands. "Scene one, take one. Actually, take two. We kind of messed up on the first take. But I think we've got it now."

Grinning, Ryan pulled Cary back into his arms. "Action!"

Epilogue

"CAN YOU SIGN my magazine, Mr. Holloway?"

Ryan glanced over from where he and the kids played Monopoly on the floor by the glittering tree. This year Tony's niece had joined them for Christmas, and fifteen-year-old Maria was fairly vibrating, unable to contain her excitement as she held out the latest issue of *Vanity Fair* and a marker pen.

From the couch, Cary smiled and put down his e-reader. "Sure. Come on, sit down. And call me Cary, remember?" He scrawled his autograph in the corner near the headline.

Hollywood Son Cary Holloway Comes Out: Are We Ready for a Bisexual Leading Man?

"And the pictures inside? Ryan signed his."

There was a four-page spread in the magazine of Cary in various poses, along with a candid shot of Cary and Ryan hand in hand at a fall film premiere—their first official event as a couple.

"Is it true that your dad hardly even talks to you anymore?" Maria asked.

Before Ryan could interject, Lisa called out from the kitchen. "Maria. Remember what we said about gossiping?"

"Sorry, Aunt Lisa." Maria appeared genuinely abashed. "Sorry, Cary. I just think it sucks."

"It's okay. I think it sucks too." Cary glanced at Ryan and gave him a tight smile.

Sucks was an understatement, and Ryan had to choke down the anger that bubbled up whenever he thought of how Cary's family had reacted to his coming out. At least his mother seemed to be softening. His father and grandfather were another story, but Cary shrugged it off. Most of the time. Some nights all Ryan could do was hold him, since there were no words.

"Can you sign my DVDs too?" Maria thrust the first two seasons of *Space Academy* at Cary. "I really wish they'd release the show on Blu-ray. Especially now that it got a two-season pickup. Everyone's talking about it. Especially about Stishi. You guys are, like, the best ev."

"And Cary's *soooo cute*," Ethan said, ducking out of the way as Maria deftly picked up a chestnut from the bowl of nuts on the coffee table and fired it across the room.

"It's true. He is pretty cute," Ryan said. "Glad you agree, Ethan."

"*I* didn't say he's cute!" Ethan protested.

"Sure you did. Besides, he's the cutest. Would you look at those dimples?" Tony added.

As Lisa, Maureen, and Jack chimed in, they all laughed—even Maria, who took five minutes to stop blushing.

Maureen yawned widely. "I think it's time for bed. Santa's on his way, and we all need to stay off the naughty list. Run and get the cookies, Amy."

Even though Amy had expressed some doubts to Ryan that morning that Santa Claus was real, she jumped up and raced to the kitchen.

It was just before midnight when Ryan and Cary sneaked back downstairs. The lights from the tree cast a rainbow glow over the room, and snow drifted down beyond the windows. They plucked the cookies from the mantel and shared the glass of milk in contented silence. Ryan couldn't believe a year had passed already.

He pressed their lips together.

"Happy anniversary."

"And merry Christmas," Cary whispered.

Hands clasped, they crept back past the mantel, where a new stocking hung with Cary's name sewn in shimmering gold.

THE END

About the Author

Keira aims for the perfect mix of character, plot, and heat in her M/M romances. She writes everything from swashbuckling pirates to heartwarming holiday escapism. Her fave tropes are enemies to lovers, age gaps, forced proximity, and passionate virgins. Although she loves delicious angst along the way, Keira guarantees happy endings!

Discover more at:
keiraandrews.com